ROBERT LUDLUM'S™

THE BOURNE DEFIANCE

THE BOURNE SERIES

Robert Ludlum's The Bourne Sacrifice (by Brian Freeman)
Robert Ludlum's The Bourne Treachery (by Brian Freeman)
Robert Ludlum's The Bourne Evolution (by Brian Freeman)
Robert Ludlum's The Bourne Nemesis (by Eric Van Lustbader)
Robert Ludlum's The Bourne Initiative (by Eric Van Lustbader)
Robert Ludlum's The Bourne Enigma (by Eric Van Lustbader)
Robert Ludlum's The Bourne Ascendancy (by Eric Van Lustbader)
Robert Ludlum's The Bourne Retribution (by Eric Van Lustbader)
Robert Ludlum's The Bourne Imperative (by Eric Van Lustbader)
Robert Ludlum's The Bourne Dominion (by Eric Van Lustbader)
Robert Ludlum's The Bourne Objective (by Eric Van Lustbader)
Robert Ludlum's The Bourne Deception (by Eric Van Lustbader)
Robert Ludlum's The Bourne Sanction (by Eric Van Lustbader)
Robert Ludlum's The Bourne Betrayal (by Eric Van Lustbader)
Robert Ludlum's The Bourne Legacy (by Eric Van Lustbader)
The Bourne Ultimatum
The Bourne Supremacy
The Bourne Identity

THE COVERT-ONE SERIES

Robert Ludlum's The Patriot Attack (by Kyle Mills)
Robert Ludlum's The Geneva Strategy (by Jamie Freveletti)
Robert Ludlum's The Utopia Experiment (by Kyle Mills)
Robert Ludlum's The Janus Reprisal (by Jamie Freveletti)
Robert Ludlum's The Ares Decision (by Kyle Mills)
Robert Ludlum's The Arctic Event (by James H. Cobb)
Robert Ludlum's The Moscow Vector (with Patrick Larkin)
Robert Ludlum's The Lazarus Vendetta (with Patrick Larkin)
Robert Ludlum's The Altman Code (with Gayle Lynds)
Robert Ludlum's The Paris Option (with Gayle Lynds)
Robert Ludlum's The Cassandra Compact (with Philip Shelby)
Robert Ludlum's The Hades Factor (with Gayle Lynds)

THE TREADSTONE SERIES

Robert Ludlum's The Treadstone Rendition (by Joshua Hood)
Robert Ludlum's The Treadstone Transgression (by Joshua Hood)
Robert Ludlum's The Treadstone Exile (by Joshua Hood)
Robert Ludlum's The Treadstone Resurrection (by Joshua Hood)

THE BLACKBRIAR SERIES

Robert Ludlum's The Blackbriar Genesis (by Simon Gervais)

THE JANSON SERIES

Robert Ludlum's The Janson Equation (by Douglas Corleone)
Robert Ludlum's The Janson Option (by Paul Garrison)
Robert Ludlum's The Janson Command (by Paul Garrison)
The Janson Directive

ALSO BY ROBERT LUDLUM

The Ambler Warning
The Bancroft Strategy
The Tristan Betrayal
The Sigma Protocol
The Prometheus Deception
The Apocalypse Watch
The Scorpio Illusion
The Icarus Agenda
The Aquitaine Progression
The Parsifal Mosaic
The Holcroft Covenant
The Chancellor Manuscript
The Gemini Contenders
The Rhinemann Exchange
The Cry of the Halidon
Trevayne
The Matlock Paper
The Osterman Weekend
The Scarlatti Inheritance
The Road to Omaha
The Road to Gandolfo
The Matarese Countdown
The Matarese Circle

ROBERT LUDLUM'S™

THE BOURNE DEFIANCE

BRIAN FREEMAN

An Aries Book

First published in the US in 2023 by G.P. Putnam's Sons,
an imprint of Penguin Random House LLC

First published in the UK in 2023 by Head of Zeus
This paperback edition first published in 2024 by Head of Zeus,
part of Bloomsbury Publishing Plc

9 7 5 3 2 4 6 8

A catalogue record for this book is available
from the British Library.

ISBN (PB): 9781803285931
ISBN (E): 9781803285894

Book design by TK
Cover design by Ben Prior/Head of Zeus
Typeset by Divaddict Publishing Solutions

Printed and bound in Great Britain by
CPI Group (UK) Ltd, Croydon CRO 4YY

Head of Zeus Ltd
5–8 Hardwick Street
London EC1R 4RG

WWW.HEADOFZEUS.COM

ROBERT LUDLUM'S™ THE

BOURNE DEFIANCE

Tskhinvali, South Ossetia Region
The past

The five-day war between Russia and Georgia had taken place years earlier, but the Treadstone agent known as Cain still saw the aftereffects of the conflict around him. He passed abandoned farmhouses with their roofs caved in by mortar fire. Tall grass grew around bombed-out rubble, and the stone walls of a lonely Orthodox church bore the pockmarks of bullets. The area felt emptied of people. Many of the refugees of the region had fled south to Tbilisi and never come home again, leaving ruins of their old lives behind them.

Cain knew he was on the right path. He could follow the trail of blood and footprints. His target was wounded, probably dying. Initially, there had only been a few tiny red drops in the white snow, but the evidence of blood came more frequently now, the stains larger. Abel was slowing down, losing strength. He couldn't be far away.

The pursuit had taken Cain north out of the town of Gori. Abel's left rear tire had blown near Tergvisi, and since then, he'd proceeded on foot through the rural countryside, making a run for Russian-occupied territory. Cain had gotten close enough to him in one of the empty farm fields to land a bullet in the man's back, but then Abel had struggled to his feet and disappeared into the trees again.

Cain and Abel.

Holly Schultz, who'd assigned the code names, had a malevolent sense of humor. She'd teamed them on Treadstone missions for years. They'd saved each other's lives often enough that they were almost like brothers. Cain had thought he knew the man well. He'd trusted him. But under the jokes, under the disguises, under the Beatles songs he whistled before a kill, Abel had been an agent with a deadly secret.

Abel was a traitor. A Russian asset.

And now Cain had been sent to kill him.

He stopped in the forest, listening to the hiss of November wind and feeling the wet flakes of snow on his eyelashes and inside his heavy boots. The snow made the whole world quiet, and in the silence, he heard movement—branches snapping—close by. It wasn't Abel. The blood trail didn't lead in the direction of the noise. He was more concerned that it was a Russian soldier. He wasn't sure which side of the border he was on, and the Russian base at Eredvi was just a few miles away.

Cain leveled his Makarov, a Russian pistol he'd acquired upon arrival in Georgia. The assassination needed to be done with a foreign gun; Holly had been clear about that. There could be no evidence of American involvement. He snapped his shoulders from side to side, his eyes hunting for movement in the trees. Then he saw a tiny face, and lowered his weapon. It was a boy, no more than nine or ten years old.

The boy came out of the trees, not looking scared. He had a dirty face, greasy brown hair that was raggedly cut, and intense blue eyes. He wore a pullover shirt that resembled a burlap sack, plus torn jeans and red rubber boots that were caked with mud. The boy took note of the gun in Cain's hand.

"You hunt that man?" the boy asked in Georgian.

Cain nodded.

"He is Russian?"

Close enough, Cain thought, so he nodded again.

The boy pointed through the trees. "I saw him go in a farmhouse over there. He's bleeding, but he has a gun, too, like you. Be careful. You kill him, okay? Shoot him dead. Kill the fucking Russians."

Cain dug some coins from his pocket and handed them to the boy. Then he nodded his head for him to run in the opposite direction. The boy thumped his chest twice with his fist in a gesture of solidarity, then vanished silently through the snow.

The farmhouse was close, not even a hundred yards away. The wooden front door was open, hanging from one hinge. It was a small structure, mostly destroyed by bombs, and he circled the place to confirm that there were no other doors, just the one way in and out. Cain smelled the smoke of a fire and the stink of boiled cabbage. As he neared the door, he heard singing from inside.

"Back in the U.S.S.R."

Abel wasn't hiding his location. He knew Cain was out there. Between the lyrics, his voice broke in alternate fits of laughing and coughing. Then he called out, his words slurring as he got weaker, "Come on in, Cain. We might as well get this over with."

Cain led with the Makarov. He moved fast, expecting a battle, but there was no gunfire as he spun through the door. Instead, he saw Abel sitting in the corner of the main room, lost in the shadows on the wooden floor. He wasn't alone. His legs were spread wide, and he had one arm around the waist of a black-haired teenage girl sitting in front of him. With his other hand, he held his pistol to the terrified girl's head.

"Hey, Cain. This is Tatiana. Say hello, Tatiana."

When the girl said nothing, Abel shoved the gun hard into her dark hair and repeated in guttural Russian, "*Say hello.*"

"Hello," she gasped.

Tatiana was undernourished, her arms and legs skinny. Her plain face was winter-pale, and tears leaked from her dark eyes. Her whole body trembled. She couldn't have been more than fifteen.

"Let her go, Abel," Cain murmured, aiming the Makarov at the man who'd once been his friend. But he didn't have a clean shot, not without risking the teenager's life. "Hurting her won't change how this ends."

"Oh, I think you're wrong. See, I know you too well, Cain. You're always a hero when it comes to women. It's your fatal flaw."

"Let her go," he repeated.

Abel managed a laugh. He leaned forward and kissed the back of the girl's head, keeping his face barely visible. It was clear that Abel had a wary appreciation for the accuracy of Cain's shooting, even with a foreign gun.

"So here we are," Abel said. "You and me. Brothers in arms."

"Here we are."

Cain studied the man's features in the shadows. Abel was a master of disguise and rarely looked the same way twice. He could be young, old, blond, redheaded, dark-haired, and have blue eyes, brown eyes, or green eyes. About the only thing that gave him away was his walk when he thought no one was looking, a strange way of gliding so that his shoulders seemed to float above his hips. But here, at the end, he was simply himself. Tall, strong, blond, blue-eyed, smart, and arrogant when he smiled.

Yes, Cain thought, seeing the truth for the first time. *He's Russian.*

Abel had been a Russian mole from the beginning. A

graduate of Putin's charm school, designed to blend in like a native and infiltrate the U.S. intelligence services. He'd played them all. Fooled them all. Cain included.

Tatiana struggled in Abel's grasp, but the man held her tight. Staring back, he seemed to read Cain's mind.

"You think they want me dead because I'm a traitor, don't you?"

Cain didn't answer.

"Well you're wrong," Abel went on. "Think about it. Why kill me? If that's what this is about, Holly would want me in a cell somewhere, so they can sweat out every secret I've given away. When they'd bled me dry, they'd trade me, use me as a bargaining chip. But send you out here to shoot me? No. They're scared, Cain. Somebody wants to shut me up. Make sure I don't talk."

More games. More *lies*!

But Cain couldn't stop himself from playing. "Talk about what?"

"Defiance."

A flash of puzzlement ran through Cain's eyes. "Defiance? That was a Treadstone mission."

"That's right, but what was the mission really about? Who ordered it? What was it covering up?"

"Are you saying you know?"

"I know enough for them to want me dead."

Cain shook his head. "You're stalling. It's too late for that. You've run out of time. Do you think the Russians are coming to save you?"

Abel's blue eyes glinted, as if laughing at a joke only he could hear.

At that moment, Cain felt a rumble under his feet. Vibrations traveled through the ground and under the floor like an earthquake. He knew what that meant. The lonely woods around the farmhouse were located near the road to

Eredvi, and heavy vehicles were thundering down that road. The Russians *were* coming. Soldiers would already be in the woods, zeroing in on their location.

"You activated a tracker," Cain concluded, thinking furiously, assessing his options.

"Of course I did. See, you're the one who's running out of time, Cain. Get out of here while you still can."

Cain tightened his grip around the Makarov. He tried to send a message to the girl, Tatiana, with his eyes, telling her to jerk sideways and give him a shot. But the teenager's face was flushed with panic, and he couldn't trust her not to swing back into his line of fire. Abel recognized his predicament. They knew each other too well.

"Go, Cain. Save yourself. You can't kill me without killing her, and I know you won't do that. If you stay, you're dead."

The thunder on the road deepened and got louder. The throb of engines carried to his ears on the still air. Through the open door, he heard men trampling noisily through the forest. There were shouts in Russian. Cain endured a moment of paralysis—*stay or go*—but then the decision was made for him. A man's body filled the farmhouse doorway. It was a soldier dressed in olive gear, with an AK-12 rifle braced against his shoulder.

The man didn't see Cain at first, and Abel shouted in Russian, "Left! Left! Left!"

In that fraction of a second, Cain swung the Makarov and fired a single shot that took down the Russian soldier between his eyes. At the same moment, he dropped to the ground, watching as Abel threw the girl sideways and aimed his gun at Cain. Abel squeezed off a shot but missed high, and Cain fired back, hurrying, choosing the fattest target. The bullet landed squarely in Abel's chest.

A fatal shot; it *had* to be fatal.

Wasn't it?

Always confirm your kill.

Treadstone.

But there was no time to do that. The cursing voices outside got louder. More soldiers were coming. Cain took three steps forward and dragged Tatiana from the floor, where she was huddled in a fetal position, and slung her over his shoulder. Together, they burst through the farmhouse door, and Cain saw another young soldier running toward them through the snow, drawn by the gunfire. The man froze, startled by their sudden appearance, and his hesitation let Cain get off a wild shot that hit the man's knee and took him down, screaming.

Cain bolted into the woods, where the trees gave him cover. He was barely aware of the weight of Tatiana draped over his shoulder. He ran, dodging around thick pines, hearing more shouts as men joined the hunt from the road. They hadn't brought in a helicopter, but he doubted he had more than a few minutes before the search headed to the sky. He reached an open farm field where there was no protection, and he sprinted across the frozen land, chased by weapons fire crackling from behind him.

One bullet seared his leg, but he didn't slow down. Another whistled past his ear. As he neared the next grove of trees past the field, the firefight intensified, and he zigzagged, feeling another near-miss that sprayed blood from his neck. When he finally reached the shelter of the trees again, he sagged to his knees, letting the girl slump to the ground next to him. He expected to hear the voices closing on him, expected to see dozens of soldiers converging on his location through the snowy field.

Instead, the gunfire stopped.

The Russians all withdrew.

At first he was puzzled, but then he understood. He'd crossed the border. He wasn't in the South Ossetia province;

he was back in Georgia, in unoccupied territory. The Russians weren't ready to start another war over a single spy.

"We're safe," he told Tatiana as he exhaled in relief. "They won't come for us now."

The girl didn't answer. He looked at her for the first time since they'd reached the trees, and he saw that her eyes were open and fixed in a look of scared surprise. Her trembling had stopped; her body was motionless. When he turned her over, he saw that a single bullet from one of the Russian rifles had landed in the back of her skull. Her black hair was matted with blood. She was dead, killed instantly.

If he hadn't been carrying her, that bullet would have killed him.

Cain got to his feet. He stared down at the lifeless teenager and felt a crushing wave of exhaustion, the weight of the world slumping his shoulders. His blood was warm inside his clothes. He needed to go, but he found he couldn't move; he couldn't leave her, not yet. He shook his head in bitter regret, and not for the first time, he hissed out a curse against the life he led.

One week later, Cain waited outside a cargo hangar at the airport in Antalya, Turkey, on the Mediterranean coast. The weather was unseasonably hot, almost eighty degrees. He wore a black formfitting T-shirt and cargo shorts as he waited for the arrival of the Treadstone jet. Sunglasses covered his eyes. By habit, he examined the faces around him, but he concluded that he wasn't being watched.

His wounds were healing now. At least the ones the doctors could treat.

Cain pressed the secure satellite phone to his ear. The signal was crystal clear. Holly Schultz, who was in Washington, could have been standing a few feet away.

"You haven't checked in about the mission," she chided him. "I had to hear from Nash that you called for the jet."

"I've been busy staying alive," Cain told her.

That silenced her complaints, but the truth was, he'd deliberately put off making his report. He'd taken three days to make his way south from Georgia, and then he'd spent the last four days at a Turkish beachside resort. He'd swum out in the sea until the land was just a smudge on the horizon. He'd drunk a lot of raki. He'd paid a prostitute to do nothing but sit in his room for an entire day and talk to him, even though he didn't speak the language. That was how Cain ran from his troubles.

But he couldn't run forever.

"Anyway, I'm back," he went on.

"And Abel?"

"I shot him."

"He's dead?"

Cain hesitated. "I think so. I didn't have time to check as the Russians moved in."

"That's unfortunate," Holly said.

"I had to act fast. I didn't figure you'd want an American agent captured in Russian-occupied territory."

"True enough," she admitted in a grudging voice. "We'll need to do a full debrief when you're back. I'll have someone meet the plane."

"Fine. Whatever." He didn't hide the hatred he felt at that moment. For her. For himself. For the whole world.

"Are you all right, David?" she asked, injecting a forced bit of sympathy into her tone. When she wanted to pretend she cared, she used his real name. David Webb. But he had been Cain for so long that his birth name had little meaning for him. There were days when he didn't even remember it.

"I'm fine," he replied, "but I had to take over one of Abel's covers as I made my escape."

"What identity are you using now?" Holly asked.

Cain squinted into the hot Turkish sunlight. "My name is Jason Bourne."

PART ONE

1

Juneau, Alaska
The present

When Sam young spotted the blond woman in the *Norwegian Jewel* sweatshirt coming into his gallery, he knew they'd found him. Yes, she looked like any of the thousands of other tourists streaming off the cruise ships every day. Her eyes went to the cheap framed prints of Mendenhall Glacier, not the handcrafted Native sculptures. She carried a plastic bag stuffed with Chinese-made T-shirts from a discount gift shop near the port. If he took her in the back and searched her, he was sure he'd find a valid cruise ship ID and a matching passport with her name and photograph. Spies didn't make obvious mistakes like that.

But she was a fake.

Cruise passengers came and went every day, but once their ship left for the next port, they were gone for good. In by eight a.m., out by four thirty p.m., depending on the tide. But this woman had been here before. Not in the gallery. She was smart enough not to kiss the dog more than once. However, Sam had learned to study and remember faces, and he was certain he'd seen this same woman outside the shop in the last couple of days.

He'd know for sure if he got a buzz on his phone. Sam's tradecraft specialty was as a computer hacker, and even though he'd been inactive for Treadstone for two years, he still kept his hand in the game. That was partly for his own protection, because when it came to Treadstone, you were never really out. He kept surveillance cameras inside and outside his Franklin Street shop, as well as on the road near his house on Black Wolf Way. He'd written an app to isolate faces from the video feeds and maintain them in a database, and with each new entry, the program ran facial recognition to look for duplicates. When it found one, it sent the information to his phone.

Buzz.

Sam felt the vibration in his pocket. He took out his phone and examined the side-by-side photographs that appeared in the notification from his app. One was the thirtysomething woman standing in his shop right now, pretending to study a display of colorfully painted Russian nesting dolls. The other was a woman with dark hair and an oilskin jacket who'd passed on the sidewalk outside the shop three days earlier. Although the second image was less focused, and she'd changed her hair in between, it was definitely the same person.

Studying the picture again, Sam was also certain that he'd seen her at a table at Mar y Sol when he'd had dinner there on Wednesday. She'd been watching him for a while.

Sam slipped his hands casually into his pockets, one hand curling around the grip of his Hellcat pistol, as he approached her. "Can I help you?"

The woman was good. A pro. She looked up with a false smile, but he could see her eyes take note of his hands, then flick up to the corner of the ceiling and spot the positioning of the security camera. He assumed there was a weapon hidden inside her gift bag. If she went for it, the question would be which one of them was faster. Sam didn't like his odds. There was something about the hawkish look in her blue eyes that made him think she'd be the better fighter.

But she was the advance scout, not the shooter. There was too much risk going after him in the middle of downtown.

"Oh, no, thank you," she replied pleasantly. "Just browsing. You have beautiful things here."

"Thank you."

"I suppose most of your business comes from the ships. It must get so quiet off-season. Do you close up for the winter?"

"No, I'm open all year, but you're right. Most of the crowds disappear as soon as the cruise season ends."

"How did you come to be in a place like this?" she asked him.

Sam shrugged. He was sure she knew exactly where he'd come from. "I don't know. How does anyone end up anywhere?"

"Oh, well, I guess you're right about that. Anyway, I wish I could afford to buy something, but you know, the family's always on a budget. T-shirts for the kids and not much else."

"That's okay," he told her. "Take your time and look around."

"I will, thanks."

She spent another five minutes in the shop, just to make it look good. As she was leaving, she called out to say goodbye, and her eyes shot another glance at the ceiling camera. Then, as the bell on the door chimed, she headed out to Franklin Street and turned toward the harbor. She didn't look through the window again. That would be the last time he saw her. But others would come soon. Tonight, most likely. She'd probably report that she'd been blown and that the assault team needed to assume he'd be waiting for them.

She hadn't fooled him, and he hadn't fooled her.

As soon as she was gone, Sam closed the shop. He assessed

his options but decided there was only one thing to do. Get the hell out of Juneau right now. Whoever was after him, he'd be outgunned and outnumbered. He didn't know how they'd found him—there were no more than half a dozen people who knew that the Arizona hacker with the Treadstone code name Dax was now gift shop owner Sam Young in Alaska—but he didn't have time to worry about how his cover had been blown.

He'd had an escape strategy in place from day one. It was time to put it into play.

Sam emptied the cash from the register. There wasn't much, just a few hundred dollars. He thought about stopping at the bank to withdraw the money from his accounts, but he assumed if they were watching the store, they'd have someone watching his bank, too, to see whether he was making a run. It didn't matter. His bank had a branch in the town of Haines. Once he was clear of Juneau, he could stop there on his way into the backcountry.

He locked the shop and hiked up the Franklin Street hill. He always parked several blocks away, which gave him time to identify any surveillance that might be waiting for him. It was a cold September day, gray and ominous, with low clouds clinging to the steep green hillsides. Drizzle spat on his face. He kept his hand around the Hellcat in his pocket, but his shoulders were hunched, just a man trudging along in the rain. His eyes took a close look at each parked car and each doorway. If they were watching him, they were keeping it under wraps. He saw no one.

Sam debated whether to go home. He had his go bag, his laptop, and more money hidden under the floorboards in his living room. He could be in and out in ninety seconds, and then he'd be on the way to Statter Harbor, where he kept his Exhilarator speedboat gassed up and ready to go. As he'd developed an escape plan—knowing a day like this would come sooner or later—he'd thought about using a floatplane. That would give him more range and speed, but the flying weather around Juneau was too iffy day by day to guarantee he could get out of town on short notice. With the Exhilarator, he could head to Hoonah or race up the channel to Haines or Skagway. Once there, he could hide out in the woods or take an SUV over the Rockies on the Alaska Highway.

He found his red Honda parked at the top of the hill near 6th Street. From there, he could see the dark water of the harbor through mist and fog. The *Jewel* was the only cruise ship docked there today, and he knew it would be gone in less than two hours. Everyone in Alaska retail knew the port times of the ships. Sam made a show of dropping his wallet, which gave him a chance to check the undercarriage of his Accord, in case anyone had planted explosives or tracking devices. He also noted the tiny red threads he'd secured across the gaps of each car door. They were still there; no one had broken into the vehicle during the day.

Even so, he held his breath when he started the engine. It caught. He didn't blow up.

Sam headed north on the Glacier Highway. He watched the mirrors and didn't see anyone following him. He decided to stop home to grab his go bag, but ten minutes later, he changed his mind. A shrill alarm went off on the phone in his pocket, which was the signal that someone had broken one of the invisible laser barriers guarding the windows and doors of his house. There were people inside. Sam pulled onto the highway shoulder near the bridge at Lemon Creek, where wooded hilltops and snowcapped mountains went in and out of view through the clouds. His breath came quickly; adrenaline surged through him.

When he dug out his phone, he activated the cameras located in the house's ductwork, which gave him sound and video of the interior. He spotted four men, all dressed in black, all armed with semiautomatics and suppressors. The faces of the men were unfamiliar, but who they were didn't concern him. What mattered was that they would take him down as soon as he came through the door.

"Should we check the computer?" one of them said through the video feed.

"Don't bother," another replied. *"He's a hacker. He' ll have it secured. We' ll take it with us and let the pros crack it. But keep your eyes open. He's bound to have backups. Maybe electronic, maybe print."*

"What are we looking for?"

"Anything about Intelsat."

On the shoulder of the Glacier Highway, Sam closed his eyes and swore. Now he understood. Now it all made sense.

Intelsat. Of course.

Seven years earlier, long before he became the Alaskan named Sam Young, he'd tapped into the feed of a satellite located in geosynchronous orbit over the Indian Ocean, and he'd modified the satellite's stored data. The order had come with a clearance code that went straight to the top. There were no names, but orders like that didn't use names. He'd known what the mission was about. Everyone in the world knew why satellite data was important at that particular moment. In the darkest part of his heart, he'd also known that sooner or later that mission would cost him his life.

Some secrets were so dangerous they had to stay buried forever.

Sam could feel the trap closing around him. They were waiting for him at home. Did they know about his escape route, too? He was only five minutes from the harbor, and all he could do was hope that they hadn't found the Exhilarator. He pulled back onto the highway, forced himself not to speed, and continued into the locals' section of Juneau, where there were grocery stores and McDonald's drive-throughs and dentist offices and churches. It was harder to spot a tail there, but as he drove, he didn't think anyone picked him up.

The sweat gathered on his neck. He kept eyeing the mirrors.

Where are they?

At each intersection, he expected to spot someone in a parked car, watching the road. There were only so many routes in and out of the city. But he made it all the way to the turn that led into the harbor, and his instincts told him he was still alone. Next stop, the boat. Then Haines. Then the inland wilderness.

He parked near the pier that led out among dozens of sailboats and trawlers. Ahead of him was the choppy water of Auke Bay, whitecaps pulsing in the afternoon wind. It was raining harder now, and he pulled a yellow slicker from the backseat and pulled up the hood. That was good. He was harder to recognize that way.

Sam made his way to the Exhilarator. He tried to keep his hands steady as he undid the tarpaulin and climbed aboard. He'd done this dozens of times, practiced over and over for a moment like this. The boat was fast, the engine new. When he fired it up, the motor growled to life, a tiger ready to stretch its legs on the water. He looked back at the parking lot, not seeing any cars pulling off the highway in pursuit.

Go!

He eased away from the pier and headed west out of the harbor. His pace was a slow putt-putt crawl through the no-wake zone as he steered toward open water. The low, dark hills loomed behind the bay, their green treetops zigzagging against the gray sky. The air got cold, and he gritted his teeth against the wind. When he'd cleared the mouth of the harbor, he unleashed the engine, kicking up white foam, the prow slapping down hard as it crested the waves. He shot between the islands and wheeled northward into the channel. He was alone out here, just him and the whales, and for the first time since he'd left the shop, he began to relax. He was on his way. He was almost free.

Then, as he passed Lincoln Island, he saw the first of the other boats.

It was waiting for him, sleek and black. If his Exhilarator was a tiger, this was a cheetah that he couldn't outrun. The boat floated out there, patiently expecting him to cut his engine, which he did. He had to think, but there was no time to think. Another black speedboat appeared around the north end of the island. When Sam looked over his shoulder, he saw two more boats closing from the south, making a pincer and cutting off his escape. He was trapped in the channel with nowhere to go.

Each boat carried two men, dressed in black, holding semiautomatic rifles. Eight to one. They didn't hurry; they knew they had him. Their engines stuttered as they began to get closer, moving in on him from four directions. This was the end. Every operative recognized that moment when there was no way out. Sam only had seconds now, just time enough to send a text. A *warning*!

He grabbed the satellite phone from the boat's storage compartment. They could see what he was doing. The gunfire began, bullets whizzing near his head. He ducked down out of the line of fire, but his shelter wouldn't last long. The other boats would be on top of him soon.

When the phone found a signal, he keyed in a number that he'd memorized years ago. It belonged to Nash Rollins, his Treadstone handler.

More shots.

The other boats rose up and down with the high waves. A ricocheted bullet broke his right wrist and knocked the phone out of his hand. Gasping in pain, Sam crawled along the deck and retrieved it. He had to tap out his message left-handed as the men appeared above him, still firing, now at point-blank range.

He heard the message go through as a rain of bullets blasted through his slicker, the rubber turning from yellow to red. His lungs began to fill with blood. When he took a breath, there was nothing there. No sweet Alaska air. Never again.

But Sam had sent Nash the warning.

One message. One word.

Defiance.

2

The first light of dawn had barely begun to break through the darkness when Jason Bourne opened the floor-to-ceiling window in his Paris apartment. Warm, humid air blew inside as he studied the empty alley of Rue Houdart below him. There was no balcony outside the window, just an ornamental iron railing and a few flowerpots filled with dying African violets. Below him, the greasy pavement was wet from overnight rain. Pigeons pecked for crumbs near an overflowing waste bin, and a solitary motorbike whined through puddles as it headed for the plaza at Rue des Amandiers.

The vandals had come back to the alley. Only a day after the white brick wall on the building across from him had been scrubbed, new graffiti had already been sprayed overnight in drippy red paint. *Aime moi deux fois*. Love me two times. It was a Jim Morrison joke, because the apartment in the 20th arrondissement was only half a block from the sprawling Père Lachaise cemetery, where the singer was buried.

Otherwise, the street looked as it did every morning. Nothing was different. No one lurked in the gated entrance below him. The typical cars were parked on the sidewalk. He'd long ago memorized every model, every license plate. Even so, Bourne felt a sense of unease, like a tiny drip of fresh paint on that smooth white wall. Once you saw it, you couldn't see anything else.

What is it?

As he stayed in the shadows behind the glass, his gaze traveled from window to window. He knew his neighbors in the building across the way. Like a voyeur from *Rear Window*, he'd studied their habits from the nighttime darkness, making note of who drank too much red wine and who was sleeping with whom. He didn't care about their private lives, but he needed to know if something suddenly changed.

A new visitor. A new threat.

Bourne had lived here since the beginning of April. It was early September now. The name on the lease belonged to a seventy-year-old widow in Lyon, and she'd been happy to lend her identity for a thousand-euro bribe. The summer had been uneventful—no Treadstone missions, no overseas hunts, nothing but Paris art museums and his relentless workouts. But his time here was winding down. Typically, he switched locations every six months. He knew that the assassin known as Lennon was still looking for him, and that meant no safe house stayed safe for long. Sooner or later, if he didn't keep moving, Lennon would find him.

But had he found him already?

Was that what Bourne sensed?

Stop it! Nothing is there!

He shook off his paranoia. He left the window and returned to the main room of the apartment. It was small, sparsely furnished, its empty walls lined with cracks and spiderwebs. The floor was covered in worn beige carpet mottled by years of stains. Normally, the place smelled of whatever takeaway dinner Jason had eaten last, but now it had a feminine, alluring fragrance, like hyacinths in full bloom. That was the smell of Abbey Laurent's perfume, which always trailed her like an erotic breath on his neck.

When he entered the bedroom, he saw Abbey naked on his twin bed in the semidarkness. She lay on her side on top of the blankets, her mahogany-red hair spilling across her face and shoulders, her left breast pushed into the rumpled sheet. One bare leg was straight, one bent at the knee. He sat down beside her and brushed back a few strands of her hair, then glided his fingertips across the hollow of her back. His touch elicited a drowsy murmur of pleasure but didn't get her to open her eyes. Abbey was typically slow to wake up. When she was alone, she routinely worked until three or four in the morning each night.

Bourne let her sleep.

They'd been together for three days. For almost a year, they'd maintained a clandestine relationship, meeting up for short visits whenever both of them could get away. Right now, Abbey had little free time in her life. In July, she'd released a novel cowritten with the famous thriller author Peter Chancellor, and the book had become a bestselling sensation. Abbey was in demand now, signing new contracts, doing events at bookstores, making appearances on television. This was her moment. He wanted her to make the most of it.

Her visibility also made it important that they keep their relationship secret, because Jason knew that any woman he was with immediately became a target.

Like Marie, his wife, who'd been killed.

Like Nova, a spy and Bourne's former lover, who'd barely escaped from Lennon.

That was why he'd never wanted to become involved with Abbey. He'd tried to distance himself from her, he'd tried to walk away, but the fact was that he was in love with her. And she was in love with him. Even so, he didn't know if that was enough to make it work.

While he waited for Abbey to get out of bed, he took a shower underneath a trickle of cold, brownish water. He braced himself against the wall and let the water drizzle down over his head. The chill brought him to life. Bourne was just over six feet tall, his lean body a taut frame of muscle and scars, his dark brown hair swept back on his head. His face was handsome and square, his skin pale, with lines deepening on his forehead. He was in his late thirties, and with each year, he bounced back more slowly from the punishment his body had endured in the last fifteen years. The pain only made him work harder.

When he was done in the shower, he shaved, running a razor over his chin by feel without turning on the bathroom light. Only his blue-gray eyes seemed to shine in the reflection, like two hard jewels. Otherwise, his features were lost in shadow, like a ghost who was barely there. That was how he preferred it. In his life with Treadstone, he'd discovered that light was a threat and darkness was his old friend.

Really, Bourne *was* a kind of ghost. Years earlier, he'd been shot on a mission in Marseilles and only survived thanks to an alcoholic French surgeon who'd gone off the booze long enough to save him. But the man who'd awakened from that injury had no memory of his life, only the lethal skills of a killer. He'd lost who he was. His childhood. His past. People he'd loved. The images that remained were nothing but disconnected fragments.

Until last year.

Last year, he'd been shot again, and as he recovered, he'd found certain parts of his past slowly returning to him. He'd remembered the traitor code-named Abel and their confrontation in the Georgian woods. He'd remembered *how* he'd taken the identity of Jason Bourne. He'd remembered that Abel had survived their encounter and gone on to a new life as a Russian assassin named Lennon. The two of them were still hunting each other.

Naked, Bourne went back to the living room.

Then, a moment later, he returned to the window.

Something drew him there, and it wasn't just paranoia. He had an instinct, a nagging sense that the picture in front of him was not right. Something was different. That instinct had kept him alive more than once, and he couldn't ignore it. His gaze traveled again from window to window, looking for any kind of change, like a blind that was usually closed but was now open, or the silhouette of a man where there should have been a woman. He looked for little things, insignificant details, because pros like Lennon only made little mistakes.

This isn't real! Stop torturing yourself!

But then he knew what his brain was telling him. The problem wasn't what was there, but what was *not* there.

The cigarette smoke was wrong.

Across the alley, two floors up, two apartments to the right—an angle that gave an uncomfortably good view of Bourne's flat—lived an old man named Hugo Gagnon. Hugo was ninety-five years old, a teenage veteran of La Résistance. Every morning, Hugo woke up early, even before Jason did, and sat invisibly in the shadows of his flat and smoked Gauloises cigarettes. The smoke blew across the short distance and right into Bourne's window.

Today the smoke was different, less acrid. An American style.

He didn't think that Hugo, at age ninety-five, had switched brands. Someone else was in the old man's apartment. Someone was there *right now*, staring back from the darkness, but he couldn't see who it was.

"Is something wrong?" Abbey asked.

She'd come up behind him, naked like he was, her red hair mussed. Her arms looped around his waist, and her bare skin pressed against him.

Bourne frowned. He stayed in the shadows, his eyes on the dark window in the opposite building. It might have been nothing. There were any number of innocent explanations, but he didn't like it. If he'd been looking to surveil his apartment, that was the location he would have chosen himself. And yet he didn't think it was Lennon. If the assassin had found him, Bourne would already be dead. So would Abbey.

Two shots from a sniper rifle through the window.

But if not Lennon, then who? And *why*?

"I'm not sure," he replied. "I better check it out."

"Check out some espresso and a chocolate croissant while you're at it," Abbey told him. Then, when he didn't laugh, she added more seriously, "What's going on? Do you think someone is watching us?"

"Maybe."

"Should we close the blinds?"

Jason shook his head. "No. If someone *is* watching us, I don't want him to know we've spotted him. For the time being, stay out of sight, and keep the lights off."

"Okay."

She'd learned not to question him when it came to directives like that. That was part of his training. Security was about taking every threat seriously.

When you lower your guard even once, you die.

Treadstone.

Jason got dressed in the darkness. Abbey slipped on a robe, and then she watched him, and he watched her. She was a few years younger than he was, and a few inches shorter, but she usually wore high-heeled boots that brought her closer to his eyes. Her body was skinny for her height, but she'd become stronger and more toned in the past year as he guided her through intensely physical workouts. She'd changed in other ways, too, from the young woman he'd met three years earlier. She walked faster, laughed louder, made love with new abandon. She was more confident, more mature, but also more cynical. A remoteness had taken over her dark eyes, which he knew only too well, because he saw that same look in the mirror himself. Living in his world meant living with compromises that most people couldn't understand. Abbey had told him she could learn to accept that, to not question the things he had to do. He wasn't so sure.

Her phone pinged with an incoming text.

"Alicia Beauvoir," Abbey said quietly when she read the message.

"About the book?"

Abbey nodded.

"You travel in elite circles now," Jason said.

She shrugged, looking uncomfortable. But it was true. Alicia Beauvoir had served as both the U.S. ambassador to the United Nations and then the secretary of state under a previous administration. Then, when she'd been presumed to be a presidential candidate, she'd retired to take care of her husband, who was battling throat cancer. He was healthy again, but rather than return to politics, Beauvoir had opted to watch the Washington games from the sidelines of her Maryland country estate. And to write books.

That was where Abbey came in. The two of them were now teaming up to cowrite a political thriller.

Jason secured his Sig Sauer in the holster at the small of his back and zipped a nylon jacket over his black T-shirt. He came up to Abbey, who'd taken a seat on the bed and was chewing on her lower lip. She had her arms crossed over her chest.

"What's up?" he asked.

"Oh, it's this new deal with Alicia. The publisher has us on a tight time frame because of their publicity plans. It could take me six or eight months. Intense work, no breaks. I don't know whether I'll be able to get away during that time."

"I figured," Jason replied.

"I don't want us to be apart that long."

"Neither do I, but it is what it is."

"Well, we've got three more days, right?" Abbey said.

"Right," he replied, wondering whether that was true. They'd made a pact to live for the day. Tomorrow was never guaranteed.

Bourne glanced out the window again. He took Abbey and guided her to a place in the living room where no one in the opposite building could see her. Light was beginning to streak through the shadows.

"Stay here," he said. "Don't go out. Keep your phone close."

"I get it, Jason."

He turned for the door, then stopped. "You know the code, right?"

"Yes, I know the code."

He didn't have to explain what he meant. One of the first instructions he'd given her was an emergency code between them. *Chicago*. The Chicago code meant drop everything, get out of the apartment immediately, get as far away from him as possible. They'd worked out a plan for her escape and gone over it multiple times.

"I'll be back as soon as I can," he went on.

She nodded with a forced smile. "Don't forget the coffee."

Bourne smiled, too, as he headed for the apartment door. Before opening it, he glanced back at Abbey, and both of their smiles bled away. Her face had a darkness in it. Their eyes locked together across the room, and somehow he thought they both knew that everything was about to change.

3

Bourne exited the apartment building near the corner of the alley. The windows next to him were barred, and there was more Jim Morrison graffiti on the redbrick walls. A couple of early-morning cars sped past him on Rue de Tlemcen. The sticky air made his black shirt damp with sweat. He checked the road, then crossed the alley and stayed close to the wall. From there, no one in the apartments overhead could see him.

He hurried along the length of the alley. His ears were pricked for footsteps behind him, and his eyes moved constantly, examining the cars and doorways. All were empty. He checked the rooflines, but the angle was too steep for a rifle shot here, and there were trees providing cover. No one else was in the alley, except a black cat sauntering across his path. Not surprisingly, the nearby pigeons had all flown away.

At the far end, he emerged into a small plaza, where early sunlight shined on the cobblestones. There were more people here, a couple of mothers with young children in hand, an old woman at a bus stop, a delivery driver unloading boxes from a truck. Traffic was getting busier as the city woke up.

He smelled fresh bread from the boulangerie two doors down, and he went inside and ordered two coffees and two *pains au chocolat*. When he emerged from the bakery, he sat down in one of the red chairs near the door. He put the white bakery bag and the second coffee on the ground and sipped his drink while he watched the plaza come to life.

If there was a trap set up for him, he'd see it soon. And he did.

It didn't take him long to realize he'd been spotted. The watcher was good, but not good enough. She was lanky and young, in her early twenties, with stringy black hair. She leaned against the window of a French restaurant and looked impatiently up and down the street, as if waiting for a car to collect her. Her thumb worked the screen on her phone, but she hadn't yet mastered the art of seeing two things at once. Every few seconds, she glanced his way, just with a flick of the eyes, but enough to give her away. She chewed gum with her mouth open, which covered the report she was making on the microphone nestled in her ear between strands of long hair.

Two more minutes passed. Bourne saw the next operative arrive, responding to the call from the woman on the street. This one was deadly.

The man was on foot. He was about thirty years old with buzzed black hair and heavy stubble on his beard line. He wore jeans, an untucked blue dress shirt, and black sneakers. Bourne knew that was a deliberate choice; black didn't show blood the way white did. You could always change clothes, but shoes were harder to switch. The man had a satchel over his right arm, and one of the zippered pockets was open. Bourne assumed the man's gun was there for easy access.

Jason glanced at him. It was natural to look at a stranger and look away. The man went into the bakery, ordered an espresso, and then took a seat in one of the chairs on the other side of the door. He didn't study his phone, unlike everyone else in Paris. Instead, he made a show of watching the plaza with a tight smile and coal-dark eyes. He noticed everyone around him except Bourne. That was a mistake, a tell; he should have looked at Jason, too.

Again, like the woman on the street, this agent was good, but not good enough. These were definitely not Lennon's people.

So who are they?

Bourne finished his coffee. He got up and left the other coffee and the white bakery bag on the sidewalk beside the chair, as if he'd forgotten it. He headed toward Rue Houdart, but he didn't return to the alley. Behind him, a metal chair scraped as the man in the blue shirt got up, preparing to follow. Jason walked past a drugstore that hadn't opened for the day, and he listened to the man's sneakers squeaking on the cobblestones and broadcasting his location as he drew closer. Another mistake.

At a fruit stand, Jason paused to examine a basket of fresh peaches. He didn't look back, but he heard the footsteps stop suddenly. Bourne called a greeting to the grocer, then continued at an unhurried pace until he reached a narrow walkway between two buildings. It led into a park; he'd checked the route many times before.

With no warning, Bourne bolted into the walkway. He anticipated the killer's reaction. Confusion. Fear. Indecision.

Keep your target off-balance.

Treadstone.

When Bourne cleared the corner of the next building, where he was invisible from the street, he ducked against the wall. He shrugged off his jacket, leaving his pistol accessible in the holster at his back. Seconds later, the killer followed. Foolishly, the man cleared the corner at a sprint without stopping, and he led with his gun. Bourne hit the man in the face with his jacket, and simultaneously swept out his legs with a swipe of his foot. As the man fell, his gun fired wildly into the air with a throaty spit. Bourne stepped on the man's wrist hard with his boot, then kicked the gun clear. He bent down, whipped away the jacket, and pounded the man's skull into the pavement.

The agent's eyes rolled back, and he was unconscious.

This was an amateur tough. A mercenary, easy to disarm. But *who* had sent him?

Bourne checked the walkway and confirmed that no one else was in pursuit. He searched the man's pockets, found no ID, then retrieved the radio receiver hanging from his ear. He listened, hearing a woman's frantic voice.

"Pierre? Pierre, où êtes-vous? Un rapport! Maintenant!"

There wasn't much time. Others would be coming soon. Bourne grabbed the unconscious man's gun, left him where he was, and ran to the end of the walkway. The path led to the far side of the building across from his own. He'd long ago stolen a key card for that building, and he let himself inside. He took the stairs cautiously, expecting an ambush. If the leader of the group was inside—hiding in Hugo Gagnon's apartment—then there should be a backup team here, placed at the various access points. But there was no one.

Bourne made it to the fourth floor. The hallway was empty. The doors on both sides were closed, but he heard voices in French as people began to wake up for the day. The squeal of the floorboards announced him, no matter how slowly he walked. Hugo Gagnon's flat was six doors down, and Jason saw that the door to the apartment hung open by a few inches.

It was like an invitation. Someone knew he was coming.

Again he checked the hallway in both directions, anticipating an assault. He had a gun in each hand now, his and the one he'd taken from the other agent.

Where are they?

The American cigarette smoke he'd smelled from his

apartment still lingered in the air. Pungent. Recent. He didn't think the flat was empty. He shouldered past the door to the opposite side, then eyed the dimly lit space through the narrow gap between the door and the frame. The morning glow of the window was in view. That window looked across the alley toward his apartment. Toward Abbey.

Something silver, mounted on a tripod, glinted near the window. A sniper's rifle?

No, a telescope.

Bourne listened. There was no movement from inside. Keeping low, he kicked the door open and waited. No one called to him, and no one fired, but he heard a muffled grunt and a scrape of wood on wood. He crossed the threshold, guns leveled, and saw the source of the noise. Hugo Gagnon sat in the corner of the room, his mouth gagged, his limbs tied to a rickety chair.

The old man's head bobbed toward the closed door that led to his bedroom.

Whoever was waiting for him was in there.

Bourne took a moment to check the window and the telescope. It was a high-magnification Orion model, and when he squinted into the viewfinder, he saw the bedroom of his apartment spring into focus. Next to the telescope, an ashtray sat on the ledge, with six butts crushed out. The surveillance had been going on for hours.

Behind him, he heard the rattle of the bedroom door. Someone was coming out and making no effort to hide it. Jason put down the second gun and aimed his Sig at the doorframe. Slowly, the door opened, but whoever was in the bedroom stayed secure behind the wall. No one emerged.

Then a voice called to him.

A voice he'd known for years, a voice that had a smoky, sultry tease whenever she talked.

"What took you so long, Jason?"

He stared at the shadows. A moment later, there she was. She had her arms in the air and no gun in her hands, as if she wasn't sure whether he'd shoot her. She was small and lithe, with thick raven hair, skin the color of rich olive oil, and a curvy body he'd traced many times with his fingers.

It was Nova.

Bourne didn't lower his gun. Nova stayed in the doorway.

"I know you don't trust me," she told him. "I get it. After what I did to you in California, I know you'll never trust me again. But I'm on your side this time. Nash sent me to get you. He's in Paris. We need to go now, both of us."

She was right. He didn't trust her.

Two years earlier, she'd drugged and betrayed him. She'd teamed up with Lennon in order to get revenge on the man who'd murdered her family, and she'd let that lust for vengeance overcome everything else. And yet Jason had protected her. He'd let her go, and he hadn't told Nash what she'd done. Despite everything, there was a connection between them that he couldn't break.

He hadn't seen her since that night, but she was never far from his mind. She'd always been unforgettable. There were even moments, making love to Abbey, when he had flashbacks of sex with Nova. The two women couldn't have been more different. Nova had a wildness about her, almost a cruelty, born of a childhood filled with death and drugs. She rarely opened a door into who she really was; she kept her true self hidden away. He understood that impulse, because he was the same way. The source of his attraction to Nova had always been the fact that they were very much alike.

Still he didn't lower the gun. She came closer, arms still in the air. If she made one false move, he wouldn't hesitate to shoot her.

"Who are the people outside?" Bourne asked.

Nova cocked her head in surprise. "What do you mean?"

"The lookout on the street. The man I took down in the walkway below the building. Who sent them?"

Her eyes widened. She took two quick steps, then stopped as his finger slid from the barrel and curled around the trigger.

"They've already made a move? Jason, we need to *go*. If they've found you, then more of them are on the way. That's why I'm here. We're being targeted. *Treadstone* is being targeted. Agents are being assassinated all over the world."

His mind screamed at him. *Don't trust her!*

"Who's behind this?" Bourne asked coolly.

"I don't know. Neither does Nash. That's the point. We need to find out."

"Where is he?"

"We set up a rendezvous point in the city. I'm supposed to take you there."

Jason nodded at Hugo Gagnon, whose eyes were wide with fear. "What about the old man?"

"We'll leave the door open," Nova said. "Someone will find him."

"You're not going to kill him?"

Nova hissed in disgust. "Of course I'm not going to kill him! Shit, Jason, I'm still one of the good guys."

"Are you? You worked with Lennon. Have you forgotten that? He wanted you to be his next Yoko."

"Yeah, and I'm *not*. I never was. That night in California wasn't about Lennon and wasn't about you. You know that."

"So where have you been for two years? What have you been doing?"

"The truth? I've been living in Athens. Mostly getting drunk on ouzo and sleeping with Greek college boys. And punishing myself for what I did to the man I loved."

Bourne didn't like Nova using the word *love*. It felt false, as if she were still trying to manipulate him. He studied her face, which hadn't changed since he'd last seen her. The full lips, the hawklike nose, the cascading black hair, the fiery green eyes. He could see the chain around her neck that held her mother's Greek coin pendant; Nova never took it off. Her clothes fit like a second skin, and where her arms were bare, he saw the tapestry of tattoos that painted her whole body. She was the same, and yet she was also completely different. Broken in ways that didn't heal. On the edge.

He didn't know if he was making a mistake, but he finally lowered his gun.

"Thank God," Nova said, her voice breathless with relief. "Let's go. They'll be coming for us."

"I need to see Abbey first."

She came and took his arm so tightly that he could feel the scrape of her long fingernails. Her gaze went to the telescope and then to the apartment on the other side of the alley. "Jason, there's no time. You'll never be able to come back here. This location is burned. You need to tell Abbey to go. To get away from here, to get the hell away from *you*. At least for a while. Right now, everything about Treadstone is radioactive."

He knew she was right, but he didn't want to admit it. He couldn't accept what he had to do.

In front of him, Nova's green eyes turned sad. "Look, she's not part of our world, Jason. She's not one of us. I know you love her in a way you never loved me. Believe me, I've been watching you. I saw your face. And hers. But if you want to keep her alive, you need to walk away."

Jason said nothing. Nova was right about that, too. He'd known it all along, and he'd been fooling himself. But it was still like a knife in his heart. He took the phone from his pocket and tapped out a message to Abbey. One word.

Chicago.

Then he crushed the phone under the metal toe of his boot.

"Let's get out of here," Bourne said.

4

The killers came for them in the cemetery.

Bourne and Nova headed side by side down a path of uneven, weed-strewn cobblestones into the heart of Père Lachaise. Jason walked forward, gun in hand; Nova walked backward, guarding them against assaults from the rear. The low morning sun cast long shadows across the city of the dead. There was no breeze, and the branches of the trees didn't move. The walls of the mausoleums on either side of them were charcoal gray from decades of soot, except where patches of mold and green moss spread across the stones.

They passed ghostly and gruesome statues: an angel spray-painted in yellow gold, leaning on a headstone; a lonely child with braided hair, kneeling and praying with fingers folded together; a prone man holding a severed head in his hands; a hideous depiction of a skinless corpse suspended in the air by thorny branches.

"This place is fucking creepy," Nova murmured.

"Yeah." Bourne put a hand on her shoulder and held her in place behind him. "Hang on. Check out that woman over there."

She twisted to see what he saw. There was a woman on

the path about twenty yards away, as frozen as one of the cemetery statues. Upon seeing her, Nova quickly swung back, anticipating fire.

"She could be just a mourner," she said.

Bourne examined the woman, who stood in front of a massive family tomb. A sprawled sculpture of a man lay across the top of a stone coffin, as if he were about to rise from the grave. The woman was tall, dressed in a gray zippered jacket over jeans, with choppy brown hair and sunglasses. She held a large bouquet of flowers in her hands, the arrangement so thick that he couldn't see her fingers.

"No," he replied quietly. "We're about to get hit."

He didn't hide his gun. Neither one of them took a step as they waited to see what happened next. The still air seemed to hold its breath. Somewhere close by, footsteps crackled on old dead leaves. Others were coming for them, unseen around the graves. He focused on the woman's mouth because he suspected she was the one calling the shots. As he watched, he saw what he expected—a flinch of her lips as she whispered a single word into her radio. *Allez.*

Go.

"Now," he hissed to Nova.

They split up as the gunfire began. The woman dropped the flowers and spun, already firing from the pistol in her hand. Nova rolled left across the stones and took cover between two large vaults. Bourne did the same in the opposite direction. Bullets kicked up stone dust around them, the noise muffled to low cracks by suppressors. The hail of fire came from two directions as more shooters joined the woman from the other end of the path. Bourne spotted at least four killers, two to the north, two to the south. Across from him, Nova held up two fingers on both hands, confirming that she'd reached the same conclusion. Nova interspersed her fire both ways, giving cover for Bourne to weave a zigzag path between the rows of graves.

The height of the stones meant no one could see him. The soft ground covered the noise of his footsteps.

Quickly, silently, he worked his way behind the pair of shooters to the north. As he closed on the path, he saw a man and a woman firing from behind low arched headstones. He leveled his barrel at the man and squeezed off a shot. A single bullet carved its way into the man's head and dropped him where he stood, but the noise alerted his partner. Before Bourne could adjust his aim, the woman laid down furious fire that forced him to dive for cover. Tree bark flew near his face; bullets landed in the dirt and pinged off graves. The gunfire got louder as the woman charged. He could hear Nova pinned down by the shooters to the south, so Bourne was on his own.

He threw himself forward, firing two shots as he did, trying to freeze the woman and drive her back. The shots came nowhere near her, but it gave him time to relocate and find shelter among the graves. So did she. When he stole a quick glance behind him, he saw no one.

Where is she?

Jason took out a black baseball cap from his back pocket. He nudged it from behind the headstone where he was hiding. Almost immediately, it drew fire, as he expected—a good shot, drilling a hole through the cap. Bourne spun the other way into the tall grass and fired back. He missed as the woman ducked out of view, but he saw that she'd taken refuge in the shadowy doorway of a mausoleum. No more than twenty feet separated them.

More gunfire erupted from Nova's direction. Three shots were clustered together, all from the same gun. He heard a feminine cry, the voice unrecognizable, but his heart skipped as he wondered if it was her. Anger welled inside him. He had to *move*, but the woman in the vault knew where he was and was primed for any attempt to escape. She wouldn't fall for a ruse again. She'd wait him out.

Jason sweated in the heat. His breath came fast. As he lay stretched across the dirt, flies landed on his face. When he slapped them off, his fingers came away with blood. He'd been hit. A fragment of stone had cut him below his ear, and he bled profusely in a ribbon down his neck. The flies soon returned, buzzing around his head and darting after the sticky prize on his skin.

Not far away, a footstep crunched in the dirt. Another killer was coming for him. Bourne lifted his gun, aiming in the direction of the sound. The light changed, and he saw a shadow flicker on the ground near a high obelisk between the trees. His finger slid around the trigger. Someone stepped out from behind the obelisk, but as Jason prepared to fire, he swore and jerked the barrel skyward. It wasn't a killer. He saw a boy, no more than twelve years old, staring at the gun with huge eyes. Even as Bourne waved him away, the child seemed paralyzed, unable to move.

The woman in the doorway didn't react in time to check her fire. A shot spat through the space between Bourne and the boy. She was a superb shot, and the only thing that saved the boy's life was a dangling tree branch just thick enough to deflect the bullet by a couple of inches. It whizzed by the boy's head, nicking his ear. In the same moment, Bourne rolled into the open from behind the headstone and unleashed a continuous stream of fire toward the mausoleum. The bullets forced the woman backward, but she had nowhere to go. Bourne kept rolling, and when he had a clear view into the darkness of the tomb door, he fired multiple shots, including one that pierced her neck. The woman had been lifting her gun to return fire, but her arm dropped, the gun dropped, and she fell forward out of the mausoleum.

"Allez! Allez!" Bourne shouted at the boy. *"Vite!"*

Finally shocked back to life, the boy ran, wavy blond hair flying behind him.

Jason wiped away dirt, blood, and flies, then scrambled to his feet. He crossed the overgrown grass and threw himself onto the cobblestoned path, prepared to fire. But the woman with the flowers was gone. So were the others. He didn't see Nova or anyone else. He took cover again on the opposite side of the trail and began making his way south.

When he reached the space where Nova had taken shelter, he saw that she was no longer there. Behind him, the headstones were built low, so he had to slither along the ground to stay out of sight until he reached an area where the land sloped sharply upward. There, uneven steps climbed the hill, making a jagged line between fallen graves. Bent low, he ran up the steps through dense foliage, his knees pumping. As he neared the top, he saw the torso of a woman's body sprawled in front of him. Her neck was a mass of blood where her throat had been cut. At first, all he saw was long black hair, and his breath left his chest.

But it wasn't Nova.

Instead, Nova rose above him, emerging from the trees at the top of the slope. She swayed, clinging to the railing with one hand, her golden face now pale. Her other hand held a bloody eight-inch knife. A dark stain matted her shirt, spreading around a burnt hole. She'd been shot in the fleshy part of her side. Her eyes rolled, her body began to wobble, and Jason ran up the last few stairs just in time to have her collapse into his arms. He propped her back against the railing.

"There's one more," she gasped. "I got two."

"Where?"

Her head tilted backward. "Up there. I broke off when I heard you coming."

"Your gun?"

"I lost it."

"Take one of mine," Jason said.

He took the knife from her hand and replaced it with the

grip of his Sig Sauer. Then he used the bloody blade to cut off a sleeve from his jacket. He rolled it up and pushed it into her other hand, and he brought the wad to her side, where he pressed her hand hard into the bullet wound. She grimaced, her face clenching.

"Keep pressure there," he told her. "Give me one minute, then fire a shot in the air."

Bourne retrieved his backup gun from the holster on his ankle and kept the knife out. He edged his way to the top of the slope, which was crowded with old graves. Broken steps climbed to a mausoleum built like a church face, with wrought iron gates. Wildflowers grew through cracks in the stone. He maneuvered his way around the side of the vault, keeping his back against the wall. Stopping to listen, he heard nothing, but he knew the last killer couldn't be far away.

In his head, he counted off the seconds. Nearly a full minute had passed since he'd left Nova, and Jason readied himself. Finally, the low crack of a gunshot snapped from the steps as Nova fired. She also screamed, a woman in pain, and Jason knew she didn't have to fake it.

The distraction worked.

Immediately, Bourne heard footsteps running from the far side of the church-like mausoleum. He twisted around the wall as a muscular blond man broke from cover. The man had both fists clutched around a machine pistol, but he was focused on Nova, not Bourne. Bourne led him with the barrel of his gun and then fired multiple times in succession, striking the man's leg at the knee and spilling him off his feet with a wail of pain. The man fired a wild burst as he fell, and he got lucky, because one bullet struck Jason's backup gun, mangling the barrel and jerking it from his hand.

The killer hit the ground like a falling tree. His MP9 skidded across the stone out of his grasp. Writhing, moaning, the man pushed himself toward the gun, and Jason ran, too, the knife his only weapon now. His boots thundered, and the leather grip slipped in his sweaty hand. When he saw the man tighten his fists around the machine pistol and twist backward, he threw himself into the air and came down hard on the man's body, sinking the knife to the hilt into the man's shoulder. The killer's body kept rotating, and the hot metal shaft of the machine pistol slammed into Bourne's face, knocking him sideways. The knife was wrenched away from Jason's hand.

The man fired. Bullets exploded on stone, and Bourne could feel the scorching heat on his face. Lashing out with his foot, he drove his boot into the man's wounded knee, and the jolt of white-hot agony froze the killer for an instant. In that moment, Bourne grabbed the knife again and slashed hard and deep across the man's wrist where it was clutched around the grip of the machine pistol. Blood spurted, and the sliced nerves immobilized the man's hand; the back of the gun slipped from his grasp.

Jason ripped away the gun and threw it aside. He pushed himself to his knees, with the blade at the man's throat.

"Who sent you? Who are you working for?"

"*Casse-toi.*" The man spat the profanity through gritted teeth.

"*Who?*" Bourne repeated, shifting the point of the knife and stabbing it into the man's knee, which elicited a howl.

Still the man told him nothing. The code of the mercenary was stronger than the pain. Never give up the people who hire you. With one more wave of fury, Bourne stabbed into bone again, but this time the man's eyes rolled back and his head lolled sideways. He was unconscious and wouldn't be awake again anytime soon.

A shadow fell across him, and he looked up. Nova was there, summoning her strength to stay standing. Her small body was framed against the trees. She bit her lip and sucked in a breath, and then she handed him his gun.

"Leave him, Jason. We need to go before anyone else gets here. And I need your help if I'm going to walk."

5

Four hours later, they sat against the wall of an empty warehouse near the train station of Noisy-le-Sec. Sunlight through the barred windows made shadow cages on the pockmarked stone floor, and thick dust clouded the air. The entire building shook whenever a train rumbled through the web of railroad tracks on the other side of the wall. This wasn't one of the usual Treadstone safe houses. Jason had never been here before. According to Nova, Nash wasn't convinced that their existing hideaways were secure, so he'd picked an alternate location run by French intelligence.

While they waited for Nash, Nova drifted in and out of sleep. Bourne had taken her to a doctor who maintained a discreet backdoor practice out of a clinic near Hôpital André Grégoire. The bullet had gone through and through, doing relatively little damage, and the doctor had disinfected the entry and exit wounds. Then he'd given her a shot for the pain. Her color was better, and she was breathing easier, but the morphine had loosened her tongue.

She had a lot to say.

"I'm sorry, Jason," she murmured as her eyes fluttered open again. Her fingers closed around his hand and squeezed.

"Sorry, sorry, sorry. I mean, for California. Shit, what a bitch I was to you. I can't believe it."

Bourne said nothing in reply. Apologies meant nothing. He knew in Nova's mind, she was genuinely sorry for betraying him, but he also knew that if the circumstances came around again, she would do the same thing.

"But the sex was great, right?" Nova rambled on. "That night? You and me. We're hot together. That never changes."

"Right," he agreed, his voice neutral.

Yes, sex with Nova had always been great. She became uninhibited in bed, like an animal set free. That was because she was so good at separating her body from her emotions. It didn't matter who she was with, whether it was Jason or some target she needed to seduce for a mission. Fucking was simply a tool for her, one more Treadstone skill. It had taken him a while to realize that it had nothing to do with making love.

Nova slept a while longer, then woke up again and kept talking as if no time had passed in between.

"Can I ask you something?"

"Go ahead," Bourne said.

"Why did you let me go? I screwed you over in California, Jason, but you came back and saved my life. Why? You could have walked away. You could have handed me to Nash or the FBI and let them stick me in a hole somewhere. Hell, you could have killed me yourself. You would have been entitled to do that. But you let me go. You never even told Nash that I was with Lennon that night."

"Maybe I couldn't betray you the way you betrayed me."

Nova flinched. He didn't often land a blow that cut through her icecold defenses, but that one did.

"Okay, point to you," she admitted. "You still have a soul, and I guess I don't. Or maybe I never did. But you got your revenge. Letting me walk away was the cruelest thing you could have done to me."

"Oh?"

"I'm no good at being out," Nova went on. "I told myself I was done with this shit, but people like you and me aren't cut out for a normal life. I need the adrenaline. Without that, I have no idea who I am. The truth is, I've been a mess for two years. I even got back into drugs. When Nash showed up at my door last month, I was actually relieved. Suddenly I had a purpose again. This is my ticket back in, you know?"

"Maybe so," Jason said.

He couldn't hide the distance in his voice.

"So you and Abbey are together," Nova continued after a long pause. "I told you she was the one for you. I told you that in London, didn't I? Like Marie. Not like me. I was never right for you. But you have to face reality, Jason. You can't walk away from this life any more than I can. You need to shut off what you feel for her. Emotion kills. You know I'm right."

"Don't talk to me about Abbey," he snapped.

But she was right. That was the simplest rule of all.

Emotion kills.

Treadstone.

The warehouse's silent alarm ended their conversation. A bright red light activated on a computer panel mounted near the door. Someone was outside. Bourne scrambled to his feet, his Sig already in his hand. He went to the steel warehouse door and checked the feed from the exterior camera mounted on the roof. A silver Mercedes had parked close to the train tracks, and he saw Nash Rollins get out. With the smoothness of a pro, Nash pretended to check his phone while he confirmed that the area around the warehouse was secure. Then he headed slowly for the door, leaning on his cane as he walked.

When Nash arrived, Jason activated the outside microphone. "So what's your favorite Clancy novel?"

"*Red Storm Rising*," Nash replied. "How about you?"

"It's still hard to beat *The Hunt for Red October*."

That was the signal that all was clear. If either one of them had said *Patriot Games*, the other would have known that they were under duress.

Bourne opened the heavy door. Nash slipped inside, taking off a fedora and smoothing back his thinning shock of unkempt gray hair. The Treadstone handler wore a loose cream-colored turtleneck—too heavy for the warm weather—and pleated brown slacks. Around his neck he wore a lanyard with a fake badge identifying him as a member of the Fédération des Cheminots, the French rail workers union.

"Hello, Jason."

"Nash."

"I heard a police report about a shooting inside Père Lachaise this morning," Nash commented blandly. "I assume that was the two of you. Are you and Nova okay?"

"Nova was shot, but she's recovering."

"Did you find any identification among the killers?"

"None."

Nash nodded, as if that was what he'd expected. His gaze swept the warehouse, and he noted Nova in a patch of sunlight against the far wall. His voice dropped to a whisper. "My apologies for bringing her back into your life without warning, Jason. I needed to find you quickly, and she was my best choice to do that. She knows you and your techniques better than anyone else. I had to avoid our usual contact methods, because I'm not sure how deeply Treadstone has been compromised."

"Understood," he replied.

"Were you with Ms. Laurent?"

"That really doesn't concern you, Nash."

The older man shrugged. "I just wanted to make sure Abbey got out of Paris safely."

"We made plans in advance," Jason said.

"Yes, of course you did."

With a pronounced limp, Nash headed into the dusty interior of the warehouse. Bourne had actually given Nash that limp three years earlier, when he'd shot the man in the leg on the boardwalk in Quebec City. At the time, Nash had been convinced that Bourne had turned, and so he had mounted a full-scale Treadstone operation to have him killed. He'd almost succeeded. For Bourne, it was a lesson in the compromised loyalties of his life. Not that he needed the reminder.

"How are you, Nova?" Nash asked when he reached the wall where Nova lay stretched on the floor.

"Hurts like hell, but I'll live."

"Were they coming for both of you? Or just Cain?"

"The primary target was Jason. They were already onto him."

"Then it's fortunate you found him when you did."

"I'm sure Jason can handle himself with or without me," she replied with a glance in Bourne's direction.

Nash grabbed a rickety wooden chair. He exhaled in relief as he sat down, as if walking and standing were both an effort. He leaned forward, balancing his chin on the head of his cane. He didn't say anything for a while—Nash always gathered his thoughts before talking—and in the interim, Bourne did another check of the exterior windows. Despite his confidence in Nash's tradecraft, he wanted to make sure the man hadn't been followed.

They'd worked together as far back as Jason's memory went—and even further, into the shadows that had been erased from his mind. Nash was fifteen years older than Jason, well into his fifties, and he had a small, tightly wound physique like a coiled spring. His face was deeply lined with wrinkles and dotted with age spots, and he had a long nose with a pronounced bump that dated back to a fight with a Chinese operative years earlier. He'd been a part of Treadstone since its earliest days, surviving all of its political purges and no-win field missions. Every agency director from David Abbott through Levi Shaw had used Nash on assignments that couldn't face scrutiny from Congress or from the civilian appointees in the intelligence community.

"Did Nova bring you up to speed on our situation?" Nash asked finally.

"I told him about the five hits on Treadstone agents," Nova said.

Nash frowned. "Six now, I'm afraid. A few days ago, I got word that one of our former tech assets, a man code-named Dax, was shot to death while he was trying to escape from his cover location in Alaska. Our people have been targets all over the world. The U.S., Europe, Asia, Australia."

Bourne returned to the wall and slid down to the floor. "Am I on the list, too?"

"Before today, I wasn't sure," Nash told him, "but the assault makes that pretty clear. The six agents who were killed go back at least a decade or more with the agency, so it's safe to assume that any of us with a long-standing history at Treadstone are at risk."

"Do you have any idea who's behind this?" Jason asked.

"Not yet."

"The people coming after us in Paris struck me as hired help, not intelligence assets," Bourne said. "Private muscle, difficult to trace."

"I agree," Nash replied. "That suggests that whoever is coming after us is working hard to keep the project off the books and to make it look like a foreign play. However, we're talking about targets who are deep cover agents. That means a very short list of people who know *who* they were and *where* they were. They found you, Jason. I don't need to tell you we keep your identity a closely guarded secret. So how did a hit team locate you?"

Bourne was quiet, but he already knew the answer to that question.

They hadn't followed him. They'd followed Abbey. Somehow they'd discovered that the two of them were involved, and they'd watched her until she led them straight to him. She was his Achilles' heel. That was one more reason why their relationship was dangerous to both of them.

"Anyway, follow it up the chain, and my fear is that this operation is being run from somewhere in the U.S. government," Nash concluded. "An inside job."

Jason frowned. "The question is why."

"I may finally have an answer to that question," Nash replied. "Or at least a partial answer. It's a place to start. Before Dax was killed, he managed to send me a text. Just one word. *Defiance*."

Nova looked up sharply. The sudden movement made her face screw up with pain. "Defiance? I was part of that mission. That was years ago."

"*Seven* years ago, in fact," Nash went on. "Dax wasn't able to give me details, or explain how he made the connection, but he obviously was convinced that there *was* some kind of connection. The first thing I did was check his history, but the relevant time period is blank. There's no record of his activities. I checked the files of the other murdered agents and found the same thing. Whatever they did on that mission was scrubbed."

"Apparently erasing the history wasn't good enough," Nova said. "Now they have to get rid of us entirely. Tie up the loose ends."

"It seems that way. Nova, what was your role in Defiance?"

"A hit. Three hits, actually."

"Who?"

"I don't remember their names, but I remember the how and where, so it wouldn't be too hard to track them down."

"Was there any connection among the targets?"

"I have no idea about that," Nova replied coolly. "It wasn't my job to know. My job was to eliminate them, so that's what I did. I have no idea who they were, and back then, I didn't care."

"Did you work with any other agents?" Nash asked.

"No. It was solo. I heard through the grapevine that multiple agents were involved in Defiance, but none of us knew what the others were doing. We were all blind. Each of us only got one piece in the puzzle."

Bourne hadn't said a word, but he felt a stabbing pain behind his eyes, and a roaring filled his ears, as loud as an aircraft engine.

Defiance!

He knew the name. He'd heard that mission mentioned twice before, both times from the same unlikely source.

Lennon.

A year ago, he'd confronted Lennon at an estate in the Hamptons, and the assassin had taunted him about an operation from their past. *They sent me on a mission. A mission that went horribly wrong.*

Defiance.

That was what Lennon had told him. And there was more.

Memories had begun to creep back for Jason—memories of his confrontation with Lennon when the assassin was a Treadstone agent known as Abel. Jason had been sent to kill him in a breakaway province in Georgia, and Abel had claimed that Defiance was the reason Treadstone wanted him dead.

"Nash, what was Defiance?" Jason asked. "What was the operation all about?"

Nash shook his head. "That's the problem. I don't know. I was never in the loop. They used our people, but I never heard details about who was involved or what the mission was. The whole operation was run above my pay grade."

"By who?" Bourne asked, but he knew the answer even before Nash told him.

"Someone you know pretty well," Nash replied. "Holly Schultz."

"It's me," Jason murmured into the satellite phone. He sat at the back of the chartered jet that was carrying him, Nova, and Nash across the Atlantic back to Washington. The cabin was dark in the overnight hours, and the hum of the engine was loud. Nova and Nash were both asleep.

On the other end of the phone, Abbey said nothing. He could feel her coolness directed at him in the silence.

"Are you safe?" he went on. "Don't tell me where you are, not on the phone. But I need to know you're safe."

Finally, she answered him. "Yes."

"Everything went according to plan?"

"I'm not in Paris anymore."

He closed his eyes in relief that she'd gotten away. "I'm sorry I couldn't be there. There was no time."

"I know the rules," she replied stiffly. "I did what you asked. I always do. What about you? Are you safe?"

"I'm fine," he said, not going into detail. "But it may be a little while before I can see you again."

"Sure."

He knew Abbey. He knew the hurt she was hiding. The distance between them wasn't just about miles. Their lives were being pulled in different directions, and he could feel it ripping them apart. A year earlier, they'd promised each other that they would fight to stay together when things got tough, but now he wondered if they'd really be able to keep that promise.

"Just so you know, I'm not alone," he added, without knowing why he felt the need to tell her that. "An old friend stopped by."

Abbey made the leap to Nova immediately, but she didn't use the name. "Her?"

"Yes."

"I see."

But he knew she didn't see. The things he'd told her about Nova had always made her jealous. "It's business between us. That's all."

"Uh-huh."

"Anyway, I need to go now. Keep your eyes open, like I taught you. That's very important. If you see anything that makes you suspicious, let me know immediately."

"I will."

"I mean it. Be careful. If these people know we're together, they may come after you to get to me."

"I understand."

"I'll check in when I can."

"Okay."

The silence between them was still awkward. He didn't know what else to say.

"I'll be in touch."

"Hang on," she told him before he could end the call. "There's one more thing. I have some advice for you about your *friend*."

"What is it?"

"Don't trust her," Abbey snapped. "And don't fuck her, either."

6

The blistering California sunshine gave a burnt glow to Tim Randall's face.

He hadn't bothered with a hat, and he'd forgotten to apply his SPF 70 sunblock. It had been six months since he'd been back home in Los Angeles, and he'd grown accustomed to the fluorescent lights of his Washington office seventeen hours a day. Now he felt like a tomato ripening to bright red on the vine.

Randall leaned against the railing at the Santa Monica Pier. Below him, on the beach, bikini-clad teenagers ran through the white surf. Multicolored umbrellas dotted the wide Pacific sand. Amid the boardwalk's carnival at his back, the screams of children went up and down with the loops of the roller coaster. Hundreds of tourists squeezed along the pier like ants tunneling through dirt, and he eavesdropped on bits of conversation in multiple languages.

Mostly he wanted to make sure that no one had recognized him. Congressional staff, unlike their bosses, could usually stay anonymous wherever they went. Even so, Randall didn't need his photo showing up on Twitter.

Not today.

No one could know this meeting had ever taken place.

Randall was dressed to blend in at the pier. He was tall, almost six foot three, and he wore a white polo shirt over his stocky chest, plus khaki shorts and sneakers with no socks. Sunglasses covered his blue eyes, and he had a handsome, chiseled face with a jutting chin. His hair was blond and wavy, parted in the middle and feathered in layers that still made him look like a surfer boy, which he'd been in his teen years. That was before he headed across the country to study international relations at Georgetown. Randall was forty now, his surfing days long behind him. Almost twenty years in DC had put twenty pounds around his middle.

Nervously, he checked his watch. It was five minutes to two, almost time for the rendezvous. The Iranian was never late.

Randall turned around, eyeing the crowd. Hamid Ashkani didn't travel alone. Armed guards, male and female, always surrounded him. That was a smart precaution for a senior official in Iranian intelligence, because a Mossad bullet might find his forehead at any moment. Randall didn't believe the Israelis would try anything on American soil, but Ashkani wasn't the kind of man who took chances.

The security detail wasn't hard to spot. On the other side of the boardwalk, a Middle Eastern couple took a selfie with the ocean behind them, then staked out a place on a bench and pretended to study their phones. Randall wasn't fooled. They were both armed and lethal. Not far away, an attractive young woman in athletic gear—wearing a Nike sports hijab—sat for a portrait by a caricaturist. Her mouth had a Mona Lisa smile, and the whites of her large brown eyes were as flawless as china. She looked tiny, barely five feet tall, but Randall assumed she could snap his neck as easily as breaking one of her long fingernails.

There were others. Three for sure, possibly four.

One large jogger, pretending to stumble, bumped into

Randall and quickly frisked him for weapons. Randall also noticed a fussy-looking older man playing with what looked like a small radio, with several black antenna probes jutting out of the top and a wired microphone leading to his ear. After a couple of minutes, he slipped the device into the back pocket of the jeans he was wearing, and soon Randall began to hear grumbles of complaint from people on their phones. Curious, Randall pulled out his phone and saw that he no longer had any cell signal.

From the other side of the pier, the old man gave him a little wink. The device in his pocket was a jammer.

Everything was ready.

Then, finally, came the man himself.

Hamid Ashkani wore a pin-striped business suit and tie, despite the ninety-degree LA sun. Years in the desert had made him immune to heat. The suit was perfect, not a wrinkle anywhere, probably handmade in London. His tie was paisley silk, his black shoes so shiny they cast reflections. Ashkani was the same age as Randall and the same height, but he didn't carry a single extra pound on his frame. He was lean, almost ascetic. He'd lost most of his hair, except for a buzzed black crown at the back of his skull, and he kept his salt-and-pepper beard neatly trimmed. He had a long, slim nose and narrow, dark eyes. He smiled with just a slight turn of his lips, and his smile had the arrogant confidence of a poker player who didn't bother hiding his straight flush.

Ashkani came up to the railing and folded his hands in front of him. His expression as he watched the grubby tourists and the young girls in their halters barely hid his contempt. He didn't look at Randall, and Randall didn't look back, but they stood close enough to speak in quiet tones, barely audible over the noisy crowds on the boardwalk.

"Timothy," Ashkani murmured, sounding like an Oxford graduate, which he was. "Salaam. How are you?"

"I'm fine."

"Really? You look anxious."

"This meeting is supposed to be off the books, and you show up in a ten-thousand-dollar suit? That attracts attention I don't need."

Ashkani shrugged. "If anyone notices, they'll assume I'm a Hollywood lawyer. But don't worry, my people are watching for cameras. You're safe, my friend."

"We're not friends," Randall replied.

The Iranian didn't look offended. "No, I suppose we are not. But even enemies can share common interests. Speaking of which, how is Senator Pine? The polls look good for him. He would appear to be the candidate to beat in next year's election. So far, he seems to be scaring other challengers out of the race."

"A lot can happen in fourteen months," Randall said.

"Yes, quite a lot. However, I have faith in you, Timothy. Or rather, I have faith in your limitless ambition. You intend to be working in the White House next year. Chief of staff, right next door to the Oval Office. Isn't that the plan? Ah, see, I know you so well. Better than your wife, Deborah, knows you. Better than those adorable children, Greta and Lucas. They're such stars at Sidwell, by the way—you must be very proud. And, of course, I even know you better than your mistress, the lovely and athletic Ms. Daria. You're not always discreet about the things you share with her, Timothy. You need to be careful."

Randall struggled to keep the reaction off his face. His nostrils flared as he sucked in air. His marriage! His *kids*! And the affair he'd been sure no one knew about. Ashkani's cultured voice only made the man's implied threat sound more savage. He was making it clear that he could blow up Randall's life anytime he wanted.

He wished he could make his own threats.

Next year, watch the sky, Hamid. There's a drone coming with your name on it.

But he couldn't, and they both knew it. Not in a year. Not ever.

"Tell me what you want," Randall snapped.

Ashkani gave him a nasty smile. "Oh, relax, Timothy. We're on the same side at this juncture. We are your *partners*, don't forget that, and partners keep each other informed when they take strategic steps."

Randall frowned. "Meaning what?"

"Meaning there are rumors in the intelligence community. Hits are being hired out to teams around the world. All of them through cutouts, all of them deniable. And all of them aimed at Treadstone agents who were involved in events seven years ago. That's hardly a coincidence, wouldn't you say?"

Even in the heat, a cold sweat formed on Randall's neck. When he said nothing, Ashkani's jaw hardened, and his cruel eyes narrowed even farther. "Did you think we wouldn't find out? I should have been your first call, Timothy. Let's be very clear. You don't make a move like this without consulting me."

"I don't work for you," Randall hissed under his breath.

"True. Our relationship goes deeper than that. I *own* you. You and your boss."

Randall sweated through another surge of impotent rage. "Maybe you do, but we share the same risks if this all comes out. We're talking about mutual assured destruction, Hamid. If *we* go down, so do you. So does your whole fucking fourteenth-century shitshow of a country. Murderers. *Terrorists!*"

"Spare me your American moral superiority," Ashkani retorted, each word as sharp as a knife. "Have you forgotten where this all started? Did you think we wouldn't take revenge for Gholami? Your boss murdered a friend of mine, Timothy. A great Iranian general, beloved by our people. And don't forget. Gholami wasn't alone at that resort. You murdered his wife, too. And his two children, ages seventeen and eleven. So before you wrap yourself up in the flag, take a good look at your own history of terrorism."

Randall bit his lip and said nothing. *Gholami!*

He hated being reminded of the name. Gholami was the evil mastermind behind suicide bombings, IEDs, and rocket assaults across the Middle East that had killed thousands. The world was better off with him dead in the ground. Even so, Randall had opposed Gholami's murder, despite everything the man had done. He'd known it was a mistake. And his *family*! His family wasn't to be touched! When they were killed, he'd warned of the consequences, but—*goddamn it!*—he'd never imagined in his nightmares the kind of vengeance they would face.

Years later, they were still paying.

Randall kept his voice calm. "Assuming something may be happening to a handful of intelligence agents—and let's face it, Hamid, intelligence is a risky business—why would that concern you?"

Ashkani shrugged. "It makes me wonder if you think you can destroy the evidence of what happened, Timothy. Perhaps you believe if you tie up all the loose ends, you can deny any rumors that come out. Let me assure you that you're wrong. We have the proof, and we can release it anytime we like."

Randall made a show of not being concerned. "Who do you think will believe it, Hamid? There are so many deepfakes today. It will look like a desperate attempt by a violent, corrupt government to smear a dedicated public official. Hell, go ahead and release it. Our poll numbers will probably go up."

But that was a bluff, and they both knew it.

"Well, shall we put that to the test?" Ashkani asked.

Randall's jaw hardened, but he said nothing. He heard the

roar of a jet engine overhead, and he glanced at the sky to watch an Airbus descending toward the runway at LAX. Then his head turned, and he studied the Iranian with nothing but hatred. "You still haven't told me what you want, Hamid."

"What I want?" Ashkani's smile broadened, showing teeth for the first time. "I want nothing at all from you, Timothy. In fact, I'm here to offer my help."

"Your help? What does that mean?"

"I mean, we both know that even if you're able to deal with the Treadstone agents, there is still a key obstacle standing in the way of your plan. Am I right? And that obstacle is considerably more difficult to deal with. The removal must be handled delicately. Absolutely no fingerprints that lead to you or anyone ... *close* to you."

"What are you suggesting?" Randall asked, unable to hide his curiosity.

"I'm offering to serve as an intermediary to someone who can solve your problem. In fact, done properly, the deed itself may actually boost your ambitions. This man is good at what he does."

"And who would that be?"

Ashkani glanced at the old man with the signal jammer, who nodded back, as if confirming there was no electronic surveillance in the area to prevent him from talking freely.

"A man who calls himself Lennon," Ashkani said. "He's the one you need."

7

Through the back windows of a white van parked on 18th street in Arlington, Bourne kept his binoculars trained on the high-rise condominium complex where Holly Schultz lived. He could see Nova, dressed in running gear, drinking from a squirt bottle in a deserted playground at the opposite end of the block. They communicated by radio. It was five thirty in the morning, half an hour before sunrise, but the sky had begun to turn shades of rose on the horizon beyond the condo towers.

Holly was an early riser. She'd typically be at her desk at Langley no later than six o'clock and probably earlier. It was a fifteen-minute drive, so Bourne expected her soon. Sugar, her guide dog, would be with her, as she always was. Holly was blind, and Sugar led the woman everywhere. Having met the dog in London two years earlier, Bourne was convinced that Sugar was superior to most human intelligence agents he knew.

"Anything?" Nova asked.

"No."

"You have her confidential number, Jason. We could simply text her and ask for a meeting."

"We're better off with the element of surprise," Bourne replied. "If Nash is right that this operation is being run by someone inside the government, then they could be watching Holly's phone. And if she's the one behind the hits, all we're doing is walking into a trap."

"Do you really think it's Holly?" Nova asked. "She's erasing her own agents?"

Bourne hesitated. "No, but she must know something about the operation back then. She did the assignments on Defiance. So we need to talk to her."

"Well, I can see her window. Twelfth-floor corner condo. Still no lights. Maybe she's sleeping late."

"Or maybe she's blind," he said dryly.

An embarrassed laugh broke through the static. "Oh, yeah."

"Next tell me about the great view she has up there," Jason added.

"Asshole."

He allowed himself a smile.

He'd been back with Nova for forty-eight hours, and he was already remembering how smoothly they worked together, how they anticipated each other's thoughts. They were more like lovers than partners. Despite her self-imposed isolation over the past two years, she'd slipped back into operational mode without missing a step. She was still the same. Skilled. Beautiful. And very calculating.

Nova hadn't forgotten that Holly was blind. She was simply playing games to draw him close to her.

Bourne refocused the binoculars on the end of the street. "We've got a limo coming."

A black town car slid silently toward them and drew to a stop in front of the locked gates that led into the condominium complex. The driver left the engine running and the headlights on, but the rear door of the car clicked open. A slim, small man in his forties, wearing a dark suit, climbed out and stood by the open door. He had thinning black hair on a high forehead and wore wire-rimmed glasses. His phone was glued to his ear.

"Do you know who that is?" Bourne asked. "He's not security."

"Yes, that's Burton Glaser," Nova commented. "Holly's executive assistant. Married, three kids, lives in Chevy Chase. Former FBI research analyst."

Jason was never surprised by the depth of Nova's intel. She had fingers in all of the intelligence agencies.

Much like Lennon did.

"I imagine he's calling Holly to say the limo's ready," he said. "Get ready. The driver is probably a pro. He'll be on the street as soon as he sees us. I'll make sure he's down while you grab Holly."

"Jason, wait," Nova interrupted.

"What is it?"

But Bourne saw the problem. Three new vehicles had suddenly arrived on 18th Street, rolling toward the condo building. All were heavy black SUVs, and he was sure they were armor-plated. The first of the vehicles passed him at high speed, and Bourne noted that the driver paid close attention to the smoked windows of the white van. The SUV headed to the end of the street, then turned sideways, blocking traffic. At the opposite end of 18th, a fourth SUV wheeled around the corner and did the same.

With the street closed to traffic, the two remaining SUVs parked ahead of and behind the town car. Half a dozen agents emerged from inside the vehicles with their service weapons already in their hands. They staked out a security perimeter, while one of the men—the oldest and obviously the leader—nodded at Burton Glaser, then headed for the locked gates and let himself inside.

"Shit," Nova said.

"Yeah. The op's blown."

"They've already got eyes on me," she told him. "There's no point in sticking around. Pick me up at the backup site in twenty minutes."

"Right."

Bourne had nothing to do but wait. He assumed that someone was running the plates on the white van, and he hoped that Nash's cover for the vehicle was good enough to stand up to CIA scrutiny. Because these men were definitely CIA. From inside the condo building, he saw the leader of the security team return, with Holly Schultz walking next to him. She had her white cane in her hand, and Sugar heeling at her side, but Holly could have followed this route in her sleep. Bourne knew that she had an amazing spatial memory for places.

Holly was a small woman with a birdlike frame, her neck so slim it hardly seemed able to support her head. At fifty years old, she kept her hair black, cut in a short bob above her ears with bangs whisking along her forehead. Her lips were bright red, her eyes dark and smart, her cheekbones high and sharp. She had a delicate Audrey Hepburn style about her, simultaneously tough as nails but also looking like a breath of wind would blow her away. She wore a white raincoat, belted at the waist, and red high heels.

The guard led her to the town car door, but as she bent to get inside, she stopped in surprise as Sugar tugged at the leash and let out one quick bark. Holly murmured something to the guard, who surveyed the area and then replied with an all-clear. A little frown crossed Holly's face, but she got into the back of the car, pulled Sugar with her, and let the guard close the door behind them.

Bourne knew what Sugar had smelled. She'd smelled *him*.

A few seconds later, the convoy departed, with the town car securely bracketed on both sides by armored SUVs. There was no way to get anywhere close to Holly. Jason waited until all the vehicles were gone, then returned to the front seat of the van and started the engine. He headed into the Arlington streets and picked up Nova at the corner of Clarendon and Ode a few blocks away.

"She knows about the hits," Nova said as she climbed inside the van. "That looked like triple her usual security."

"Yes, and she also thinks that *she's* on the list," Bourne agreed. "She's a target, which tells me she's not the one coming after us. But that means it's going to be hard to get close to her."

Nova smiled. "Well, we do have a plan B."

"What's that?"

"Me. As in me and Burt Glaser. Holly's assistant."

Bourne stared at her. "You know him?"

"Sort of. I slept with him a few years ago. He was a research admin with the FBI then. He was married and needed some good sex, and I needed a look at his laptop while he was in the shower. Time for a little déjà vu."

"Do you think he remembers you?" Jason asked.

Nova stuck out her tongue at him. "Oh, trust me, darling. He remembers."

The meeting had to look accidental. Bourne didn't want a warning getting back to Holly.

Nova reached out for help to one of her former contacts at Interpol, a French forensic scientist named Claude who'd spent a year working a global drug case with the FBI. Burton Glaser had been assigned to the same case for the bureau's Information Management Division. Claude agreed to send an email to let Glaser know that he was in town and would enjoy meeting up for a drink at the Ritz-Carlton that night.

An hour later, Claude called back to say that Glaser had

agreed. Then Nova booked herself a high-floor suite at the same hotel.

That evening, a few minutes after eight thirty, Bourne and Nova took a table in the cocktail lounge called Quadrant. They ordered drinks and chatted in low voices. Nova had chosen a little black dress that emphasized her long legs and the numerous tattoos embroidering her bare arms. At nine o'clock exactly—he was a punctual man—Glaser took a seat at the black stone bar. He had a briefcase with him. The bartender put a glass of red wine in front of him, and Glaser checked his phone and then reviewed the people around him, the way a former FBI man would. It took only a few seconds for his stare to land on Nova.

"Happy memories are stirring," she told Bourne with a smile, without looking back at the man at the bar.

They gave it twenty more minutes. Nova still acted as if she hadn't noticed Glaser at all. As the time passed, Glaser kept checking his phone impatiently, and eventually he tapped out a text that Nova suspected was directed to Claude. In another couple of minutes, Claude would write back to apologize that he wouldn't be able to meet him.

"Time for you to go," Nova whispered to Jason.

Bourne got up from the table and shook Nova's hand like a coworker saying good night. Left alone, Nova simply sipped her drink, studied her phone, and waited for Glaser to approach her. She knew he would.

It didn't even take five minutes.

"It's—Caitrin, right?" Glaser said, appearing at her table. He stood with his glass of wine in his hand and eyed the empty chair across from her. "I'm Burt Glaser. We met a few years ago. It is you, isn't it?"

Nova's stare drifted from her phone to the man in front of her. She studied him with the suspicion of a single woman in a bar, and she let just the right amount of time pass before her face smoothed out in recognition. "Oh, Burt. Sure. Well, this is a surprise. What a pleasure to see you again. What are you doing here?"

"I was supposed to be meeting someone, but he just texted to say he's a no-show."

"Too bad."

"What about you? What brings you back to DC?"

Nova rolled her eyes. "FERC meeting about pipelines."

"Oh, yeah, you were in oil and gas, weren't you?" Glaser asked. "For Shell?"

"Good memory. Seems to me you were with the bureau, right? Judging by your suit, I assume you still are."

Glaser smiled. "Actually, I've relocated. Different agency, still in the government."

"Ah." The knowing look in her dark eyes said, so it's one of *those* agencies. The ones you can't talk about.

She didn't invite him to sit down. She wanted him to make all the moves. They parried small talk back and forth for another couple of minutes, and then he asked if he could join her. She made a point of checking her watch before she said yes, but a few minutes after that, they were leaning close to each other across the table and sharing an expensive bottle of Russian River Valley pinot noir.

By midnight, they were kissing in the elevator on the way to her room.

When they got inside, Nova didn't turn on the lights. Instead she used the glow from the city to set a romantic mood. She crossed to the hotel phone by the bed because there was a light flashing to let her know she had a message. She checked it—she'd left a voice mail for herself earlier in the day—and then put the phone down and scowled.

"That was my boss. He needs a document from our London server before the meeting tomorrow. I need to log in and forward it to him. Won't take two minutes." Then she looked around the hotel room and swore. "Fuck, I don't have my laptop. I was using it in the car, and I forgot it under the seat. I don't suppose you have a PC with you, do you?"

Glaser hesitated, his mouth creased in a frown.

"Oh, yeah, hi-ho, security," Nova said. "I get it. Look, you can watch me, okay? Literally, it will take two minutes. Tell you what, I need to do a couple of things in the bathroom, know what I mean? Before we can get busy. If you boot up your laptop, I swear, I'll be in and out of my VPN in a flash."

She headed for the bathroom, and she was sure that Glaser was horny enough not to spoil the mood by turning her down. As she waited, she checked her phone and loaded the video feeds from the cameras she'd secreted around the room. In less than a minute, she had the code for Glaser's briefcase lock and the password for his computer.

She returned to the hotel room wearing only her panties. In the darkness, she hoped he didn't notice or comment on the stitches from the bullet wound, but she had an excuse prepared in case he did. But Glaser never got past the view of her breasts, and his hands got busy right away. She let him fondle her from behind as she loaded up a fake Shell VPN on his laptop—courtesy of Treadstone—and when she'd downloaded and forwarded a convincing analysis of leakage issues on a Utah crude oil pipeline, she kissed him again, then poured them more drinks from the minibar.

This time she added a narcotic to his wine.

Glaser slumped backward onto her bed, unconscious, a couple of minutes later. His mouth hung open, and he snored. Nova carefully put his glasses on the nightstand, then removed all his clothes. Whenever he awakened, she wanted him convinced they'd had sex. She also straddled him and took several photos that showed their bodies together, without any that identified her face. If he ever suspected that she'd hacked his laptop, she wanted blackmail material to keep him quiet.

Then she put her dress back on, reopened Glaser's briefcase, and booted up his laptop. She began to paw through the calendar files that Glaser maintained for Holly Schultz—the personal calendar, not the official one synced to the government computers. When she spotted a pattern that looked promising, she called Jason.

"How's your friend?" Bourne asked.

"Sleeping like a baby. And in case you're wondering, I didn't fuck him."

"I wasn't wondering."

Nova frowned. He could at least have been a little jealous. "Anyway, I'm looking at Holly's calendar. She's got some interesting entries a couple of times a month. No location listed, just the name MOM."

"She's visiting her mother?" Bourne asked.

"No, according to her contact folders, her mother lives in Seattle. But there's an entry for Marcus O. Matthews."

"As in General Matthews? Joint Chiefs?"

"Right. As in married General Matthews, wife a hotshot lawyer, splits her time between DC and New York. He's got a big old mansion in McLean. I also found several receipts from a high-end lingerie store called Le Bustiere Boutique, with several deliveries made shortly before her visits to MOM."

"You're thinking an affair," Jason said.

"I'm thinking an affair."

There was a long pause on the phone. "Well, when's Holly supposed to go there next?"

"Two days," Nova replied. "Saturday night."

8

Bourne heard the scrape of the deadlock being undone at the home of General Marcus O. Matthews in McLean, Virginia. Holly Schultz was letting herself inside with a key. He heard the sharp three-legged tap of stiletto heels combined with Holly's white cane, as well as the scratch of a dog's claws on the hardwood floor. Sugar had joined Holly on her midnight rendezvous.

He sat in the dark in the general's library, which had a high ceiling and smelled of leather and cigars. The air was cool, with a draft blowing from the vents, and a light drizzle outside spat against the windows.

In the foyer, Holly called the general's name, announcing her arrival in a throaty voice. "Marcus?"

When there was no response, she tried again, suspicion creeping into her tone. "Marcus? Hello?"

Then Sugar yelped one single bark at a specific pitch, obviously a warning. Bourne heard a whimper and more urgent scratching, as if the dog was dragging Holly in a new direction. Not upstairs to the bedroom, as he assumed was her usual route, but toward the library, where Jason was waiting for them.

Holly's voice turned low and cautious. "Who's there?"

She let go of the leash, and the dog charged into the library ahead of her. Sugar's initial growl at the presence of a stranger switched to a happy yip as she associated the smell in the house with Bourne. The dog skidded to a stop in front of him, and he rubbed her ears as the yellow Lab got on her hind legs and licked his face.

In the doorway, he saw Holly's shadow. Without her eyes, her other senses examined the room like a kind of radar. "Cain? Is that you?"

"Yes," Bourne replied.

"Of course it is."

Holly walked confidently into the library, knowing the layout of the furniture in the house by heart. She dropped down into a leather armchair near the fireplace and snapped her fingers. Instantly, Sugar left Jason and returned to her master's side. Holly put a single finger on the dog's nose, a kind of discipline, and Sugar sank down to the floor with a whine, as if apologizing for bad behavior.

"I get that she loves you, but she's not supposed to trust anyone but me without prior consent," Holly commented. "Also, just so you know, with the right command, she'd rip your throat out."

"I don't doubt it."

"I've got a panic button, Cain. There are agents around the house who can be inside in seconds. I thought about using it, but honestly, I wondered if it might be you. I've been expecting you to show up, given what's happening. Actually, I'm pleased to know that you're still alive."

"And trying to stay that way," Bourne said.

"Where is Marcus? I trust you haven't harmed him."

"The general is fine, other than a case of wounded pride. He's tied to a chair in the bedroom upstairs. I can leave him that way, if you're into that sort of thing."

"Funny. Do you want to tell me how you found out about us?"

"It doesn't matter," Bourne replied.

"In other words, Burt was indiscreet."

"This is Washington. There are no secrets in Washington. The point is, I'm here, and we need to talk."

Holly sighed. "I'm not sure what I can tell you, Jason."

"You obviously think you're at risk. You don't go anywhere these days without a major-league guard detail. You must have some idea why they're coming after all of us."

"It's about Defiance, obviously," Holly replied. "I know that much. Since you're here, I assume you do, too."

"How did you figure out the connection?" he asked.

Holly drummed her fingers along the arm of the leather chair. She bent down and put a finger firmly on Sugar's nose again, and the dog snapped back to attention beside her with a happy bark. "Get me some brandy, do you mind, Jason? By the way, I assume you've got the lights off, and you might want to keep it that way. If my agents outside see you, they're likely to get nervous. The wet bar is in the corner if you can feel your way there."

Jason did as she asked. He found a bell-shaped glass and a bottle of Rémy Martin, and he poured a generous dose and brought it to her. Holly swirled it, smelled it, and then took a sip, inhaling as the warmth filled her chest. Her body seemed to relax in the darkness, uncoiling like a spring.

"I suspected early on that this had something to do with Defiance," she acknowledged finally. "That was the only common denominator among the targets. I knew that meant my head was on the chopping block, too."

"Nash thinks it's an inside job. The orders are coming from someone inside the government."

"Very possibly," Holly agreed.

"So who's running the operation?"

"Unfortunately, I have no idea."

"I find that hard to believe."

"Oh, you know how the game is played, Jason," she snapped with a sigh. "You don't ask for names on missions like this. In fact, you don't *want* to know names. The less you know, the less you can say when you get pulled in front of a congressional committee or a grand jury. You get approval codes to authorize expenditures and personnel, and that's all. If you receive the necessary approvals, then you stop asking questions."

"Except someone at your level doesn't take anonymous orders," Bourne said. "Somebody contacted you. Somebody you knew."

"You're right, but typically A hands it off to B, and B hands it off to C, and C doesn't have a clue who A is. In this case, I was C. Defiance came to me from the deputy director of NCS. He leapfrogged several of my superiors to put it directly in my hands. That's not standard protocol, but like I say, he had the right approvals. I didn't need anything more than that, not if I wanted to keep my job and keep moving up in the agency. So I did what I was told."

"Who was the DD?"

"At the time, it was Vic Sorrento. He retired last year. I don't know who gave the orders to Vic, and I didn't ask. At that level, it can come from anywhere, not just from within the agency."

"What do you mean?" Bourne asked.

"Military. NSA. Elected officials. A favor for an ally, the UK, Israel, whoever. What I do know is that seven weeks ago, Vic Sorrento drowned while on vacation in Costa Rica. The police down there said it was an accident. Undertow got him. Me, I don't believe in top CIA personnel having *accidents*."

"Someone like Sorrento must have made a lot of enemies during his career," Bourne pointed out. "It didn't have to be about Defiance."

"Agreed. Plenty of foreign actors may have wanted a little payback for Vic's work over the years. But Defiance was a very unusual directive. I've had my radar up ever since then to make sure it didn't come back and bite me in the ass. When I heard about Vic, Defiance was the first thing that popped into my head. With him dead, the trail to Defiance stopped at B. He must have known who A was, but now he's not around to tell anyone."

"And that was what tipped you off?"

"No, but that was the first domino to fall. A couple of weeks later, I heard about a Treadstone agent getting hit in Hong Kong. Inactive, we hadn't used him in five years. But he was on the Defiance list. That was enough to get me to bring armed security wherever I go."

"So you still have a list of Treadstone agents who were involved in the mission?"

"Of course. I picked them myself."

"What were they supposed to do?"

"Are you not hearing me, Cain? *I don't know!* Vic came to me and said he needed multiple deep-cover assets for a sensitive cover-up operation. That's all he told me. Some of it was technical—people like Dax, hackers who could penetrate highly secure servers and manipulate the data without leaving any bread crumbs. Some of it was wet work. That meant people like Nova. But I didn't hand out the actual assignments. I gave Vic names and authorization codes, and he arranged the contacts himself. All I knew was that Treadstone was being used to cover up something big. I have no idea what it was."

"Nova says her assignment involved three separate hits, but she doesn't know why they were targets."

"Then she knows more than me," Holly replied. "I didn't even know who the targets were."

"I need that list of agents," Bourne said.

Holly tilted her chin and stared blankly at the ceiling. Her nostrils flared as she inhaled. "For what purpose?"

"Multiple agents went on multiple missions. No one knew who else was involved or what they were doing. If I can backtrack and figure out what their assignments were, then maybe I can figure out how they fit together. That will give me a clue about what Defiance really was. And who ordered it."

She nodded. "Okay. I'll get you a copy of the list."

"How many names are on it?"

"More than twenty."

"And all of them are now at risk?"

"I assume so," Holly said. "The ones who are still alive."

"Why didn't you reach out with a warning? You left us twisting in the wind."

Her face showed no remorse at the bodies left in her wake. "I was mounting my own investigation, so I didn't want to tip my hand. Trying to locate and contact the various deep-cover agents would have exposed what I was doing."

"You've been mounting your own investigation? What have you found?"

"Nothing that's likely to help you. I went after Vic's files, his phone records, his credit card receipts, anything that might tell me about his off-the-books meetings during Defiance. I hit a brick wall. Whoever mounted the operation has covered their tracks well. If there's an answer to be found, it's in the field. Just like you say."

Bourne nodded. "I assume I'm on the list, too."

"Actually, no."

He stared at her, puzzled. "Why not?"

"You were being trained for a different assignment. The one that would ultimately lead to your being shot and losing your memory. When Vic came looking for names, I didn't give him yours."

"But they came after me in Paris," Jason pointed out. "Why would they do that if I wasn't part of Defiance?"

"I have no idea."

Bourne paced in the darkness. It didn't make *sense*! He was on the hit list, and yet he'd never taken part in the mission itself. For some reason, the people behind Defiance thought he knew something that could take them down.

Why?

Then he understood. He knew the reason.

"*Abel* was on the Defiance list," Jason said quietly.

"Yes."

"You sent me after Abel. You pulled me off my other mission to go after him. Highest priority. Urgent assignment. Why?"

"You *remember* that?" Holly asked, and Bourne thought he saw a twinge of concern on her face. He was pretty sure she preferred him being in the dark.

"Some things from my past are coming back," Jason told her. "You sent me to kill him."

"Yes, and you failed," she retorted like a disappointed schoolteacher. "Abel survived and went to the Russians. He became *Lennon*."

"But why did you need him dealt with so quickly? Normally, you'd watch him. Play him. See where he would lead you."

"We did watch him. We surveilled him for months, but we were concerned he was going to run. And he did. So we had to move fast."

"Was that all?" Bourne asked.

"What do you mean?"

"I mean, who ordered the hit to move ahead on Abel? Was it Vic Sorrento?"

Holly pursed her lips. "Yes, in fact, it was."

"*Jesus!*" Bourne exclaimed. "That didn't raise red flags with you?"

"Jason, I'm where I am in the agency because I know when to ask questions and when to shut up. You could afford to learn that yourself."

Bourne shook his head. "Abel was right all along. I wasn't sent after him because he was a Russian spy. I was sent because of Defiance. And now they're afraid of what he told me when I went out there to kill him."

9

The noise of traffic on i-395 growled over the rain on the other side of the motel parking lot. It was after midnight. The cheap third-floor room in Alexandria was dark and warm. Bourne and Nova lay next to each other on the queen bed, both of them fully dressed. She was smoking, something she'd given up years earlier but had obviously gone back to while she'd hibernated in Greece. The ceiling fan blew smoke around the room, and the fan motor rattled as it spun.

The two of them were getting ready to separate again. They'd agreed that it made sense to pursue Defiance from different angles, but he suspected that Nova wasn't happy about it. She was thinking about their past, just like he was. For Jason, any memories were intense, because he'd lost so many. But he remembered everything about Nova in particularly vivid detail. Their passionate, illicit affair, violating every Treadstone rule. Their naïve plans for the future, fantasies of an ordinary life that was impossible in their worlds. And then the worst memory of all—seeing Nova shot in Las Vegas, seeing Treadstone agents carry her body away, spending two years thinking she was dead. When she finally showed up again, nothing was the same, and it never would be the same.

Forget the past! The past doesn't exist!

He ignored the warmth of her body inches away.

"Did Vic Sorrento give you the assignments on Defiance?" Bourne asked, his voice flat. "Did the targets come from him?"

Nova took a while to reply. He listened to a quiet hiss as she exhaled, and he knew she was dragging her mind out of the past, too.

"Oh, hell, no. You think someone like Sorrento would get his hands dirty passing off black jobs? He probably used half a dozen cutouts to distance himself from it. As I recall, some Indian guy in a suit showed up next to me at a pub near Waterloo. Gave me a piece of paper, three names, three cities. Two were in the U.S., and one was in Germany. The guy used all the right codes, so I knew the orders came from Treadstone."

"What was the reporting procedure?" Jason asked.

Another long pause. More smoke. "I memorized a phone number to call when the jobs were done. A male voice answered, and I let him know we had closure on all three. For all I know, the guy on the phone could have been Sorrento. But it doesn't matter now."

"How long did the jobs take?"

"Nine weeks. They wanted accidents or disappearances. No obvious violence. They got what they were paying for, but that took me some time."

"Have you tracked down the names of the targets?"

Jason heard the word leave his mouth with a sour taste, because it flowed so naturally. *Targets*. Not victims. You couldn't think of them as victims. Victims were real human beings, whereas targets were simply avatars in a video game who could be erased from the screen.

"I've found two so far," Nova replied. "The German was a mechanical engineer, did lots of consulting for Mercedes, Airbus, Siemens, the big European manufacturers. Wilhelm

Hopf, age forty-one. It took a while to figure out the best way to eliminate him, but eventually I sabotaged his car. He lost control on the Autobahn at about a hundred miles an hour. The second target was a DC cop. Billy Janssen, age twenty-five. He was only in his second year on the force, a patrol cop busting drunks and hookers. With him, I got lucky. He left his house the first day I was watching him, and I had the opportunity to stage an accident on a steep hiking trail. As for the last target, I'm still trying to unearth who that was. I set it up as an OD in the Tenderloin in San Francisco, but it didn't get any press. As I recall, he was a Berkeley college student. He was twenty-one."

"A college student?" Bourne asked, shaking his head.

"Yeah."

"And you have no idea how the three fit together?"

"There were no obvious connections that jumped out at me while I was planning the operations. I'll start digging around and see what I can turn up. But I'm not sure what kind of common thread I'm likely to find among a DC street cop, a German engineer, and a California student."

Bourne nodded in the darkness.

What *was* the connection?

Holly was certain that Defiance had been a cover-up, a mission used to hide evidence of something big. An operation that needed to be buried. But Nova was right. Jason couldn't fathom what would link these random targets together. Their ages, professions, and locations didn't line up at all. He saw no clue about the truth behind Defiance, but no doubt that was the point. Split up the agents and the kills. With each agent holding only small pieces of the puzzle, no one could see the big picture.

"What about you?" Nova asked. "Where do you go next?"

Bourne thought about the list Holly had given him of Treadstone agents assigned to Defiance. He'd only recognized about a third of the names. The others had never overlapped with him on missions; most of their work was solitary. The agents represented multiple specialties—everything from forensic accounting to electronic surveillance—and he knew they were located in countries around the world. Most would be in hiding now, almost impossible to find. He could work with Nash to zero in on their likely covers, but that would take time, and he had a shortcut in mind.

One of the names on the list was a retired agent he'd connected with three years earlier during the Medusa operation. His name was Teeling, and he lived on a boat in the Bahamas. Jason had already booked a charter flight to Nassau for the following day.

And yet he found himself reluctant to tell Nova where he was going. In his head, he heard Abbey's voice. *Don't trust her*.

Nova sensed it. Her words spat from the darkness.

"Fine, don't tell me. It's probably better that way. If they catch one of us, they can squeeze us to find the other. Let's not pretend we're anything but two agents who are stuck working together, okay? File me away in the blackness with all of the other shit you've erased from your life."

He heard her stab her cigarette into an ashtray.

"I'm going to find Teeling," he said finally. "He's in the Caribbean."

Telling her the truth didn't change the harshness he felt from her.

"Well, good."

"We can meet up again in a few days and compare notes," Bourne said. "Between the two of us, maybe we can figure out what this is all about."

"Yeah, maybe," Nova agreed.

"We should get some sleep."

"Yeah."

She got out of bed. He listened to the rustle of her clothes as she undressed. There was enough of a dim glow from outside the motel room to see her body as she stripped off her top, her jeans, her bra, and her panties, until she was naked. The pendant around her neck glistened in the light. When she got back into bed, he smelled the perfume of her skin over the acrid cigarette smoke. She lay close enough for her bare leg to glide against him and for her fingers to lace with his hand.

He felt attraction to her rise in him like a rogue ocean wave. It would be so easy to reach for her, and he knew that was what she wanted him to do. Just like the last time. Two years ago, in California, they'd had wild sex on another rainy night in another hotel room. And then she'd drugged him and gone off with Lennon.

"We're good together," she murmured. "I mean, we used to be, Jason."

"I know that."

She didn't say anything more. The invitation to make love to her was clear without the words, and she knew him well enough to know that he wanted her. But when he didn't move or kiss her, when he didn't take her body in his arms, she let go of his hand. She turned on her side, facing the opposite way. Not long after, he could hear the steadiness of her breathing as she slept. Nova was someone who never looked back.

Jason didn't sleep for a long time. He lay with his eyes open in the darkness as he revisited his relationship with her from the beginning. All the passion, all the dreams, all the mistakes. In the morning, when light finally streamed into the motel room, he glanced at the other side of the bed and saw that Nova was already gone.

10

Abbey texted Jason again. This was the fourth time she'd tried to reach him since they talked on the phone after she left Paris, but she still got no reply. There was no indication that he'd even read her messages. She didn't know if he was out of reach because of Treadstone or if he was ghosting her again, the way he'd done after their breakup in Quebec City.

Either way, she heard him loud and clear. *You're alone now*.

She uttered a low curse, as if that could shake him from her mind. The curse was directed more at herself than at Jason, because she was the fool who'd fallen in love with him and decided that she couldn't live without him. He'd warned her that they were doomed from the start, but she hadn't wanted to believe it.

Anyway, she had her own life to lead now. This was the life of a successful novelist.

She sipped orange juice from a crystal glass and stared through the solarium windows at the green hills surrounding Alicia Beauvoir's farm. The farm was located down a dirt road outside Tuscarora, Maryland, on five hundred acres bordering the Potomac River. Calling it a farm made it sound rustic, but in fact, it was a sprawling multimillion-dollar estate, nearly six thousand square feet, which housed no one but Beauvoir, her husband, and the staff that maintained the grounds. There was a large red barn on the property that had been converted into a museum showcasing Beauvoir's three-decade political career. The only animals who lived here were horses. Beauvoir loved to ride, and she and Abbey had had their first conversation about cowriting a thriller while on horseback near the river. The only crops that grew on the grounds were apple trees and flower gardens. Everything about the estate was precise and manicured, which was also true of Alicia Beauvoir.

Beauvoir had suggested that Abbey stay at the estate while they worked on the book. Despite being only an hour from Washington, the former secretary of state rarely went into the city anymore. Her husband had recovered from his bout with cancer, but still needed care that required Beauvoir to be close to him. She also didn't want Abbey hiking back and forth between the farm and her shabby little apartment, particularly when the two women shared a habit of staying up until the middle of the night as they did their work. Abbey was happy to agree. Looking around the sunroom, she decided she could get used to living in the lap of luxury, with breakfast pastries waiting on a silver tray every morning, European coffee pressed to perfection, and three or four freshly squeezed juices to choose from.

"Good morning," a voice said crisply behind her.

Abbey turned to see Alicia Beauvoir join her from the library with a brisk, decisive walk. That was how she did everything, with a clipped confidence that broached no hesitation. Beauvoir was in her early fifties but had the looks and energy of a woman years younger. Even Abbey, in her mid-thirties, sometimes found it a challenge keeping up with her. Beauvoir was tall and slim, with sandy hair that curled up at her shoulders, and she wore it parted on the side so that it flowed over her high forehead like a blond waterfall.

Everything about her face was sharp—a sharp, pointed chin, sharply defined cheekbones, a nose like the blade of a knife, and very sharp, very smart blue eyes. Abbey didn't think she'd ever met a more intelligent woman, but along with that intelligence came impatience with lesser mortals. She was charming until you disappointed her, and then her tongue became venomous.

"I've been thinking about the assassination attempt at the UN in chapter seven," Beauvoir announced without prologue as she poured strong black coffee and then selected a berry tart from the pastry tray. "That's not working for me. We need to change it."

Abbey had gotten used to the fact that her cowriter didn't sugarcoat her opinions. She'd assumed when she first agreed to the book project that Beauvoir would be like most celebrity writers, happy to let the real novelist do the work, as long as they could stick their name on the cover and take home most of the royalties. But that was not the case with Alicia Beauvoir. She wanted to be involved in the smallest details of the novel, and Abbey was a little jealous to find that many of Beauvoir's thriller ideas were even better than her own.

"It's totally unrealistic," Beauvoir went on, sipping coffee with her brow knitted. "Plus, the UN isn't where any of the real power is. They're mostly entitled clowns taking three-hour lunches over Silver Oak wine. I think we should consider using the Chinese embassy as the venue for that section. More dangerous, more shadowy espionage."

Abbey reworked the jigsaw puzzle of the plot in her mind. "I think that would work."

"You'll get started on that today? Put together detailed notes we can look at tonight."

"I will."

"Also, about the sex scene in chapter two," Beauvoir continued.

"Too explicit?" Abbey asked.

"No, no, no, the opposite. Too tame. We need to shock people, make it really twisted. Murder in chapter one, plenty of hot fucking in chapter two. That'll make Sarah at the *Times* sit up and take notice. 'Oh, my God, Alicia Beauvoir was the secretary of state, and now she's writing about cock rings and toe sucking.'"

Abbey choked a little on her orange juice. "Yes, okay."

A smirk crossed Beauvoir's face. "Did I shock you, too, Abbey?"

"No, no, I'll turn up the heat, sure," Abbey replied, although her lip curled with an unpleasant fantasy of Jason sucking Nova's toes. Something told her that Nova was exactly the kind of woman who could make a man do that.

Beauvoir sat down at a marble table near the solarium's west wall. Abbey refilled her glass of juice and joined her. Outside, streaks of cirrus clouds made shadowy lines across the sloping green fields. In the closest valley, half a dozen ducks landed with splashes and squawks in a small pond. It was a happy, idyllic environment, which made the chaos of DC feel far away. But Abbey couldn't stop thinking about Jason.

"Is something wrong?" Beauvoir asked.

Abbey focused again and forced a smile. "Oh, no, I'm fine."

"Come on, Abbey. You've been distracted about something since you got back from Paris. Did the trip not go well?"

Abbey's first instinct was to brush the question aside, but that didn't usually work with Alicia Beauvoir. "Honestly, no."

"Boyfriend trouble?"

"You could say that."

"Do you love him?"

"I do."

"Does he love you?"

"I think he does, but it's complicated."

Beauvoir snapped her jaws around a bite of strawberry

pastry. "Well, this may sound harsh, Abbey, but you're young, you're smart, you're pretty, and you're on the verge of a big breakthrough in your career. If the man you love today isn't right for you, you'll have plenty to choose from in the future."

Abbey stared out the windows. She supposed that was true, but hearing those words out loud made her incredibly sad.

Beauvoir's face softened, and she seemed to realize she'd said the wrong thing. "Sorry. I can be a bull in a china shop when it comes to emotions. But don't mistake that for not caring."

"I know. Thank you."

"My daughter was a lot like you, Abbey. That's one reason we get along so well. You remind me of Ellie. Very smart, very courageous and headstrong, but not always blessed with good judgment about men."

"Guilty," Abbey agreed with a smile.

She felt surprised and pleased by Beauvoir's comparison to her daughter, because she knew Beauvoir didn't say such things lightly. This was also sensitive ground, so she was careful not to pry. Nothing melted the ice queen faster than talking about Ellie. There were photos and paintings of the girl everywhere around the estate, and Beauvoir's charitable foundation was named for her only child. Abbey knew the story from her research. Ellie, twenty-two and already following in her mother's political footsteps, had been spending a summer in Israel doing onsite research for a UN human rights committee. On a hot Friday night, she'd gone to a Tel Aviv nightclub, and she'd been twenty feet away when a Hizballah suicide bomber detonated himself at the club door. Seventeen Israeli young people died in the blast. So did Ellie Beauvoir.

Abbey saw a faraway look come and go in Alicia's eyes. It happened a lot when they were working together, just a little break in the woman's concentration, but it never lasted long. She was sure she was thinking about Ellie.

"Anyway, let's pause on the book for a few minutes," Beauvoir suddenly announced with a check of her watch. "There's a speech starting soon that I want to see. Senator Pine is doing a fundraiser at the Ritz. He's live streaming his remarks on his website."

"Okay."

Beauvoir dabbed at her mouth with a napkin, then strode from the solarium and returned seconds later with an iPad Pro. She mounted it on a keyboard and navigated confidently with a few taps of her fingers, which were tipped by long burgundy-colored nails. The iPad screen showed an empty podium in a hotel ballroom.

"I assume it's the usual stump speech, but you can tell a lot from a person's delivery," Beauvoir said. "Particularly with a man like Don. He's all about the voice. If his poll numbers look good, he can't hide the arrogance."

"Well, his poll numbers have definitely been looking good," Abbey replied.

Beauvoir pursed her lips thoughtfully. "Yes."

"In a year with an open nomination, I would have expected a tight race, but Pine seems to have the field mostly to himself," Abbey went on.

"Yes," Beauvoir said again, but Abbey didn't think she was listening.

"Do you miss being part of it?" Abbey asked.

This time there was no answer at all. Beauvoir's gaze was fixed on the iPad screen, studying the empty podium and seemingly running through a thousand political calculations in her mind. Abbey knew she'd asked the wrong question. In order to miss something, you had to have left it behind, and she didn't think Beauvoir had really left the political game. She might be happy staying home in her country estate, but that didn't mean she'd given up her influence. Abbey had seen her spend hours on the phone, pulling strings and making connections around the world. Her hand was still in the race, even if her name wasn't on the ballot. Even so, Abbey found it depressing, because it still seemed as if women politicians had to do much of their work behind the scenes, rather than out front.

"Ah, there you are, Don," Beauvoir murmured.

Senator Don Pine of California made his way to the podium in the Ritz ballroom. The sound on the iPad came to life with an enthusiastic round of applause. Behind the microphone, Pine raised his arms as if to quiet them, but in fact, he basked in the adulation. The crowd sensed his approval, and the applause got louder and continued for several more minutes. The longer it went on, the wider the senator's grin became.

"The shame about the people we get as presidents," Beauvoir commented wryly, "is that they all do so *want* to be president."

Abbey knew that was true of Senator Pine.

He certainly had the look of a president. He was tall and slightly stooped, a former basketball player who was now almost sixty. His dark hair was swept back with a couple swaths of gray near his ears. Abbey couldn't help but wonder if they'd poll-tested how much gray to leave in when they colored his hair. He had a politician's easy smile, but his dark eyes were icy and calculating. Abbey had interviewed him for a magazine article two years earlier, and he'd given her a bone-crushing handshake, then answered her questions with a strange mix of flirting, condescension, and progressive sensitivity. As a California Democrat, he was far enough to the left that some people joked that he'd fallen off the coast into the ocean. However, he was also a former Top Gun pilot who could out-tough his most conservative challengers on Russia and China. He'd been laying a road map to be elected POTUS since he was thirteen years old.

For the next fifteen minutes, Abbey listened to the senator's speech along with Beauvoir. It was good, full of carefully scripted applause lines, but she noticed that it was a big-tent kind of speech. It said a lot about how far ahead the senator was in the polls that he felt no need to feed raw meat to the base.

"I'm tired of Democrats and Republicans living like they're in two different countries. My friends, we've only got one America."

Cheers.

"I've been to war, and I' ll tell you this. We lose wars when we don't know what we're fighting for. Well, I can tell you exactly what I'm fighting for and who *I'm fighting for. People. The American people. Every single family in every single state from New York to Wyoming and from California to South Carolina."*

More cheers.

Even before it was over, Beauvoir clicked off the sound. She watched Pine gesticulate in silence, his arms waving. Then she slapped her iPad shut and stared at the wide-open land surrounding the farm.

"Smooth, isn't he?" Beauvoir asked, not looking back at Abbey.

"Very smooth."

"He knows he's winning," she added.

"Obviously." Then Abbey went on. "Are you for him or against him?"

Beauvoir chewed the last bit of tart on her plate carefully and finished her coffee before saying anything. "I haven't decided yet."

Abbey thought that was unusual, because Beauvoir seemed to have a fixed opinion in mind about everything. She rarely held her fire. "You know the media will be hounding you for what you think. Getting your endorsement is probably the last obstacle in Pine's path. You could stop him if you wanted to."

"I guess the question is whether it's worth stopping him," Beauvoir replied. "Ah, well, it's probably a moot point. Even if I didn't like Don, he has the nomination nailed down. No one's going to make a serious challenge."

Abbey cocked her head. "Why is that?"

Beauvoir tapped a finger against the side of her nose. "Before he ran for the Senate, Don spent five years as head of the CIA. Everyone is scared to death of him around Washington. Don Pine knows where all the bodies are buried."

Tim Randall watched from the back of the ballroom as senator Pine made his way off the stage to a final round of applause. It had been a good speech. A *presidential* speech. Randall had worked around politicians for his entire career, and he'd seen candidates for the top job come and go. There were lots of people who wanted to win, but very few with the brains, balls, and nerve to outlast the other pretenders.

One thing Randall knew about Don Pine: the senator would chew off his arm to be president of the United States.

Pine's face was creased with a big smile as he threaded his way through the crowd, shaking hands with all the right people as aides tried to nudge him to the door. That was how it went at every event. Randall had learned to take Pine's long goodbyes into account when preparing the senator's schedule. Pine fed off the energy of supporters like a kind of political vampire, sucking out every last drop of blood before moving on to new prey.

It took another twenty minutes before the two of them were finally seated together in the back of the town car, returning to the Capitol. Behind the smoked windows, the smile vanished from the senator's face, and his jaw hardened. His skin was flushed from the heat of the room, and he loosened his collar and tie. A few dark strands of hair broke free of the mane swept back over his head. He grabbed a bottle of San Pellegrino sparkling water from the limousine fridge and drank it all, then stretched out his long legs. His knee bounced impatiently, still burning off excess energy. Pine was never content to stay still for any length of time.

"Could you feel the hunger in there?" he asked. "Fuck, that gets me hard."

"It was a good event," Randall agreed.

"What's next?" Pine demanded, snapping his fingers. "Come on, go, go, go."

"You have a meeting with the majority leader on the Big Tech bill."

"Google and Meta are going to shit over that one. And then?"

"Interviews. CBS. CNN. MSNBC. The narrative is converging around you being the prohibitive front-runner for the nomination."

Pine worked his thumb around the dimple in his chin as his political instincts kicked in. "So what's their angle? Let me guess. Where did this unanimity come from in a party where the nomination process is typically a circular firing squad?"

Randall gave a tight smile. "Pretty much."

"Okay, how do I dismiss the other clowns without sounding like a prick?"

"I'm not sure you need to worry about that. Don't mention them. Let the reporters draw their own conclusions."

"All right. I like that. I'll just keep playing the giant in a land of dwarves."

The senator's chief of staff offered up a hesitant cough. "But there's one person we should talk about before the interviews."

"Who?"

"Alicia Beauvoir."

"What about her?"

"She's conspicuously neutral," Randall said. "That hurts us. You've wrapped up key endorsements among the party leadership, but not from her. People are starting to ask why. You'll get questions."

Pine shrugged. "Do I look like I care about Secretary Beaver?"

"Her voice carries a lot of weight. Especially with women."

"Well, if she thinks she can play the party's high priestess, fuck her. She can stay neutral for all I care. Hell, she can endorse someone else. Whoever it is, I'll crush them."

"There's no point having her as an enemy," Randall replied carefully. "The press loves process stories and Democratic civil war stories best of all. A feud between you and Alicia will stomp on our message. We're getting a lot of traction from the kumbaya unity pitch, and that won't play if we get into a pissing match with another leading Democrat."

The senator rolled his eyes. "I know you have history with Alicia, but Jesus, Randall. You really think I'm going to suck her dick?"

"I'm saying she can be a problem for us if she chooses to be. So use the interviews today to talk her up. You're anticipating productive conversations with her. You respect her policy instincts. That sort of thing."

Pine shook his head. "Alicia's too smart for that shit. Plus, if I talk publicly about how important she is, I'm handing her the knife if she decides to stab me in the back."

"No, it makes you look like a consensus builder by bringing her into the media discussion before they start asking questions. Plus, it makes her look petty if she holds back her endorsement at that point. After she pledges allegiance, it doesn't matter whether you actually consult her at all."

Pine snorted. "Fucking Beaver."

"The point is to keep her out of the war," Randall insisted. "If she decides to torpedo you, things will get ugly. We'll still probably win, but we'll be bloodied going into the general. That's the last thing we need. There's no point in having her standing in your way if we can figure out how to neutralize her."

The senator fixed Randall with his dark eyes. "Neutralizing my opponents is what I pay you for, Tim."

"Yes, I know."

"Are we very clear about that?"

"Crystal clear," Randall replied.

"I don't care what you have to do. I expect you to take care of anyone who gets in my way. Especially Alicia Beauvoir."

11

The heat of the Nassau sunshine burned on Bourne's neck. The sticky air pasted the purple tie-dyed shirt he'd bought at the airport to his torso. A cheap plastic gift bag dangled from his hand, and he wore a baseball cap low on his forehead. He'd taken a cab from the terminal at Pindling to Junkanoo Beach, and now he walked along the white sand amid hordes of cruise ship tourists snapping up cheap souvenirs. The blue harbor water was as still as glass, barely offering up lazy waves. In the park next to him, the fronds of palm trees drooped limply. He pretended to sip sky juice from a half coconut as he navigated around oiled bodies stretched out on wildly colored beach towels.

Behind his amber sunglasses, his eyes watched the dozens of people around him. Before heading for Teeling's catamaran, he'd wanted a chance to scope out the area and check for surveillance. That was a good thing, because he'd already been spotted.

First, at the airport, a Bahamian police officer had done a doubletake on seeing Bourne's face in the terminal. Word had obviously gone out to look for him; he was on a list. Now, at the beach, a Black kid about twenty years old was following him from a safe distance. The kid was tall and muscled, with glistening skin, and wore a skin-tight white tank top. Wired earbuds stretched to a device in the pocket of his baggy shorts, and Jason could see his lips move as he reported on Bourne's route.

The question was, *who* was on the other end of the microphone? If the kid was an advance scout for another hit team, Jason didn't want to lead them straight to Teeling. Assuming Teeling was still alive.

Bourne needed a diversion.

Ahead of him, half a dozen Nassau boys, none of them more than ten, kicked a soccer ball around the sand. As they played and ran with loud shouts, another boy outside the group drew a bead on a group of middle-aged tourists. This other boy was older by a couple of years and was beanpole skinny, with wiry hair growing straight up from his head. He was obviously the ringleader of this little group. The kid flagged the younger boys with a flick of his index finger, then gestured toward a bearded American in his fifties, who stupidly had his wallet and passport jutting out from the rear pocket of his khakis. With a smooth kick, one of the young boys lofted the soccer ball into the air, where it thumped into the bearded man's head. He staggered and reacted angrily, and the kids surrounded him in an instant, groveling and apologizing. Meanwhile, from behind, the older boy dove at the scene like a crafty seagull, picking the man's pocket and melting back into the crowd. It would probably be several minutes before the man realized his wallet and passport were gone.

Bourne caught up with the boy with a few long steps, then locked a hand on his shoulder. Looking back, the boy opened his mouth to shout for help—another practiced technique when in need of a getaway—but Bourne lifted his tie-dyed shirt just far enough to show off the silver gleam of the Sig

Sauer shoved into his belt. Immediately, the boy clamped his lips shut, and his eyes widened into two big orbs of fear. Panicked words spilled from his mouth.

"Hey, man, you want the guy's shit back, you got it. He a friend of yours, you take it. I don't want trouble. Just let me go, no harm done, 'kay?"

"Keep it," Bourne told him with a shrug. "Tourists should be more careful."

The boy's eyebrows shot skyward. "For real?"

"For real." Bourne grabbed a fifty-dollar bill from his pocket and slipped it into the boy's hand. "But I want your help with something."

"Yeah, no problem, man, what you need?"

"There's a guy about thirty yards behind me. Don't look at him, but tell me if you see him. White T-shirt, earphones, muscles."

The boy nodded eagerly. "Yeah, sure. I got him."

"You know him?"

"No, man. He ain't local. I know everybody 'round here. Haitian, maybe. Fucking Haitians do a lot of dirty work."

"I need about thirty seconds where he's not looking my way. Can you and your friends arrange that?"

The boy's lips spread into a wide white grin. "You bet. No problem. Thirty seconds is what you need, thirty seconds is what you got. But a white guy's got a gun, I figure he can pay a hundred bucks, not fifty."

Jason chuckled and found another bill. "Man knows how to make a deal."

The boy pocketed the extra money and winked. Then he slapped his hand over Jason's palm. "Close up your fist, man. Gotta make it look like you buying drugs. Tough guy seen us together, don't want him expecting a trick."

"Good thinking," Bourne replied with a smile.

He kept walking, eyeing his escape route off the beach.

Thirty seconds later, he heard a loud disturbance behind him as the soccer brigade descended on his pursuer. Without looking back, Jason shifted course and crossed the sand to an adjacent stretch of parkland. Behind the thick trunk of a palm tree, he stripped off his tie-dyed shirt and replaced it with a red polo shirt from inside the plastic bag. He stripped the baseball cap off his head and pulled a leather satchel from the gift shop bag, then stuffed the hat and bag inside the satchel. Casually, not hurrying, he wandered toward the parking lot that led into town. He didn't look back until he'd climbed the slope of Cifford Park and was hidden by the trees.

His stalker in the white tank top was nowhere to be seen now. But Bourne assumed others would be looking for him soon.

He zigzagged among the downtown streets and cut through an old cemetery, where the crumbling stones were dotted with orange mold. The neighborhood was mostly deserted. When he was well east of the cruise ship wharf, he made his way back to Bay Street, which was a couple of blocks from the water. This was the industrial section of the harbor, where container ships were offloaded. Many of the buildings still showed the damage of Hurricane Dorian, their façades ruined, their windows covered over with metal shutters that had done little to stop the sea and wind. He passed girly bars, spice shops, and a pink-walled bakery making rum cakes. Finally, the street swung back to border the harbor, and he saw bridges leading to and from Paradise Island and the towers of the Atlantis casino.

Ahead of him were a dozen piers crammed with boats ranging from downscale fishing trawlers to sleek hundred-foot yachts. He located the pier he'd visited three years earlier and made his way to the slip where the Treadstone agent named Teeling kept a catamaran that he'd used for years as his retirement home.

Except now the slip was empty. The *Irish Whiskey* wasn't there, and neither was Teeling.

Bourne looked up and down the pier. Not far away, he spotted a midsize white powerboat, where a woman with long brunette hair sunbathed facedown across the prow. He approached the boat but didn't announce himself. The woman wore a revealing thong bottom, and the ties of her bikini top were undone, exposing a long stretch of bronzed skin and the ripples of her spine. She was fit and trying to look young, but forty was in her rearview mirror. As she rolled onto her back, the loose cups of crocheted fabric barely contained breasts that looked too gravity-defying to be natural.

"If you want a show, buy a ticket," she said, sensing his presence without opening her eyes.

"Actually, I'm looking for someone," Bourne said. "I was hoping you knew him."

The woman stretched out her arm languidly and picked up a pair of sunglasses that she slid over her face. She propped herself up on her elbows and took a good look at him in the sunshine. Her lips bent into a smile.

"You got a name?" she asked. "My mama said never talk to strangers."

"Briggs," Bourne replied. "Charlie Briggs."

"Nice to meet you, Charlie Briggs. I'm Meredith."

The woman pushed herself up so that she was sitting at the front of the boat. She reached around to her back to retie the bikini top, and in the process, she gave him a peekaboo look at her dark nipples that wasn't accidental. Her legs dangled off the boat, pedaling slowly back and forth. Standing closer to her, he smelled rum wafting off her breath.

"So who are you looking for?" Meredith asked.

"A man who owns a catamaran that usually docks here. The *Irish Whiskey*."

"Oh." She drew out the word, making her voice sound like a purr. "You're a friend of Teeling?"

"I am."

"Teeling doesn't have many friends."

"We used to work together. Have you seen his boat today?"

"No, he headed out on the water a few days ago. He hasn't been back."

"He say where he was going?"

"He didn't."

"Anybody with him?"

"Don't think so. Like I said, Teeling's kind of a loner. Tough old guy. Looks like he was in a few wars."

"That's him," Jason agreed.

"Well, I don't know where he is, Charlie Briggs, but if he comes back, I'll be sure to tell him you said hey."

"It's important that I find him quickly," Bourne said. "You ever hang out with him, Meredith? He ever take you anywhere around town?"

"Oh, sure, we go out now and then. Me, I usually prefer younger men, not salty dogs. I like Teeling, though. Tells good stories, and he's not shy about pouring the whiskey until the bottle's empty. But that's all it is between us."

"Did he take you anywhere special?" Bourne asked. "Any place where people seemed to know him?"

Meredith pushed her sunglasses to the end of her nose. "Teeling avoids the tourist dives. He prefers local clubs. A lot of times, him and me are the only whites in the place. Teeling doesn't dance, but he likes to see me out on the floor."

"Like where?"

"Like maybe I could show you rather than tell you," she purred again.

"Or you could just tell me."

Her mouth pouted. "Aw. Now I can't remember."

"Then I guess you better show me," Jason said, surrendering.

"All righty then," Meredith announced happily, licking her tongue around her lips. She took off her sunglasses and lay back across the boat again, her legs slightly spread. She closed her eyes and caressed the line of her chin. "Pick me up at ten. The club doesn't open until ten. And you better dress better than that, Charlie Briggs."

At ten thirty that evening, Bourne escorted Meredith down an alley perfumed by the smells of bougainvillea flowers and vomit. He saw a drunk body slumped in front of the barred doorway of a warehouse whose metal walls were streaked with rust. Shards of glass glinted on the pavement underneath one of the building's broken windows. A prostitute on her knees leaned into the open door of a pickup truck parked near a collapsing chain-link fence. When Jason glanced behind him, he could see the lights of one of the Paradise Island bridges, but the island's glamour felt far away.

The club was called Fat Sadie's, although several of the painted letters on the sign had chipped away. The window holes on the stone walls were filled with cinder blocks, and rather than an actual entrance, a loading dock led to open wooden doors. Someone had placed a wrought iron chair near the dock to help the girls in high heels make the climb. From inside, a steel soca beat thumped like an explosion into the street. When Meredith heard it, her hips began to writhe, and her arms waved as if she were hoping to take flight. She'd already been half drunk when he picked her up at the boat.

Bourne climbed onto the loading dock, then lifted Meredith behind him. She'd poured her body into a pink dress that ended at her upper thighs, and she wobbled a little as he set her down. She planted a wet kiss on his lips, then wiped away the lipstick she left behind. Her fingers smoothed the shoulders of his black jacket.

"You clean up nice."

"Thanks."

He led her inside, where the dance floor was a seething mass of bodies. Red and yellow strobe lights played across the fog cloud that made the faces go in and out of focus. Meredith in her low-cut dress got a lot of attention. So did Bourne, because he was the only white male in the club.

"Teeling," he shouted in Meredith's ear over the calypso music. "Who do I talk to?"

"The bartender," Meredith shouted back. "Claton. He's always here. If anyone knows Teeling, he will. But how about we dance first?"

"We'll dance later."

He took her elbow and made a path through the crowd. In the waves of light and fog, hard eyes everywhere watched them go. The drums beat louder and faster, and the arms and legs of dancers flailed, bumping against them. Meredith bumped back, her skin already wet with sweat. With each step, Bourne expected to see a knife or a gun coming at him out of the cloud. This was a bad idea.

Then it got worse. At the bar, Meredith waved at the back of a Black man who was mixing cocktails in hurricane glasses. Her voice screeched, still not much more than a whisper over the throbbing music. "*Claton!*"

Claton turned, and Bourne recognized the muscled twentysomething kid who'd followed him at Junkanoo Beach.

"Shit," he hissed under his breath.

Bourne slid his hand into his pocket and curled his fingers around the butt of the Sig he was carrying. A few feet away, Claton's hands slipped into the baggy pockets of his white cargo pants, and Jason knew he had a gun, too. As the bartender approached them warily, Bourne watched, ready to draw and fire if the kid's arms twitched at all.

"Go dance," he told Meredith.

She stared at him. "What?"

"Dance. I'll watch you. That's what Teeling does, right?"

"Well, sure."

Meredith didn't need to be asked again. With a happy scream, she waded onto the dance floor, and soon she was surrounded by men running their hands over her body. Bourne kept one eye on her to make sure she was okay and one eye on the bartender, who was now standing right in front of him.

Claton leaned forward, putting his mouth near Bourne's ear. "Are you fucking crazy, Cain? Coming here? You got a death wish?"

Bourne's head cocked with surprise. Claton was *Treadstone*.

"You were following me," Jason said, trying to recover. "Why?"

"I was watching your back," Claton snapped. "Teeling said you might show up like a damn fool. Don't you know you're a fucking target on this island? Why do you think he cleared out of here?"

"I need to find him," Bourne said.

Claton shook his head. "No way."

"Teeling can lead me to whoever's behind this."

"Not according to him. He says he doesn't know shit." Claton wiped sweat from his forehead. "You shouldn't have come here."

"Where *is* he?" Bourne asked.

The young bartender's gaze traveled nervously around the club. He kept both hands in his pockets, as if expecting an ambush. Bourne studied the place, too, noting through the dance floor fog that Meredith seemed to have forgotten him entirely. Everyone else stole glances at Bourne, but he couldn't separate real threats from the naked hostility directed at a non-islander.

"Meet me at the end of the bar," Claton said.

The kid gestured for one of the other bartenders to take over. When the man gave him a quizzical look, Claton nodded at Bourne, then rolled his eyes and closed one nostril with a finger and snorted. The implied message won a laugh from the other man: *Stupid white tourist needs some coke.*

Bourne shoved through intertwined bodies to the other end of the bar, where Claton led him through a door to a dirty metal stairwell. The beat of the music followed them in a muffled pound through the walls. Claton ran lightly up the stairs in his worn sneakers, and Bourne stayed closely behind. On the second floor, another door opened onto a narrow uncarpeted hallway. Dim lights flickered automatically to life as they moved. Cockroaches scattered, and a snake slithered past them.

A red light on the ceiling marked a security camera that was watching them.

"Teeling's *here*?" Jason said.

"We took out the catamaran overnight a few days ago," Claton explained. "It's docked on a nearby island owned by some rich Russian. Then Teeling and I took a Zodiac back here. Hide in plain sight, right?"

Sometimes the best place to hide is where everyone is looking for you.

Treadstone.

They marched down the hallway side by side. There was a wooden door on the far end that looked ready to collapse inward, but as they got closer, Jason saw that the outer door was a ruse. The hinges and locks were heavy and new, and he spotted a glint of metal that suggested a steel door hidden behind the wood.

Bourne got ready to knock, then stopped when he heard a drunken, screeching voice behind them.

"Hey, where you going, Charlie Briggs?"

He and Claton both spun.

Meredith stood by the stairwell door, legs planted solidly atop her high heels, looking in her miniskirt like Modesty Blaise. By the time Bourne processed the CZ Bren 2 semiautomatic rifle cradled in her arms, she'd begun to fire.

12

"*Cain!*"

The shout came from the steel door behind them, which had swung open. Frantically, Teeling gestured them inside, but staccato fire from the other end of the hallway froze them in place. Bullets ricocheted off the floor and walls. Claton grunted in pain as burning metal lodged in his shoulder, and a spray of blood across the hallway spattered Bourne's face. For an instant, Meredith paused her shooting, because she wasn't alone anymore. Two more gunmen burst through the stairwell door, and as they did, Bourne drew his Sig and laid down fire that forced them backward. Then he hurled Claton through the open doorway and hit the ground himself and rolled inside.

The door stayed open. Jason heard the thunder of running feet as the killers charged, lured down the hallway. More bullets rained into the room, breaking glass and kicking plaster dust from the walls. Teeling winked, then hoisted a CTS flash grenade down the hallway and kicked the heavy door shut behind it. On the ground, Bourne clapped both hands over his ears, but even so, the twin bangs from the hallway slammed him like thunder. On the other side of the door, the blinding flash and deafening noise brought the killers down with heavy thuds, their brains scrambled.

"That won't hold them for long," Teeling barked. "Come on! The window!"

They all leaped to their feet. Claton staggered, his hand clamped over his bloody shoulder. The three of them ran to a single window covered by a metal hurricane shutter. It took a few seconds for Teeling to unlock it, and in that amount of time, rifle fire began again from the hallway. Bourne heard a guttural curse as the killers discovered that the door was made of reinforced steel, then a scream as a ricochet struck one of them. The voice was male; it wasn't Meredith.

Teeling rolled back the shutter and secured an emergency escape ladder against the sill. The metal steps unwound toward the street below.

"Claton, you first," Teeling said. "Can you make it?"

The young Black man looked insulted by the question and began to squeeze his body through the frame. With one arm mostly limp at his side, he used his other hand, which was sticky with blood, to grasp the rungs of the ladder. Slowly, he lowered himself halfway down, then lost his grip and fell the short distance to a cluster of rosebushes growing on the side of the building. He stumbled to the street, then looked up to the window and waved them down.

"Now you," Bourne said to Teeling.

The older agent didn't argue. For a man well into his seventies, he remained spry. He thrust one leg over the sill, then the other, and with his hands on the ladder chains, he slid down like a firefighter to land nimbly in the dirt.

Bourne began to follow, but before he could climb outside, an explosion shuddered through the small apartment and knocked him to the ground. The metal door crashed inward, its hinges and large chunks of the accompanying wall blown apart by two detonations of C-4. Smoke and dust made a choking cloud that poisoned his lungs when he inhaled. Dizzy, Jason crawled, his gun in his hand, as two shadows spilled through the open doorway. Their rifles fired wildly, spraying the interior.

His eyes blinked as he struggled to see through the haze. He stayed low, and the first of the gunmen practically ran right over him. Bourne spilled him off his feet, then clawed for the man's skull and wrenched it sideways until he heard a sickening crack. He stripped away the rifle and rolled onto his back, his gaze shifting as he tried to spot the other killer above him.

More gunfire erupted, so close he could feel the heat of the bullets. He slithered through the acrid cloud, then bumped into something on the floor. His hands found warm skin and a wet pool of blood.

A body.

Dead.

Bourne heard a familiar voice. Teeling shouted at him, and Jason saw the old man leaning through the window with a smoking Glock in his hand. He'd climbed back up the ladder and taken out the other shooter.

"Cain, come on, let's go!"

Shaking his head in admiration, Bourne pushed himself to his feet and slung the strap of the man's Bren rifle around his neck. He ran to the window and waited until Teeling slid down the ladder again, then dropped to the ground, taking the impact through his knees. He followed the older agent to the street, where Claton was waiting for them. Smoke filtered through the open window, but below, he could still hear the soca beat pounding uninterrupted from the club. No one seemed to have noticed the battle over their heads.

"Not bad, old man," Bourne said.

"Who you calling old?" Teeling asked, then nodded up the street. "I've got a car a few blocks away. Best we get off the island fast. Claton, is the inflatable still hidden near Bonefish Pond?"

"Yeah, right where we left it."

"Where are you planning to go?" Bourne asked, but he didn't have time to wait for the answer. His brain shot him a warning, detecting movement behind them, a scrape on dirt, the swish of a rifle strap. Not even looking back, he piled his shoulder into Teeling, taking both of them down just as bullets whistled past their heads. From the ground, Bourne glanced toward the lights of the Paradise Island bridge and saw the woman who called herself Meredith. She hadn't gone into the apartment with the other two; she'd backtracked down the stairs and emerged through the club door.

Claton wasn't fast enough.

Meredith shot him in the neck, then the forehead, and his body collapsed like a balloon leaking air. Her torso swiveled, her barrel taking aim at Bourne and Teeling. Her first shot missed low, bouncing off the cracked pavement of the street, and that gave Bourne enough time to squeeze off one shot with the Bren that drilled into her stomach. She looked down in shock at the blood turning the tight pink fabric of her dress burgundy red.

Bourne fired again. He hit her in the breast this time. She tried to raise the rifle and fire back, but she no longer seemed capable of holding the weapon. It slipped away and fell to the street. She swayed, her knees buckling, then collapsed face-first. Jason got to his feet and walked over and turned her on her back. Her dress was a mass of blood and dirt, and she'd broken her nose as she fell. Her ample chest swelled as her lungs tried to gulp air, and her eyes seemed to roll around in her head.

"Who do you work for?" Bourne asked.

"Fuck you, *Cain*," she gasped.

"Are there others on the island?"

But a last bubble of acid and blood spewed out of her mouth. She was gone. He felt a hand on his shoulder, and Teeling was beside him.

"Time to go, my friend."

Teeling steered the zodiac across calm, dark water. They'd left Nassau behind them, and now they were alone under the stars, with no landmarks on the horizon. Even so, Teeling seemed to know exactly where he was going. Every now and then, he checked his phone, and Jason saw the glow of a compass, which told him they were heading southeast away from the island.

"Where are we headed?" Bourne asked.

"I know someone who can get us out. Me to another island. Aruba, maybe. You to wherever you want to go next."

"Claton mentioned a rich Russian."

Teeling smiled. "Remember when you looked me up three years ago? I said one of my old Soviet-era comrades retired down here. Let's just say he took a lot of money with him when he left. He's got a speck of land near Black Point, built himself a mansion, flies around the Caribbean in a helicopter. We get together every now and then to rehash our glory days. Once you're out of the game, the old battles don't seem to matter anymore. We drink vodka, play poker, lie about how many girls we fucked. At least I hope he's lying, because otherwise, Jesus."

The Treadstone agent grabbed a canvas bag from the damp bottom of the Zodiac. He undid the flaps and removed a bottle of Irish whiskey that matched his name. He undid the cork and took a swig, then handed it to Jason, who did the same. The drink went down incredibly smooth and spread out like a warm river through his chest. He put a hand over the side of the small boat and let it drag in the water. Even in the near total silence, his ears rang from the music of the club and the explosions in the upstairs apartment.

Close up now, with time to really focus on his face, he could see that Teeling had aged in the few years since he'd last seen him. He didn't know if the man had crossed eighty yet, but that age couldn't be far away. His body had sunk into a bony mass of wrinkles, his skin like cocoa from constant exposure to the sun. His long gray hair was tied in a ponytail, and he'd shaved the bushy mustache he'd previously worn. When he spoke, his voice sounded like the scrape of steel wool.

"Anyway, I need to move on," Teeling said. "Too bad. I've had a good run in Nassau. Sucks about Claton, too. He was a good kid. Inexperienced, but we all start out that way. I don't know, except maybe you, Cain. You've always been an old soul. I laughed when Claton told me how you ditched him at Junkanoo."

"I wish I'd known he was working for you," Bourne said.

"Well, I wanted to see if anyone was following you. He said no, but was he wrong? Where did you pick up the Black Widow?"

"She was hanging out on a boat near yours. She was obviously waiting for you to come back. Or maybe they guessed that I'd come looking for you."

"And who the fuck *are* they?" Teeling asked. "I got the word that we all had targets on our chest, and that's when I went into hiding. But nobody seemed to know who was calling the shots."

Bourne drank more of the whiskey, enjoying the smooth burn. "Do you remember a mission seven years ago codenamed Defiance?"

Teeling's face turned dark. His eyes narrowed into slits. He slowed the Zodiac until it was barely moving, just bobbing with the open water. His eyes turned up toward the starlit sky, and he shook his head. "Ah, shit. Yeah, I remember. Always knew that one would come back to bite me in the ass."

"Do you know what it was all about?" Bourne asked.

The older man shook his head. "No, all I knew was my piece of it. But I was a good boy. I did what I was told."

"Seven years ago," Bourne reflected. "Weren't you already retired by then? You were out, or as out as you can get with Treadstone. Why did they approach you? Why did you even take the job?"

"Yeah, I was done, but you know me. I keep my hand in wherever I go. Contacts, local assets, whatever. I figure I live longer if I know what might be coming at me. Anyway, I wasn't in Nassau at that point. I was living on Réunion island in the Indian Ocean, had a condo overlooking the water in Saint-Denis. I mean, you can't get much more remote than that. I hadn't heard a word from anyone at Treadstone in three years. Then one day I was hanging out with my flask on the seawall in Le Barachois, and some guy sits down next to me. He had the look. I knew without him even giving me the codes that he wanted me to do a job."

"What was it?" Bourne asked.

Teeling frowned, not answering for a while. The sea around them was silent. Then he said, "A hit, what else?"

"Who?"

The old man wore a pained look that Bourne knew well. He had the face of an agent who knew the rule was to take orders, do the job, not ask questions. Some, like Nova, never had a problem with that. Others carried the scars.

"Who was it?" Bourne asked again. "Knowing the target may help me figure out what was behind Defiance. That will lead me to whoever's coming after us."

"The target's name was Ronny Dunstan," Teeling replied with a sigh.

"Should that mean something to me?"

"Nope. Didn't mean anything to me, either."

"Was Dunstan on the island, too?"

Teeling nodded. "Yeah. I assume that's why they approached me, even though I was technically out. It's not like I needed the money, but I got the feeling if I said no, they'd bring in someone else and add *me* to the hit list."

"This Ronny Dunstan. Did you check him out?"

Bourne knew that wasn't procedure. The *who* was important. The *why* didn't matter. Or at least, it wasn't supposed to.

Confirm the identity. Do the job.

Treadstone.

But he was pretty sure, looking at the old man's face, that Teeling had broken the rules. Maybe that was a luxury he'd allowed himself in retirement. It was also insurance if anyone started asking questions.

"Sure, I checked him out," Teeling admitted.

"So what was his story?"

"Man, I still don't have a fucking clue. That's what bugs me. Ronny Dunstan was a beach bum. Twenty-two years old. Transplant from Manchester in the UK, liked to wear Manchester United T-shirts. No money. He crashed on a friend's couch most nights or slept on the sand. Kid didn't even have a phone. His passport said he hadn't left the island in months. And yet Treadstone needed him dead. The whole thing made no sense. I mean, it wasn't hard to do. Ronny never figured some old geezer like me would cut his throat. I planted some drugs on him after I did it. The heroin trade was ramping up back then, so nobody batted an eye about the murder."

"But you don't know what made him important?" Bourne asked.

In Jason's head, he was adding Ronny Dunstan, UK beach bum, to a list that included a German mechanical engineer, a

DC police officer, and a Berkeley college student. Four targets from around the world, different ages, different professions. Dunstan seemed to be the unlikeliest of all.

What linked them? Why had they been killed?

What was Defiance?

"No, I came up empty," Teeling replied from the other side of the Zodiac. "I figured maybe Ronny saw something. Wrong place, wrong time, that kind of thing. But I don't know what the hell it was. As it was, I asked too many questions. People noticed. I came home one day and found that my condo had been searched. They weren't subtle about it. I got the message to back off. That's when I left Réunion and headed to Nassau."

"Well, they're going to know you and I have talked," Bourne said. "They'll assume you told me all of this."

"Yeah, I'd expect a welcoming committee when you get to the island," Teeling told him. "You're following the right track, but I'm not sure what you're going to find. All I can tell you is that Treadstone doing the hit on Ronny was like sending in Tom Seaver to pitch a Little League game. If you want the truth about Defiance, you need to figure out why they sent a guy like me to take out a nobody like him."

13

"Ronny Dunstan," Bourne repeated to the owner of the alley-side bistro two blocks from the beach in Saint-Denis. *"Il a travaillé pour vous. Vous vous souvenez de lui?"*

The impatient Frenchman, who was mincing garlic in the hot, crowded kitchen and cursing out his sous-chefs at the same time, shook his head. No, he did not remember Ronny working for him. He barely remembered the people who worked for him now.

Bourne took out a photograph of the body from the crime scene. He'd acquired it for two hundred euros from a pretty young secretary in the Commissariat Central. She'd also given him a look at the archived file from the murder investigation conducted by local police. The unsolved file was thin, but it did list a few businesses around Saint-Denis where Ronny had worked part-time in the year before his death. The bistro on Rue de Nice was one of them, but even after seeing the photograph of Ronny's dead face, the owner had no recollection of the kid who'd washed dishes for him seven years earlier.

"Non, non, non," the man insisted, waving Bourne away. *"Il n'est personne."*

He's a nobody.

That had been the story for three days wherever Jason went since he'd arrived on Réunion island on the other side of the world. No one in Saint-Denis remembered Ronny Dunstan. He'd come and gone without anyone even noticing he was here.

So why had it been so vital for Treadstone to send Teeling to kill him?

Bourne bought a takeaway croque monsieur, then headed toward the beach to eat lunch. Bright sun shined from a cloudless sky, and the sea breeze was salty and strong. In other towns, real estate this close to an ocean view would have included a lineup of million-dollar homes, but here in Saint-Denis, he found downscale apartments with rust-stained walls overlooking the water. He sat on a stone wall above the sand, not far from where Ronny Dunstan had been found in the surf, seaweed draped around his body. He could imagine Teeling heaving the bloody knife into the moonlit ocean, then casually walking away.

His passport said he hadn't left the island in months.

Whatever had happened to make Ronny a target had happened right here. But what on earth could the kid have seen in this remote place?

Réunion island was just a tiny French outpost of volcanoes jutting like jagged teeth from a verdant rain forest. It wasn't even a thousand square miles in size, with fewer than a million people living along the ring of its coastline. To the west, a few hundred miles away, was the much larger island of Madagascar and then the mainland of Africa. To the east was nothing but five thousand miles of Indian Ocean heading toward Australia. For a beach bum like Ronny, this would have been paradise, but few other outsiders had reason to come here.

He was a nobody!

And yet Ronny was somehow also part of a conspiracy that reached high into the U.S. government, a conspiracy that triggered the murders of Treadstone agents around the world seven years later.

What are they trying to cover up?

Bourne stared at the vast blue ocean that looked ready to swallow up the whole island. The gusty wind threw heavy waves onto the beach, and the crowns of the palm trees swirled and danced. He ate his ham and cheese sandwich and thought about the first half of the puzzle he was trying to solve. What could Ronny have seen or heard on the island? Jason had already been to the library and looked up archived copies of the local newspaper, *Journal de l'île de la Réunion*, for the entire month preceding Ronny's murder. He'd found no unusual events on the island that made headlines. No deaths or disappearances, no celebrity tourists, no government visitors, no multinational conferences. Overall, the island had no strategic significance. There was simply nothing here worth killing over.

Then he thought about the second half of the puzzle.

How would anyone even have *known* that Ronny was a threat?

Had he been recognized somewhere he shouldn't have been? Had he told someone about something he'd seen or heard? But the kid didn't even have a phone.

Bourne found himself at a dead end. Seven years after his murder, Ronny Dunstan may as well have never existed at all. And yet someone must have known him and been aware of his death. He must have had friends on the island. A girlfriend. *Somebody*.

When Jason finished his sandwich, he wandered down the beach through the palm-lined park known as Le Barachois. Near the main street, he approached half a dozen cannons pointed out toward the bay like stiff old soldiers. A French mother watched her two children climbing on the cannons and making *boom* noises as if they were firing on pirate ships. The children were both boys, not even ten years old, their brown hair wild and messy. They looked like brothers, and they were dressed alike, both of them wearing T-shirts for the French soccer team Olympique Lyonnais.

Then Bourne remembered.

Manchester.

According to Teeling, Ronny had come to the island from the UK and often wore Manchester United jerseys. That kind of obsession didn't fade no matter how far away he moved from his hometown. So where would an English transplant go if he felt homesick and wanted to watch his favorite team play football?

It took Bourne less than half an hour asking questions on the street to identify a pub known as the Wessex, where UK expats congregated. He found it six blocks away in a rundown alley crowded with cars parked on the sidewalks. In apartments on either side of the small bistro, people hung their laundry over the balcony railings to dry. Inside, he found a handful of wooden tables clustered around a bar that served warm pints of English bitter. A flat-screen television was mounted near the ceiling. It was midafternoon, and the place was mostly empty, with just a few people lingering over plates of sausage and chips.

The bartender poured him a London Pride. He was a huge Black man with an untamed beard, and he wore a Chelsea jersey. He'd only been on the island for five years, but he told Jason that many of his regulars were long-timers who would be straggling in as it got dark and the soccer games started back home.

So Bourne waited. He nursed his beer, then ordered another. When the evening crowd began to arrive, the bartender tuned the satellite television to a Premier League game between

Arsenal and Tottenham. Bourne's casual questions for the new arrivals turned up no one who remembered Ronny Dunstan, not until a wizened old man with a smoker's cough took a seat at the end of the bar and ordered "anything but Boddies." Like Ronny, the man wore a T-shirt for Manchester United, and the dirty red fabric hung loosely on his scrawny chest. His white hair sprouted in wild curls, and he wore black glasses with thick lenses. The bartender whispered that the man's name was Arthur. Bourne waited until a seat opened up next to the man, and then he sat down and bought Arthur another pint.

It wasn't hard to get him talking. Jason had spent several weeks in Manchester on a Treadstone mission, and he introduced himself using his cover as an architectural historian who'd worked on the renovation of the Victoria Baths. Arthur, who'd left the city twenty years earlier, rambled on with the passion of someone who missed his hometown. The old man was still pissed about the betrayal of Boddingtons being sold to Anheuser-Busch two decades earlier, and he offered up stats on Cristiano Ronaldo from memory.

Finally, Bourne steered the conversation to Ronny.

"I have some good friends in Manchester," he told the man. "When they found out I was coming here, they asked me to follow up on a boy from the old neighborhood. His name was Ronny. Ronny Dunstan. He came here to hang out on the beaches, but apparently he got killed. Murdered. Sounds like it was an ugly thing. His parents never got any news from the police about what really happened or who did it."

Arthur took off his glasses and cleaned them on his red T-shirt. "Aye, Ronny, sure, sure. That was years ago."

"You knew him?"

"Oh, aye, Mancunians have to stick together," the man insisted. "Not a lot of us here."

"Well, do you know what happened to him?"

Arthur drew a finger across his throat and stuck out his tongue.

"That's awful," Jason said, giving a little academic fussiness to his voice. "I was told the police thought drugs were involved. Heroin, that was what they told his parents."

"Sure, that's what they said, but that was shite. Never saw Ronny touch drugs, sure never saw him sell any. He was into vitamins and organics and such. Always ordered the fucking veggie meal, like anyone does that in a pub. Used to tell me if I knew what was in the bangers, I'd never eat them. Hell, they could fill 'em with pig's dick for all I care."

"If not drugs, then why would anyone kill him?" Bourne asked. "He was just a kid, wasn't he? In his twenties?"

"Yeah, he was. Nice kid, too, I liked him. As to why he got killed, that's a damn good question. Police had their head up their arse on that one, for sure. Nobody seemed to care."

"Do you have any theories?"

"Me, nah, not like I'd have any clue."

"Was anything going on in Ronny's life? Did he tell you any stories before he was killed? The thing is, I'd love to be able to tell my friends something."

Arthur took a slug of his bitter, wiped his mouth, and replaced the mug heavily on the bar. There was a wild cheer from the bar as Arsenal scored on Tottenham. Arthur followed the replay on the television screen, then grunted and looked away. He rubbed his chin, which was in need of a shave.

"There was the whole buried treasure shite," Arthur murmured finally. "But I don't see how that could make any difference."

Bourne cocked his head. "I'm sorry, what?"

"Aw, Ronny came in a couple weeks before he was killed, was full of himself, talking about finding buried treasure. Said how it was going to make him rich and famous. I didn't put any stock in it."

"What kind of treasure?" Bourne asked.

Arthur shrugged. "No idea. What could anybody find around here? We're in the middle of nowhere. Plenty of pirates in the Indian Ocean years ago, so I don't know, maybe something washed ashore. A gold doubloon or shite like that."

"Did he say where he found it?"

"Oh no, big secret, that was all he said. Ronny didn't want people finding out."

Bourne tried to make sense of it.

Buried treasure.

He was sure the treasure didn't have anything to do with pirates. He was also sure that whatever Ronny found had led to his murder not long after. The coincidence was too great to be anything else. But Teeling's mission had been to kill Ronny, not torture him for information about whatever he'd found. Either that meant someone already *knew* what Ronny had found, or they didn't want Teeling to know what it was.

Or both.

"Did Ronny have any good friends?" Bourne asked.

"Not that I saw. I was as good a friend as he had, and he didn't tell me shite."

"What about a girlfriend?"

Arthur stroked his white stubble again. "Yeah, yeah, there was a girl from Madagascar. Zaina, I think. They were hot and heavy for a while. She worked here as a waitress, liked the tips when the footy crowds came in. But she quit the place right after Ronny kicked it. Maybe it reminded her too much of him, who knows."

Or maybe she didn't want to be next, Bourne thought.

"Any idea where I could find Zaina?" he asked.

Arthur shook his head. "Not a clue. Haven't seen her in years. Went home to Africa, for all I know."

Bourne clapped a hand on the man's shoulder. "Well, thank you, Arthur. How about I buy you another pint for the road?"

"I won't say no to that."

Jason signaled the bartender, who was standing nearby, and he waited until the man had placed another ale in front of Arthur before turning away. He pushed into the dense crowd and headed for the street door of the Wessex, but before Bourne made it outside, he felt a hand on his shoulder. When he turned around, he recognized the Black bartender, who'd followed him from behind the bar. The big bearded man nodded for Jason to continue to the street. When they were together under the flickering pub lights, the man lit up a vape pen and leaned casually against the stucco wall. His breath smelled of the beer he'd been serving all day.

Jason waited.

"I heard you talking to Arthur," the bartender said finally through the steam of his vaping.

"You've got good ears," Bourne replied. "It was pretty loud in there."

"Hey, you know what they say. Bartenders listen to your problems. So you find what you were looking for? Info on this Ronny guy?"

"Some," Bourne said. Then he went on after a pause. "Is there anything you want to add?"

The man sucked loudly on his vape pen. "Maybe."

"How much does 'maybe' cost?" Bourne asked.

"Let's say two hundred," the man replied.

Jason extracted two bills from his wallet, and the euros disappeared into the bartender's pocket.

"I heard Arthur mention a girl named Zaina," the bartender went on. "You looking for her?"

"I am."

"Well, there's a Zaina who goes to our church," he told Bourne. "Don't know if it's the same girl, but she comes from

Madagascar, like Arthur said. Pretty, mid-twenties. I've had a go at her, but she prefers white boys. This Ronny was a white boy?"

"He was."

"So maybe she's the one you want."

"Do you know where she lives?" Bourne asked.

"I don't, but it can't be too far from the church. I see her walking home sometimes after mass. She volunteers in the evenings, so she may be there right now. You may be able to catch her."

"What church?"

"Our Lady of Deliverance."

Bourne nodded. "Thanks."

He turned to leave, then stopped as he heard the bartender call after him. "Hey, man, one other thing. A little bonus for you."

"What is it?"

"Watch your back. You're not the only one looking for her."

Bourne felt a chill in his blood as he took a step closer. "What do you mean?"

"I stopped at the church today on my way to work," the man told him. "Light a candle. Chat up the old people. It's what you do. When I was there, I heard a man talking to the priest. He was asking about Zaina, too."

"What did the man look like?"

"A little like you," the bartender replied, eyeing Bourne up and down. "Like a man who means business."

14

It was after nine o'clock when Bourne arrived at our lady of Deliverance.

The church face loomed over a small plaza built on a peak above the white city. Dark hills rose behind the church, and the expanse of the ocean lay below it. A full moon had crested the horizon, bathing the façade in an unearthly glow. Four sharp turrets aimed at the sky like rockets, and a single sharp gable dominated the exterior, with a giant rose window in its center and a statue of Christ at its peak. Tan-painted mortar mixed with rough gray flagstones. There were three arcades leading to the doors, and Jason used the center door to slip quietly inside the church.

He wore a light jacket, his hand curled around the Sig in his pocket. He was taking no chances.

The interior was cool, with dark stained glass looming on the walls and above the altar. High stone columns on both sides led beneath an arched ceiling that was painted like the nighttime sky. Light in the church was low except for a few sconces on the walls, and he stayed in the shadows on the east aisle, where he could remain unseen. There were a dozen people in the pews, some seated, some on their knees. Most were in their fifties or older, and he saw no one who matched the description of Zaina.

Even in the peaceful stillness of the church, he felt a sense of urgency. Someone else was already hunting for the girl. If they got to her first, the next link in the chain to Defiance would be cut off.

How did they find her so quickly?

But Bourne knew. Treadstone agents weren't the only targets of the cleanup operation. The mission was obviously larger than that. They were going back to the original victims, making sure no loose ends were left untied, no secrets at risk of being revealed. It didn't even matter what their targets knew or didn't know. Anyone close to Defiance was at risk.

Including Ronny Dunstan's girlfriend.

He heard a murmur of voices, amplified by the acoustics of the church. It was only a few words and a little musical laughter, but then a man spoke very clearly. He was on the far end of the aisle, but Bourne heard him as if they were standing next to each other.

"Thank you, Zaina."

Bourne focused his gaze on two people near the altar. One was an older, bald Caucasian priest robed in white. The other was a woman with mahogany skin. She was short and small, with bony limbs, and she had wiry black hair tied tightly behind her head and colored with streaks of gold. She had prominent cheekbones on a narrow face, and her smile was wide and bright. She wore a simple white dress that came to her knees; it looked handmade. As Bourne watched, Zaina curtsied to the priest, then made her way up the center aisle.

He followed her out the door into the night.

She crossed the empty plaza toward steps that led down the hillside to the street below. The wind rustled her white dress. She seemed unconcerned by her surroundings and didn't look back to see Bourne trailing her on the other side of the plaza.

He studied the area around her, but for the moment, he saw no threats.

Zaina took the steps at a bright pace, and he could hear her singing under her breath. The lights of Saint-Denis apartment buildings glowed below them, and the night air had turned colder with the ocean breeze. When Zaina got to the street, she continued downhill along a narrow sidewalk. Stone walls bordered the street, level with the treetops that rose from the lower ground on both sides. Bourne walked softly, making no sound with his shoes as he slowly closed the distance between them.

At the base of the hill, Zaina turned left toward the ocean, which he could see several blocks away. The Saint-Denis River paralleled the street, and a low metal fence separated the sidewalk from the grassy riverbank. Zaina stayed near the fence, and the street beside her was crowded with parked cars. She was maybe twenty yards ahead of him, still unaware of his presence. When he studied the lineup of cars, his eyes focused on a green Renault parked near a stone electrical pole. The pole had a streetlight at the top, but the light was out, the glass shattered.

Down the street, all of the other lights were on.

Bourne smelled exhaust and heard the low rumble of an engine. His heart raced with adrenaline.

Immediately, he sprinted forward. He knew what was about to happen, but he was too late to stop it. As Zaina passed the car, the back door flew open. A man bolted from inside, crossed to the riverbank in two steps, and wrapped her up in his arms. She didn't have time to scream as he yanked her off her feet. In the next instant, he'd thrown her into the back of the car, and he jumped in behind her, pulling the door shut as the driver swung the wheel hard and swerved away from the curb.

Bourne veered into the street. In one smooth motion, he

drew the Sig from his jacket pocket, aimed low, and squeezed off a shot as the Renault accelerated away from him. The first bullet careened off the asphalt and hit the chassis with a sharp metal ping. The second shot exploded the right rear tire. Lurching, the Renault crunched down to the pavement with a grinding noise and a shower of sparks. The driver tried to keep going, but the vehicle slammed into a retaining wall and shuddered to a stop. The Renault's front door swung open. The driver rolled out to the street and came up firing from his knees, but Bourne was ready for him. He fired twice, both shots hitting the middle of the man's chest like the kick of a mule. As the driver dropped the gun, Bourne fired again with a kill shot into his forehead. The man slumped sideways.

His partner in the backseat was smarter.

When the other door of the Renault opened, Zaina came out first. The man who'd grabbed her off the street followed, holding her tightly with an arm around her breasts and a gun pressed to the side of her head. Bourne had no clear shot. He could see Zaina's face, shadowed by the nearest streetlight, and her eyes were huge white orbs of terror and confusion. She had no idea why she'd been attacked or what was going on.

Bourne walked slowly toward them, the gun level in his outstretched arms.

"*Arrêtez!*" the man shouted, but Bourne kept coming.

"*Je la tuerai!*" he insisted.

"No, you won't kill her," Bourne replied, matching the man's French. "If you kill her, then I'll kill you, like your friend here. But if you drop your gun and walk away, then I'll let you go, and you live to fight another day."

"Fuck you," the man hissed. "Do you think I believe that?"

Bourne shrugged. He was close to them now, no more than ten feet between the hot barrel of his gun and the man's face, which was mostly hidden behind the short woman in front of him. "You can believe what you want, but from where I'm standing, you don't have many options."

"If you shoot, I shoot, too!" the man snapped. "You want her alive, but I don't care about that. My job is to kill her."

In his tight grasp, Zaina moaned at those words, her body wriggling to escape. She sucked in a breath and tried to scream, but the man lifted his other arm from her chest to tighten it around her throat. He choked off her cry.

"Shut up, you little bitch, shut up, shut *up*!"

The man's eyes danced nervously, shooting to the windows in the nearby apartment buildings, where lights had begun to blink on like Christmas trees. Silhouettes appeared behind the curtains.

Someone shouted to the street. *"Qu'est-ce qui ce passe?"*

"They're calling the police right now," Bourne told the man, his voice hard and calm. "I figure we have about thirty seconds before we hear sirens. Do you really want to be here when they show up? Do you think your people will let you live if you're arrested? But you have a choice. You can let Zaina go and run away. I told you, I won't shoot."

The man's eyes blinked furiously. He was looking for a way out of a no-win situation. In the distance, Jason heard the wail of sirens; it hadn't even taken as long as he'd expected. The man in front of him heard them, too. Bourne anticipated the killer's next move, because there was only one. Surrender wasn't a choice; neither was walking away.

First the man would push Zaina toward him, trying to throw Bourne off-balance.

Then he'd shoot them both.

Jason watched the man's arm, still wrapped in a choking grip around Zaina's throat. He waited for the flinch, knowing it would come any second.

There!

The killer stripped away his hand and drove his body

into Zaina's back, forcing her to stumble forward. His other arm was already straightening, leveling his pistol and aiming toward Bourne. But Jason wasn't there anymore. He'd already leaped sideways, firing as he did, one shot clipping the killer's ear with a spray of blood, the other burrowing into the shoulder of his gun arm. The killer aimed again, toward Zaina this time, who'd fallen to her hands and knees on the pavement right in front of the man. It was an easy shot, and the killer was already squeezing the trigger when Bourne fired again, drilling through the man's forearm and eliciting a wild cry of pain. The gun fell.

Eyes wide, the man ran, one arm dangling uselessly at his side and trailing blood in his wake. Jason let him go; he didn't fire again. There was no time. He ran to Zaina and helped her to her feet, holding her by the waist to keep her from falling as her knees buckled. Down the street, near the ocean, he saw the swirling glow of lights. The police were coming; they'd almost reached the intersection.

"*Venez avec moi,*" Bourne whispered in the girl's ear. "*Maintenant.*"

Her huge brown eyes stared at him. She barely understood; her whole brain was in shock. "*La police?*"

"The police can't help you. There are people who want you dead, and if they know you're in the hands of the police, they'll be able to find you and get to you. You need to stay with me."

Zaina stared at the dead body of one of her kidnappers on the street and at the growing pool of blood. "*Pourquoi?*"

Why?

Why was this happening?

"Ronny," Bourne replied. "Because of Ronny."

Her voice went soft. "Ronny. *Mon Dieu.*"

But something about her dead boyfriend's name got through to her. She didn't have the strength to walk on her own, but she didn't resist as Bourne helped her stagger in the opposite direction, away from the sea, away from the police. They reached the bridge over the river, and he kept them low as they crossed. When they reached the other side, he shot a glance backward to see one of the island squad cars screeching to a stop near the murder scene. But the darkness kept them out of sight. With another few steps, they were out of view, and as Zaina got stronger, they walked faster, and then they ran. He led them through zigzag turns for half a mile, where the streets were mostly empty. When he was sure they wouldn't be found, he slowed. They were on a drab city street, walking beside water-stained building walls and closed storefronts.

"I have a car," he told her. "I can get you out of Saint-Denis."

"Can we stop at my apartment?" she asked him. "There are things I need."

"I'm sure they're watching your apartment. If we go back there, they'll come after you again."

"Who?"

"I don't know."

Zaina shook her head. "And this is because of Ronny? After all this time?"

"Yes."

She smoothed her white dress and made it as presentable as she could. The fabric was dirty and torn in several places. The happy face he'd seen in the church had grown more serious. Her smile was gone. Her dark eyes were thoughtful, and in the nighttime shadows, she was very pretty. She took a deep breath, her breasts swelling as she inhaled the ocean air. She studied the run-down streets as if she knew she was unlikely to see them again.

"Well, Ronny warned me," Zaina said. "He said people might come. But it's been so long. I assumed it had all been forgotten. I should have left years ago. I should have gone home to Madagascar. It's easy to disappear there. Can you get me back there?"

"I can."

"I suppose you want to know about Ronny first," Zaina said with a little twitch of a frown.

"Yes. I need to know what got him killed."

In the distance, they heard more sirens. Zaina shivered.

"I don't know what it was. Not really. He wouldn't tell me the truth. He said I was in danger if I knew too much. But he found something—something he said the whole world was looking for. I don't know what it was, but I know where he hid it. I can show you. He buried it near the beach."

15

They walked along the white sand in the first light of dawn. The wide beach on the island's southeastern coast was deserted and quiet, except for the raucous chatter of tropic birds in the trees. Drooping palms lined the shore, and beyond the fringe of sand was the dense, humid rain forest. They'd hiked past ribbons of waterfalls on a dirt trail from the nearest highway to reach the coast. High above them they could see the sharp green slope of one of the island's dormant volcanoes.

Overnight, the wind had grown strangely still, as if the island were holding its breath. Beside them, the vast stretch of the Indian Ocean lapped in lazy surf over their bare feet and quickly erased their footsteps. Bourne wore cargo shorts and no shirt, his shoes dangling on the laces around his neck, a satchel slung from his shoulder. His gun was in an unzipped pocket, easily reached. He also carried a shovel loosely in one hand, so he could go digging for buried treasure.

Zaina led the way. She'd told him that she hadn't been back to this beach since Ronny's death seven years ago, but she seemed to know exactly where she was going. He'd stolen some clothes from a laundry line for her to wear, including the tiger-striped bikini that now clung to her bony frame. Her skin was smooth and dark, her body more like a teenager than a woman in her twenties. Her face had the distracted look of someone who was searching her memories and going back into her past.

Jason knew that look well.

"This was one of our favorite places," she told him without pausing her quick steps. "We'd come here to swim. To listen to the birds. He would read to me from his favorite books. I remember he found a copy of a book called *Travels in Alaska* by an American named John Muir. He translated it into French for me as he read it; he was good with languages. It was strange, listening to a description of snowy mountains and glaciers while we lay on a blanket on the beach."

Her mouth bent into a sad smile.

"You still miss him," Jason said.

"Yes, I do. I loved him."

"What was he like?"

"Oh, Ronny was a free spirit. Not tied down by anything. Not even me. I never expected our relationship to last forever. He worked only until he made a few euros, and then he quit and lived on the beach until he needed more. He said it was all about living a natural life. Being a speck of a human being on a speck of an island in the middle of a huge ocean. Ronny called it a reminder of where we really fit in God's universe. I liked that."

"You met him at the Wessex?" Bourne asked.

"Yes. Ronny liked to talk about important things. Most boys don't like to talk, but he had a lot of ideas about life. The environment. Religion, too. I'm very Catholic, and I told him there could be no sex if we weren't married. I was only eighteen then. We'd kiss, nothing more. He never pushed me. That was unusual compared to other boys I'd known."

"How long did the two of you go out?"

"A year."

"So what happened?"

Zaina stopped on the beach. Her head bobbed back and forth, making sure they were still alone, but no one else had come to this empty stretch of sand in the early hours. She put her hands on her narrow hips and stared out at the ocean. "The treasure hunt happened," she said. "That changed him."

Jason cocked his head. "I don't understand."

"Ronny became obsessed with finding some kind of treasure. After a while, that was all we did together. I asked him about it, I wanted to know more, but he wouldn't tell me what he was looking for."

"Why did he think this treasure was on the island?"

"It started because of an online friend he had in California. He used to sign on to message boards on a computer at the library. Beach, climate, science groups, that kind of thing. He met someone online a few weeks before he was killed. They chatted all the time. I think the whole treasure hunt came from him. It was his idea."

Bourne's senses grew alert. "Do you know who this friend was?"

"No, but he was a lot like Ronny. Organic, natural, spiritual, another beach lover. I think they were the same age or close. Ronny never mentioned his name, but he said this friend was going to school in California. He was studying oceanography and was very active in climate politics. They talked a lot. Like I say, Ronny enjoyed talking about things."

California.

Jason saw two of the threads in the mystery finally twist together. He'd found a link between Ronny Dunstan and another of the Defiance victims. Someone Nova had killed.

A college student at Berkeley.

"Was Ronny political, too?" Bourne asked.

"Not really. Not before he met this person. After that, he began to talk a lot about conspiracies. About how governments around the world were keeping secrets from us, exploiting the earth, raping the planet for profits. I didn't like hearing him talk like that. And not long after, Ronny started looking for the treasure. He said his friend in California had been doing research, analyzing ocean currents, and he thought there was a good chance some of the treasure would end up on Réunion."

"But you don't know what this treasure was?"

"No. Ronny never told me. He said it would be dangerous if I knew, and I thought that was silly talk, but look what happened to him. This friend encouraged Ronny to go looking on the beaches and not to tell anyone what he was doing. So that's what we did. He and I spent hours here on the east coast, just walking up and down the sand mile after mile. Ronny even bought a metal detector. He was sure he would find it."

She stopped again. Jason waited.

"And he did," Zaina said. "He told me he found it. This was on one of the trips he made by himself, while I was working. It was on this beach right here. He found it and buried it. But he took me back here the next day, because he said somebody else needed to know where it was in case something happened to him. I thought the whole thing was crazy. But a month later, they found him dead near Le Barachois. The police said it was drugs, but that was a lie. It was the treasure, just like Ronny said. As soon as it happened, I quit the Wessex. I was scared."

"Did Ronny tell anyone else what he'd found?" Bourne asked.

"Well, he told his friend in California, I guess. He said they were making plans about what to do next."

Jason shook his head. Ronny had shared his discovery with a college student at Berkeley on the other side of the world. In doing so, he'd shared it with the NSA, the FBI, the CIA, the Russians, the Chinese, and everyone else surveilling the not-so-secret forums of the internet. Not long after, both Ronny and his friend had wound up dead.

"Did he tell his friend where he hid it?" Bourne asked.

"I don't think so. Ronny said I was the only one who knew."

"And are we close?"

"Oh, yes. We're here."

She took Jason's hand and led him away from the surf up the white sand. Ahead of them, two tall palm trees leaned together, making a kind of triangle. One was notably fatter than the other, and on the trunk of the larger tree, Bourne noticed a small *X* that had been carved into the trunk with a knife and had grown wider in the intervening years until it looked like a kind of spider.

X marks the spot.

"Ronny said he buried it there," Zaina said.

Jason looked up and down the beach. They were alone, the sun still low on the ocean horizon. He noted a line of debris and shells down the sand and concluded that they were far enough from the high-tide line that anything hidden here would have stayed hidden over the years. Below him, between the trees, was Ronny's treasure.

He pushed the blade of the shovel into the sand and began to dig. Zaina stood nervously next to him, chewing on a fingernail and shifting her weight from one leg to the other. In the warm air, as his arms pumped, Jason quickly began to sweat. Drips of moisture poured down his face and chest. A few minutes later, he'd created a hole a foot deep and still found nothing. A few minutes after that, he'd expanded the pit to almost two feet deep, and was beginning to wonder if Zaina had been wrong and Ronny had confided the secret to someone else, who'd already recovered the treasure.

Then with his next thrust, metal hit metal.

He stared into the hole, seeing a small patch of gray steel. With new energy, Jason expanded the pit around the metal fragment, but he had to work for another hour to uncover the entire artifact. It was large, at least six feet on all sides, roughly triangular in shape. When it was completely exposed, he could see a jagged edge that had been torn apart under extreme pressure, and there were blackened scorch marks that made part of the steel look like charcoal. There were no markings, nothing to identify what it was.

But Bourne knew. The timeline clicked in his head, and he knew exactly what this was.

"Son of a bitch," he murmured.

It had been one of the great mysteries of the past decade.

Seven years earlier, a Boeing 777 jumbo jet carrying 227 passengers, most of them Americans, had taken off from Tambo Airport in Johannesburg on its way to the United States. The plane, operated by a South African carrier called Crown Air, had headed across the continent, and as it passed from the mainland over the waters of the South Atlantic, it had vanished. Disappeared. Its transponder signal blinked off. Satellites lost it. Radar failed to track it. It took off, and it never landed, and years of searching in the vast ocean had turned up no evidence of what had happened to bring the plane down or where the crash had even occurred.

Conspiracy theories had followed the mystery ever since.

Sabotage.

Terrorism.

Suicide.

Mechanical failure.

Even aliens.

What really happened to Crown Air Flight 1342?

No one knew the truth, because no one had ever found any trace of the wreckage. The jet had gone down without a trace.

Except Bourne now realized that someone knew. Months after the flight vanished, thanks to the drifting currents of the Indian Ocean, Ronny Dunstan had found part of the plane right here on Réunion, and he'd been killed to keep the secret. Along with many others, from then until now.

The deaths had begun on the plane, but they hadn't stopped there.

Defiance was about a missing jet.

PART TWO

16

The assassin known as Lennon climbed out of bed and crossed the plush carpet of the condominium in the darkness. He went to the heavy curtain, which was shut. That was how he always kept the curtains, wherever he was. Pushing the paisley fabric aside by a couple of inches, he glanced across the East River at the New York skyline. It was two in the morning, but the city that never slept was alive with lights. Then he looked down from the twentieth-story condo window. Directly below him, he could see Center Boulevard where it ran along the river near Gantry Plaza.

Lennon brought a compact pair of Bushnell binoculars to his eyes and focused on the handful of cars parked near the plaza. The black Mercedes was gone. It had been there when he'd arrived for his rendezvous at six o'clock. It had still been there at eight, at ten, and then again at midnight, but now it was gone. So maybe the vehicle was innocent. Maybe it had nothing to do with him.

Even so, Lennon had stayed alive all these years by taking nothing for granted. He suspected the condo was being watched. There were no listening devices or cameras inside—he always did a thorough check when he arrived—but this surveillance felt like an old-school operation. By leaving a car on the street where he wouldn't miss it, they weren't even trying to hide their pursuit. They wanted him to know they were there.

But who were they?

The Americans? Unlikely. Not with a single vehicle on the street. The FBI and CIA never failed to overcomplicate their espionage. They relied on too many people, too many devices; they may as well have posted a list of their targets on Facebook. Treadstone was better at the game, but Treadstone had other problems. They were hiding inside their shells like scared turtles because of the assassinations. So he didn't think it was them.

The Russians? No, they knew better than to babysit him.

So who?

"Come back to bed," said a smoky voice from the darkness. "Fill me up again."

Lennon crossed the bedroom, finding his way without light. He reached for the nightstand and found his cigarette lighter where he'd left it next to his Ruger. With a flick of his finger, he cast a small flame, illuminating the naked woman sprawled across the messy sheets. Nazanin was barely thirty and looked even younger. Her raven hair was wavy and long. She had a full mouth, made to be kissed, and black, teasing eyebrows. Her huge eyes—sad, like most Iranian eyes—studied him with erotic hunger. That was one of two reasons Lennon had made love to Nazanin off and on for more than ten years. She was voracious in bed, with an uninhibited desire that matched his own.

But, more important, she was also the wife of a senior minister in Iran's United Nations delegation. Her husband had a big mouth to match his big ego, and he liked to share information with his much-younger bride. Every few months, when the minister returned to Iran and Nazanin was left alone, Lennon paid a visit to the man's condo for sex and secrets.

Of course, Nazanin had no idea who her lover really was. It would have stunned her to learn that he was a killer and a spy. To her, he was a blond British entrepreneur named Simon, with oil and gas interests in Tehran and distant links to the royal family. He'd been grooming her ever since she joined the delegation as a teenage secretary, because he'd spotted in Nazanin exactly the right combination of sensuality and ambition that would assure her of a powerful husband. Putin had wanted a pipeline into what the Iranians were saying and doing behind his back, and Lennon had provided it.

Back then, he was still officially a Treadstone agent known as Abel, but he'd been playing both sides of the street since the beginning.

Nazanin nudged closer to him in her languid way. She reached her skinny fingers, which were heavy with jeweled rings, between Lennon's legs and began to awaken an erection from him.

"Again," she said in a demanding, dominating voice.

Lennon was tempted. Nazanin was very good in bed, and he didn't know when he'd be back with her again. But the black Mercedes worried him enough that he decided to cut the night short. He needed to go.

"I have to shower," he told her, "and then I have to return to my hotel to pack. I'm sorry, my love. I have an early flight out of JFK."

Nazanin sighed and shifted her hand to between her legs. "Leaving me to finish by myself? That's not like you."

"Next time."

He bent down and gave her an open-mouthed kiss, tasting her tongue. Then he left her in bed and went to the bathroom, where he closed the door and turned on the light. The lavish master bath was overdecorated like the rest of the condo.

Black marble tiles were etched with geometric patterns, and paintings and bronze sculptures of horses filled the counters and walls. Nazanin's husband was a skilled horseman.

It took Lennon only five minutes to shower, pummeled by body sprays on three sides. He toweled off, then turned off the bathroom light and waited a few seconds for his eyes to adjust to the darkness again. When he slid open the door to the bedroom, he knew instantly that something was wrong.

The curtains were open now.

Nazanin knew better than that.

Before he could retrieve his Ruger from the nightstand, the bedroom light flashed on, blinding him. When he could see again, his brain absorbed several things at once. First, his gun was already gone. Second, Nazanin was dead, a round red bullet hole in the middle of her forehead, her eyes still open, her hand still nestled between her legs.

And third, two men waited for him, both with pistols and suppressors aimed at his chest from opposite sides of the bedroom. They were young, tall, and dark, with olive skin and heavy beard lines, and they were dressed in black.

Lennon made no effort to cover himself or resist. He knew when an opponent had the upper hand.

So it would end like this, in the bedroom of one of his lovers. He'd always indulged a faint curiosity about the moment of his death, who would do it, when it would come. He'd assumed there would be a final confrontation between him and Cain and that only one of them would survive. He wondered idly if Cain was still alive. Perhaps the assassins had already come for him, too.

He waited for the gunfire, the muffled cracks that would end his life, but they didn't come. Instead, oddly, the two men retreated from the bedroom, leaving him alone. A few seconds later, he heard the condo door open and close. Then his senses detected something else. Cigar smoke.

He wasn't alone.

Not bothering with clothes, Lennon continued to the living room, drawn by the smoke and the further odor of musky cologne. When he turned on the light, he saw an Iranian man sitting in a leather armchair, watching him with the faintest smile and sipping brandy between puffs of his cigar. Lennon knew him because he'd memorized the biographies of nearly every senior Iranian intelligence officer. Hamid Ashkani. Dapper, charming, ruthless. Ashkani wore the suit of a businessman, and he didn't appear to be armed, but Lennon had no doubt that the killers who'd shot Nazanin could return to the condo in a split second if Lennon made a move against their boss.

Iran. That told Lennon everything he needed to know. This was about Defiance.

And Gholami.

"Hello, Hamid."

"Lennon," the man said in his husky accent.

"Was that necessary?" Lennon asked, nodding toward the bedroom. "Killing the girl?"

"Oh, we've known about you and Nazanin for some time. I've kept the matter private, assuming it would be useful to us at some point. Alas, this time we had to inform her husband about the affair. He insisted on a degree of vengeance for his humiliation."

"Well, revenge is your specialty," Lennon commented.

Ashkani gave the smallest shrug of agreement.

"So why am I not dead, too?" Lennon asked. "You've been eliminating agents all over the world. I must be on your list. And I know much more than any of the others about the truth behind Defiance."

"Yes, you do. Thanks to Nazanin."

"Thanks to her husband not being able to keep his mouth shut," Lennon corrected him. "He's the one you should be taking out."

Ashkani pursed his lips. "True enough. In good time. But in fact, you are wrong about the recent assassinations. It's not *our* list, my friend. We have no list. You're perfectly safe from us."

Lennon kept his expression impassive, but inwardly, his mind churned with surprise. He was safe from them? *Impossible!* The Iranians should want him dead more than anyone else. Even with Russian protection, he'd wondered for years when they would come for him.

But he was *safe*?

That could mean only one thing. *My God, they don't know! They don't realize it was me. Me and Cain!*

A resort in Cyprus!

"Then why are you here?" Lennon asked calmly, showing nothing of his inner thoughts.

"I have an assignment for you," Ashkani told him.

Naked, his muscles rippling, Lennon walked to the wet bar and calmly poured himself a brandy from the bottle that Ashkani had used. He took the crystal tumbler to another chair and sat down, eyeing the Iranian from across the room. "I don't work for you, Hamid. You know who I work for."

"Indeed. But I can promise you this will be the most lucrative assignment you've ever undertaken."

"Money isn't my concern," Lennon said. "I have plenty of money."

"Then I can sweeten the pot in other ways."

"Oh?"

"Yes, if you do this, it's likely that you'll have an opportunity to confront someone you very much want to find. You can finally bring your rivalry to an end."

Lennon swallowed the whole brandy, got up, refilled the glass, and sat down again. He didn't have to say the name out loud or ask who Ashkani meant. They both knew.

Cain.

After a long stretch of silence, Lennon said, "If the assassination list isn't yours, then why are you involved?"

"Call it a favor for a friend."

"Who?"

"Is it necessary for you to know?"

"If you want my help, yes it is. I don't work in the dark. There are too many risks when silent partners are involved."

"All right. That's fair. His name is Timothy Randall. If you don't know who he is, you can find out readily enough. But I'll be your only contact. The two of you should have no communication at all."

"I prefer it that way," Lennon said. "And the target? Who do you want me to kill?"

Ashkani gave him the name, and Lennon tapped a finger against his lips thoughtfully. The Iranian noticed his hesitation.

"Can you do it?" Ashkani asked. "I realize it's a big ask."

"Oh, I can get it done easily enough. That's not the problem. But I'm not sure the Russians will approve. They may fear that the blame will come their way, and Putin won't be happy about that."

"In fact, that's why we want you," Ashkani replied. "You're an expert at placing the blame elsewhere. If you do your job well, then no one will suspect Russian involvement at all. Or ours."

"Or your silent partner's," Lennon said. "Mr. Randall."

"Very true."

"And the timeline?"

"A month. Is that possible?"

"Everything's possible. I'll need some support to get it done. A staging area close to DC."

"I'm sure that can be arranged. So will you accept?"

"If I do, what guarantee do I have that I won't end up on the assassination list once the job is done?"

"Quite simply, you will have Timothy's balls in your pocket," Ashkani replied.

Lennon chuckled and swirled the brandy in his glass. He didn't say yes, but that didn't matter. Saying nothing was his tacit agreement. He knew that saying no would bring the killers back into the room. It was literally an offer he couldn't refuse. He would take the job, or he would leave the condo in the same body bag with Nazanin.

The Iranian knew they had a deal. Ashkani simply smiled, got to his feet, and smoothed the lines of his suit. Their business was concluded. He left his glass on the wrought iron coffee table in front of him, and he nodded toward the bedroom. "Don't worry about the girl. Cleaners are on their way. They will take care of her."

"Of course."

Ashkani left, and Lennon was alone.

He returned to the bedroom, still surprised to be alive. Nazanin stared back at him with her wide, dead eyes. He felt nothing about her murder. No regret. No loss. The Iranians had done him a favor; sooner or later, he would have had to kill her himself. It had been a while since she'd provided any useful intelligence, and despite her sexual prowess, he had other sources of release. Whenever he needed erotic stimulation, Yoko was available to him.

But seeing Nazanin made him think back to his days as Abel.

To his mission for Defiance seven years ago.

The target is an American scientist who goes by the name of Mallory Foster.

He'd been given no explanation for the assignment, not that he needed one. The only requirement of the job was that it look like an accident, with no hint of foul play that might invite a police investigation. If he had been nothing more than Abel, a Treadstone agent, he would simply have followed orders. But he'd also been a Russian mole, and the whole operation made him curious. It hadn't come through normal Treadstone channels. It came with the right code words and authorizations, but with nothing else to suggest why it had to be done.

That made him want to know more.

So before he forced alcohol down Mallory Foster's throat and staged the car accident that killed her, he'd gotten information out of her. She talked easily. She *wanted* to talk, like a kind of confession. She told him everything. About the emergency phone call she'd received in the middle of the night. About the limousine ride to a state-of-the-art government laboratory. And the *timing*! The timing definitely couldn't have been a coincidence. She'd known the truth as soon as she saw the headlines the following day.

That was what had sent him to talk to Nazanin. The whole thing smelled of Iran. Of vengeance for Gholami. Nazanin had known nothing about Iranian intelligence operations, and even her husband—boasting fool that he was—knew enough to stay silent about something this evil. But Nazanin had given him one name. A name she'd overheard while her husband was on the telephone. When she'd asked him about it, he'd gone into a fury and told her to forget she'd ever heard it.

One name.

Khalaji.

Lennon knew exactly who Khalaji was. The name confirmed all of his suspicions.

Rafi Khalaji had been the copilot on Crown Air Flight 1342.

17

The flight from Ivato airport in Madagascar—where Bourne left Zaina, hoping the assassins wouldn't find her again—brought him four hours later to hot, humid Johannesburg. The next day, he boarded a transatlantic flight to Washington, DC, with one connection in Atlanta. That meant he was following the identical route of Crown Air Flight 1342 seven years earlier, when it detoured into the twilight zone. However, Bourne's journey went off without a hitch, and he landed at Dulles a few minutes before noon.

Being back in Washington made him think of Abbey. He knew she was nearby, working on her book with Alicia Beauvoir. They hadn't spoken since their tense phone call on the Treadstone jet, and he found himself tempted to go to her apartment, to see her and take her to bed. But he shut down that desire. For now, it was safer if he left Abbey alone.

Instead, he checked in at the Watergate Hotel, then walked through Foggy Bottom to the park at the heart of Washington Circle. He staked out a spot on one of the benches underneath the trees, where he had a view of George Washington in his tricornered hat, seated atop a prancing steed. He took pictures like a tourist as he surveyed the people around him, and he concluded that he wasn't being followed or watched. Not yet.

His contact showed up on schedule at two in the afternoon.

Ray LeBlond worked as the chief technical adviser for international aviation affairs at the National Transportation Safety Board. Bourne had known him for five years. They'd met when LeBlond was on-site in Egypt, investigating the midair failure of an Airbus engine that had forced the unscheduled stop of a Delta flight in Cairo. One hundred and seventy-two passengers got off the plane, but only one hundred and seventy-one got back on a different plane six hours later. The missing man, a physician working with Human Rights Watch, later turned up near the Libyan border with his throat cut. Bourne and Nova had worked with LeBlond to determine who had sabotaged the flight, and the evidence led them from a Turkish flight mechanic to a Syrian colonel, who'd masterminded the operation to keep the doctor from testifying about Syrian military attacks on Christian schools.

LeBlond asked no questions when the colonel was never seen again.

For a man with the last name LeBlond, there was nothing blond about him. His hair was thick, dark, and full, and he wore a bushy black mustache. He was a third-generation Hispanic American from South Texas who had spent fifteen years in the Air Force before switching government careers. He was tall and much heavier than when he'd been in the military, with a prominent belly jutting over tan khakis. He wore a baby-blue dress shirt and a striped knit tie with a square bottom. He sat on the opposite end of the bench and began pawing through his lunch bag without looking over at Bourne.

"Hello, Ray," Jason said.

"Mike," LeBlond murmured as he popped a couple of Doritos into his mouth.

When they'd met, Bourne had been using the cover name

of Michael Dallin, and he'd kept that cover with the man ever since. LeBlond knew perfectly well that Mike wasn't his real name. He didn't know what agency Bourne worked for, but he knew enough to realize the kind of work that Bourne did.

"Last time we talked, you said I should have a word with the security folks at da Vinci Airport in Rome," LeBlond went on. "Tell them to toughen things up."

"Yes, I remember."

"They thwarted a suicide bomber six days later. I was quite the hero over there. The director sent me a case of very expensive Barolo."

"I'm glad to hear it."

"I don't suppose you want to tell me how you knew about the bomber?"

"Afraid not," Bourne replied.

"Well, I'm grateful anyway. I still have a bottle or two of the Barolo left if you want me to send you one."

"That's okay, but thanks."

LeBlond gave him a quick sideways glance. "So what's going on? Are you here to give me another security heads-up?"

"No. This time I need some information."

The man licked some of the red chili dust from the chips off his fingers. "About?"

"1342," Bourne said.

"Ah, fuck," LeBlond hissed with a little sigh. "You trying to get me killed, Mike?"

"What makes you say that?"

The big man shrugged. "Rumors get around. An awful lot of people who were part of that investigation came to strange ends. Heart attacks, strokes. Lots of accidents. A few disappearances. It felt like the Bermuda Triangle. We joke about it, but let me tell you, nobody pushes too hard to join the task force."

"And do you think that's all a coincidence?" Bourne asked.

"Well, generally I don't believe in conspiracy theories, but now here *you* are, Mike. That makes me think there's something to it."

"So what can you tell me?"

LeBlond shook his head. "Not much. Seven years later, and not fucking much. Crown Air 1342 took off from Johannesburg with two hundred and twenty-seven people on board, bound for Atlanta and then DC. For four hours, the flight was normal. Four hours of a seventeen-hour flight. Dead normal. We know it made it to open water over the South Atlantic, but then its transponder went off. No onboard communications, Wi-Fi disconnected, no routine electronic updates. The thing up and vanished."

"How is that possible in this day and age?"

LeBlond scowled and crumpled the empty paper bag beside him into a ball. "You didn't get this from me."

"Of course not."

"Someone on the plane took it offline," LeBlond told him. "Shut everything down."

"This was deliberate?" Bourne asked.

"Oh, yeah. The disappearing act wasn't because of mechanical failure, or radio failure, or a bomb, or missile, or loss of oxygen debilitating the crew and passengers. No way. Someone *wanted* the plane to go silent, and trust me, that's not easy to pull off. Whoever did it had to have very specialized knowledge of the plane's systems."

"So what happened after it went off the grid?"

"We got a couple of automated satellite pings, not enough to pinpoint location, but enough to tell us that the plane was being *flown*. It flew for a while. Maybe several hours. Then we think it was deliberately crashed, probably straight down, extreme speed, in a way that minimized the debris field. We still have no clue exactly where it was done. It's a big fucking ocean out there, Mike."

"So one of the pilots did it," Bourne concluded.

"Yeah. Had to be. Either the lead guy, Shaheen, or the copilot, Khalaji. I mean, okay, maybe one of the passengers managed to take over the controls, but we think that's unlikely. If there had been a takeover attempt, odds are they would have had time to get off a distress call to alert somebody. There was nothing like that."

"I read a couple of articles suggesting that the lead pilot, Shaheen, was mentally ill," Bourne said. "Depressed. Marriage falling apart. Alcohol issues. He'd been crashing planes on his video game simulators. That kind of thing."

LeBlond sighed. "Yeah, I read that, too."

"You don't believe it?"

"I don't know what to believe. Somebody on board made that plane disappear, but the mystery didn't stop there. Ever since, the investigation has gone nowhere. The cover-up has been every bit as ruthless as what took place on that jet."

"How so?"

LeBlond's nervousness increased. His face got a little twitch, and he looked around the park to see if anyone was nearby. "Why do you care, Mike? Why are you asking about this now?"

"Because people are still being killed. I'm trying to find out why and figure out how to stop it."

"Well, I don't want to be the next victim," LeBlond said.

"I get it. We never talked."

Ray rubbed a meaty hand across his forehead to wipe away a sheen of sweat. "Okay, so here's the thing. Everywhere we turned, we got stonewalled. Witnesses unavailable, missing, or dead. Records lost or destroyed. That depression shit about the pilot? It came in thirdhand from cops in Cape Town. We never saw the source material, never talked to anyone who could verify his behavior."

"What about Khalaji, the copilot?"

"Same thing, but the opposite story. A family man, three kids, solid as a rock. But we couldn't get access to his wife to ask any questions. She took the kids and left, went off the grid. The airline records said Khalaji was a Qatari national, but we couldn't even confirm *that*. It was all too good to be true. His background looked manufactured. A cover identity. I'm sure you know how that works."

Bourne smiled.

"To me, it felt like somebody was serving up Shaheen as a fall guy," Ray went on, "but my gut tells me Khalaji was really the one behind it. I think he was a terrorist mole, probably had been in place with the airline for years. And I don't think he was alone on that plane. Our investigation of the passengers turned up two Iranians who used fake passports. The story was, they were refugees looking for asylum in the U.S. Yeah, maybe. Or maybe they were there to deal with any issues among the passengers."

Bourne frowned as he considered the implications of what LeBlond was saying.

Iran.

The Iranians certainly had the ruthlessness and technical skill to pull off a terrorist coup of that magnitude. But why take such an enormous risk? If their role came out, the American public would demand a military response. Plus, there was no way the Iranians were behind Defiance itself. The cover-up operation was born in the USA. It didn't make sense.

"What else?" Bourne asked.

"We tried going after Intelsat data that might have given us a track on the plane's route after it went dark," LeBlond said. "The last radar pings hinted that the plane was changing direction. If that was true, it would explain why all of the searches turned up nothing. Maybe we were in the wrong place, you know? Hell, maybe the wrong ocean. It's possible they turned south out of the Atlantic toward Antarctica or even into—"

"The Indian Ocean," Bourne said.

LeBlond's bushy eyebrows shot up. "You know something?"

Bourne didn't reply, and LeBlond's mouth puckered with unhappy curiosity.

"Anyway, it was a dead end," the man continued. "We got nothing off the satellites. Except our tech people are convinced the data from Intelsat was manipulated. Altered, falsified to cover up the change in course. I mean, modifying encrypted global satellite data, that takes skill and access. You know who can do that?"

"The government," Bourne said.

"Exactly. This felt like a government snow job from day one. The left hand ties the right hand behind its back. No offense, Mike, but it was the kind of thing people like you could pull off."

Bourne nodded, because LeBlond was right. Yes, it was exactly the kind of thing Treadstone could pull off. And they had. Now the agents behind the cover-up were being eliminated, too.

"Anything more?" he asked.

"Like I said, people learned not to get too curious. Curiosity killed the cat. There was a lot of chatter online about a high death rate for anyone who was too close to the investigation. I figured it was bullshit, but now I don't know. When you add it all up, all the people who died, it makes you wonder. There was this independent group of engineers and researchers. They called themselves the 1342 Truthers. These were pros from around the world. The U.S., UK, Australia, India, France, Germany. They didn't believe the manure the government was shoveling, and they set out to examine the record themselves. Well, eight of the original twelve members died within a year. Eight. I mean, there was no pattern, no foul play, but come on. *Eight.*"

"Wilhelm Hopf," Bourne murmured.

"What? What did you say?"

"Wilhelm Hopf," he repeated in a louder voice. "Was he one of them?"

LeBlond's golden face looked several shades paler. "Yeah. Hopf was a mechanical engineer from Germany. He was one of the first of the truthers and one of the most outspoken. He died in a car accident on the Autobahn six months after he started speaking out about the missing jet."

Bourne closed his eyes. He didn't bother correcting LeBlond. Yes, Hopf had died on the Autobahn, but there had been no accident.

Nova had killed him.

When Bourne returned to the Watergate, Nash Rollins was waiting for him. The old Treadstone agent sat by the window in Bourne's room, a Glock in his lap and binoculars around his neck. He held a glass of whiskey in his hand that he'd poured from the minibar. His gray hair was even messier than usual, and his face was deeply flushed.

"Everything okay?" Bourne asked.

"I caught one of them," Nash said, eyeing the street below them. "But where there was one, I figure there might be more."

Bourne shook his head. "I checked the area, and we're clear for now. There's no one outside."

Nash relaxed. He took the Glock from his lap and placed it on the window ledge. "That's a relief."

Jason poured whiskey for himself, then dragged a second chair to the window. "So you grabbed one of the assassins?"

"Yes. I'd like to tell you it was skillful tradecraft, but honestly, I got lucky. He was waiting for me in a parking lot on H Street. He would have taken me down, but a car backfired and startled him. He missed. I was able to return fire and get him in the stomach. I had a few minutes to ask questions before he died."

"He talked?" Bourne asked with surprise.

Nash shrugged. "Let's just say I wasn't polite. Anyway, he was one of the team that went after Dax in Alaska. In addition to the execution, they were supposed to remove anything in Dax's house relating to data he gathered from Intelsat. Not just technology. They were afraid he'd left printouts behind to cover his ass."

"Had he?"

"No. Dax was a good boy. The killer didn't have a clue what Intelsat was, but as soon as I heard the name, I figured this was about—"

"Flight 1342," Bourne said.

Nash cocked his head. "You know about that?"

Bourne nodded. He briefed Nash on everything he'd learned from Teeling in the Bahamas and then on Réunion island about Ronny Dunstan's treasure hunting, including his discovery on the beach. He concluded with the speculation offered by Ray LeBlond about what had really happened to the missing jet.

"An Iranian connection?" Nash mused.

"Could be. Except that raises as many questions as answers. Why would anyone in the U.S. government be protecting the Iranians? Someone is going to a hell of a lot of trouble to make sure Iran doesn't get blamed for the crash."

"You think Holly knows more than she's telling us?"

"No, this time I think she's really in the dark. Vic Sorrento was the one who gave the actual orders on Defiance, but he's dead. There must be others who were involved in mounting the operation, but we don't know who they are. Regardless, they'll be keeping their mouths shut and their heads low."

Nash glanced out the hotel room window, where night

was falling across Washington. "What did you do with the fragment of the plane you found?"

"I buried it again. For now it's safer in the ground."

"Agreed."

"Have you heard from Nova?" Bourne asked.

Nash nodded. "She's in DC, too. She's trying to find out more about that cop who was on her hit list. Billy Janssen."

"Good. I can explain her other two victims, but not that one. I want to know how a street cop like Janssen found himself in the middle of this."

Nash eyed him from behind his whiskey glass. "What about you? What's your next move?"

Bourne didn't answer immediately. He had been thinking about that ever since he'd left Ray LeBlond in the park. Someone in the government was running Defiance, but no one was talking. So he had to look for answers elsewhere.

If you need to spy on your friends, talk to your enemies.

Treadstone.

"Who knows more about what goes on at the CIA than the CIA?" Bourne asked.

Nash's face broke into a little smile. "The Russians? You plan to talk to the Russians?"

"Exactly."

18

The old man in the 6XL Mickey Mouse t-shirt groaned as he settled into the shuttle that returned tourists to the parking lots of the Magic Kingdom. Multiple chins draped over his sweaty neck like steps into the water of a swimming pool. His large, misshapen nose resembled a potato, right down to two moles that looked like eyes. He was seventy years old, but his thinning gray hair had been colored and filled out with black plugs that made him look a few years younger. He wore sunglasses despite the late hour, and his distinctive wild eyebrows were now carefully trimmed. The dark beard was fake, applied whenever he went out in public. It wasn't really much of a disguise to anyone who knew him, but he didn't think the FSB sent many agents to surveil Space Mountain.

The name on his Florida Resident Annual Pass to Disney World read Maksim Sepp. If anyone asked about his accent, which had all the Slavic thickness of Dracula, he told people he was a Ukrainian émigré escaping the war. Nobody questioned that. In reality, his name was Fyodor Mikhailov, and until three years earlier, he'd been in charge of anti-American Russian intelligence operations. Then his grandest strategy of all—the Medusa operation—had been blown apart by Jason Bourne and Nash Rollins.

Rollins had offered him the choice of a cushy defector's life in Florida or a bullet in the head in Moscow's Lubyanka prison. Fyodor had opted for the beach.

As the Disney shuttle rocked through the huge parking lot, he found his heavy-lidded eyes drifting shut. Only a few tourist families had joined him on the postclosing tram. By the time they reached the Goofy lot, he was the last person on the shuttle. He eased his enormous girth out of the tight row of seats and waved at the pretty blond girl with the microphone who'd been chirping at them since they left the park. *My God,* he thought, *these Disney people are perky.*

Fyodor stayed where he was as the shuttle departed. He put down a plastic shopping bag and took a moment to light a Djarum Black clove cigarette. He stood in the darkness, puffing, while his eyes examined all of the cars that were parked around him. That was the price of exile. Sooner or later, someone would be waiting with a pistol and a suppressor. The Russians didn't bother going after all their old spies, but Putin was unlikely to forgive *him*. One night he was going to die a violent death.

But apparently not tonight. The handful of parked cars near his electric Hyundai SUV looked empty.

Fyodor trudged across the pavement, finding it an effort to lift up each foot. He loved riding the rides—it made the little kids laugh, seeing the huge old man wedged into the roller-coaster seats—but by the end of the day, he always felt his age. His breath came heavily as he sucked air and cigarette smoke into his lungs. He reached the SUV and used his fob to unlock the driver's door. He'd parked under one of the high streetlights, as he always did. He glanced into the backseat—confirmed it was empty—then squeezed his bulk behind the wheel. It was a pain in the ass, driving himself. For years in

Europe and New York, he'd had a driver, but the Americans had told him that a driver would attract too much attention. Which was bullshit. They were just too cheap to spend the money. So now he drove his own SUV.

With his cigarette still in his left hand, Fyodor pushed the button to start the engine. It came to life silently, and he opened the window, letting in the sticky Florida night air.

That was when he felt the gun barrel jab into the back of his head.

Fuck!

He'd gotten careless. In the old days, he would have checked the far back of the vehicle, not just the backseat. He flicked his cigarette casually out the window, then lowered his left hand toward the Makarov that he kept taped to the side of the driver's seat. But he wasn't surprised to find that the killer had already found it and removed it.

Fyodor rumbled a sigh out of his huge chest. "So are you here to make it quick, or does the Moth want me to suffer?"

"Relax, Fyodor," said a voice that had the cool strength of granite and steel. "I'm not here to kill you. I just want to talk."

The Russian reached up to the rearview mirror and adjusted it to show the handsome, shadowy face of the man behind him. He hadn't seen that face often, but he knew who it was. "Well, well. Cain."

"American life seems to be treating you well," Bourne said.

"It would treat me better with more money," Fyodor replied with a shrug. "Can you tell Nash that? The pittance of an allowance I get barely covers the occasional hooker. And do you know what Viagra costs for an old man on Medicare?"

"Try generics," Bourne suggested.

Fyodor scoffed. He stripped off his sunglasses and rubbed his tired eyes. "Should I be concerned that you found me so easily? Florida is a big state, but if you can find me, Putin can, too. Even Nash isn't supposed to know exactly where I am."

"If you want to stay anonymous, change your cigarettes," Bourne advised him. "The flavored ones are illegal here, but Nash remembered how much you liked them. It wasn't hard to narrow down black market purchases of clove cigarettes online."

"Ah well, we all have our weaknesses," Fyodor acknowledged. He had no intention of giving up his Djarums. "I have a long drive to get home, Cain. What do you want? I'm out of the game. I don't own a computer, and I don't read the newspapers anymore. If you're looking for dirt on my comrades, there's very little I can give you."

Bourne holstered his gun and leaned across the front seat. "This information goes back several years. Back when you were still in play."

Fyodor's trimmed eyebrows arched in surprise. "Oh, yes? What are we talking about?"

"Defiance."

"Ah," he said, drawing out the word. "Of course, of course. I admit, I was surprised in all of my debriefings that no one ever asked me what I knew about it. Then again, perhaps I'm not so surprised. Lennon always said that the Americans were desperate to sweep that mission under the rug."

"Lennon told you about it?" Bourne asked.

"In the most general terms, but that's all. Lennon never reveals secrets to anyone unless it is in his interest to do so. That's one of his trademarks, you know. He's an oyster hoarding his pearls. He collects information and keeps it locked away to use as currency whenever he needs something. Even with Putin, Lennon had a reputation for sharing only what was absolutely necessary. He claimed it made him more valuable in the long run."

"So what *did* he tell you?"

"About Defiance? Only that it was connected to the disappearance of that jet. The one out of South Africa."

"Did he say how he knew that?"

"Another of his sources, that's all."

"Lennon was still working for Treadstone when the jet disappeared. Did he say what his role in Defiance was? I assume it was a hit."

Fyodor shook his head. "I'm sorry, Cain. He told me nothing about that."

"Well, the Russians must have done their own investigation into 1342."

"Yes, of course we did. It was quite the mystery, and as a rule, we don't like mysteries. But wherever we went, it seemed as if someone was one step ahead of us, shutting down sources. Later, Lennon acknowledged that Treadstone was involved in doing just that. Even so, we had our own suspicions."

"Such as?" Bourne asked.

"Our theories involved the copilot on the flight. Khalaji."

"What about him?"

Fyodor shrugged. "Khalaji's identity was manufactured. That was pretty much an open secret among the intelligence communities, but no one knew who he really was. Me, I'm convinced he was an Iranian agent. A longtime sleeper. In fact, I found records in our archives regarding a young Iranian who went through Russian intelligence training camps. Though I couldn't say for certain, I'm pretty sure it was Khalaji. We weren't happy. If that came out, it would have made it look like we were involved, when we were not."

"So you believe Iran brought down the jet," Bourne said.

"That is what I think, yes."

"Why would they take a risk like that? If it was traced back to them, the response would have been catastrophic."

Fyodor let his contempt hiss through his lips. "Do you think they care? Fucking martyrs. This was about vengeance. Vengeance is everything to them. Iranians never forget a slight, particularly from the Great Satan. Surely you remember the incident the previous year?"

He studied the American and then recalled the man's background. This was the fractured agent. The one with no memory.

"Or perhaps you don't, Cain. Lennon told us about you. A bullet erased who you were. Erased your life."

"This incident," Cain said impatiently, giving nothing away. "What was it?"

Fyodor pursed his lips. "Does the name Gholami mean anything to you?"

He watched a strange uncertainty pass like a cloud across Cain's face. Briefly, the man squeezed his eyes shut, his brow furrowing as if he was in pain, his mind hammered by distant thunder.

"Gholami," Cain murmured.

"Ah, so you do remember something."

"He was an Iranian general."

"Correct."

"He was killed. With his family. Assassinated at a resort in Cyprus."

"Exactly. A black op. No one claimed the kills. The CIA spread rumors that Mossad was behind it, and yet the Iranians were convinced that it was an American operation. Anyway, you cannot imagine the fury his death unleashed in Iran, particularly given that his wife and children were murdered with him. Me, I'm convinced that 1342 was their retaliation. Children for children, Cain. Of the many Americans on that flight, several dozen were teenagers touring South Africa as part of a church choir group."

"It's still a huge gamble," Bourne said. "If proof ever came out that the Iranians were involved—"

"But it hasn't, has it? That can't be an accident. For some

reason, the Americans are as determined to hide the truth as the Iranians."

"Why?"

"I do not know, Cain."

"Do you think Lennon knows?"

"Well, if not all of it, I am certain he knows more than he told us. Like I said, the man hoards secrets. Plus, he played both sides for a long time. If you want the truth, you'll need to ask him yourself. But good luck with that. Lennon is as much of a ghost as you are. It won't be easy to find him."

Next to him, Cain was silent, his face brooding. Fyodor's eyes narrowed until they were heavy slits.

"Unless, of course, you already know where he is. Do you?"

"No, I don't," Cain replied with a strange shadow in his voice. "But I know someone who can get him a message. After that, I'm sure Lennon will find me."

19

Nova parked the Kia minivan where the street dead-ended in a dark jungle of trees. She'd stolen the van two hours ago in DC. Now she was miles away in the suburb of Camp Springs, Maryland. With her binoculars, she studied the brick house two doors down. There was a car in the driveway and a light on downstairs, but she couldn't see anyone inside. She wasn't expecting trouble, but Nash had told her about the assault on the woman named Zaina—former girlfriend of one of the Defiance targets—on Réunion island. If the assassins had come after her, then they might come after the wife of Billy Janssen, too. So Nova was taking no chances.

She got out of the van. The crickets were loud. A breeze rustled the trees, but there were no other sounds in the neighborhood. And yet she had a bad feeling. The pricking on her neck told her she was under surveillance—but when she tried to pinpoint who or where, she came up empty. If anyone was nearby, they were hiding in deep cover.

Did they want to kill her? If they had a laser scope, she'd already be dead.

Did they want to abduct her? They needed more resources for that, and she saw no assets in place.

You're being paranoid.

Nova checked the Glock inside the coat of her gray business suit. Then she walked slowly down the street, her footsteps muffled by dead leaves in the gutters. Her eyes checked each house, each car. She saw no one, but her instincts got louder.

Someone's here.

She walked up the driveway and climbed the porch steps to the front door. It was a one-story house built on a slope, so she assumed there was a basement level that led out to the wooded backyard. A blue light outlined a Ring video doorbell, so Lori Janssen had probably been alerted that she'd arrived. She rang the bell anyway, and footsteps approached from the other side of the door.

A pretty brunette in her thirties appeared in the doorframe. She was several inches taller than Nova, slim and athletic, dressed casually in jeans and a loose DC police sweatshirt. Her smile was pleasant but wary as she opened the screen door.

"Mrs. Janssen?" Nova said, drawing a fake identification badge from her suit. "I called earlier. I'm Corinne Foster with the FBI."

"Oh, yes. Come in, please."

Nova followed the woman into the living room, which faced the street. The first thing Mrs. Janssen did was sweep the curtains shut, as if she didn't want neighbors spying on her conversation with the feds. Nova glanced around the room, taking note of a few framed photographs above the fireplace. Two of them were turned facedown, but the other pictures showed a handsome young man wearing a police uniform. It had been several years since the mission, but Nova recognized Billy Janssen.

She recognized the man she'd killed with a blow to the head.

Nova inhaled sharply and felt a little sick. She'd trained her heart to be ice-cold. She did her job; she didn't ask questions. But it was different being here. Billy Janssen was a victim in this house, not simply a target. So was his widow.

Mrs. Janssen directed Nova to the sofa. Then she sat down in an armchair and adjusted her sweatshirt uncomfortably.

"I'm puzzled as to what you want, Ms. Foster," she said. "You said on the phone that it had something to do with Billy. He died years ago. I really don't see why he'd be of interest to the FBI after all this time."

"Some questions have arisen about his death," Nova said.

"Questions? I don't understand. Billy fell from a cliff near Harpers Ferry. It was an accident."

No, Nova thought. *I crushed his skull with a rock, and I pushed his body over the cliff so the fall would hide what I' d done to him.*

"Well, I don't mean to alarm you," she said. "It's probably nothing. You see, we've received new intelligence about certain terrorist activities in DC during that time period, and some email communications refer to the death of a police officer. So we're going back to review any law enforcement fatalities that occurred that year, even accidental deaths, just in case something was missed."

"Oh, I see."

Something flickered in Mrs. Janssen's face. Nova wasn't sure how to interpret it. The woman tugged at her long brown hair, and her dark eyes examined the closed curtains and the house's locked front door. Then she checked her watch and glanced over her shoulder at the doorway that led to the kitchen.

"You don't sound surprised by this information, Mrs. Janssen," Nova told her.

"What? Oh, no, I'm shocked. I'm sure you must be wrong. Billy had nothing to do with terrorists."

"It's not a question of that. For all we know, he heard

something, or saw something, or was simply in the wrong place at the wrong time. And as I said, it's also quite possible there's no connection at all."

"Well, how can I help you?" Mrs. Janssen asked. "What do you want to know?"

"I was wondering if Billy talked to you in the weeks preceding his death about anything unusual he may have encountered at work."

"Nothing at all," she said quickly. Too quickly.

The woman adjusted her sweatshirt again, as if it was uncomfortable. She took another look toward the kitchen. Nova heard alarm bells going off in her head.

"Is everything all right, Mrs. Janssen?"

"Fine."

"It's just that you seem nervous."

"No, I'm not nervous. But you come in here asking questions about my husband's death after all this time, and now you're talking about him being involved with terrorists. What am I supposed to think?"

"No one believes Billy was involved with terrorists," Nova said.

"Well, good, because he wasn't."

For a third time, Mrs. Janssen glanced at the kitchen doorway.

"Do you have something on the stove?" Nova asked.

"What?"

"You keep looking toward the kitchen. I thought maybe you were afraid something was going to burn."

"Oh! No, actually, the dog's out back. I thought I heard him barking. He probably wants to come in. Sorry, do you mind if I go check on him? Sometimes he runs off."

"Not at all," Nova said. "Go ahead."

"Thank you."

Mrs. Janssen practically leaped to her feet. She disappeared into the kitchen with quick steps, and Nova heard the sound of the back door opening. She listened to the woman's footsteps going outside, but she didn't hear Mrs. Janssen whistle or call a dog's name.

There had been no barking. Nova looked around the room and saw no dog toys, no dog hair on the furniture, no dog bowls near the bathroom. The house didn't smell like a dog.

Because there was no dog.

Why is she lying?

Nova got off the sofa and parted the curtains to look out at the street, then closed them again. She walked quickly to the doorway and glanced into the kitchen, but there was nothing out of place. The back door was still open. Mrs. Janssen was still outside. Biting her lip with concern, Nova returned to the living room, examining everything for some clue as to what was really happening in this house. Furniture. Artwork.

Pictures!

She went to the fireplace, where the widow kept a row of photographs of her late husband. Billy's smile taunted Nova. *Murderer!* But two of the pictures were facedown, and Nova lifted them up.

Her breath left her chest.

Billy Janssen's wife was with him in these photographs. His wife, petite and blond-haired, with blue eyes.

Not the woman who'd opened the door.

Nova grabbed for her gun, but she was too late. The woman was back in the living room now, framed by the kitchen doorway, her sweatshirt caught on the empty holster clipped over her belt. She held an FNX-45 Tactical with an Obsidian suppressor pointed at Nova's chest at the end of her rigid, outstretched arms.

"Stop," the woman demanded. "Take out your gun with two fingers, put it on the ground, and kick it away. You flinch, and I fire."

Nova took a split second to assess her options and concluded she had none. She did as she was told and disarmed herself. With a little kick, she nudged her gun a few feet across the carpet.

"Where is Cain?" the woman demanded.

The question genuinely shocked Nova. "Cain? I have no idea."

"Where *the fuck* is he?" she asked again. "I know he's here."

"I came alone," Nova insisted.

"My men are *gone*," the woman hissed. "No one's out back. No one's out front. If they're not here, then I assume they're dead. Tell Cain that unless he shows himself, I'm going to put a bullet in your forehead. You got that?"

Nova thought quickly.

Was it possible? Was Jason *here*?

"I don't know where Cain is," she said again. She was about to add: *You might as well shoot*. But she didn't. Standing where she was, she felt the slightest change in the atmosphere of the house. A hiss of wind flew up the fireplace. Under her feet, the floor shifted, barely enough to notice. The woman with the gun was too focused on Nova to realize what was happening. Behind her, in the kitchen, someone had entered the house.

"I can call his phone," Nova said calmly.

Can you hear me, Jason? Are you there?

"It won't do you any good, though," she went on. "He'll ignore the call. Cain hates me. I betrayed him. Fuck, he probably has me blocked."

"Call him."

"And say what? That you want to kill me? He'll tell you to do it."

"Call him."

"My phone's in my inside pocket."

"Then take it out slowly so I don't have to blow your head off."

Nova held her hands up, fingers wide. Slowly, she peeled back the lapel of her suit, then used two fingers to extract her phone. She found the unlabeled number for Jason's private mobile device. As she tapped the number, she readied herself. Tensed her thighs. Measured the distance between herself and the woman. Watched how she was standing and holding the gun, anticipated which direction she would turn.

Ten feet away, in the kitchen, came an explosion of sound. The climactic unleashing of "Stairway to Heaven." Jason's ringtone.

The woman with the gun flinched in shocked surprise. Just for an instant, but that was enough. When Nova saw the twitch of her muscles and the momentary shifting of her eyes, she sprang in one smooth motion across the space between them. Her left hand shoved the gun upward as it fired, blasting plaster from the ceiling. Her right hand hammered like a piston into the woman's throat, hard enough to crack cartilage and choke off her air. The woman fired once more, harmlessly, yielding another cloud of dust, and Nova clamped her teeth down over her wrist until the woman screamed and dropped the pistol to the floor. Gagging, she stumbled backward, frantically pushing Nova away. Then she knelt, grabbing for her ankle.

A backup! Another gun!

Nova threw herself sideways. The noise and char of gunfire filled the room. One shot, two shots, three shots. But it wasn't the woman firing. She was facedown on the floor now, dead, two shots in her back, one in the back of her head. Standing over her, smoke curling from the barrel of his Sig, was Jason.

20

They found Lori Janssen in her bedroom closet at the back of the house. She'd been shot, and she was bound and naked, her mouth gagged to muffle her screams. Her eyes were open, frozen in her final moments of terror. Bourne could see circular wounds all over her torso. The killer had used a lit cigarette to get her to talk.

Nova stood next to him. He felt darkness radiating from her. The agent he'd known in the past had been a model of cool, utterly free of emotion. But two years alone—since Lennon, since California—had changed her. She looked unsteady, at risk of losing control. He didn't like it.

"Fuck," she murmured, her voice trembling. "Fuck, look at her. I murdered her husband, and now *look at her*!"

"You didn't do this," Bourne reminded her.

"Does that matter? Does that make any difference? If they told me to do it, I'd do it. If that was the job, I wouldn't ask questions. I never do. Would you? Would you do this, Jason? Torture and kill an innocent woman?"

He hesitated, but he couldn't lie. "No."

"And that's the difference between us. You still have some semblance of a soul. I sold mine a long time ago."

"Nova, we don't have time for this. It's awful, but it's done. If any of the neighbors heard shots, the police will be here soon. We need to move quickly."

But Nova was in a different world, disconnected from reality. "I liked the crack of his skull."

"What?"

"When I killed her husband, I hit him. I cracked his head open. The sound turned me on. I get off on it. I always have. That's who I am, Jason."

"*Nova.*" He took her by the shoulders and twisted her body roughly toward him. "Focus. Listen to me. If you need to have a breakdown, fine, you can do it later when we're back at the hotel. Right now, we have about two minutes to figure out why they tortured this woman instead of just killing her."

Slowly, the wildness in her expression faded. Her eyes grew cold again, feelings draining away. She brushed her black hair out of her face. "Sorry. I freaked out. It won't happen again."

"Forget about it," he said. "Now think. Help me. Why the interrogation? What did they want from her?"

"They must have thought Billy told her something."

Bourne shook his head. "If she knew anything, killing her would have taken care of that. They must have been afraid that she *kept* something. That there was something in the house that they couldn't let fall into the wrong hands."

"Well, if that's true, it could be anywhere."

Jason looked around the woman's bedroom, studying the dresser drawers and the shelves of the closet over her head. Where would Lori keep memories of her husband? Where would she hide something? Then he stopped and took a second look at the room and realized there had been no search. There was no sign of disruption. The house hadn't been turned upside down, because the woman who murdered Lori Janssen already had what she wanted.

"She broke," he said. "Whatever she had, Lori told the killer where to find it."

Nova frowned. "So maybe it's still on the killer's body."

Bourne led them back to the living room. He knelt beside the body of the woman on the floor and squeezed his fingers inside the pockets of her jeans. They were mostly empty, no identification, nothing except a spare clip for her FNX. He checked her shoes, then undid her belt and squeezed her jeans down to her thighs. Her underwear was empty, and nothing was taped to her skin.

But when he pushed up the woman's sweatshirt, he found what he wanted. Tucked into one of the cups of her bra was a slim plastic flash drive.

Whatever was on it had gotten Billy Janssen killed.

"Come on," he said, securing the drive as he got to his feet. "Let's go out the back."

Together, he and Nova retreated to the porch behind the house. The densely wooded yard was nearly pitch-black, and he used a penlight to guide them through the neighborhood. No one saw them or stopped them. They left Nova's stolen car where it was, and they made their way through a park along Henson Creek and found Bourne's car a mile away.

Half an hour later, they were back at the Watergate.

Nova said nothing during the drive back to the hotel. She finally talked when they were alone with the hum of the elevator.

"How did you find me?" she asked.

"Nash."

Nova nodded. "Were there others? Did I miss the others?"

"Two," Bourne said. "One out back, one near your car. I dealt with them."

She shook her head in disgust with herself. "I'm slipping, Jason. I felt them, but I didn't spot them. They would have taken me out. Either in the house or when I got back to the car."

"They didn't," Jason said.

She fell silent again. When they reached his hotel room, she went to the window and looked out at the city lights with her arms folded tightly across her chest. She seemed consumed by her thoughts and doubts. Jason set up a laptop and inserted the thumb drive into one of the USB slots.

When he checked the contents of the drive, he found a single MP3 sound file.

"Come on, let's check it out," he said.

Nova left the window and stood stiffly behind him. He kept the volume low as he started the playback, which was a low-quality recording captured from a podcast. Bourne kept tabs on online conspiracy chatter, but he didn't recognize the host as anyone who had a large following. It didn't matter. Whatever the show was, whenever it had been broadcast, the government would have been listening.

"This is Zeno! And welcome to another shocking episode of Zeno's Paradoxes. *As you know, we've spent the last several weeks digging into the conspiracy behind Flight 1342. Tonight we have an exclusive interview with a witness who can* prove *what many of us have long suspected—that the U.S. government knew what was happening on that plane long before it ever disappeared from radar. Who is this witness? Well, for obvious reasons, we can't give you his real name—let's just call him John—but we can tell you what he does. He's a cop. A Washington, DC, police officer."*

"Billy Janssen," Bourne said.

"Why would he go on a fringe conspiracy podcast?" Nova asked.

That was the first question out of the host's mouth.

"John, listeners are probably wondering why you're talking to me. You're a cop. You could go to the FBI. The Justice Department. Even your superiors in the police department. Why tell your story here?"

Bourne heard Janssen's voice for the first time as it crackled through the computer speakers.

"Because I'm scared, Zeno. I'm scared for myself and for my wife. I kept quiet for days after it happened. Maybe I didn't want to believe what you just said, that the government knew what was going to happen to that plane. But after a couple of weeks, I decided I had to say something. In fact, I did go to my lieutenant. I told him what I saw, because I thought maybe the FBI would want to talk to me, like I could help with their investigation. After I did, there was a car outside my house that night. Someone was already watching us."

"But you don't know who?" the host asked.

"I don't, but it had to be someone in the government," Billy replied. *"They also tapped my phone. I figured they were looking at my email, too. I' d kicked a hornet's nest, and it scared me to death."*

"And what's your story, John? What did you see?"

A long, staticky pause stretched across the recording, as if Billy Janssen knew he was crossing a line from which there was no going back.

"John?" the host said. *"John, are you still with us?"*

"Yes. Yes, I'm here. It happened on a Tuesday night. Late. Actually, I guess it was Wednesday, because it was after one o'clock in the morning. I was on a routine patrol, cutting through Rock Creek Park on Military Road. All of a sudden, out of the woods on my right, a man bolted into the lane. I nearly hit him. In fact, I was afraid I did hit him, because he stumbled over the median and collapsed in the road. So I stopped to check on him."

"Was this man alive?"

"Yes, he was, but he was practically incoherent. Based on how he was dressed—and how he smelled—I figured he was homeless. He started telling me this story about being chased. He said men in suits—men with guns—were following him

through the park and trying to kill him. I didn't believe it. I assumed he was high on something, but—"

Billy stopped.

"But?" Zeno prompted him.

"But then I heard something in the woods where the man had come from. It was dark, so I grabbed my flashlight and shined it that way, and I caught a glimpse of someone backing away, disappearing into the trees. The light flashed on something metal, and I could see he was armed, just like the man said. Not just a pistol, a serious assault rifle, could have been an SR-16. It happened quickly, but I know what I saw. It distracted me, so I didn't even notice the homeless man running away. I tried to follow him, but a couple of cars passed in the opposite lane and slowed me down. By the time I made it into the woods on the other side, he was gone."

"What did you do then?"

"I took my cruiser into the park to see if I could figure out what was going on. I got to a point where the road was closed. Blocked off. The feds had it shut down, and sure enough, there were agents with guns guarding one of the parking lots. Usually, we get alerts about that kind of thing, but there was nothing on the books for that night. I couldn't get close enough to see what was going on. I showed my badge—didn't matter. They told me to leave, and they weren't polite about it."

"Did you leave?" Zeno asked.

Again Billy hesitated.

"No. *There was just something that felt off about it. The agents didn't show me any ID. They didn't tell me who they were, what agency they were with. I didn't like it. So I drove off in my patrol car, but then I parked somewhere else. I hike RCP all the time, so I know the trails. I backtracked on foot and worked my way to the parking lot through the trees. I was real quiet. I didn't want them finding me."*

"What did you see?"

"Two limos. There were two limos in the parking lot. Unmarked, no logos. I don't know who was inside, but there was some kind of meeting going on. In the middle of the night? With federal security protection? Whoever was there, they had some pull and some clearance, I'm telling you. And you know, this is DC, that kind of thing happens. Normally, I would have written it off as a Deep Throat thing and let it go."

"But you didn't."

"No."

"Why?"

"Because the news about Flight 1342 broke less than twelve hours later."

The host let a dramatic silence stretch out on the show. Then he said, *"You think the two events are related?"*

"I do. I mean, come on, a coincidence like that? No way. My first thought was—okay, some big shots were talking about what to do after the plane went missing. That makes sense. But when the news came out, I put together a timeline. I figured out when the plane first took off and when it broke contact about four hours later. That was in the media, they couldn't hide it. I compared it to the timeline in DC."

"What did you discover?" Zeno asked.

"Those two limos in Rock Creek Park? Whatever that meeting was, it was happening right after the plane took off from Johannesburg. I mean, it had to be within minutes of takeoff. That was before *the plane broke its flight plan. Before! At that point, nobody had any reason to think this was anything but an ordinary flight, right? There were no problems, no strange communications. That means somebody knew, Zeno. Somebody knew that plane was going to go rogue. They knew before it happened."*

The recording ended abruptly. It stopped there.

Nova's hands were on Jason's back. She'd begun to caress

his neck with her sharp fingernails. It felt casual, but Nova never did anything casually. "What do you think?"

Bourne replayed the last few seconds of the recording. "I think Billy was right. Someone knew about this from the beginning. And someone is desperate to keep the truth about that flight hidden."

"So what do we do?"

He hesitated, because he knew she wasn't going to like it. "I need you to set up a meeting."

"With who?"

"I talked to a Russian contact. He thinks Lennon knows the truth behind Defiance. Or at least part of it."

Nova's hands stiffened on his shoulders, her sensual touch evaporating. She broke off and went to the hotel window, and it was several seconds before she said anything more. "*Lennon?* You want me to reach out to Lennon? Do you know what he fucking did to me, Jason?"

"Yes."

"He tortured me. He *broke* me."

"I know."

"I betrayed you because of him."

"Believe me, I know what I'm asking," Bourne said. "But we need to find him."

"What makes you think I even have a way to reach him? You're so sure I've stayed in touch with an assassin?"

Bourne said nothing, but they both knew the truth. Of course she had a way to reach him. Even if she'd wanted to break the connection between them, she couldn't. On some level, Lennon still controlled part of her mind. He would have left the door open, knowing the day would come when Nova would walk through it.

But forcing her to admit it also felt like twisting the knife when she was already down.

"Okay," Nova said finally, without looking at him. "There's

a cutout he uses at a Starbucks in New York. I'll send a message."

"Good."

"I don't know how long it will take. It could be a few days."

"That's okay. There's something else I need to do first."

"What?" Nova asked.

"Whoever's behind Defiance is in DC," Bourne said. "They need to know we're getting close, that we've made the connection to 1342. We need them scared, off-balance. We need to rattle some cages right here in the city."

Panic is an asset. Panicked people make mistakes.

Treadstone.

"How do you plan to do that?" Nova asked.

Jason was slow to say the name out loud. He didn't want to involve her in his world, not again, but he had no choice. "I have to talk to Abbey."

21

Jason knocked on the door of abbey's Washington apartment. He wondered how she would react when she saw him again. He half expected her to slap his face and send him away. Then the door opened, and she stood there dressed in the sleeveless white T-shirt and panties in which she usually slept. Her bare skin was smooth and perfect, and her breasts pushed out the cotton shirt, ending in hard points. Feathery strands of her red hair fell across her forehead and cheeks. She studied him through dark, tired eyes. It was six in the morning, and knowing Abbey, she'd only been asleep for a couple of hours.

"You," she murmured.

"Yeah. Me."

"You're alive."

"Yeah."

A long silence stretched out between them, and their tension was caught somewhere between desire and anger.

"How's your friend?" she asked finally, with an edge in her voice.

"Fine."

"Did you fuck her?"

"No."

"Would you lie to me if you had?"

"No."

"Okay then," Abbey said.

She grabbed him by the shirt and pulled him into the apartment and kicked the door shut with her bare foot. Getting on tiptoes, she kissed him hard on the mouth, and the mint taste on her breath made him think she'd already known it was him when she heard the knock on the door.

"Take me to bed, you son of a bitch," she whispered in his ear.

So he did.

An hour later, they lay next to each other in her bedroom under a slowly spinning ceiling fan. They were both out of breath, their naked bodies glistening with sweat. Her fingers curled around his hand and held it. Her smile was easy and satisfied as she looked at him. *Damn it, that smile!* He could never resist it.

"Hello there," she said, because they hadn't spoken since he'd carried her to the bedroom with her legs wrapped around his hips.

"Hi."

"I thought we were supposed to be staying apart."

"Yeah, I thought so, too."

"I'm not complaining," Abbey said.

"How goes the book?" he asked.

"Really good. It's going to be great. Actually, you're lucky to find me here. Most nights I've been staying with Alicia at her estate in Maryland. We're both late-night people, and it's easier than going back and forth every day. But I needed to do some research in the city, so I stayed here last night."

"Lucky thing I came when I did."

Abbey's eyes narrowed, and she propped herself up on one elbow. "I don't believe in luck when it comes to you."

"What do you mean?"

"I stay in my place one night, and that's when you show up? You knew I was back here, didn't you? You've been watching me."

"Yeah, for a couple of days," Jason admitted.

"Why?"

"To make sure you were safe."

"Because of Paris?" she asked.

"Yeah."

"Are you going to tell me what Paris was all about?"

"You know the rules," Jason said. "I can't."

"I get it, the less I know, the better. Well, the rules suck. What the hell is going on?"

"I can't tell you anything, Abbey. I'm sorry."

But he put a finger over his lips, which brought a puzzled expression to her face. He signaled toward the nearest doorway, and together they left the bed and went into the bathroom. Jason turned on the shower, and when the water was warm, he pulled her in with him and closed his arms around her naked body. They kissed again, but Abbey could read in his face that this wasn't about sex.

"Not that I mind the shower, but what's going on?" she asked. He didn't need to tell her to whisper. She knew that already.

"We need to be careful what we say in your apartment," Jason replied.

Abbey cocked her head. "Why? Do you think my place might be bugged?"

"I know it is."

"What?"

"I searched it yesterday while you were at Alicia Beauvoir's. Sorry. I found listening devices in the living room and the bedroom. Audio, not video. They can hear us, but they can't see us."

"Oh, well, that's a relief," she said sourly. "Are you saying you left the bugs there? Why didn't you get rid of them?"

"Because I don't want whoever's on the other end to know I found them."

"So they were listening to us in bed?"

"Yeah. I should have told you."

Abbey's face creased with a frown, but then she laughed. "If I'd known I was performing, I would have moaned louder."

"Sorry," he said again.

"So who is it? Who's doing this?"

"I don't know."

"You don't think it's Alicia, do you? Why would she care? I'm already with her most of the time anyway."

"I have no idea who it is. But I'm sure they want to get to me through you. The thing is, now they know we're together again, so we can't stay here for long. I have to go, and you have to go, too. Don't come back here. Not for a while. Stay with Alicia or stay at a hotel until you hear from me again."

Her face turned serious. "Jason, what is going on? What was Paris about?"

He told her.

He told her everything. In other circumstances, he would have kept the truth from her, because the Treadstone rules were there for a reason. The less she knew, the safer she was. But this time he needed her help. If he was going to pull her into Defiance, if he was going to make her a part of this, then she deserved to know why.

"1342," she reflected when he'd told her the story, from Paris to Madagascar to DC. "Jesus. After all this time. I can't believe it. And you think Iran brought the plane down? They did this?"

"I do, but there's more to the story. Something else is going on, something that started closer to home. It wasn't the

Iranians who organized Defiance, and they're not the ones coming after Treadstone now."

"Then who?" Abbey asked.

He continued to hold her close, and her dark eyes stared up at him, intense and curious. The shower soaked her red hair and cast a damp sheen on her face. "You can help me find out," Bourne said, "but I'm reluctant to ask you."

"Why?"

"It may put you in an uncomfortable position."

"I thought you already did that," she said with a smoky tease.

"I'm serious. This is dangerous. I don't want to involve you."

She kissed him again. "But you need me, right? Okay then. I'm a big girl. Tell me what you want. I'm in, Jason. I always am."

The operative known as Yoko sat on the steps of the New York Public Library with her back against the platform that supported one of the stone lions. She had a notebook computer balanced on her lap, and she tapped the keys at lightning-fast speed. Her blue eyes focused on the screen from behind round wire-rimmed glasses, and her matching blue hair hung in long bangs down the forehead of her small, round face. While she typed, she kept an eye on the hordes of people coming and going on the crowded sidewalks of Fifth Avenue. Sometimes Lennon tested her. He would send someone to take her picture, and she had to be able to tell him who it was. If she failed, there was punishment.

Admittedly, Yoko liked his punishment. Sometimes she failed his tests on purpose, in order to savor the pain he doled out.

He had named her the new Yoko—his second-in-command—

four months earlier. She liked the perks of her position, the power, the violent assignments, the occasional sex. But she also knew that she was only the latest in a long line of women to serve his needs, and she was aware of the risks that came with the role. The previous Yokos were all dead. Everyone close to Lennon was a target.

Yoko was small, barely five feet tall, and only nineteen years old. Age and size didn't matter. She'd made her first kill—poisoning a Russian dissident on the London Underground with the prick of a fake fingernail—by the time she was thirteen. At fifteen, she'd slept with a member of Parliament and blackmailed him into changing his vote on trade legislation. At seventeen, she'd infiltrated a band of climate extremists and led bombings across Germany and France. At that point, Lennon had concluded that her profile was too high to stay in the UK and Europe, and he'd moved her across the pond to set up shop in the U.S.

Now he'd made her the lead in setting up their biggest mission ever.

She'd been on the library steps since four o'clock in the afternoon. It was now midevening, almost dark, and the library would be closing soon. When the people around her thinned, she'd have to find a new location. She was logged in to the government account of FBI Special Agent Michael Green, whose password she'd stolen while staying in an adjoining room in a Denver hotel. She didn't think the FBI was likely to detect her hacking—or if they did, to pinpoint her location that quickly—but just in case, she always did her research in public places where she could melt into the crowds if she saw the feds coming.

On her screen, the email database showed a list of death threats made against U.S. politicians and prominent government figures. For each email, Special Agent Green had compiled a risk assessment analyzing the seriousness of the threat and attaching a bio of the sender and any known associations with extremist or terrorist groups. It was a long list. In her first couple of hours on the library steps, Yoko had identified half a dozen possible targets for Lennon's operation, but all of them had flaws that made them questionable choices.

Until now. Now she was pretty sure she'd found her man.

His name was Walter Pepper. She couldn't stop giggling when she saw that he was a former Marine sergeant. Lennon was going to love that. Sergeant Pepper now worked as a taxi driver in Maryland, and he'd sent more than a hundred emails to members of Congress about his grievances with the state of the country. None included actual threats, but it was impossible to miss the undercurrent of violence. *Keep going like this, and real Americans will rise up just like our forefathers did to take back our country from people like you.* On social media, Pepper followed pages for extremist organizations with names like the Liberty Soldiers and Sons of the Minutemen. He'd posted a picture of himself holding up a Colt Python revolver and a shooting range target, with the center blasted away.

Yoko studied the man's photo. Sergeant Pepper was in his early thirties, with a shock of messy brown hair, a scraggly beard, and a short, skinny frame. He had a scar across the middle of his forehead, angry dark eyes, and a mouth with a mean scowl. A tattoo on his chopstick forearm showed a colonial flag—don't tread on me, with a coiled snake—held in place by an old-fashioned M1 carbine.

Yes, he was perfect.

She checked her watch again. It was time to go. She packed up her backpack and skipped lightly down the library steps. She made her way south on Fifth, dashing across the streets as the lights changed and drawing wild horns from the taxis gunning through the intersections. At 23rd, she turned right and made her way to the subway, where she took the F train in the opposite direction. She got off at Lexington and 63rd, confident she hadn't been followed.

There was a Starbucks immediately on her right, and she slipped inside only ten minutes before it closed. She had made that side trip once a week for the past two years, and her order was always the same, almond milk honey flat white with an extra shot of honey. Same order, same barista, week after week. No variations.

But that night, it finally changed.

When the barista called her name to hand over her tall cup of coffee, he also gave her a package of madeleine cookies that she hadn't ordered. Yoko didn't react or look surprised. Her tradecraft lessons were clear: Any night could be the night when the signal comes. Assume it's going to happen when you walk in the door. Always be ready.

Yoko smiled, thanked him pleasantly as if this were an ordinary evening, and left the coffee shop. It was dark now. She ate the madeleines a nibble at a time and sipped her coffee as she followed a random route through the shadowy Upper East Side streets that led toward the river. She had no permanent address. This week, she was staying at the Bentley Hotel near the Queensboro Bridge. Every week she switched hotels, and she never used the same hotel twice. Again, tradecraft.

When she got to her room, she knew Lennon was waiting for her. The curtains were shut, the lights off, the way he always insisted. She could smell his presence and hear his breathing even if she couldn't see him, and her body reacted with a surge of erotic adrenaline. She said nothing. Nothing needed to be said. Slowly, she took off all her clothes and let them drop onto the carpet, and then she felt her way to the bed in the darkness. There he was, naked like her, already aroused and ready. She kissed him, stroked him, felt his need. Lennon didn't visit often, but when he did, she knew the mission was coming soon. Thinking about the violence ahead excited her even more.

"I found him," Yoko murmured, giving him updates on her research like a kind of foreplay. "His name is Walter Pepper. He's perfect. He's the one. Fuck if he wasn't a sergeant, too. Sergeant Pepper."

He didn't acknowledge what she'd said or even laugh at the joke of the man's name. His hands were already busy, making her breathless, making her nerve endings come alive. She eased back onto the bed and spread her legs wide, and his body moved over her like an invisible, animal ghost.

"One more thing," she whispered as he slid easily inside her. "The signal came at the Starbucks tonight. Nova wants a meeting."

22

Bourne watched the gray-haired man in the suit emerge from the private day school on South Carolina Avenue. Five minutes earlier, he'd seen the man accompany his two children, ages ten and thirteen, into the building. Now he returned alone. The man's car, a silver Lexus, was parked on the cobblestone street. He watched the man take the steps to the sidewalk, then calmly cross the street and walk across the green grass into the park, where Bourne was waiting on a bench.

He sat down next to Bourne, tightened the silk tie at his neck, and pinched the end of his long nose with a sniff. He snapped open a copy of the *Wall Street Journal* and crossed his legs as he began to read. Bourne noticed that the man's leather shoes were impeccably polished, shining under the morning sun.

"I'll be honest with you, Cain," the man murmured, his British accent still intact despite decades in the U.S. He didn't look away from his newspaper as he spoke. "Seeing someone like you near my children's school does not make me happy. If you're going to show up unexpectedly, I'd prefer you do it elsewhere."

"Understood," Jason replied, "but you're a hard man to find alone."

The man gave a little shrug of his shoulders to acknowledge that was true. "Well, for what it's worth, my oldest boy wants to be a spy when he grows up. Maybe you'd like to speak at career day."

The man's thin lips bent slightly to indicate that he was joking. Bourne smiled, too.

Gerald Addison had been the Washington editor of the *Financial Times* for twenty years. He knew everyone in DC, and there were few rumors that didn't cross his desk. To Addison, information was like a cryptocurrency spiking in value. He accumulated nuggets of facts, hints, whispers, and speculations, and used them to break stories that no one else had. He was in his mid-fifties but still wrote many of his exposés himself, in addition to doling out assignments to his team of reporters. Jason had occasionally served as an anonymous source for Addison, in order to make sure that certain stories got told correctly. In return, he'd also turned to Addison for information.

"So are you giving or taking this time?" the man asked. "Things are a bit dry at the moment. I wouldn't mind a tip."

"Actually, this situation is a little unusual," Bourne said.

Addison's eyebrow nudged upward to show his curiosity. "Go on."

"I need a favor."

"Such as?"

"I'd like to start a rumor," Bourne said.

Addison pursed his lips. "I see. And is this rumor true?"

"No."

"Well, I'm afraid I'm not in the business of spreading disinformation," Addison informed him. "I know it's quite en vogue in certain circles of the media these days, but I'm old-fashioned about the truth."

"I'm not asking you to lie. Only to ask a couple of questions with the right people in the right places. You can phrase it in such a way that you're not vouching for the truth of the underlying statement, just wondering if people have heard a certain item of gossip. You can even suggest that you don't believe it yourself."

"And nonetheless, by doing so, I feed the rumor," Addison concluded.

Jason nodded. "That's right."

"Hmm. Interesting. Well, without saying yes or no, what is this about?"

Bourne smiled to himself. He'd known Addison couldn't resist the bait. "Are you familiar with Abbey Laurent?"

"By reputation, yes, of course. I was always a fan of her reporting, but now she seems to have found a new passion. I loved the novel she did with Peter Chancellor. Candidly, I've also heard *your* identity linked to Ms. Laurent, going back to the Medusa affair a few years ago. People suggested that the two of you had a personal relationship. Is that true?"

"Off the record, yes."

"That seems rather dangerous for her."

"It is."

"Does she know you're here?" Addison asked.

"She does. And she agreed with what I'm asking you to do. Although, to be honest, she doesn't like this any more than you. She's a fan of the truth, too."

"I guess that's a bit ironic, given her new occupation. But there may be more truth in certain novels these days than in nonfiction."

"That's why I'm here. Abbey is following in Peter Chancellor's footsteps. She's writing ripped-from-the-headlines fiction where people wonder if that's how it really happened. Breaking open conspiracies that may be real."

"Color me intrigued."

"You also know that Abbey is cowriting a novel with Alicia Beauvoir, right?"

Addison nodded. "Of course. I've known Alicia for years. That seems like a savvy move for both of them. Abbey gets realism and credibility for her next book, and Alicia gets some pop culture fame to make her more human and less of an ice queen."

"Have you heard what their book is going to be about?" Bourne asked.

"I haven't. That seems to be a closely guarded secret, which only contributes to the speculation."

"I can think of a topic that would be right up Abbey's alley," Jason said.

Addison's eyes narrowed. "Can you now? What would that be?"

"What really happened to Flight 1342."

"Ah, the missing jet," Addison mused. "What an intriguing idea."

"Of course, I'm sure she'd change the flight number, the details, make it fictional. But everyone would wonder if she was exposing the truth, wouldn't they?"

"They would. And what do you suppose her angle would be in a book like that?"

"She might suggest that certain people in the American government knew the crash was going to happen *before* the plane disappeared."

"More and more intriguing," Addison said. "*Is* that what Abbey and Alicia are writing about?"

"I didn't say that."

Addison folded up his newspaper and shook his head in amusement. "But perhaps I should make some calls and see if anyone else has heard about this rumor? Is that what you're suggesting?"

"You're the reporter. That's up to you."

"Well, perhaps I will. I can think of at least one scandalmonger who would love to post the story, true or not." Then Addison turned and looked directly at Bourne for the first time. "I know you're accustomed to hazards in your own world, my friend, but I hope you're not playing a little too fast and loose with Ms. Laurent's life."

"Abbey made this decision herself," Jason replied. "I didn't force her. In her own words, she's a big girl. But believe me, I know the risks."

The intermission crowd outside Kennedy center mingled around Tim Randall as he sipped his scotch. He was in demand. The chief of staff to the odds-on favorite for the Democratic presidential nomination was always in demand. A White House staffer had buttonholed him at the urinals to discuss Senator Pine's confirmation vote for a deputy secretary in the Treasury Department. A DC circuit judge had dropped broad hints about his interest in a possible Supreme Court vacancy the next year. Randall was noncommittal with both of them, making no promises. Instead, he made his way slowly through the crowd, eavesdropping on the buzz of conversations. Listening without seeming to listen was a key political skill. More deals got done at Kennedy Center than in Capitol Hill cloakrooms.

The ambitious circuit court judge was soon replaced by a Republican congresswoman from Texas talking about energy policy. Randall paid more attention to her than the others, but only because she was a beautiful blonde with a reputation among staffers for being very loud during sex. Texas women might be gun nuts and fascists, but damn, they could fuck. He tried to multitask, pretending to listen to her thoughts on U.S. refinery capacity while also admiring the way her breasts spilled out of her black dress. At the same time, he spied on the dialogue between the FBI director and the attorney general, who were standing outside the concert hall a few feet away.

The congresswoman's breasts were winning until an isolated fragment of conversation drifted to his ears.

"I hear it's about Flight 1342."

Jesus!

Randall kept a fake smile pasted on his face as the Texas blonde rambled on, but he focused all of his senses on the two men near him. He tried to contain his shock. What were they *saying*? What was this *about*?

He picked up only a few isolated words, but what he heard filled him with fear.

"Book."

"Exposé."

"Conspiracy."

And then worst of all: "Beauvoir."

Around the lobby the theater lights flashed on and off. The second half of the concert was about to begin. Like a slow wave, people began returning to their seats, and the conversation between the FBI director and the attorney general faded into noise as the two men pushed farther away from him.

"I suppose we should go back in," the congresswoman purred. She looked a little upset that Randall wasn't focused on her breasts anymore.

"Actually, I'm afraid I'll have to miss the rest of the concert. Duty calls."

Randall forced another smile, then fought the oncoming crowd to make his way outside the building into the cool night air. He began running searches on Washington news sites and quickly found a banner headline on the feed of a DC blogger. He read the article and couldn't believe it. He read it again, as if the words might change, but they didn't.

It was *impossible*!

Randall reached into the pocket of his tuxedo jacket and

grabbed his other phone. This was his burner phone, the one outside the reach of government archivists, the one that congressional committees and DOJ investigators would never know existed.

"It's me," he hissed. "We've got trouble. Get online. *Now!* "

23

Alicia Beauvoir didn't slow down near the end of her daily run through the riverside hills that surrounded her Maryland estate. Her arms and legs pumped even faster, and her breathing was fast and loud. She always ran hard, especially on the last leg, timing herself to keep track of her performance. If she was off her desired pace by even a few seconds, the next day she ran even harder.

When she reached the paver patio near her Olympic-size swimming pool, she took a seat in one of the wicker chairs. A folded towel was waiting on the glass table beside her to wipe away the sweat from her brow. There was also a bottle of Fiji water in a chilled wine cooler. She took her pulse to note how rapidly her heartbeat returned to its resting rate, then gulped down a short drink of water.

Glancing at her wrist, she focused on the red dragonfly tattooed on her skin. On one of its wings was the name *Ellie* in script. Her daughter had loved dragonflies, and as a little girl, she would shriek with delight whenever one landed on her finger. As foolish as it sounded, Beauvoir couldn't help but think whenever she saw a dragonfly that Ellie was paying her a visit. It didn't matter that ten years had already passed since the Hizballah bomber had taken her daughter away from her. Everything she did, she still did for Ellie.

Her slim briefcase was waiting with four daily newspapers and a summary of the day's political and policy updates. She reached out to pull the briefcase closer, but she didn't have a chance to open it. Instead, she saw a slim Filipino man cross the patio with a silver platter on which he'd placed her iPhone.

"Senator Pine for you, Madam Secretary. He says it's urgent."

"Thank you, Tipo."

She waited until the servant had returned inside the house, and then she put the phone to her ear. "Don, good morning."

The senator didn't waste time on small talk. His growl erupted from the speaker. "What the fuck, Alicia?"

"I take it you've seen the rumors," she said calmly.

"Of course I have! Are you kidding me? You're writing a thriller based on 1342?"

"Take a breath, Don. I don't want you having a stroke."

"Don't bullshit me, Alicia. Is it true?"

Beauvoir sighed. "No, for heaven's sake, it's not true."

The senator stayed quiet for a long beat. "Are you serious? The reports are wrong?"

"They're completely wrong. I have no idea how those rumors got started. The plot has nothing to do with 1342."

"Then why are you out there with a canned press release that says no comment? Why aren't you denying it?"

"It's called publicity, Don," Beauvoir replied. "You of all people know how the game is played. If I say the media reports are wrong, then the story goes away. In this case, wrong or not, I don't want the story going away. Have you seen the Amazon ranking for preorders? A blank page, no description, no excerpt, no cover art, and we're already at number nine on the Kindle bestseller list. Do you think I'm going to say no to that?"

She could almost smell fire breathing out of the dragon's mouth as Pine snarled at her. "So did *you* leak this rumor?"

"No, I already told you I didn't. Maybe if I'd known what it would do to juice sales, I would have. But it wasn't me."

"Then who? I want to know what's going on, Alicia. What's your game?"

"There's no game, Don. I promise you."

He didn't seem to hear her denial. "You know perfectly well that this is going to light up all the conspiracy nuts again. They're going to rehash the old stories. Fox will have a panel of yahoos out there claiming that the CIA was behind the jet's disappearance."

"No one seriously believes that," she replied.

"The media doesn't care about what's true! This shit brings ratings, so they'll blast it all over the news. I'm asking you again, what's the game, Alicia? Is this somehow designed to embarrass me?"

"Of course not."

"Have you changed your mind about the election?" Pine went on. "Are you planning to run against me? You're the only one who poses any real threat. Do you think I don't know that?"

"Don, I haven't changed my mind," Beauvoir insisted. "When we met last year, you told me you were planning to go after the nomination, and I wished you Godspeed. I said I had no interest in the nomination, and that's still true."

"But you haven't endorsed me."

Beauvoir hesitated. "No, I haven't."

"Why not?"

"We talked about that last year," she reminded him. "We agreed it would look like we were clearing the field too early. Another smoke-filled cloakroom deal to shut out the voters. You needed to win this on your own, Don, and you have. Everyone says the nomination is yours to lose."

"Yeah, that's the point. It's mine to *lose*. Nobody's voted yet. We're months away from the first primary. Polls don't mean a thing until then. I know how fucking easy it is for a front-runner's momentum to deflate, and there you are sitting on the sidelines with a pin waiting to prick my bubble."

"I'm *not* going to challenge you, Don."

"Then endorse me," Pine snapped. "It's not last year anymore. The race is far enough along to choose up sides. If you think I'm way ahead, then let's get the party coalescing around me so I can train my fire on the Republicans. Your endorsement would give me the establishment nod to go along with the progressive activists. You'll make sure women stand with me, too. The general election is going to be close. Let's not blow it."

Beauvoir didn't say anything for a while. She took another drink of Fiji water and admired the country view on the rolling hills of her estate. The white cloth towel was soft on the back of her neck, and her sweat had dried.

"Trust me, Don," she said finally. "When we're at the convention next summer, I'll be the good party soldier. I'll deliver a rousing speech to support you as the nominee."

"So why wait?"

"Because I have relationships with all of the candidates. I can't be seen picking sides."

"Bullshit. What's the real reason?"

Her voice changed. She could be sweet, generous, and polite, but she never let an adversary forget who they were dealing with. "Okay. Since you insist, here's the real reason. Your allegiance is to yourself and your ambition first and the country second. The voters may choose you, and if they do, I'll respect their decision. But *until* they do, I'm not going to stand up and tell them you're the right choice for the times, when I simply don't believe that."

"Are you going to endorse someone else?" Pine asked.

"No. I told you, I'm staying neutral."

She heard him breathing into the phone, and she knew he was furious. When he spoke again, his tone was ugly and dark. "You really *don't* want me as an enemy, Alicia."

"Is that a threat?"

"It's a promise. Take me on, and you're asking for war. If you come after me, I will destroy you."

The senator hung up, leaving only silence and dead air.

Beauvoir replaced the phone on the silver tray. She took another drink of her Fiji water and then tapped her manicured index finger thoughtfully on her lips. Then she raised her hand to summon her servant Tipo from the house.

"Get hold of Ms. Laurent," she told him. "Tell her I want her at my house in an hour. If it's sixty-one minutes, I tear up our book deal."

Abbey arrived fifty-five minutes later.

She'd been waiting for Beauvoir's call ever since the news had broken the previous night. Jason had said he wanted to shake up Washington by spreading rumors about her book, and she knew the blowback would start with Alicia Beauvoir. Of course, she could have told Jason no. He'd half insisted that she turn him down, that she think about the risks. They both knew he was throwing a hand grenade into her career. Beauvoir might walk away, abandon the project, and leave Abbey's reputation in ruins. That was in addition to the physical danger. But Abbey still found it hard to give up Jason's world when he asked her to be a part of it. More than that, she found it impossible to give up *him*.

When she got to the solarium, the former secretary of state was waiting for her. Beauvoir directed Abbey into a chair with a single finger, like a teacher with a misbehaving student.

"Was it you?" she asked flatly.

Her voice had the chill of a Quebec January.

Abbey opened her mouth to answer, but Beauvoir interrupted her before she had a chance to say anything.

"*Was ... it ... you?*" she asked again.

Abbey took a deep breath and lied. Well, she told herself it wasn't technically a lie. The story hadn't actually come from her. Jason was the one who'd set the rumor in motion. "No. It wasn't me."

"You did not leak this story?"

"No."

"Do you know who did?"

"No," she replied, which *was* a lie, but she had no choice. "I have no idea. I was as shocked to see it online as you were."

"Then where did it come from?" Beauvoir demanded.

"I don't know."

"I find that hard to believe, Abbey. I really do."

"I'm sorry, Alicia, but obviously, we both know that the book *isn't* about Flight 1342. I mean, I would never leak anything about the plot without your permission, but regardless, I certainly wouldn't start a rumor that's false. It makes no sense."

She heard herself talking, and she knew her voice was convincing. No hesitation, no tremble as she said it. She'd learned the tools of the trade from Jason. She'd become good at lying. On the other hand, she was dealing with a politician who knew the art of the lie better than anyone.

Beauvoir frowned. "Well, it's true that I can't see what you'd hope to gain from it."

"Exactly," Abbey replied with a silent wave of relief.

The older woman loosened her arms, and some of the frozen tension in her body seemed to melt away. She went to one of the solarium windows. "I'm surprised you didn't ask me the obvious question, Abbey."

"Which is?"

"If it wasn't you, was it *me*?" Beauvoir said.

"I never thought that for a moment. Was it?"

"No."

"Well then, it's a mystery," Abbey said.

Beauvoir's lips pursed. "The *who* may be a mystery, but certainly not the why. That part of it seems pretty obvious. We're being used."

"I don't understand."

Beauvoir glanced at her from the windows with a frown, and Abbey wondered if she was overplaying her part by acting too naïve.

"Someone's flushing the ducks to the hunter," Beauvoir said. "Whoever leaked this story is looking to scare people into thinking that our novel will expose secrets about Flight 1342. It's actually a clever strategy. Sow panic. Panicked people make mistakes."

Abbey heard Jason's voice telling her the same thing. That was another of his Treadstone rules.

"*Are* there secrets about the jet?" she asked. "You were secretary of state back then. Do you know what really happened?"

"You don't have clearance for the things I know," Beauvoir replied, her voice steely again. Then she softened and shook her head. "But in this case, there's nothing to tell. I don't know anything at all. However, one thing I will tell you is that we both need to be very careful from now on."

"Why?"

"Because it doesn't matter whether we're really writing about the plane. Even if we deny it now, people won't believe us. If someone thinks we know more than we do, then we may wind up with targets on our chests."

24

Tim Randall waited until after dark and then headed out of Washington. He used a car from the GSA fleet and made sure there was no official record of it being taken out of the pool. There was always a bureaucrat ready to help a Senate staffer who needed a vehicle for a confidential meeting.

It was a long drive, nearly two hours. He continued northward through Baltimore and past the towns of Abingdon and Aberdeen. When he finally crossed the bridge over the Susquehanna, he left the interstate and followed the back roads. By then, it was nearly midnight. His route led him around the inlet of the North East River, where he turned south and had to slow down to avoid making wrong turns. He used a paper Rand McNally atlas to figure out his course—his phone was off, and he wanted no GPS record of his search—but in the dark, all the roads looked alike.

Then, under the moonlight, he spotted a small yacht harbor branching off the river. He switched off the car's headlights and turned onto a dead-end street beyond the water. There were two houses in the middle of a sloping green meadow that looked toward the harbor. Both were dark. He continued to the second property—a ranch-style farmhouse with red siding—and drove into the grass behind the house, where the car was out of sight from the road.

He shut down the engine and got out. There was a barn behind him on the fringe of a thick stand of woods. Wind off the river rustled the trees, and on the far side of the house, he heard the clang of sailboats bobbing in the harbor. Back here, the moonlight didn't reach him, and he felt blind. He could barely see the outline of the house, but it looked deserted.

Randall wasn't sure what to do next.

The instructions delivered to him at a DC café by one of Hamid Ashkani's men had only taken him this far. Now he was on his own.

"Hello?" he murmured into the darkness.

There was no answer, but Randall felt the hairs rise on his neck, as if someone was close to him that he couldn't see. Or maybe it was an animal from the forest. He half expected to hear the snarl of a wolf.

"Are you there?" he called.

He took a step toward the house, then froze when something hard pressed into the back of his skull. Randall realized it was the barrel of a gun.

"Jesus!" he exclaimed too loudly. "I'm unarmed! You don't need to do that!"

"Keep your voice down," came a quiet hiss.

"Sorry," Randall whispered. He was uncomfortably aware that the gun stayed where it was, pushed against his head. "You're Lennon?"

A long silence followed before he heard any kind of reply.

"This meeting is ill-advised," the man said.

"That couldn't be helped."

"Everything was supposed to go through Ashkani. He gave me the target. There wasn't to be any direct communication between us. That's in both of our interests, Mr. Randall. That's how you stay out of prison and I stay alive."

"I understand."

Randall didn't turn around. In the darkness, he wouldn't have been able to pick out details of the assassin's face, but he was taking no chances. He stared into nothingness and held his body perfectly still, his arms slightly out, making no moves. He didn't want to give the man any reason to shoot him, and he knew Lennon wouldn't hesitate to fire if he suspected even the hint of a trap.

"Then why are you here?" the killer asked.

"The situation has changed. There's an emergency."

"What is it?"

"Haven't you heard? It's all over Washington. The media's picking it up, too. Everyone is talking about this book about 1342. It's a *lie*! But that doesn't matter. All the old stories are coming up again."

"You're a fool, Mr. Randall," Lennon said. "Yes, I know about the rumors, and I know who's behind them."

"Who?"

"This is *Cain*. He's obviously the one who leaked the story."

"Jesus! Why?"

"To get you to panic," Lennon snapped. "To get you to make a mistake. Which is exactly what you're doing. You're playing into his hands. Are you sure you weren't followed out of Washington?"

"I—I have no idea. For God's sake, I don't know how this *insanity* works for people like you!"

"That's why we were never supposed to meet. You arranged this safe house so that I could plan the assassination, and now you may have led Cain right to me. He could be coming through those woods behind us; he could have a nightscope trained on both of us right now. Do you not understand that? For me, the *smart* thing to do is kill you and then disappear. There's no upside to me in your staying alive, Mr. Randall."

Randall's knees turned to rubber, and his voice grew

choked. "I don't *think* I was followed! I mean, it was dark, wouldn't I have seen something? Headlights, anything? And there's no way anyone could know I'm involved!"

Finally, the pressure of the gun disappeared from the back of his head.

"Relax, Randall. I had one of my people on you the whole time. There was no one else trailing you, but next time you may not be so lucky. If Cain was following you, you wouldn't have a clue until it was too late. Now tell me what you want so you can get out of here before I change my mind."

Randall tried to catch his breath. He knotted his tie a little tighter, trying to remind himself that *he* was the one with all the power. People in Washington groveled before him, flattered him for favors. But he was a long way from DC, and he knew he was nothing next to a man with a gun.

"It doesn't matter that the rumors about the book are a lie," Randall said, keeping his voice steady. "It's still a huge risk. It may flush out people who know something. We've been trying to shut it all down, but there are bound to be others who have some clue about what really happened. This may bring them out of the shadows."

"So what do you want me to do?"

"Move up the timeline. The hit needs to come sooner."

Lennon exhaled loudly, and there was annoyance in his tone. "Doing it the way you want, making sure the blame goes elsewhere, takes time. We have someone in mind, but moving faster adds risk. Ashkani said I had a month."

"Not anymore," Randall insisted. "We can't wait. You're a pro, aren't you? You're being paid for results, not excuses."

He spoke more harshly than he intended. He heard the assassin's steady breathing in the darkness, and he knew he'd made a mistake.

"I mean, can you do it?" Randall continued quietly, trying to soften the blow. "I know it's a big ask."

A hint of a smile crept into Lennon's voice. "When and where?"

"I'm setting up a meeting," Randall replied, exhaling in relief. "It should happen then. At the estate. I don't know the exact date, but it will be within a week, no more. I can get the information to you through Ashkani."

"Do you have a burner phone?"

"Yes."

"We'll use that to communicate on the day."

"Yes, okay."

"We never meet again," Lennon said.

"No. Never."

"Now get the hell out of here, and go back to Washington."

"Wait, there's one more thing," Randall said.

Lennon's voice grew impatient. "What is it?"

"The target. I want to add someone. But it shouldn't change the plan, not really. I'll make sure they're together."

"Who is it?"

"The writer," Randall replied. "We need to get rid of the writer, too. Abbey Laurent."

25

At one in the morning, abbey returned to Washington.

She wasn't driving her own car. Jason had warned her that street cameras would track her license plate, and if anyone was looking for her, they'd know where she was as soon as she entered the government zone. So she'd checked with a House staffer who was away in her home district in Ohio for several weeks. She'd borrowed her friend's Tesla, which also gave her the added benefit of parking privileges on Capitol Hill.

The quiet streets made her footsteps on the sidewalk sound loud. She stayed on Constitution Avenue, passing in and out of the glow of streetlamps. The Capitol dome shone through the park trees. The air was still, with no breath through the leaves, and the temperature had finally turned colder. Every few steps, she stopped, looking over her shoulder. She felt watched, but she saw no one nearby, even when she peered carefully into the shadows.

Paranoia!

This was crazy. But Jason had told her—and so had Alicia Beauvoir—that people would be coming after her. Her apartment was bugged. They were looking for her car.

Abbey had a purse over her shoulder and a compact Glock 19 inside it. Jason had given it to her and trained her in how to use it. She always kept a round chambered, ready to fire simply by pulling the trigger. For her whole life, she'd hated guns, but now she was glad to have protection with her.

What was that?

She stopped again, spinning in a circle. The Senate park loomed beside her, its trees like dark soldiers. Not far away, a figure came and went through the lights, casting a shadow that was swallowed up as he moved away. She told herself this was DC. There was security everywhere all night long. The man was Park Police. He wasn't watching *her*.

Or was he?

Stop it!

Abbey accelerated her pace. At New Jersey Avenue, she walked down the middle of the deserted street, with the park on both sides. There were a few cars in the diagonal spots, and she remembered what Jason had told her about looking for tells that someone was hiding inside. Steam on the glass. Windows cracked open. The barest movement in the chassis as someone shifted. As far as she could tell, the cars were empty. Regardless, she slid her hand into her purse, and her fingers curled around the butt of the Glock.

When she reached Louisiana Avenue, there was more late-night traffic. She was only a block from the Hyatt Regency, and when she got to the hotel, she took the escalator down to the lobby level. There was a man in a business suit lingering in one of the comfortable bar chairs with a phone in his hands. He looked up, saw her, and looked down again. She saw no recognition in his eyes, but she still wondered if he was watching her. Waiting for her to arrive.

Jason had told her during their tradecraft training that a professional *will* look at you in circumstances where it would seem strange not to. But he'll feign disinterest, so stay alert.

Two strangers in a lobby in the middle of the night would naturally glance at each other the way that man did.

Did it mean nothing—or did it mean she was under surveillance?

Abbey hurried to the elevators. The doors opened, and she heaved a sigh of relief as she rushed inside and collapsed against the back wall. She punched the button for the top floor. The doors began to close, but then, out of nowhere, a hand sliced between them and they reopened. Involuntarily, Abbey let out a little scream.

Jason walked inside.

When the doors closed again, she kissed him, and then she slapped him hard.

"You scared the shit out of me!" she protested loudly. "You said you'd be waiting in the room."

"I was following you," Bourne said. "I wanted to make sure you were okay."

"So was that you in the park? I saw someone in the trees."

"No, it wasn't me, but I tagged him, too. He was Park Police. You were fine. But if you felt watched, that's good, because I *was* watching you. Your instincts are kicking in."

"What about the man in the lobby?"

"He's one of mine," Jason said. "He'll be there all night."

Abbey shook her head. "Jesus. This world of yours."

"I know."

They got to Abbey's room, which looked out across New Jersey Avenue toward another hotel. When she went to turn on the lights, Jason intercepted her and told her to leave it dark. She shrugged, then went to the minibar and opened a bottle of wine. She raised the bottle in his direction, but he declined. Not bothering with a glass, she took a swig from the bottle. She went to the hotel window, expecting Jason to stop her, but he didn't. There were a few lights on in the other hotel, but it was the middle of the night. She could see curtains drawn across some windows, but others were open.

"It's the dark rooms you worry about, right?" she murmured. "Watchers don't turn on the lights. They sit in the darkness with their telescopes and binoculars."

"That's right."

"And guns."

"Sometimes."

"Do you think we're being watched?"

"Yes," Jason said.

Abbey turned to him in surprise. "You know that? Who is it?"

"It's Nova," he replied, looking unhappy to tell her. "I asked her to keep an eye on the hotel room."

"*Nova.*"

"She's the best, Abbey. You don't have to like her, but we need her."

"Is she listening, too?"

"No. We put in a motion sensor, but that's all."

Abbey stared at the other hotel. It was probably all in her head, but knowing that Nova was out there, she could feel the fiery intensity of the woman's stare looking back at her. She wondered which of the hotel windows the woman was behind. They'd never met, but that didn't matter. She knew Nova from Jason's descriptions of her. Small, lithe, incredibly sexual. The jet-black hair, the wild tapestry of tattoos. Looking across the street, Abbey struggled to keep her feelings off her face. This was more than jealousy. She disliked Nova—*hated* her—for everything she'd done to Jason and for how much he'd once loved her. And she was sure Nova felt the same way about her.

She took another swig from the bottle of wine and hoisted it in a mock toast for Nova to see. Then she turned away from the window. She was about to close the curtains to give them privacy, but Bourne stopped her.

"It's better if we keep them open," he said. "If there's a problem, Nova can get backup up here quickly. If she can't see inside, then she doesn't know what's going on."

Abbey scowled. "So she watches us all night."

"It's security. Nothing more."

She felt an immature annoyance that her rival was spying on their every move. It made her want to have sex with Jason in full view of the window just to spite her. But she couldn't bring herself to do that.

"The rumor's everywhere," she said. "Everyone's talking about our book and 1342. How will you know if your plan is working?"

"Hopefully, someone will reach out to you," he replied. "That's what we're waiting for."

"Who?"

"I don't know. And I don't know which side they'll come from. It could be someone who wants to see how much you already know. Or it could be someone who wants to tell *you* something."

Abbey frowned. "Alicia says you put a target on our chests."

"Well, she's right. They were already at your apartment today. A team of assassins."

"Oh, my God! Are you *kidding*?"

"No. It may have been the same team that's chasing me because they realized we're together again. Or they could be coming after you because the rumor went public. Either way, the danger is real."

"Well, I knew the score when I agreed," Abbey replied. "What did you do? Did you stop them?"

"I didn't want them to know I'd spotted them, but I got pictures. Nash has the photos. So do Nova and the agent downstairs. They won't get close to us here. You didn't tell anyone where you were staying, did you?"

"No. Nobody knows."

"Good. The room's booked under a false name, but that's not a complete guarantee. They could still track the signal on your phone. It won't get them to this room, but it could get them close to the hotel."

"That's why the precautions? The surveillance?"

"Yes."

"But don't you want me to turn off my phone?" Abbey asked.

"No. If someone reaches out to you, I want them to get through."

"What do we do until that happens?"

"Sleep," Bourne said.

"Because sleep is a weapon," she said, parroting words he'd said to her in the past.

"That's right."

"Well, you sleep. I can't. Not with *her* out there."

They stretched out on the bed, and Abbey stared at the ceiling in silence. She didn't feel tired, but somewhere along the way, her body took over and her mind gave in to exhaustion. Soon she found herself dreaming of being chased. It was a violent dream, and she called for Jason to rescue her, but he wasn't there. The next thing she knew, a trilling bell jolted her awake. Her eyes blinked; her brain was in a fog. There was a terrifying shadow looming above her, and she was scared until she realized Jason was standing over the bed.

Her phone was ringing.

"Jesus, what time is it?" she asked.

"Two."

"Who's calling?"

"Unknown number," he said.

"Should I answer it?"

"Yes."

She took the phone from him. She hesitated only a moment,

then switched it to speaker mode as she answered. "This is Abbey Laurent."

Whoever was calling took a long time to say anything.

"Hello?" Abbey said. "Who's there? Who is this?"

"Is it true?" a man's voice asked. "Are you writing a book about the jet? About 1342?"

"Who are you?" Abbey repeated.

"You're dragging it all up again. Goddamn it! I've spent years trying to forget. But I can't pretend anymore."

"Tell me," Abbey urged him. "If you know something, talk to me."

In the silence, she heard what sounded like crying.

"My wife," the man said finally.

"What about her?"

"Her name was Mallory. Mallory Foster."

"Was she on the plane?"

"No, but she's dead. They killed her."

Abbey glanced at Jason, who nodded at her to go on.

"Tell me your name," she said.

"It's Dennis. Dennis Foster."

"Dennis, what happened to your wife? What happened to Mallory?"

"They said it was an accident. They said she was drunk. But that was bullshit. Mallory hadn't had a drink in years. I knew they were lying. I knew, but I didn't say anything. She told me I should stay quiet. She said otherwise they'd come after me, too. But Mallory knew she was in danger. She said if something happened to her, if there was some kind of accident, I shouldn't believe it."

Dennis Foster choked on his tears. Then, coughing, he went on.

"They murdered her. They murdered Mallory because of that jet."

*

Nova's phone pinged with a text message from Bourne.

Meeting in one hour. Anacostia River Trail. Need backup.

Nova got ready. She was dressed all in black, a Lycra top clinging to her torso and seamless leggings down to her ankles. She strapped on two holsters, one behind her back, one across her stomach below her breasts, both loaded with matching VP9s. Then she shrugged on a loose gray overshirt and buttoned it to hide her weapons. She grabbed a leather bag in one hand, in which she kept backup guns and magazines, plus smoke grenades and flash-bangs. Bourne hadn't told her how wet a reception they could expect.

She called the lobby and asked the valet to get her car. She promised him an extra two hundred dollars if it was there in less than five minutes.

That left her a few seconds to steel her mind for what came next. Before every mission, she gave herself a brief silent time to purge her feelings. To step outside herself. She knew she had a reputation in the intelligence community for being cold. A cold lover. A cold killer. A cold human being. Her Treadstone handlers thought she'd left all of her emotions behind years earlier on a boat in Greece, when her parents had been killed by terrorists while she hid under the bed. But that wasn't true. She still felt everything deep into her soul. She was still Greek. She'd simply learned how to lock that scared little girl in a closet and not let her out until the violence was done.

The seconds ticked away.

She spent that time thinking about Abbey Laurent. She'd seen her before—secretly, in Paris, without Abbey or Jason knowing they were under surveillance. She'd watched them laugh together. Like a voyeur, she'd even watched them make love. She'd watched Abbey take for herself everything that Nova once had, and it had driven her crazy with envy. There had been moments, when Jason was gone and Abbey was alone, that Nova had been tempted to steal across to his Paris apartment to slit Abbey's throat.

In, out, a few seconds was all she needed to kill her. Then Jason would be hers again.

It was *so* tempting. One time, she'd gotten as far as his apartment door before she'd wrestled the devil back inside her head.

Tonight Abbey knew Nova was out there. Bourne had obviously told her. Abbey had stared through the hotel window as if there were some electrical connection between them. There had been something in Abbey's eyes, a kind of jealousy, fury, bitterness, and hatred to match her own. That was the reality between the two of them. They both loved Jason, but only one of them could have him.

Standing there, Nova also felt a premonition in the pit of her gut that Defiance would end with one of them dead. Abbey or herself. Winner take all.

It was time to go.

But before she could leave, there was a knock on her hotel door. Nova spun. In one fluid motion, she had a VP9 in her hand, barrel aimed across the room, her arm rigid. Killers didn't knock, but it was also three in the morning. No one should be here.

"Who is it?" she called harshly.

"Flowers for Miss N."

Nova actually laughed. That was so transparent it made no sense. But she heard the nervous voice on the other side of the door and knew she was dealing with an innocent, not a professional. She went to the side of the door, then checked the peephole and saw a kid who couldn't be more than eighteen. He wore a red uniform and carried a bouquet of white lilies wrapped in plastic.

She opened the door.

"What the fuck?" she demanded. "It's the middle of the night. Do you usually make deliveries in the middle of the night?"

The teenager shook his head. He looked scared. He had greasy blond hair and a face sprinkled with pimples and blackheads. "The man said you'd be up."

"What man?"

"I don't know. He didn't give me a name. But he paid a lot."

Nova took the flowers. She found twenty dollars to hand the kid as a tip. When she closed the door, she unwrapped the package. As she expected, it was just flowers. Anything else, any kind of threat, was too obvious. What bothered her was that someone *knew* she was at this hotel in this room, which shouldn't have been possible. Jason was the only one who knew that, and he damn well wasn't sending her flowers.

That left only one other person with the skills to find her when she didn't want to be found. Nova grabbed the small envelope taped to the vase and opened it. There was a card inside with a handwritten note.

The Iroquois, New York. Two days.

L

26

The moon cast a milky glow over the slow-moving water of the Anacostia River. Tendrils of fog had begun to gather in the lowlands with the damp cool of the early morning. Green fields bordered the river and led toward dark groves of trees, which were blurred by the mist. The park atmosphere felt oddly rural so close to the heart of the city, but not far away, the lights of a few cars sped across an overpass at Highway 1, reminding them of where they were. It was four in the morning, and Jason stood next to Abbey in the middle of a footbridge over the water.

"Will he come?" she asked him.

"Someone will come," Bourne replied. "Whether it's him or not, I don't know. That's the question."

"Why meet here, do you think? I don't like it."

"He says he lives nearby. There are records for a Dennis Foster in Bladensburg. Assuming he is who he says he is, then he's probably familiar with the area."

Abbey went to the bridge railing. "Is *she* here, too?"

Jason knew she meant Nova. "Yes. She's near the trees on the north side. My other man, Grant—he's the one from the hotel lobby—is on the south side."

"Are you expecting trouble?"

Assume your plan will go wrong.

Treadstone.

"The key is to be ready for trouble if it happens," Bourne said. Then he tapped the receiver in his ear as he heard Nova's whispered voice.

"Someone's coming."

"He's on his way," Jason told Abbey. "Stay here."

Bourne walked to the north end of the footbridge. His Sig was ready, but he chose not to keep it in his hand. In the trees fifty yards away, he saw a tiny light go on and off. That was the signal from Nova, telling him where she was. He studied the paved walking trail ahead of him and saw a dark figure separate from the cloud of fog. Whoever it was approached slowly and nervously.

"Do you see anyone else?" he murmured into his microphone.

"Negative," Nova replied.

"Just us," Grant added from the other side of the bridge.

The dark figure took shape as he got closer. Jason saw a man in his forties, tall and thin, with dark hair tied back in a ponytail and wirerimmed glasses. He wore a jacket over a polo shirt and khakis. His hands were empty, but his clothes were loose enough to hide weapons. The man came within twenty feet of Jason, then stopped and removed his glasses and wiped steam from the lenses. He put them back on and seemed to see Bourne for the first time. Obviously scared, the man took a quick step backward on the trail.

"Who are you? I called Abbey Laurent. I told her to come alone!"

"I'm here to keep us all safe."

"I only want to talk to her!" the man insisted.

"You talk to both of us, or you talk to nobody. That's the choice, Dennis."

The man took another look into the fog and darkness. He shook his head with indecision. "I tried to get out of my house without being seen. But I don't know. I think people have been following me. Is that crazy?"

"No, it's not, but if you're right, that means we should wrap this up fast."

"Yeah. Yeah, okay."

Dennis Foster came forward, and Bourne stopped him at the end of the footbridge. He frisked him, then checked the man's Maryland driver's license to confirm who he was. Jason led him onto the bridge, where Abbey was waiting. The three of them stood over the water, but Dennis looked reluctant to break the silence. Jason didn't like the delay. With each minute that passed, Nova and Grant checked in through the receiver in his ear, and for the moment, all was clear. But he didn't know how long that would last.

Abbey sensed Jason's urgency. "You called me, Dennis. Let's not waste time. What do you want to tell me?"

The man's eyes went back and forth between the two of them. "You're really writing a book about the missing jet?"

"I am," she lied, and Bourne was impressed at the smoothness in her voice. She was getting good at lying. "I write fiction, but sometimes fiction is the only way to tell the truth. I want this story to be as close as possible to what *really happened*. We put out the story about the plot to find people like you. People willing to talk."

"I don't have any details. Not really."

"You mentioned your wife. Mallory. You said they killed her. Do you know who they are?"

"No. And I don't know why, either. Except—"

On the bridge, Dennis Foster wet his lips and stared at the trees. The man coughed a few times, then took off his steamy glasses again and wiped them.

Bourne waited. Listened. Watched. His instincts grew alert.

"All clear," Nova reported in his ear.

"All clear," Grant added a moment later.

Abbey put a hand on the man's shoulder. "Dennis, go on. Please."

"The day before the plane disappeared, Mallory got a call in the middle of the night," Dennis finally continued. "I think it was one, maybe two in the morning. She said she had to go. A car came to pick her up."

"Who called her?"

"She couldn't say. I was used to that. Mallory had top secret clearance, so I didn't know much about what she really did. I'm not even sure *she* knew who was on the phone. I gathered that sometimes in her job there were simply code words. Authorizations. If you get a certain code, you don't ask questions, you just do it."

Like Treadstone, Bourne thought.

"How long was she gone?" Abbey asked.

"Three or four hours."

"Did she say where she went?"

"No, but when she came back, she looked shaken. I'd never seen her like that. She was so pale she was almost white. I asked her if she was okay, but she wouldn't talk to me. Instead, she just—she just went to the bathroom and threw up."

"And this was the day before 1342?" Bourne asked.

"It was the day before the news broke. When Mallory got the call, the plane was already in the air. I—I checked on that later. I was curious about the timeline, because it didn't seem like a coincidence. Whoever called Mallory did it like two hours into the flight. Before she got back home, the plane had already veered off course."

Bourne thought about the podcast interview with Billy Janssen.

Those two limos in Rock Creek Park? Whatever that meeting was, it was happening right after the plane took off from Johannesburg. I mean, it had to be within minutes of takeoff.

All connected.

All part of Defiance.

There was a secret meeting in the park in DC. Two limousines. Soon after that, someone called Mallory Foster.

"Did you ask your wife about it?" Bourne said.

"She wouldn't tell me even if she knew," Dennis replied.

"Yes, but you already thought the timing was suspicious. Come on, Dennis, did you ask your wife whether there was a connection between what she did that night and the missing jet? What did she say?"

Dennis looked stricken. "She told me never to talk about that. She said to forget all about it. But after that night, Mallory changed. She was scared. She'd whisper that the house was bugged, that people were following her. She said if something happened to her, I shouldn't say anything about the call that night, because they might hurt me, too. I thought she was paranoid. Except then came the accident, just like she said. I knew it wasn't an accident. But I did what she wanted. I stayed quiet. Until now."

"All clear," Nova reported again.

"How long after the jet disappeared did Mallory's accident happen?" Abbey asked.

"A few weeks."

"What did—" Abbey began, but Bourne stopped her with a hand on her shoulder.

"Wait." He barked into the microphone, "Grant, report."

Bourne heard nothing.

"Grant, *are you there*?"

There was silence on the radio.

Shit!

He knew what was about to happen.

Jason immediately pulled Abbey down to the deck of the

footbridge, and an instant later, gunfire erupted like fireworks around them. In the barrage, a bullet struck Dennis's chest, and blood began to ooze in a dark stain across his polo shirt. Dennis looked down at himself, stunned and disbelieving, unable to move. Another round of gunfire burnt the air, and Bourne took hold of Dennis's belt and dragged him out of the line of fire.

"Nova, cover us ... *now*!"

Flickers of flame burst from the north side of the bridge as Nova returned fire. With the assailants momentarily pinned down, Bourne shouted at Abbey to run. He did the same, half carrying Dennis Foster as he followed behind her, blocking her from the gunfire at their backs. They made it off the bridge, and he could see Nova sprinting toward them from the trees. Her assault had bought them time, but not enough to get away. Dennis couldn't walk on his own. He was seriously wounded.

"Abbey, get out of here," he told her. "Take the path, go *now*."

"And leave you? Fuck that. I'll help you with Dennis."

He didn't have time to argue. Jason took the man's right side, and Abbey took the left, and they walked Dennis up the trail, his feet dragging. Behind them, Nova staked out the bridge, preventing the killers from crossing, but she couldn't fend them off for long without help. There was too much land in the park and not enough time to escape, so Bourne shifted direction and led Abbey into the nearest grove of trees. He settled Dennis down with his back against a tree, and he took Abbey's hands and shoved them into the man's chest. Dennis howled with pain. Blood bubbled around Abbey's fingers.

"Keep the pressure up," he told her. "I'll be back. Do you have a gun?"

"Yes."

"If anyone comes near you, use it."

He ran before she could say anything more. A hail of bullets chased him across the green field, and as the ground exploded in bursts of grass and mud, he dove and rolled. He crawled across the remaining space to take up position at the bridge next to Nova.

"I count four shooters," she told him. "I took a fifth man down."

"How's your ammo?"

"Plenty if it comes to that, but we're outgunned."

"Keep them occupied. When you hear me count you down, fire on *one*."

Bourne rolled away again as bullets screamed over their heads. He used the muzzle flashes on the other side of the river to pinpoint the four men who'd emerged from the trees. Then he slid face-first down the grassy bank into the water without a ripple, using the bridge to shield himself from view. His clothes were soaked, weighing him down. The river wasn't deep, and the current wasn't strong, but the thick mud of the bottom clung to his shoes, so he floated, only his eyes and nose above the water. With the barest kick, he nudged forward, a tiny ripple forming in the river behind his head. At the opposite bank, his body emerged slowly, dark and dripping, like a sea monster coming ashore.

He unholstered his Sig and threaded a suppressor. Crouching, he took silent footsteps up the rocks, then drew a bead on one of the killers, who was stretched on his stomach in the field no more than thirty feet away. Under the moon, the man's face was visible in a sheen of white. Bourne braced himself on the bridge span, then whispered into the microphone.

"Three ... two ... *one*."

Bourne and Nova fired simultaneously. He took one low, muffled shot; she unleashed a torrent, covering the noise of his gun. His lone bullet tunneled into the forehead of the killer. The others around the man didn't realize he was down.

Bourne dropped back to the ground. He slithered like a

snake through the wet grass, away from the three men, who were closing on the bridge. As he neared the trees, clammy fog descended on him, keeping him invisible. Shifting direction, he worked his way behind the team of killers and took aim at the nearest one.

"Three ... two ... *one*."

Again they fired simultaneously. His aim was true, but this time, one of the other killers noticed the man falling and shouted a warning to his partner. The two retrained their aim, forcing Bourne to zigzag toward the trees. Their semiautomatic rifle fire chased him and then spilled him off his feet with a round that seared his calf. Jason fell, rolled, and fired; then he rolled and fired again. His wild shots had no chance in the fog, and he found himself in the center of fire from two directions as the assassins trained their weapons on him. The bullets kicked up dirt as they closed on his body.

He was unprotected in the middle of the grass. There was no way out and nowhere to go.

Then, through the fog's milky cloud, Nova charged across the bridge with a guttural shout. It was two on two now. One of the assassins turned to exchange fire with Nova, and the other kept his rifle on Bourne, who rolled away until he found cover behind a tree. The rifle fire hammered the bark and filled the air with dust.

Over the thunder, he heard Nova's voice in his ear.

"Bang."

Jason knew what was coming next. He crouched, covered his ears, and closed his eyes, but he could still see the flash of light and feel the earthquake of the flash-bang. In the next instant, he spun from behind the tree, firing. The nearest killer was dizzy, and Bourne mowed him down with two shots. The second, closest to Nova, was coming off his knees, but Nova was on her back, still disoriented. Jason fired but missed in the fog and darkness. He ran, then cursed as he pulled the trigger again and found himself with an empty magazine. The last killer staggered toward Nova. Bourne leaped as the man raised his gun arm, and they collided as the gun went off. Intertwined, they landed hard, and Bourne's hands viciously twisted the man's head until he heard the ugly snap of bone cracking. The man was still gasping, dying, as Jason kicked away the rifle and crawled to Nova.

She was already pushing herself up. "I'm fine, go, go!"

Bourne ran across the bridge. Fog had consumed the river, turning the night into a dense cloud. He couldn't see in front of him, and the milky dampness left him struggling to find the trees. He didn't know which way he was heading, but when he called Abbey's name, he heard her voice from only a few feet away. The grove at the fringe of the field took shape, and as he got closer, he saw Abbey with her Glock in her hands, just as he'd told her. Even realizing it was him, she seemed unable to lower her arms, and he had to bend her elbows and then carefully peel the pistol from her fingers.

"We're okay," he said. "How's Dennis?"

Abbey shook her head mutely, unable to speak. Bourne swore. He checked the body, but Abbey was right. Dennis Foster was dead.

"We need to go," he told her. "We can't be found here."

Wearily, Abbey nodded and got to her feet. He could see that her hands and clothes were covered in blood where she'd tried to keep Dennis alive. They limped through the fog arm in arm, Bourne favoring the leg where the bullet had wounded his calf. As they neared the bridge, the white cloud lifted enough that Nova was clearly visible in the moonlight, watching them go. She couldn't have been more than twenty feet away. Jason felt Abbey tense, and he watched the two of them study each other, both frozen where they were.

The spy and the writer. Two women he'd loved.

Neither said a word.

Then the fog blew down over them again, and Nova was gone. He heard the soft thud of her footsteps running away.

He took Abbey down the trail that led out of the park.

"I'm sorry about Dennis," Jason said.

She didn't reply.

"Was he able to tell you anything more?"

Abbey's arm tightened around his waist. She inhaled sharply, then seemed to fight off her shock. "He did, but I don't know what to make of it."

"What did he say?"

They didn't slow down. There was no time to slow down.

"I asked him about Mallory," Abbey said, her voice regaining its strength. "I wanted to know what she did for the government."

"What did he say?"

"He said she was a scientist."

"Something to do with aeronautics?" Bourne asked.

She took a long time to answer him. "No. That's what I thought he'd say, but no. Mallory didn't know anything about jets or engineering."

Bourne was puzzled. "Then what did she do?"

"She was a virologist. Infectious diseases. Her specialty was bioweapons."

27

Bourne watched the black town car pull off Constitution Avenue across from the Washington Monument. He broke from the crowd of tourists and crossed the sidewalk toward the curb. The limo's back door opened and he climbed inside, shutting the door behind him. Just as quickly as the car had stopped, the vehicle accelerated into traffic again.

Holly Schultz was waiting in the backseat. So was her yellow Lab, Sugar, who whimpered with delight when she saw Bourne. Holly gave the dog a tap, and Sugar scrambled across the limo to lick Jason's face. After a few seconds, Holly snapped her fingers and Sugar returned to her original position, laying her head on a quilted towel that protected Holly's suit from yellow dog hair.

"I got your message," Holly said.

Jason settled into the backseat and watched the National Mall passing beside them. "Then you know what I've found so far. Defiance was about Flight 1342."

"So it seems."

"Did you already know that?"

She shook her head. "No, I was in the dark about it as much as you. Although, back then, the timing of the operation did make me wonder. The disappearance of the jet was still big news at that point. But I concluded it was safer not to indulge my curiosity by asking too many questions."

"Who would benefit from a cover-up?" Bourne asked.

"That depends on what really happened to the jet. I have no information that would point you to anyone in particular. As I told you, I got instructions to provide a list of Treadstone agents who were available for a mission. My orders came from Vic Sorrento, but Vic's dead. And he certainly wasn't the one calling the shots."

Bourne frowned. "What about Mallory Foster? Were you able to find out anything more about her?"

"Yes, she's an interesting case," Holly replied. "Someone tried to turn her into a nonperson, but I was able to connect the dots based on her accident. Mallory Foster was just a cover identity, of course. If her husband knew her area of research—and based on what you told me, he did—then she violated half a dozen federal laws simply by telling him. But it did help me find out who she was. Her real name was Letitia Brown. She was one of our foremost experts on infectious diseases and genetically modified bioweapons. She had a very distinguished résumé, including a couple of UN fact-finding missions investigating genocide in Somalia and Syria. I read her assessments regarding the possibility of ISIS creating highly transmissible viruses with enhanced fatality rates. Scary stuff."

"So what would Mallory—or Letitia—have to do with 1342?" Bourne asked.

Holly shrugged, as if contemplating the worst horrors of the world meant very little to her. "I can think of only one reason, can't you? Someone thought there was a plague on board that flight."

"Is that possible? Could a virus have killed everyone on the plane?"

"Why not? The consensus seems to be that the plane flew on for a long while before crashing, but there could be various explanations for that. Remember what happened to that golfer years ago? No one was alive on board, but his plane continued to fly until it ran out of fuel. With as little evidence as we have, we can't be sure what was really going on aboard 1342. It's possible the pilot knew what was happening—maybe passengers were already dying—and he opted to take the plane down at a point where wreckage couldn't be recovered and no land population was at risk."

"Without telling anyone what was going on?" Bourne asked.

"Perhaps he did, and the record's been covered up. There are plenty of people in Washington, from the White House to Congress to the Pentagon, who would conclude that information like that was too sensitive to disclose."

Bourne hissed in disgust. "Even if it meant hiding the truth behind the deaths of American children? There was a church choir group on that flight, right? Dozens of teenagers."

"Especially then," Holly replied, with a tut-tut in her voice that told him he was being naïve.

And Jason knew he was. He stared out the car window at the government buildings around them, all of these white stone monuments to secrecy and power. No one wanted to know what really went on behind the walls. No one wanted to hear about the compromises that had to be made. The sacrifices. The brutal choices.

He thought about what Abbey had said to him. *Jesus. This world of yours.*

"Who killed Mallory Foster?" Bourne asked. "Which Treadstone agent did the hit?"

"Cain, I told you, I provided a list of agents and authorizations," Holly snapped impatiently. "That's all. I wasn't part of Defiance. I didn't make any of the assignments, and I don't know who did. That trail went cold years ago. There's no way for me to know who did what."

He knew she was lying this time. Hiding the truth.

"The accident that killed Mallory Foster happened in DC," he reminded her. "Are you really saying you don't know which Treadstone agents were in Washington at the time? But that doesn't matter. I'm only interested in one agent, and I know you were already watching him. You told me you were."

Holly frowned and said nothing.

"Abel!" Bourne continued. "Abel was on the Defiance list. You told me you'd been surveilling him for months, because you were afraid he was passing information to the Russians. So you knew where he was throughout the mission. Was he in Washington when Mallory Foster was killed?"

Holly stiffened. Sugar growled a little, sensing the tension in the car. "All right. Yes, Abel was in DC during that period. So were at least three other agents on the Defiance list, but you're correct. It seems likely that Abel did the hit on Mallory Foster. On the night of her accident, he lost my men using a series of clearance maneuvers. He's good at that, just like you. We didn't pick him up again until he returned to his apartment the following morning."

"And before he killed her, he got information out of her," Jason concluded.

"That's certainly possible."

"But you knew nothing about it."

"That's right. I didn't know any of this until you told me about Mallory's death."

He tried to penetrate the mask that Holly always wore. "Let's say I believe you. One thing still doesn't make sense to me. Why send Abel on the Defiance mission? If you didn't trust him, if you thought he was a Russian spy, why put him on the list?" Then he thought about it and answered his own question. "You added him *because* you had him under surveillance. You wanted a back door to figure out what the mission was all about."

Holly nodded. "I don't like having my people co-opted and not knowing why. I wanted information without being too obvious about it. But like I told you, Abel must have smelled the tail. I never found out what he was really up to."

Bourne stared at Holly across the car. "What else?"

"I'm sorry?"

"You know something more. This isn't the time to hold out on me, Holly."

"All right. It didn't seem to have any special significance at the time. I thought it was routine, not necessarily connected to Defiance. But maybe I was wrong. Immediately after what we now think was the hit on Mallory Foster, Abel flew to New York."

"Why?"

"He'd been cultivating a foreign source there for some time. Cultivating in Abel's usual way—as a lover. We knew about it. He'd filed reports about her. Her information had proved useful to us, so I was happy to see him continue the relationship. Of course, in retrospect, he probably shared it all with the Russians, too, given that we think Abel was already a double agent."

"Who was the source?"

"A low-level secretary in the Iranian UN delegation," Holly told him. "She'd recently married one of their senior ministers. As such, she was in a position to hear a lot of sensitive government secrets."

Bourne felt the pieces coming together.

Iran!

The trail kept leading back to Iran. The Russians had been convinced that the Iranians were involved in the disappearance of 1342. And immediately after the murder of Mallory Foster,

Abel had flown to New York to gather intel from his best-placed source on Iranian clandestine operations.

That was no accident. No coincidence. It all fit together. And yet too much was still missing.

"Who is she?" Bourne asked. "This source Lennon had at the UN. What's her name?"

"Nazanin."

"I need to see her."

Holly shook her head. "Alas, that will be difficult. Her body was pulled out of the Hudson a few days ago."

Bourne felt the door slamming in his face. A few *days*! He'd been that close!

Another murder. Another loose end tied off. One by one, someone was cutting all the threads that led back to Defiance.

Except one.

The one place left to hunt for the truth was with a man who wanted him dead. A man he'd chased around the world for two years. A man whose identity he'd taken for himself as he escaped from South Ossetia.

Abel. Lennon.

The original Jason Bourne.

28

When she arrived in New York, Nova stayed in her room at the Iroquois Hotel, waiting for Lennon to make contact with her. Instead, the entire day passed, and no one did. There were no phone calls, no messages, no knocks at the door, no deliveries of flowers. He had to know she was there, so why was he making her wait?

But she knew. Lennon was doing what he always did. Playing with her head. Driving her crazy. Torturing her the way he had two years ago.

She still woke up in a sweat sometimes, reliving the night when he'd kidnapped her and bound her to a wall. She could hear his voice in her ear and feel his hands exploring her body. He seemed to know her better than she knew herself, knew just how to evade her defenses and get inside her head. And all along, he'd played a bizarre soundtrack to her surrender, the same Beatles song booming through hidden speakers. "Strawberry Fields Forever." He'd used that song to crack through the wall she'd built to keep out her pain and reach out to the little girl hiding under the bed while her parents were murdered.

In the end, he'd won. He'd broken her. He'd made her

betray Jason. And ever since, she and Lennon had shared a psychic connection that she couldn't seem to sever. It was always with her, that voice in her head, that song on repeat in her mind. There were nights when she swore he actually came to her room, like a drug-induced dream. And yet in the morning she woke up alone.

It disgusted her to admit that she missed him. She needed him.

By evening, she couldn't wait in the hotel room anymore. She put on a black dress and went downstairs to the bar, a speakeasy called Lantern's Keep. It had a Sinatra vibe, like a moody, low-lit getaway for gangsters to meet their girls. Dark wood columns adorned the walls, and the wooden floor made her high heels tap like machine-gun fire. She chose a stone table in the corner, near a painting that reminded her of a Degas dancer. She ordered a multicolored martini and drank it alone. Then another.

It occurred to her that she was falling apart.

When the waitress brought her fourth drink, she heard music from somewhere. The woman was leaning over to put the cocktail in front of her, and Nova caught a few strains of a song. It was so low and muffled that it was almost impossible to hear, but the music made her sweat. Her memories blew up. She was tied to the wall again.

"Strawberry Fields Forever."

"Did you hear that?" Nova asked.

The waitress looked at her. "Hear what, doll?"

"That song."

"Sorry, I didn't hear a thing."

Nova's pulse raced. Her gaze went from table to table. The bar was crowded with well-dressed New York couples engaged in hushed conversations, the nightly seductions under way. She checked every man's face, knowing she was dealing with a master of disguise. Was he here? If he was, would she recognize him? Most of the men met her stare and sent an invitation back, even those who were with other women. It was always that way. She was Nova. She could have any man here.

But was one of them *Lennon*?

She heard it *again*!

Just a snippet of the lyrics about living with eyes closed. And then again, about nothing being real. The chorus, forever, forever, forever.

Where is it coming from?

Was she going mad?

No one else reacted; no one looked around; no one seemed to hear it. Was he using a directional speaker, shooting the sound only at her?

Nova blinked rapidly and felt dizzy. Her fists tightened. Was it the drink? Had he put something in the drink? She scraped the chair back and got up suddenly from the table. She threw money on the table, then walked out, feeling as if she were now being watched by everyone in the bar. Instead of going back to her room, she headed out of the hotel onto 44th Street, where the night air was cool. She had no coat, and she shivered, but she walked along the deserted sidewalk to clear her head.

Automatically, her eyes checked the cars and doorways. She saw no one in the darkness.

Then she heard it again.

The fucking *Beatles*! The same song, the same John Lennon voice singing the John Lennon lyrics. This wasn't her imagination. She stopped on the street, trying to isolate the source of the music.

It was coming from a construction site across the street.

Scaffolding clung like an Erector set to the stone wall of an apartment building that was being gutted and renovated. A fine mesh net hung from the roof to the sidewalk. Nova crossed the street and found that the plywood door leading to the interior had been opened, a heavy padlock dangling from a latch. Inside, she saw nothing but shadows, but she heard the music beckoning her to enter.

Nova reached under her skirt, where she had her Glock holstered to her thigh. She took it in her hand. Did Lennon think she was a fool? Did he think he could play games with her head and she'd forget to bring her gun wherever she went?

She entered the building, then swung the wooden door shut behind her. The darkness was complete; it was impossible to see. A fine plaster dust coated the floor and hung in the air, and she coughed. She took her phone from her purse and switched on the flashlight, which provided a dim light so she could walk. The ground floor had been stripped down to its concrete walls and columns, and it was empty except for the tools the construction crew had left behind. A rat scurried away when it was exposed by her light.

The song came from above her.

Near the back of the building, steps led to the higher floors. Nova picked her way to the stairs and climbed carefully in her heels. The music got louder. When she reached the third floor, she heard the song clearly behind the stairwell door, and she pushed it open. The flashlight wasn't strong enough to illuminate more than a few feet in front of her. She kicked off her heels, then walked toward the middle of the building. There was sharp debris under her feet—rocks, screws, nails—but she didn't care. The heels slowed her down.

Near the wall facing the street, in an open window frame that had once held glass, she found wireless speakers playing the song, broadcasting it to the nighttime street below her. A cool breeze blew inside and rustled her hair. With a disgusted flick of her hand, she pushed the speakers off the ledge. They crashed onto the wooden floor of the scaffolding below her, and the music came to an abrupt halt.

In the sudden silence, she realized she wasn't alone. Someone was standing right behind her now. She spun, aiming the Glock, shining the light at whoever was there. She expected to see *him*. Lennon. How would he look this time? Would he be wearing a disguise, or would he let her see the man behind the mask?

She hated how she felt. Scared. Excited.

But it wasn't Lennon. It wasn't a man at all. A small, short teenager—even shorter than Nova—stood ten feet away, pointing a gun at her. The Russian Grach looked huge in the girl's tiny hands. Nova's flashlight shined on a mop of turquoise bangs and reflected in round metal glasses. The girl wore a short-sleeved tie-dyed T-shirt, black drainpipe jeans, and yellow high-top sneakers. In the glow of the flashlight, her skin was pale white, except for a tattoo creeping from her elbow toward her shoulder. Nova knew tattoos, and with a quick, automatic glance, she took note of two things.

First, the design showed a liberty or death flag held in place by a shaft that was actually an old M1 carbine.

And second, the tattoo was fake.

"Who the fuck are you?" Nova demanded.

"I'm Yoko."

Nova gave her a dismissive sneer. "You mean the latest Yoko, don't you? You're part of an endangered species, little girl. Yokos come and Yokos go. I've killed several of them myself."

"Well, you won't kill me," the girl snapped. "But maybe I'll get to kill you ... *Nova*."

"Don't waste my time with empty threats. Where's Lennon?"

"He sent me."

"Go back and tell him I don't talk to little girls."

"You wanted a meeting, you got a meeting. What do you want?"

"I only talk to Lennon," Nova insisted.

A sly grin crossed Yoko's face as she heard the urgency in Nova's voice. "Jesus. He was right about you."

"About what?"

"You're obsessed with him. He's in your head. You want him so bad you can taste it."

"Fuck off."

But the girl with the gun was right. Nova hated to admit it, but she was disappointed—*humiliated*—that Lennon had sent someone else, that he hadn't come to see her himself. She was so sure he would. Bourne had insisted that Lennon would never show up, but she'd been supremely confident that he would come when she called. But Yoko was here instead, and that sent her a message. Lennon was the one in control. He still held all the power over her.

Yoko stepped forward, their two guns practically touching. "Do you want to know what it's like to sleep with him? I fuck him all the time. I'll bet that makes you jealous."

Nova's fist squeezed shut. She spat the words at her. "Just go tell him that Cain and Nova want a deal."

"What kind of deal?"

"He tells us about Defiance. We call a truce. Cain stops hunting him."

"Lennon's not afraid of Cain. Just like I'm not afraid of you."

Nova's anger was like pent-up pressure hunting for a release. She wanted to teach this punk kid a lesson.

"Lennon should be afraid of Cain. And you should definitely be afraid of me, little girl."

Nova yanked up the hem of her short skirt and calmly reholstered her Glock on the inside of her thigh. Yoko hesitated, thrown off-balance by Nova's odd surrender. In the next instant, Nova unsheathed a four-inch ice pick from the thigh holster and impaled it in Yoko's wrist from the veins all the way through to the other side until it poked out like a bloody spike. The girl never saw it coming. As Yoko screamed, Nova peeled away the Grach and struck it backhanded across her face, breaking the girl's nose. Then she grabbed her jeans at the belt and pulled her forward, dizzying her with a blow of forehead against forehead, bone to bone. Nearly unconscious, Yoko slumped, knees buckling, and Nova threw the girl off her feet and followed her down to the ground. With one knee on her skinny chest, Nova crammed the Grach into the girl's open mouth, hearing the crack of chipped teeth and a gurgle of vomit as Yoko gagged deep in her throat.

"Do—not—fuck with me!" Nova told her. "Now, you crawl back to Lennon and tell him the next time I call, he better show up himself instead of sending *the help*."

She yanked out the gun and hit the girl again, across the skull this time, and Yoko's eyes rolled back in her head as she fell unconscious. Nova got to her feet, swaying a little, and brushed herself off. It took all of her self-control not to pull the trigger, but she needed Yoko alive. She looked around the dark, dusty floor of the construction zone and wondered if Lennon was watching, if he'd seen the whole thing.

If she hunted in the shadows, would she find a night-vision camera?

It didn't matter. She called out to him anyway.

"I'm serious about the deal, Lennon. I meant what I said. Give us Defiance, and you're free. Otherwise, Cain will kill you."

When Nova got back to her hotel room, Bourne was waiting. He sat in the corner, his Sig in his lap, a crack of city light shining on his face through the curtains. He noted the blood on her dress.

"Are you okay?"

"Fine." Casually, she pulled the dress over her head. She wore nothing underneath except the gun holster, which she untied and dropped heavily on the hotel bed. She noted with satisfaction that his eyes took notice of her naked body, moving from tattoo to tattoo, lingering on her breasts.

"You were right. Lennon didn't come."

Bourne shrugged. "Who was it?"

"The new Yoko. A fucking teenager."

"And?"

"I taught her a lesson."

"Hard or soft?"

"Hard, but not enough that she won't recover."

"It's not smart to make enemies like that, Nova," Bourne said.

"Well, I guess I just don't have your self-control, Jason."

"Did you plant the tracker?" he asked.

Nova gave him an annoyed look. "Yes, of course I planted the tracker. It's inside the flap of one of her sneakers. So now we follow her and let her lead us straight to Lennon."

29

The tracker showed Yoko retreating to a hotel eight blocks away, where she stayed overnight. The next morning, Jason was waiting across the street to follow her on foot.

The app on his phone provided a red dot to monitor her movements, but the streets were crowded enough that he allowed himself to stay within visual range. The girl's Easter egg–blue hair made her easy to spot, and Jason didn't think she was likely to recognize him. Her first visit was to a doctor's clinic and then to a dentist's office to repair some of the damage to her wrist, nose, and mouth. Nova hadn't been lying about the beatdown she'd delivered. Yoko's face was a rainbow of colors.

"Any sign she knows you're on her trail?" Nova asked through the radio. She was circling the area in a Toyota SUV.

"No."

"What about Lennon?"

"No sign of him yet."

After her medical appointments, Yoko took an outdoor table at a tapas restaurant on Spring Street. Bourne watched from the corner of Broadway. The girl was alert, carefully observing the people around her. A quick look at her eyes made Bourne realize that this Yoko was much more intelligent and capable than Nova realized. She may have gotten a lucky drop on the girl once, but there was a reason this teenager had become Lennon's number two agent. When her eyes brushed across Bourne on the street, she took no apparent notice of him, but he knew she'd registered him as someone to watch. Rather than risk discovery, Jason backed out of sight and relied on the remote tracker on his phone.

He wouldn't let her see him again. She'd remember his face.

Forty-five minutes later, when she was done with lunch, Yoko was on the move again. He gave her a two-block head start, then followed. The girl used smart tradecraft, changing direction randomly, crossing the street without warning, backtracking on her route, and making regular stops to clear the area behind her. Again, despite her age, she was obviously a pro. Without electronic surveillance in place, she would have lost him or spotted him.

Her evasive maneuvers lasted an hour. When Yoko seemed satisfied that she wasn't being followed, she turned into a parking garage between Houston and Bleecker. Bourne radioed Nova to pick him up, and from inside Nova's black Highlander, he monitored the exit with binoculars. Ten minutes later, he caught a flash of the girl's blue hair as she left the garage. She was behind the wheel of a beat-up Ford Fusion.

It was midafternoon. Yoko led them west into the Holland Tunnel and then continued through Jersey City to Newark, where she merged onto the southbound 95. The signal on the tracker was strong, and Nova let the distance between the two vehicles increase to almost half a mile. Yoko stayed on the interstate for the next two hours, heading through New Jersey and passing south of Philadelphia and Wilmington.

Then, shortly after she crossed into Maryland, the tracker showed Yoko turning off the freeway. She took a two-lane highway through the town of North East and followed the river southward for several miles. When the map showed her passing a small inlet, he saw the movement of the red dot freeze.

"She's stopped."

Nova slowed. A couple of minutes later, they approached a yacht harbor where dozens of motorboats and sailboats bobbed in the quiet water. She pulled onto the dirt shoulder of the road, and Bourne checked the map. According to the tracker, Yoko was close, but he didn't see the Fusion parked near the pier.

"There it is," Nova said.

She pointed past the harbor to a shallow slope of country meadow that led to a rambler farmhouse with red wooden siding. The house was surrounded by a weathered picket fence and set against a dense stand of trees in back. Bourne spotted the Fusion parked in the driveway near the house. He saw Yoko climbing out of the car. With her hands on her hips, she took a careful look around the area, but she didn't appear to notice the Highlander parked on the other side of the harbor. Then she turned and walked up to the front door.

The girl used a key and disappeared inside.

Bourne studied the house. It looked ordinary, but it *wasn't* ordinary. The windows had an odd, dark cast, and he suspected the glass had been taped or painted black on the inside. He noted surveillance cameras near the roofline angled to cover every approach. If someone got near the house, whoever was inside would know it. He also spotted the gleam of late-afternoon sunlight reflecting on the fender of a pickup truck parked between the house and a barn near the trees.

Someone else was already inside the house, waiting for Yoko to arrive.

"Lennon's in there," he concluded.

"This looks like a staging ground," Nova said.

"Count on it," Jason agreed. "He's getting ready for a hit."

Bourne saw no other vehicles near the house and no evidence of guards outside. The whole area felt strangely still, almost deserted. There was no wind in the trees or on the calm water, and even the sailboats docked in the harbor barely swayed. As peaceful as it was, Bourne didn't like it. Something felt wrong. Yoko had done exactly what he wanted; she'd led them to Lennon. But he'd learned never to underestimate the assassin.

"What do you want to do?" Nova asked.

"Drive past the house. As soon as we're out of sight, pull off the road. We'll come in through the trees in back."

Nova steered the Highlander onto the highway. She continued past the boat harbor up a shallow hill, and as they passed the farmhouse on the other side of the fields, Bourne took another look to see if there were guards monitoring the area. He saw no one. A few seconds later, when the house disappeared from view, Nova bumped the SUV off the road and drove across soft grass into the woods. She parked, and they both got out. Nova headed for the rear of the truck to grab their weapons, but Jason held up a hand, stopping her. He listened, still expecting a trap.

There was nothing.

Sometimes paranoia is just paranoia.

Treadstone.

They armed themselves with Black Rain Spec15 rifles, which Nova had acquired for them in New York. If they encountered resistance, it would be heavy, and he wanted them prepared. And yet, as they made their way silently through the woods, he saw no signs of a welcome party. No guards. No trip wires. Ahead of them, not even a hundred yards away, he spotted the shadows of the barn and the farmhouse. The quiet of the place had an ominous feel.

He checked the tracker again. Yoko was inside, but she

wasn't moving. The red dot stayed fixed in place somewhere in the middle of the house.

What's going on?

They used the barn to cover their approach. Bourne took one side; Nova took the other. Near the corner of the barn, he deployed a snake camera attached to his phone to surveil the rear of the farmhouse. The back windows, like the ones in front, had been taped over on the interior of the glass. So had the back door. He saw four spy cameras mounted along the soffit, creating an overlapping view of the back of the property. There was no way to cross the short stretch of green grass between the barn and the house unseen.

"Take out the cameras," he murmured into the radio.

They timed their assault, each pivoting around a corner of the barn with their rifles propped against their shoulders. With two pulls of the trigger and two loud snaps, Bourne took out two of the cameras, and Nova did the same. Then they pivoted back under cover. If Lennon was watching from inside the house, he was blind now—but he knew he was under attack. They couldn't allow him time to regroup.

"*Go.*"

Bourne stormed across the grass. He focused on the house's back door, which was located up four steps in the middle of a white porch. As he neared the porch, he swung the rifle toward the nearest back window and fired several shots that shattered the glass. To his right, Nova did the same. He wanted a diversion; he wanted Lennon to think they were coming through the windows. Then he charged up the porch steps, firing at the hinges and flattening the door with the weight of his shoulder. He crashed inside the house, hit the floor and rolled left, and came up firing in a semicircle. His aim was low; he wanted to wound, not kill. Nova entered behind him and did the same on the right side of the house.

When the dust and smoke cleared, he saw in the shadows of the broken windows that the house was empty.

Empty!

There was no furniture. No maps. No weapons. No equipment. If this had been a staging area, it had been cleared out.

So why had Yoko come here?

He checked the tracker. It showed that she was still in the house. Based on the layout, she was at the end of the hallway in front of them, in a bedroom behind a closed door.

But it made no sense.

With a hand signal, he motioned Nova into action, and they riddled the closed bedroom door with a hail of bullets. Then they charged down the corridor and into the bedroom, only to find that it was empty like the rest of the house.

Almost empty.

He spotted the green dot of a camera in a corner of the ceiling. They were being watched. Remotely, from somewhere else, *not* from inside the house. Quickly, he lifted his rifle, fired one shot, and disabled it. The bedroom had two windows, but both had been painted over, leaving no light to come inside. In the darkness, he grabbed a penlight and shined it around the bedroom. Nova did the same, and their crisscrossed beams came together in the middle of the floor.

"Fuck," she hissed.

The tracker she'd planted on Yoko sat in the middle of the floor.

"She knew," Bourne said. "She knew we were following her all along. She went in the front of the house and right out the back, where we couldn't see her."

"Why?"

"To get us here. To—"

Suddenly, Bourne understood.

"Run!"

Nova hadn't grasped the danger yet. He grabbed her by the arm and bodily threw her out of the bedroom in front of him. She lost her balance, then corrected herself and skidded down the hallway. Now she knew; they both knew. Jason followed, steps behind her. They'd almost reached the back of the house when he heard a shrill ringing from the bedroom.

They'd run out of time.

"Down down down!" he shouted.

He dove onto Nova's back and took her to the floor and covered her with his body. In the bedroom, the ringing of a cell phone completed the circuit on an IED, and the interior of the house exploded. A concussion wave washed over him, hammering his face into the floor. Blood poured from his nose. The walls disintegrated into plaster and powder; all the windows shattered outward; the ceiling collapsed like rain around them. Smoke filled his lungs, and he felt the heat of fire on his skin. The back door was only a few feet away. As the house disintegrated, he lurched to his feet, pulling Nova with him and staggering into the open air. They stumbled down the steps, then collapsed dizzily as a second explosion pitched them forward into the grass.

Bourne rolled onto his back. His gaze struggled to focus as the world did somersaults. The entire house was burning, flames spitting like dragons through the broken windows, ash floating into the trees. The walls buckled and bowed, collapsing in a fountain of sparks. Some landed on his arms like hot, stabbing needles. Next to him, Nova's face was streaked with charcoal, and tears leaked from her stinging eyes.

"Come on," he told her urgently. "Quick. Let's go."

They couldn't stay here. They had to get away, get back to the Highlander, get out of the area. He struggled to his feet and helped Nova up. Behind them, flames had already arced over their heads like shooting stars onto the roof of the barn, and it had begun to burn. The nearest trees were on fire, too.

"Come on," he said again.

Nova held his hand, and he led her away, both of them limping. Smoke lingered in a choking cloud around them, and they bent over and kept their arms over their faces as they retreated into the woods.

From a sleek speedboat bobbing in the north east river, Lennon watched them go. Even through the binoculars, they were nothing but two tiny figures disappearing into a gray fog. But they were alive. The bomb had gone off as planned, but it had failed to kill them. Once again, Cain had slipped through his fingers.

Next to him, Yoko hissed in disgust. "Lucky bitch."

Lennon shrugged. "There's no such thing as luck. They won, we lost."

"Just as well," Yoko retorted. "Next time I want to be face-to-face with her. Do you see what she *did*? Look at me!"

Lennon traced the bruises on Yoko's face, and then he twisted her wrist and put his thumb hard on the wound where the spike had punctured through flesh and bone. She winced with pain. "You'll heal, my dear. But I told you, never act out of revenge. Revenge makes you careless."

"You're right. I'm sorry."

He patted her cheek. "Good."

"What do we do now? How do we go after them?"

Lennon put away the binoculars in a cabinet on the speedboat. He sat on the white leather chair behind the boat's wheel and slipped sunglasses over his face as he eyed the calm water. "We don't have to go after them. Trust me, Cain and Nova will be coming after us. We'll get another chance with them sooner or later. In the meantime, we have other priorities. We have to introduce ourselves to our new friend."

Yoko smiled. "And his Lonely Hearts Club Band?"

"Exactly."

Lennon shoved the silver throttle forward to full. The engine growled, and the boat rose high in the water and then shot southward down the river.

30

Every few minutes, the thunder of a navy super hornet taking off from NAS Pax River made the bar shudder wildly, as if a tornado were about to come through the walls. The wooden floor shook, the glasses rattled, and the neon lights of the beer signs flickered. Louie, the owner, kept a heavy bottle of Russian vodka on a shelf behind the bar, with an empty fighter pilot's helmet slung below it. If the vibrations of a Hornet pitched the bottle into the helmet, then everyone drank shots for free until the vodka was gone.

That night, as Walter Pepper heard the roar of a jet rocketing into the sky, he lifted his mug in a toast and bumped it against the glass of his best friend, Jake DeRusha.

"Fuck, yeah!" Walter growled as the fighter stormed overhead, turning east with a burst of speed toward the Atlantic. His beer sloshed over the rim, and foam ran across his fingers. "Go kick some commie ass!"

"Fuck, yeah!" Jake agreed loudly.

The two men sat at the end of the bar near the dartboards and pool tables. That was where they always sat. It was tradition. Everyone knew to leave those stools open, even on crowded Friday nights, because sooner or later Walter and

Jake would show up and expect their usual seats. They'd order thirty-two-ounce mugs of MGD, flirt with the girls, and yell at the television sets over the bar. The regulars knew to leave them alone.

Walter and Jake had grown up in the town of Bramwell, West Virginia, population three hundred. Walter was short and wiry; Jake was tall and ripped. They were childhood next-door neighbors who'd hunted wild turkeys together, gone to summer Bible camp together, and discovered porn and Jenna Jameson together on a computer belonging to Jake's brother. When they got out of high school, they'd joined the Marines together, too. They'd both dreamed of storming beaches and both wound up replacing parts on jet engines instead. They'd been assigned to the Marine Aviation Detachment at Pax River, and they'd expected to stay Marines until it was time to collect their pensions.

And then, for Walter, it had all gone to shit.

A year ago, he got word from the MAD's sergeant major that he was being involuntarily separated from the Corps. Just like that. It blew him away. According to his superior, Walter talked too much about what leftists were doing to America and to white people in particular, and that included making slurs about the commander in chief. His "extremist views"—that was what Sergeant Major Crane called them—were making people on the base uncomfortable, and the Corps wanted him gone.

Walter couldn't believe it. Fourteen years of service, fourteen years of patriotism and loyalty, and goodbye, Pepper. So now he was stuck driving a cab. All because he loved his country.

He didn't blame Sergeant Major Crane. He didn't even blame the Marines. It was the politicians in Washington who were trying to turn the military into a bunch of pussies. That was what people needed to understand. Jake had warned him years ago that he needed to learn how to keep his mouth shut, but Walter believed in his First Amendment right to say whatever the fuck he wanted. Now that he was Walter Pepper, civilian taxi driver, he'd been doing just that. His letters to the worthless assholes in DC had earned him half a dozen visits from the FBI, one from the Secret Service, and two restraining orders from members of Congress. Walter kept them framed on his wall like medals.

Fuck all of them. Their time was coming. It was coming *soon*.

Walter ordered another MGD. When Louie brought it, Walter took a long swallow and wiped his mouth, then swiveled on his stool to survey the rest of the bar. His feet dangled a couple of inches above the floor. It was almost midnight, which was when the fights usually started and the hookups began. A Stones song played loudly from the jukebox. He and Jake knew almost everyone here, because most of the regulars were squids from Pax River. A little farther down the bar were three Navy wives whose husbands were on assignment in the Gulf. Jake claimed to have scored with the hot redhead, but Walter didn't believe it. Right in front of him, half a dozen E-1s played drunken pool. None of them could have been more than eighteen, and they were starting to get rowdy. Soon Louie would have to take them by the collars and drag them outside and remind them of the facts of life. Nobody messed with Louie.

And then there was the girl in the corner.

She was new. She wasn't local. Walter had never seen her before. Involuntarily, his lips pursed into a silent whistle.

"Shit, would you check that out," he murmured to Jake.

Next to him, his buddy popped salted peanuts into his mouth. Jake had a military look, with a shaved head and a Jason Statham physique. "Check what out?"

"The hot chick," Walter said.

Jake swiveled, and he whistled, too. “Nice.”

The girl sat at a table by herself. She was young—she looked barely legal—but her blue eyes had a mature, smoldering directness. Her white face was round and pretty, her lipstick bright red. She had bangs dyed like jet-black satin, and her hair was half covered by a leather beret adorned with the number *88*. She wore a loose white tank top and obviously no bra underneath, and a jean jacket that was covered with patches about motorcycles and guns. Her fingers, which were wrapped around a glass of white wine, were long and pointed and tipped in black polish.

Best of all, the girl was looking straight at Walter. She didn’t hide her interest. No girly games for this one. Walter lifted his beer mug at her, and she winked and tipped her wineglass back at him.

“Fuck,” Walter said, drawing out the word. “How about that?”

“Go talk to her,” Jake told him.

“Ya think?”

“Yeah, I think.”

Walter pushed his Pax River baseball cap back on his head, letting his forehead scar show. Somehow he thought this girl would like scars. He slid off the barstool and took his beer mug with him, and he kept his eye on the girl as he navigated the crowd. Her smile—just lips, no teeth—got broader as he got closer.

“Hey there,” he said, taking the empty chair next to her. “You’re new around here, huh?”

The pickup line sounded lame even to him, but the girl didn’t roll her eyes.

“Actually, I stopped in to meet a friend,” she said.

“Oh, yeah? Girl or guy?”

“Guy,” she said, rubbing one sharp fingernail along the line of her jaw. There was something really hot about the gesture.

"He stand you up?" Walter asked. "I can't believe any guy would stand you up."

"No, he just arrived."

Walter looked over his shoulder toward the bar door with faint disappointment. "Yeah? I don't see anybody."

"He's you, Walter," the girl said. "I came here to meet you."

Walter's eyebrows bunched together with suspicion. She knew his *name*?

"Me? What do you want with me? Who the fuck are you, a fed?"

The girl laughed, showing her white teeth this time. "Hardly."

"Then what do you want? How do you know who I am?"

"Oh, we know a lot about you, Walter," she told him. "We've been watching you for a while. Ever since the Marines betrayed you for having the balls to tell it like it is. You're our kind of people, Walter. But we think you can do more for the cause."

Walter cocked his head and pulled at his messy beard. She had him intrigued now. "What cause are we talking about?"

The girl nudged her jean jacket off her shoulders and let it drape across the chair behind her. Underneath, she wore only the tank top, which gave him a look at her skinny body and a tease of milky side boob. But mostly he noticed the tattoo on her arm, and he knew that was what she wanted him to notice. It matched his own tattoo, showing a don't tread on me flag held in place by the barrel of an M1 rifle.

"Jesus, you're with the Liberty Soldiers?" he said.

"Just like you."

"So what's your name?"

"Names aren't important," she replied. "What's important is what we believe. And what we *do*."

"Okay, so what do you want me to do?"

The girl looked around the bar. "Not here. There are too many people here. Let's go back to your place."

"You know where I live?" Walter asked.

"The Liberty Soldiers know everything about you." Then her stare shifted to the bar, where Jake was watching them, a big grin plastered on his face. "Your friend, Jake. Do you trust him? He's seen us together."

"Fuck, yeah, Jake's one of us," Walter replied. "He keeps a low profile because he doesn't want to get his ass kicked out of the Corps like me. But Jake's a true believer. We go way back."

"Text him. Tell him we're hooking up. You'll reach out to him in the morning. Perhaps we can find a role for him, too."

"Sure. Okay."

Walter tapped out a quick text to his friend, and when Jake read the message, he sent a winking emoji back as a reply. Then he shot Walter an obscene gesture as Walter followed the girl out of the bar. In the gravel parking lot by the highway, she accompanied him to his cab, which was an old Ford Taurus decorated with flags and military bumper stickers. He got behind the wheel; she got in the front seat next to him.

"Are you armed?" she asked.

"Hell yeah. Always. Smith & Wesson nine-millimeter."

"Excellent. You're well trained?"

"I fire at the range every week."

"How about rifles?"

"I keep several in my basement," Walter said. "AR15 types mostly."

"Accuracy?"

"I may not be a sniper, but I'm pretty good."

"Would people remember you at the range?"

"Sure. Everyone knows me. Why?"

The girl didn't answer his question. "Drive home. Park in the garage. Leave the lights off when we go inside."

He did as he was told. He felt a surge of adrenaline—a surge of purpose—that had been missing from his life for years. The Liberty Soldiers knew *him*. They'd come to *him*. This girl meant serious business. He could feel cold determination radiating from her, a kind of icy violence in her eyes. It turned him on.

"So what's the mission?" he asked when he pulled into the cul-de-sac two miles away, where his house butted up to the trees. Around him, the houses of his neighbors were dark because it was almost one in the morning. Nobody saw his taxi arrive.

"I said, what's the mission?" Walter asked again.

"Assassination," the girl replied calmly.

Walter felt his stomach turn upside down, and he swallowed hard. He tried not to let his voice crack with nervousness. "Fuck, yeah. Who?"

But she said nothing.

When he parked the taxi inside the detached garage next to his Ford Explorer, she directed him across the short walkway to the house. She made sure no one was watching them. He unlocked the side door and went in first, and everything inside his house was dark. It was *too* dark, even with the curtains closed. That was weird. Usually the streetlight on the cul-de-sac cast a glow through the fabric. But not now.

Something else was wrong, too. There was music playing. The Beatles. "Sgt. Pepper's Lonely Hearts Club Band."

What kind of sick joke was this?

Walter felt uneasy, as if he'd made a really bad mistake. Who was this girl? He reached around to the small of his back to grab his Smith & Wesson, but she was expecting that move. In the darkness, she grabbed his wrist and shoved his arm up his back, far enough that if he resisted, she'd break it. With a hook of her foot, she dropped him to his knees, and her other hand grabbed his hair and pulled his head back, exposing his neck.

There were footsteps in front of him.

Someone walked closer, and he felt the cool metal of a blade across his throat.

Then the lights went on.

A tall man stood there. In *his* house. He had wavy blond hair and hypnotic blue eyes, and he was dressed in black from head to toe. His gloved hand held a knife, which had a long, sharp blade, but he made no effort to break the skin of Walter's neck. Instead, he took the knife away, retrieved the Smith & Wesson from Walter's holster, and then sat down in Walter's ratty tweed recliner.

The man crossed his legs. He smiled at Walter with a smile that managed to be both sadistic and jolly at the same time. He hummed to the music.

"Easy, Yoko," he murmured to the girl, who held Walter's arm so tightly that tears leached from his eyes. "Remember, we don't want any obvious damage to our friend here. Nothing the medical examiner would find."

Walter thought he would piss his pants.

Medical examiner?

Behind him, the girl loosened her grip slightly, but she still held Walter so that he couldn't move at all. He looked around at his house and realized that everything was different. The furniture had been pushed aside. The glass of the windows had been taped over so no light could get in. And on the walls, his movie posters had been replaced by enlarged photographs of politicians with blood drawn on their throats and their eyes cut out and targets scrawled over their faces.

Shit, shit, shit!

"Who are you?" he gasped, dragging the words from his throat. "Jesus, what do you want with me? You're not from the Liberty Soldiers!"

The blond man kept humming to the Beatles and didn't answer. His graceful fingers explored the Smith & Wesson, then pointed the gun across the short space at Walter's face.

"Fuck, man!" Walter exclaimed, squirming at the sight of the barrel. "What do you want? Jesus, don't kill me, man!"

Finally, the humming stopped. The man laughed and lowered the gun. He switched off the music, but somehow the silence felt worse.

"Relax, Walter," the man told him. "You've been leading a worthless life up until now. All that anger, all those hollow threats, and no place for any of it to go. But I'm going to change all that. I'm going to make your dreams come true. By the time I'm finished, you'll be the most famous man in America."

PART THREE

31

Bourne and Nova lay next to each other in the back of the highlander with pistols cradled loosely in their hands. They were parked at the end of a dirt road in a nature center east of Washington, close to the waters of Whitehall Bay. The windows were open so they could hear anyone approaching in the darkness. The SUV still smelled of smoke from their escape from the burning house, and their skin was slick with greasy remnants of ash.

They'd intended to trade off sleeping for a few hours, but Bourne's usual ability to sleep anywhere had failed him. He could tell from Nova's breathing that she was awake, too. As a result, the night had gone slowly. Waiting time was always the slowest time.

On past missions, they'd talked to each other at moments like this. Bourne had opened up about losing his memory, about not knowing who he was, about struggling with his identity. Nova had talked about her past, too. The deaths of her parents. The violence and drugs of her teenage years. She'd been dark and troubled long before her abduction by Lennon, and she still was.

That was the irony for both of them. Jason wanted to remember his past, and Nova wanted to forget hers.

He couldn't deny there was still heat between them. Even after everything she'd done to him, the lies, the betrayal, it would have been easy to pass the night and defuse the tension with quiet, urgent sex. He knew that was what she wanted. She would tell him it meant nothing, that it was purely physical. The trouble was, she was right. Sex had never meant anything to her. It had taken him far too long to realize that.

It was never like it was with Abbey.

She seemed to read his mind as she spoke to him from the blackness of the Highlander. "I shouldn't tell you this, but I had a premonition about me and Abbey."

"A premonition?"

"I'm Greek. We believe in those things."

"So what was it?"

"She and I can't both survive this mission. We can't both survive *you*. One of us is going to die."

Jason didn't know what to say.

He wondered if Nova expected him to say that was crazy, but he couldn't. He felt stalked by death without the need for premonitions. Or maybe she wanted him to say that he couldn't bear to lose her, but he couldn't say that, either. If he looked in his heart, he couldn't bear the idea of losing *Abbey*. He was sure Nova knew it.

He let the moment go by in silence as he listened to the waves off the bay through the open windows.

"So what is Lennon up to?" Nova wondered, her voice clouded by a distant sadness. "Or was this whole thing just a trap for us?"

Bourne had been thinking about that all night. "No, there has to be more to it than that. Using the house was too elaborate for a trap. You were right. It was a staging ground. There's a kill coming, and it must be soon."

"Who's the target?" she asked.

"In DC? It could be anyone."

Nova was quiet for a while. He listened to the clicks as she disassembled and reassembled her pistol by habit. The darkness didn't matter. She routinely did it with her eyes closed, and she'd already done it half a dozen times during the course of the night. He knew that was how she calmed her nerves.

"Do you think this is linked to Defiance?" she asked finally.

"Someone brings in a Russian assassin to make a kill in Washington? At the same time that Treadstone agents and anyone else with ties to that jet are being hunted and murdered around the world? No, the timing isn't random. Whoever is running Defiance wanted a pro for this job."

Outside the Highlander, a faint lightness opened up the trees. Dawn was coming soon, and it was a reminder of time ticking away. He didn't know if the hit would be today, or tomorrow, but it wouldn't be long.

"The tattoo," Nova announced suddenly.

"What?"

"When I confronted Yoko in New York, she had a tattoo on her arm. To me, it looked fake, and believe me, I know tattoos."

"What was the design?" Bourne asked.

"An old flag held up by a rifle. Liberty or Death, Don't Tread on Me, the coiled rattlesnake. It looked familiar to me, like I'd seen it in an FBI alert not too long ago. I think it may be associated with some kind of extremist group."

Bourne frowned. "Lennon's trademark is shifting blame. Remember in London two years ago? He played an elaborate ruse with the Gaia Crusade."

"You think he's doing the same thing here?" Nova asked.

"I think it's worth checking out."

"Okay. I have a few bridges I haven't burned with the

FBI and DOJ. I'll see what I can find out about the tattoo and whatever group may be behind it. Maybe it leads us somewhere."

"Good."

"What about—" Nova began, but then she cut off her words as Bourne squeezed her hand sharply.

Outside the Highlander, they saw a flash of headlights. That was followed by the rumble of a car engine. It was too early for anyone to be visiting the park. He didn't have to give Nova directions; they slipped into operational mode automatically. The SUV shifted under their weight as they skidded forward and slipped through the open tailgate. Both still had their guns. Bourne went into the trees; Nova headed in the opposite direction.

The vehicle approached, its tires scraping over rocks. The lights shut down with the engine, and a car door opened with a click. The location of the car blocked their escape. Bourne saw the gnarled figure of a man, a shadow among other shadows, barely visible in the predawn gloom. He also heard the snap of a gun slide. Then he heard the uneven tap of shoes on the rocky ground, along with an extra rhythmic tap that matched the footsteps.

Jason knew what that noise was. A cane.

Down the road, a flashlight went on and off. Short, short, long, short. That was the Treadstone greeting. A few seconds later, Nash Rollins appeared near the Highlander, his wounded leg dragging. His gun was aimed and ready, but he lowered it when he saw Bourne and Nova closing on the vehicle from both sides.

"Good morning, you two," Nash said pleasantly as he holstered the gun. "I assumed it was you, but I came prepared just in case."

"How did you find us?" Bourne demanded.

Nash sat down heavily on the open tailgate. "It was easier

than you think, Jason. I heard about the bombing in North East a few minutes after it happened. We had reports thirty minutes after that of a man and woman matching your descriptions escaping the scene in a black Highlander. We had to get the local cops off the scent, but after that, I figured you'd head to DC. That meant crossing the Chesapeake Bay Bridge. We laser-tagged you as you crossed and followed you here. I've had security outside the park all night."

Nova rolled her eyes. "You could have brought coffee."

"Next time. First things first. Are you both okay?"

"Mostly," Jason replied. "Lennon lured us into a trap."

Bourne gave him a quick summary of the previous day's events, as well as their speculation about Lennon's plans. Nash took it all in, then leaned forward with his chin on the end of his cane.

"A hit near DC," he murmured. "And you think there's a connection to Defiance?"

"Nothing else makes sense," Bourne said.

"Well, I have an interesting wrinkle to add to that," Nash continued. "Although I don't quite know what to make of it."

"What is it?"

"That house in North East that Lennon blew up. I did some research on it. I was curious who owned it and why anyone would have chosen that particular location as a hideout. Lennon could have simply killed the owners and taken it over, but that's always a risk in a small town. Neighbors and police might get curious."

"What did you find?" Bourne asked.

"I found a house with a very interesting history," Nash replied. "The deed is registered to a man named Chris Vaccari in Lansing, Michigan. Only trouble is, there's no such man. I found someone by that name in New York, but he has no ties to Maryland and doesn't own any property here. So I kept digging, looking into property taxes, utilities, deliveries, whatever. I bumped up against a whole lot of shell companies and missing records. Whoever owned this place definitely didn't want to be found. And then, as it happened, I got lucky in our own backyard."

"How so?"

"I ran a search through our own database. Treadstone."

"*Treadstone* owns the house?" Nova asked.

"Not quite. But we handled security there on an operation almost a decade ago. The CIA had a highly placed Chinese mole who was on a visit to Philadelphia, ostensibly to negotiate a joint venture with a bioscience company. Agents smuggled him out of the city for a debriefing, and they took him to *that house*. The interview was done there. The CIA was afraid of assassination attempts if the Chinese found out where he was, so several of our agents monitored the scene."

"You're saying Lennon had access to a *CIA safe house*?" Bourne concluded.

"That's right. It's been vacant for years, but somehow Lennon found out about it. And that's not even the most curious part. I checked our reports from the scene back then, which included the usual roster of people in and out. One of the names jumped out at me, but as I say, I don't quite know what to make of it."

Bourne frowned. "Who was it?"

"The CIA director. And now U.S. senator and presidential frontrunner. Don Pine was in that house."

32

The imposing white-gray façade of the capitol dome loomed above Don Pine.

Not far away, he heard a drumbeat of protests in front of the Supreme Court building. The area around the eastern steps was empty, blocked off by security blockades that kept the public at a distance. Capitol Police roamed the area, wearing green vests and holding serious rifles. When Pine had asked them about the increased security, they'd mentioned a spike in threats from yet another extremist organization, so the police were limiting access out of an abundance of caution.

Pine appreciated the privacy. He held the phone close to his ear—no official phones for this call—and waited impatiently for Alicia Beauvoir to pick up. He wasn't used to being put on hold. It must have been a full five minutes before he heard her say, "Hello, Don."

"Alicia," Pine breathed into the phone, swallowing his rage and replacing it with California sunshine. "I appreciate your taking my call."

Her voice was cool. She'd always been immune to his charm.

"I admit, I'm surprised to hear from you. It seems to me we said everything there was to say last time we talked. Remember? When you threatened me?"

"Yes, I know. I'm calling to apologize about that. I could blame it on the stress of the campaign, but the fact is, there's no excuse. I'm sorry."

She sounded amused now. "An apology? How unlike you."

"I overreacted, and I regret it. Truly."

"All right," Beauvoir replied. "Apology accepted. Thank you. Now can we move on to the real point of your call? What do you want, Don?"

"I want to talk about your endorsement again," Pine said.

He heard a sigh on the line. "I think I made my thoughts on that clear."

"You did. Crystal clear."

"Then what else is there to say?"

"I'd like a chance to make my case. In person. You said ambition was more important to me than what I want for the country. I understand why you might think that, but you're wrong. And I think we both know that unity between the two of us going into next year's campaign will be vitally important for the party. We won't win if we're divided. So I'd like to talk about what it would take to get you on board with my candidacy."

Beauvoir didn't answer right away. "Are you planning to offer me something? Because I'm not interested in cabinet positions, Don. I'm happy where I am."

"Well, I can think of several options worth your consideration. However, that's not a discussion I want to have over the phone. Can we meet?"

There was another long pause.

"I think you're wasting your time."

"Maybe so, but give me an hour to change your mind."

"Yes, all right, fine," she replied finally, her voice impatient.

"Come to my estate tomorrow for lunch. Shall we say one o'clock?"

"I'll be there. Thank you, Alicia."

Pine hung up the phone.

He nodded at Tim Randall, who was standing next to him on the Capitol plaza. He handed the anonymous phone back to his aide. "Okay, Randall. I sucked my dick for her. Now what?"

"Now we figure out her price tag," Randall replied.

Pine hissed in disgust. He didn't like being manipulated, and he didn't like groveling. "Fine. This is your plan, so I'll play along. We do what it takes to get her endorsement. We trot her in front of the cameras. But after that—"

"After that, we take her off the board," Randall replied.

Alicia Beauvoir put down the phone and pinched her lips together in a tiny smile. "Perhaps we picked the wrong plot for the book after all," she said to Abbey. "If Flight 1342 can shake up Don Pine this much, then we're clearly onto something."

"Maybe we can do that for the sequel," Abbey said, only half joking.

She sat in front of her laptop at a table across the room from Beauvoir's huge walnut desk. Her notes file was open so that she could take down whatever stream-of-consciousness thoughts came out of her coauthor's mouth. But she wasn't really paying attention to the book. Her mind was far away.

She was thinking about Jason.

She was supposed to see him at the hotel that night, but his voice on the phone had sounded dark. He'd warned her: *Watch your back. Don't go anywhere alone.*

Abbey felt as if her world and Jason's world had merged. She was writing a novel, but Flight 1342 wasn't fiction. It was real, and people were being killed because of it. Someone had died right in front of her.

And Jason. What about Jason? She didn't know what came next for the two of them. She didn't know what she wanted. Or maybe she did—maybe she'd begun to face some hard truths—and that was what scared her.

She wasn't aware of how long she'd stayed quiet, but from the other side of the office, Beauvoir called to her, breaking the silence. "Abbey?"

Startled, Abbey looked up from her computer. "I'm sorry. What?"

"You seemed far away. You've been staring off into space for five minutes."

"I guess I'm just caught up in the plot."

Beauvoir gave her a look that said there was no point in lying. The former secretary of state got up from the desk and came over and sat down next to her. "Try again," she said. "What's going on?"

"I'm distracted," Abbey admitted.

"Is this still about that boyfriend of yours?"

"Partly."

"Well, he must be very good-looking to have someone like you so rattled," Beauvoir said with a smile.

"He is."

"So who is he? You've been very mysterious about him."

"I can't really say," Abbey replied.

"Is he in government?"

"Sort of. Yes and no. It's not safe for me to talk about him. I'm sorry."

"Ah, he's one of *those*," Beauvoir said with a gleam of understanding. "You realize I still have a top secret clearance, don't you? Whatever you know, I probably know, too. And anything you say goes no further than me."

"It's more complicated than that."

"Fair enough. Subject dropped. All I'll say, Abbey, is that I have a lot of personal and professional experience with intelligence agents. That world can be very exciting. Very attractive. At least for a while. But it's not easy sharing your life with a man who can only share a small part of his life with you. In many ways, my husband has experienced the same thing in reverse. I can't tell you it's been easy. In fact, sometimes it's exceedingly lonely for both of us."

Abbey blinked and had to look away to stop herself from crying. She didn't want to cry in front of Alicia Beauvoir. But Beauvoir had put a finger on exactly what Abbey was feeling. Lonely. Even when she was with Jason, she felt lonely, unable to penetrate the shadows he kept. The shadow of things he had to keep from her. The shadow of the past that he didn't even remember.

Suddenly, she realized she was weary of keeping secrets.

"It was him," she blurted out to Beauvoir.

"What?"

"He spread the rumor about the book. About 1342."

Beauvoir's face hardened like a wax figure at Madame Tussauds. "You lied to me, Abbey. You *knew* where this story came from."

"I'm sorry. Yes, I did. I didn't feel like I had a choice. He told me lives are at stake. People are being killed. He's trying to stop it."

"Who *is* this man?" Beauvoir asked again.

"I can't tell you that, but I can tell you that I trust him with my life. He's *saved* my life more than once. He's a good man."

Beauvoir sighed. "I know you mean well, Abbey, but in this universe, there's no such thing as *good*. Everything involves compromises. There are no decisions that are simply right or wrong, moral or immoral. All you can do is weigh the options, choose one, and then live with your decision. I suspect this man would be the first to tell you the same thing."

"He's said that to me more than once," Abbey agreed. "But he *is* a good man. I know him. In some ways I know him better than he knows himself."

Beauvoir tapped one of her fingernails slowly on the table. "Well. I can't see how this ends well for either of you, but that's not my call. But tell me, why the rumor about 1342? What did this man hope to accomplish?"

"Just like you said," Abbey replied. "To flush the ducks to the hunter."

"And did it work?"

She nodded. "Only too well. An innocent man died because of it. I was with him when it happened. It was—horrible."

"Who was he?" Beauvoir asked, her face creased with concern.

"His name was Dennis Foster. He called me because he saw the rumor about the book. He thinks his wife, Mallory, was murdered because she knew something about what happened to the jet."

Beauvoir pursed her lips. "Mallory Foster? I don't know that name."

"Jas—my friend—says that was just a cover identity. Her real name was Letitia Brown. She was a scientist."

Beauvoir's eyes widened. "Letitia? My God, I knew Letitia. I worked with her when I was at the UN. She was involved in several multinational scientific teams that I coordinated. She's *dead*? I never heard anything about that. But I suppose I never had occasion to deal with her after I went to State."

"Her husband said she was called out on some kind of secret assignment while 1342 was in the air. He doesn't know what the assignment was, but something about it terrified her. He said his wife was sure that she was going to be killed because of what she knew. And a few weeks later, she was."

Beauvoir shook her head. "As I recall, Letitia's specialty was virology. What would that have to do with 1342?"

"We don't know. That's the problem." Then Abbey closed the laptop and leaned closer. "Do you know anything more about this woman? Anything that would help us?"

Beauvoir frowned. "I can't tell you anything for certain. What I *can* tell you is that Letitia occasionally referenced assignments—in an oblique way—that I couldn't correlate with her résumé."

"What does that mean?" Abbey asked.

"Well, I took it to mean that she'd been involved in classified research. She had a secret life. Her official employer was the university—Johns Hopkins, I think—but my guess was that she also had some kind of relationship with an intelligence agency. Probably the CIA. Of course, I never asked her to confirm that."

"The CIA?" Abbey asked.

"Yes. Does that help?"

"I—I don't know. But I think so. Thank you."

Abbey opened up the laptop again, but her hands sat frozen above the keyboard as if she'd forgotten how to type. Beauvoir squeezed Abbey's shoulder in a surprisingly warm gesture. Usually, their relationship was strictly professional.

"You need to go to him, don't you?" she asked. "This mystery man of yours."

Abbey hesitated, but then she nodded. "I'll come back later tonight, and we can work as late as you want. But I feel like this is something he should know right away."

"Go ahead," Beauvoir replied. "We're already making good progress on the book. A few hours of delay isn't the end of the world. Get back here as soon as you can, and you can stay the night as usual. Actually, I was going to interrupt our work for a while anyway. I have a meeting coming up with the director of Homeland Security."

Abbey, who was already packing up her things, stopped in surprise. "Homeland Security? Is everything okay?"

Beauvoir shrugged. "Oh, it's nothing that should alarm you. I'm not worried. Apparently, they're seeing an unusual amount of online chatter involving threats against current and former officials. Including me. Trust me, this is the kind of thing that happens all the time. But the director asked to brief me about it."

"What kind of threats?" Abbey asked.

"It's another far-right organization. White supremacists and twisted patriots, the usual thing. In the end, most of these groups are toothless tigers, but apparently this one has posted some pretty specific threats recently. They call themselves the Liberty Soldiers."

33

Trees hugged the country road, making a kind of tunnel that was barely wider than the Ford Explorer that Lennon was driving. A few of the trees had begun to put on their autumn colors, like farm girls dressing up for a dance. Lennon kept the windows of the SUV open, with cool twilight air blowing inside. He had the radio off, but he whistled "Nowhere Man" through his teeth. Under the truck, loose rocks scraped and crunched. He drove slowly, barely twenty miles an hour, examining the topography. Sight lines. Observation posts. Backups. Places where things could go wrong.

Looking for the perfect spot.

Through the trees, wide-open fields rolled over the low hills. The lazy water of the Potomac was no more than a mile away, and the sun had already dipped low enough to cast long shadows. He'd driven back and forth along this road six times, narrowing down locations, weighing pros and cons. In all that time, he'd only seen a handful of other vehicles. The land outside Tuscarora was isolated ground, with nothing but a few lonely farmhouses dotting the fields. And yet the bustle of Washington was an hour away. It was the ideal place for rich politicians to retire.

Politicians like Alicia Beauvoir.

Once more, he passed the unmarked dirt road that led to her estate. It wound into the fields, disappearing over a hill. There was no sign, no gate, nothing to advertise who lived on the other side of the hill. And no security cameras. Those came later, but not here, where the neighbors might complain. Lennon slowed and eyed the road carefully, then drove another half a mile, where the river road emerged from the trees into open land near a small lake. Two rutted tractor tracks led around the water across the green field. On the other side of the lake, he saw a farmhouse and barn, with a high tower for power lines built behind it. In the trees near him, he heard the cackle of crows.

Lennon stopped. The truck engine was still running. He backed up the Explorer to where the trees ended and parked in the dirt, near the trunk of a fat oak tree. Tightly wound hay bales were lined up on the border of the field. He climbed down and examined the land in every direction. Where he was, the road sloped as it headed back toward the dirt road he'd passed earlier. A vehicle cresting that hill wouldn't see the Explorer until it was practically on top of it, and even then, the oak tree and hay bales made it mostly invisible.

This was the place.

Tomorrow, this was the place.

Then his eyes squinted as he noticed a small cloud of dirt and dust rising over the field. A vehicle was approaching from the farmhouse. As it drew close to him, he saw a dirty white pickup truck with a covered flatbed. There was a painted logo on the door that read DAWSON FARMS. An old man—at least in his seventies—was behind the wheel. The pickup pulled up next to Lennon, and the old man rolled down the window and leaned out. He had a completely bald head, almost chocolate brown from days in the sun. His face was stern and wrinkled, and his gaze studied Lennon with frank suspicion.

"Help you?" the man asked, which wasn't really an offer of help.

Lennon's mouth bent into an easy smile. "I'm fine, thanks. This your land?"

"Yup."

"Oh, sorry. I didn't mean to trespass."

"Uh-huh."

"Nice place," Lennon added. "Beautiful area."

"What brings you round here? You lost?"

He said it in a way that made Lennon think the man had been watching him go back and forth on the road for a while. This farmer didn't miss much, and he didn't trust strangers. That was a problem.

"No, actually, I'm scouting the area," Lennon told him.

"Scouting for what?"

"I'm in real estate. I've got a client looking for a place around here."

"Nothing's for sale that I know of."

Lennon shrugged. "Oh, everything's for sale for the right price."

"Uh-huh," the man said again.

"You lived here long?"

"Forty years."

"Well, that's long." Lennon gestured toward the door of the pickup. "Dawson Farms. You're Dawson?"

"That's me. Mel. Wife's Catherine."

Lennon approached the truck and extended his hand, which the man shook with a firm grip. When Lennon glanced into the pickup, he noticed the barrel of a shotgun in the passenger seat. Mel Dawson was taking no chances. Lennon was conscious of the various weapons secured around his body, any one of which would take care of Mel Dawson in a few seconds, long before the man could grab his shotgun. But Lennon glanced across the small lake toward the farmhouse and saw a woman on the sprawling front porch watching them through binoculars. No doubt that was Catherine Dawson. A busybody, like her husband. She had too much time to alert authorities if Mel didn't turn the truck around soon and head home.

"Anyway, I should be getting back to Washington," Lennon said.

Mel's face was still a blank slate. The farmer's hand drifted toward the rifle. "Don't think you mentioned your name."

Fuck! This one was smart.

Lennon sighed and changed his strategy on the fly. He'd planned to invade the farmhouse overnight and take care of the Dawsons, but he decided he couldn't wait until then. There was an outside chance they might make phone calls to the wrong people. He let his smile bleed away, and he met Mel's stare eye to eye. "You're right. I didn't."

"Never met anyone in real estate who didn't push a card in my hand and tell me their name," Mel went on.

"You're right about that, too."

"I was in Vietnam. I know military when I see it, friend. What are you, private security? FBI?"

"You're a sharp man, Mr. Dawson," Lennon replied.

"Got any ID?"

"Of course."

Lennon always had ID. Typically, he carried six IDs with different identities, depending on the cover story he needed. He reached into his back pocket for a worn leather wallet, and he flipped it open to show Mel Dawson. The farmer took his time examining it closely.

"Tom Cassidy," Mel said. "Homeland Security."

"That's right."

"This about Alicia Beauvoir?" Mel inclined his head toward the hills behind them. "Around here, we know all our neighbors. That dirt road back there leads to her place. We get a lot of limos through here."

"I bet you do. Yes, the secretary has been receiving some threats lately. Sorry for the cloak-and-dagger, but Ms. Beauvoir likes us to keep a low profile."

"Uh-huh."

"Since we're talking, let me ask you. Have you noticed any unusual activity around here lately? Seems like you keep a close eye on things."

"Nothing out of the ordinary."

"What about strangers coming and going?"

"Other than you? No."

Lennon nodded. "Okay. That's good. The thing is, your land borders hers. We'd love to station a couple of men in the fields that overlook her place for the next few days. With your permission, of course."

Mel's eyes had a strange way of not blinking. The lines on his bald brown forehead tightened. "Maybe I'll just call Alicia about that first."

"Sure, of course, you do that." Lennon glanced at the farmhouse, where Catherine Dawson continued to watch the two of them through her binoculars. "Tell you what, how about we go back to your place? You can call Alicia. Then I'd love to get a tour of your property. I want to make sure nobody's been out here surveilling the Beauvoir estate. Odds are, they'd leave a trail."

Mel took a long time to answer, but then his stoic face softened just a little. "All right. We can do that."

"Thanks. I appreciate your help." Lennon put his hands on his hips and took another admiring look at the evening shadows spreading across the fields. "This really is a beautiful place up here, Mel. I bet you get potential buyers knocking on your door all the time."

The farmer shrugged. "Yeah, we could make a fortune if we sold, but we're not going anywhere. Not while we're still alive. They'll have to take me and Catherine out of here feetfirst."

Lennon eyed the shotgun in the truck. "Good to know, Mel. Good to know."

Jake Derusha was puzzled. Where the hell was Walter?

He nursed the dregs of his second tall beer as he sat on his usual stool in the bar near NAS Pax River. The stool next to him was empty. It was almost ten o'clock, and Walter was a no-show. That wasn't like him. Walter could have had shingles on his ass, and he'd still sit down and order his MGD. Jake had tried calling and gotten no answer. He'd tried texting, but Walter hadn't even read any of his messages.

Fucking weird.

Jake scrolled backward on his phone to the last message Walter had sent him the previous night. *Going home with the girl. She's one of us. Talk to ya in the a.m.*

Okay, so Walter had gotten lucky. Good for him. The girl was hot as shit, no denying that, and if she had a daddy complex, so much the better. Jake wasn't going to begrudge his buddy a one-night stand, but what exactly did he mean?

She's one of us.

And why had Walter been ghosting him all day?

"Hey, Louie?" Jake called down the bar. "You seen Walter at all? He been in here? Did he call you or anything?"

Louie, the owner and bartender, rumbled toward him. Jake was no small guy, but Louie was even larger, built like a WWE wrestler with a muscle-bound torso and no neck. His gray hair was cut in a flattop. He was in his fifties, and he'd spent his whole life in the Navy before retiring to open the tavern.

"Walter?" Louie said. "Nah, haven't seen him. I was gonna ask you where he was."

"No idea, man. I don't get it," Jake grumbled. "You see the girl he left with last night?"

"Enough to see that she was out of Walter's league."

"Yeah, no kidding. Who knows, maybe they're still fucking."

Louie snorted. "If Walter was fucking twenty-four hours ago, I figure they've been done for twenty-three hours and fifty-eight minutes."

"I hear you," Jake replied with a chuckle. "So do you know who this girl was?"

"I don't. Not a local. But I guess she was his type."

Jake cocked his head in surprise. "What does that mean? Walter said something like that, too."

Louie tapped a meaty index finger on Jake's forearm tattoo, which was the same tattoo that Walter had. They'd gotten them together at a meeting of the Liberty Soldiers on some country farm two years earlier. For Jake, the meeting had been about shooting off guns and talking smack about the deep state. He didn't take it seriously, but the others who were there sure did. They were scary as shit with their beady eyes and their white power salutes. He'd warned Walter not to get too close to them.

"Really, the girl had the tattoo?" Jake asked. "You sure?"

"I was checking out her tits, man," Louie chuckled, "and the ink was right there on her arm, so it was hard to miss."

Jake shook his head. "Huh. I don't get it."

"Well, I imagine Walter will be in here sooner or later making up stories about last night," Louie said with a shrug. "You want another beer?"

"Yeah, why not?"

But Jake wasn't so sure about Walter showing up. He had a weird, creepy feeling about all of this. While he waited for Louie to pour his next beer, he tapped out another text. *Proof of life, man. Come on, where you at?*

His phone told him the text had been delivered, but he waited and still didn't see a verification that Walter had read it.

So he texted one more time.

Seriously, brother. You okay? I'm getting ready to call the cops here.

He put his phone facedown on the bar and took a long swig from the ice-cold mug that Louie put in front of him. A few seconds later, his phone buzzed like a mosquito, and he grabbed it.

His texts had finally been read. This time, Walter replied.

Chill, dude. All's well. Still busy with the girl if you know what I mean. Walter added a winky emoji after the message.

The text didn't make Jake feel better. In fact, he felt more convinced now that something was wrong. *Chill, dude?* Walter was about as likely to use an expression like that as he was to put a Kamala bumper sticker on his taxi. Jake took his phone, and this time, he called Walter instead of texting.

The phone rang and rang, and there was no answer. Jake thought: *Come on, Walter, what the fuck? If you just texted, why aren't you answering?*

Then, not even a minute later, another text arrived, but this time it came from a different phone number. Jake didn't recognize it.

We need to meet, man. There's big trouble.

Jake hesitated as he read the message, then texted back: *Who is this? Walter? That you?*

Yeah, it's me. Got a pay-as-you-go today. Think the feds are watching my other phone.

What the fuck, man?

I need help, buddy. How fast can you get to Lancaster Park?

Jake drank down as much of his beer as he could in a single swallow.

Ten minutes, he sent back.

See you there. Thanks, man.

Digging in his wallet, Jake fished out a twenty-dollar bill

and left it on the bar for Louie. He slid off the barstool and headed for the door with a little unsteadiness in his walk. He should have hit the head—the beer was galloping through him—but Walter sounded panicked, and Jake didn't want to waste time.

Outside, a steady rain made the night even darker as he hurried to his F-150. He shot off down the highway, but he didn't have far to go. Lancaster Park was only a couple of miles away, just a community park and playground. The Pax River softball teams played there sometimes. Not even five minutes later, he swung off Willows Road into a deserted parking lot that led to the green fields. He leaned forward, squinting through the windshield wipers to see what was ahead of him.

There was one other car parked in the lot, and he recognized it immediately. It was Walter's Ford Taurus taxi, painted as yellow as the sun.

Jake pulled his truck next to Walter's cab and got out into the rain. The water poured down his bald skull and soaked through his clothes. He pulled on the driver's door of the Taurus, but it was locked, and when he wiped away enough of the rain from the windows to peer inside, he could see that the car was empty. But when he checked the hood, the metal was warm.

"Walter?" he called, looking around the park. "Walter, you there?"

There was no answer.

He tried again, his voice louder. "Hey, Walter, it's Jake."

He checked his phone and found no more messages from either number. He tried sending a text to the burner number—*I'm here, where are you?*—but the message bounced back as undeliverable. When he dialed the phone, he got an error telling him that the number was out of service.

What the fuck?

Walter had used that phone fifteen minutes ago, and now it was dead?

Jake trudged into the fields, his boots sinking into wet grass. The rain got heavier, and the cold rain on his wet clothes reminded him how much he needed to piss. He was practically dancing now. He crossed the soccer field and followed the sidewalk that led beside the trees, and he kept calling Walter's name and getting no response. And yet his buddy couldn't have gone far if his engine was still hot.

Where the hell was he?

Was this some kind of joke?

"This ain't funny, Walter!" he shouted.

Behind him, in the trees, Jake heard movement. A branch snapped; the weeds rustled. He spun around, waiting for someone to break from the woods. He took a step closer. "Walter? That you?"

Nothing. No one was there. The woods were quiet again, except for the thump of the rain. Even so, Jake got that same creepy feeling, and he backed away. His heart began to beat faster in a rush of fear and adrenaline, so loud it was like a drum in his ears. He kept wiping his eyes, trying to see better, but the rain blinded him. And *Jesus*, he needed to piss. It was so bad he was ready to unzip and water the ground. But even worse, his bowels were loosening, running through his insides like a river.

Jake was worried now. Something was going on, something really bad, and he didn't like it. He was ready to go back to his truck, go home, go back to the bar, go anywhere except this park. Fuck Walter, fuck whatever mess he was in. But he couldn't leave. They'd been best friends since they were five years old.

"Walter!" he shouted again, half impatient, half afraid. "Come on, man!"

He walked deeper into the park. Behind him, he heard the

noise again, like someone following him through the woods. But that was crazy. It was a fucking deer. Or a squirrel. He ignored it. Ahead of him, he saw a small white stone building, and he breathed a little sigh of relief, because that was where the park's restrooms were located.

Jake ran to the men's room—thank God it was open—and he switched on the lights inside. It was cold and dank, with a sewery smell, but he didn't care. There was one stall, and he hustled inside and barely had his pants down before his bowels unloaded.

Fuck, that was close.

Then the noise of the rain got louder. The bathroom door opened again. The lights went off.

Jake sat there in the dark, not knowing what to do. *Walter, stop playing games, man!*

Footsteps. He heard footsteps. Jake scrambled to his feet and zipped up his jeans. The toilet was totally black; he couldn't see a thing. Silently, he opened the stall door, but he was disoriented, not remembering which way to go. He could hear his breathing, but he could hear someone else's, too.

Ahead of him? Behind him? He didn't know.

Jake slid his hand into his pocket and pulled out his phone. With a push of the button, he turned on the screen, which made a tiny glow, enough to show him the white floor and the sinks and the glass mirrors on the wall. There was nothing in front of him. No one was there.

Then he turned around.

The last thing Jake saw in his life was that hot-as-shit girl from the bar raising Walter's Smith & Wesson and pointing the barrel at his face.

34

Bourne walked Abbey to the parking lot near the capitol where she'd left her friend's Tesla. They'd spent the evening in her room at the Hyatt, and now it was almost midnight. The smell of her perfume lingered on his skin, and he could taste her on his lips. They'd made love twice, wildly, silently, but with a kind of darkness lingering between them. It was as if they both sensed that this might be the last time. He'd found himself memorizing every inch of her body, every expression on her face, as if she might get lost in the ether where the rest of his past resided.

For now, he pushed those thoughts out of his head. Abbey was his weakness, and he couldn't allow any weakness to stop him.

"Tell me what Alicia said," he murmured as they walked.

"Jason, I already told you," she replied with a frustrated sigh, because he'd made her repeat it multiple times. "Alicia knew Mallory Foster through the UN. She thought Mallory—or Letitia Brown, that was the name she knew—had some kind of secret life. That her work at the university was mostly a cover for her real job."

"And she thought her real job was with the CIA?" he asked.

"Yes."

"Did she say why? Did she have any proof?"

"I don't think so. She's just been around enough spooks to know who they are. She figured out what *you* did without my saying a word about it. There aren't many secrets in Washington that she doesn't know, Jason. But if you need confirmation about Letitia, can't you go to your own people? To Nash? Or to Holly Schultz?"

He shook his head. "If Letitia was working for the agency, she was doing it off the books. I doubt there was any record of her activity that they could access. Even if there was, I'm sure it was erased after she was killed."

"And do you think this is important?" Abbey asked.

Jason nodded. "I think if we could figure out exactly what Mallory Foster was doing that night, we'd know what Defiance is all about."

Abbey took his hand. She led him to a bench in the darkness, and he sat down next to her. The white glow of the Capitol wasn't far away. A cool breeze snaked through the trees like a whisper. He studied the shadows and caught a glimpse of movement, a silhouette that came and went. He knew it was Nova. He'd asked her to follow them, in case the killers came back. But he didn't tell Abbey she was out there. Even the mention of Nova's name set Abbey on edge.

"The CIA connection means something?" she asked.

Bourne didn't deny it. Abbey was already in too deep to keep the truth from her. "Yes."

"What?"

"Well, in part, the connection is Lennon," Bourne said. "He's been involved in Defiance from the beginning, back when he was in Treadstone. He's the one who killed Mallory Foster, and I think she told him her secrets. If so, then Lennon knows the truth, or at least a big part of it. Now he's back in play, and we're pretty sure he's got a new target in DC. Nova and I tracked him to a safe house. A *CIA* safe house. So I think whoever's pulling the strings on Defiance is in bed with Lennon, and the trail leads back to the CIA."

Abbey frowned, as if she'd suddenly remembered something. "I'm sorry, Alicia said one more thing. I should have told you before, but it had nothing to do with Mallory Foster. I mean, it was offhanded, just a joke—"

"What did she say?"

"She said maybe we picked the wrong plot for our book. She said if the story about 1342 could make Don Pine freak out, then we must be onto something."

"*Don Pine?*" Bourne asked. "She mentioned Pine specifically?"

"Yes, she said the rumors about our book had him shaken."

"What else did she say?"

"Nothing. That was it. I heard her end of a conversation with him, that's all. It sounded like he was pushing to get her endorsement. Alicia didn't mention 1342 during the call, but afterward, that was when she made the joke. So clearly she thought it was on Pine's mind. I got the impression she thought Pine was trying to get the rumors out of the headlines."

Bourne said nothing.

His mind raced through the possibilities. Don Pine, reincarnation of J. Edgar Hoover. Don Pine, U.S. senator from California. Don Pine, front-runner for the Democratic presidential nomination.

Why bring back Defiance years later?

Why tie up loose ends with murders around the world?

A presidential campaign was a hell of a motive.

"How did they leave it?" Bourne asked. "What happened on the call between Pine and Beauvoir?"

"They're meeting tomorrow at her estate to talk about her endorsing him."

"Do you think Beauvoir will do it?"

"I have no idea. I know she detests him personally. But this is politics."

Bourne's face darkened.

"A meeting tomorrow," he reflected. "Will you be there?"

"Well, I won't be at the meeting itself. I have nothing to do with that. But I'll be working on the book at her estate. Why?"

"Because one of the top assassins in the world is active in Washington right now, and a meeting like that is a prime target for him."

"He's not coming after *me*, Jason," Abbey said.

Bourne grabbed her hand. "Abbey, Don Pine thinks you are working with Alicia Beauvoir on a book about Flight 1342. If he's involved with Defiance—if he's the one behind all of this—then you're *both* targets."

"Lennon would have to be crazy to go after us there," she told him. "Alicia's already reviewing security at the estate and looking to tighten things up. She met with the head of Homeland Security about it today."

Jason's eyes narrowed. "Homeland Security? Why were they involved? Because of the meeting with Pine?"

"No. Alicia said there's been an upsurge in extremist threats lately. Some group called the Liberty Patriots. Or Liberty Soldiers. Something like that."

Bourne's fists clenched, and his eyes squeezed shut with a wave of certainty. He felt all the threads coming together, and he didn't like where they were leading him.

An extremist group.

The *tattoo* that Yoko was wearing. *Liberty or Death!*

Liberty Soldiers.

It was a classic Lennon diversion, pointing blame for a hit somewhere else.

"Abbey, I want you to stay here tonight," Bourne insisted, not letting go of her hand. "Go back to the hotel. Keep out of sight for a few days."

"I can't do that."

"I don't want you anywhere near Alicia's estate, not until this is *over*!"

"I'm sorry, but no," she repeated. "Look, I know you want to protect me, but I promised Alicia I'd come back tonight. We have work to do. Don't you get it? This is my life, my career, my future. I've already put it at risk by lying to her, and I won't walk away from this project." She stopped, biting her tongue, as if she was struggling to say what came next. "Besides, let's face it, Jason."

"Face what?"

Abbey reached out and put a soft hand on his cheek. Her eyes were full of sadness. "With you, it's never really over, is it?"

35

Nova stood in a darkened corridor of the Smithsonian's National Museum of American History and stared through the glass display case at a man's stovepipe hat. Originally glossy silk, time had worn down the fabric until it looked almost like polished brass in the museum light. Abraham Lincoln had worn that top hat at Ford's Theater on April 14, 1865.

"Lincoln wore a hat like that once when visiting the battlefield, too," a voice said next to her. "The soldiers had to warn him to take it off. Any Confederate rifleman spotting that hat would have known who it was."

Nova glanced at the man who'd come up beside her. He was in his forties, as tall as Lincoln at six foot four, with a bowl cut on his black hair that made him look like a monk. His face was square, his ears sharply pointed. He wore a dark blue suit, white shirt, and a red tie with an American flag tie clip. In Washington, that suit was practically a required uniform for lawyers.

"You'd look good in a hat like that, Keith," Nova said.

"You think so?"

"Sure, you would have fit in back then. Me, I probably

would have been some kind of homeless fortune teller. Reading palms. Speaking in tongues. That kind of thing."

"I don't know," the man replied. "I see you working your magic behind enemy lines. Once a spy, always a spy, Nova."

"Smooth talker."

Keith took her by the elbow, and they left Lincoln's hat to the tourists. They made their way through halls of presidential trivia until they found a corridor of the museum that was dark and still mostly empty. She knew Keith was reluctant to be seen with her. Keith Farley was a deputy assistant attorney general in the Department of Justice, in the investigative section that focused on domestic terrorism. They'd worked together on an arms-trafficking case when Nova was at Interpol, but they'd fallen out over a Michigan white supremacist who was trafficking young girls as well as guns.

Keith had wanted to leverage the prostitution charges to blow a multinational gunrunning operation wide open.

Nova had wanted to kill the bastard.

Soon after their argument, the white supremacist had been found dead in an Amsterdam alley with his throat cut and his genitals sliced off with a pair of garden clippers. If Jason had asked her "hard or soft," that death would definitely have qualified as hard. Keith had suspected—correctly—that Nova had conducted the execution. He'd never reported her for it, but he'd also never worked with her again.

"I appreciate your seeing me," Nova said.

"I said I'd give you ten minutes," Keith replied in a chilly tone. "We've used two minutes talking about Lincoln. You have eight left."

"Fair enough. Then I won't waste time. Tell me what you know about an extremist group that calls themselves the Liberty Soldiers."

Keith sucked his upper lip between his teeth. His face looked unhappy. "Why?"

"You first," Nova said. "Who are they?"

"Well, right now, I'd compare them to Rich Strike."

Nova cocked her head. "I don't understand."

"Rich Strike came from the back of the pack to win the Kentucky Derby. Almost nobody saw it coming. That's how it feels with the Liberty Soldiers. They came from nowhere, they weren't on anybody's radar, and yet suddenly they're the only group that anybody wants to talk about. Including you, apparently. I'd like to know why that is."

"Lennon," Nova told him. "Lennon's why."

One of Keith's thick eyebrows arched. "He's active?"

"We think so."

"In the U.S.?"

"Yes."

"Who's the target?"

"We don't know. Not for sure."

"What's Lennon's connection to the Liberty Soldiers?"

"He could be using them as cover."

"In other words, setting them up to take the fall for the hit?" Keith asked.

"Exactly. You know that's how he operates. The thing is, we think someone in the government may be running Lennon this time."

"In the *American* government?"

"That's right."

Keith frowned. "Who's we? You and Cain? Is this another fucking Treadstone operation? Those rogue bastards are constantly going off the reservation and leaving us to clean up their mess."

"Even if I could tell you more, you wouldn't want to know the details," Nova replied. "Now I've showed you mine, Keith, you show me yours. What do you know about the Liberty Soldiers?"

The lawyer glanced both ways down the museum corridor.

"We've had them in our database for about three years, but they've never made waves. As far as we could tell, they were all smoke, no fire. The FBI didn't even bother trying to get an informant inside. Then all of a sudden—literally just in the last few days—we've seen a shitload of chatter about them online. Like they've got an op planned, something big. You think this could be Lennon?"

"Could be."

"What makes you so sure?" Keith asked.

Nova slipped her phone from her pocket. She'd done her best recreation of the tattoo she'd seen on Yoko's arm, and she showed the image to Keith. "I saw something like this on a Lennon operative. Do you recognize it?"

"Yeah. That's from the Liberty Soldiers, all right. They've all got that tattoo."

"Where do they have cells?"

"I told you, we don't have a lot of hard information. Our intelligence has been limited because we didn't consider them a serious threat. The FBI has been scrambling to catch up, but they haven't been able to tie their recent activity to any particular cell. Then again, if you're right about Lennon, there's no cell. It's all misdirection."

"Yeah, except Lennon's going to pin the blame on *somebody*," Nova pointed out. "He always serves up a suspect for us. Usually dead. That's the link in the chain I want to find. If we can nail down *who* he's trying to use, then maybe we can find the target and find Lennon, too."

Keith's hesitation told her that he knew something but he didn't want to share the information.

"I really shouldn't help you," he said stiffly. "You have no authority here. And Treadstone methods—"

"Come on, don't play games with me. I know you don't approve of how we do things, but if you think the fucking federal bureaucracy is going to move fast enough to stop this, you're kidding yourself. Your best shot at getting Lennon before he makes the hit is *us*. So tell me what's going on."

Keith shoved his hands in his pockets. "There was a murder."

"When?"

"Yesterday. Last night."

"Last night," Nova hissed. "Where was this?"

"About ninety minutes south of here," Keith said. "Cops got a call about a body in a park restroom not far from NAS Pax River. Shot in the face. This guy had a tattoo that matched the Liberty Soldiers. Fortunately, someone in the local police was a nerd about reading DOJ bulletins. He recognized the logo and called us."

"Well, the vic can't be Lennon's fall guy," Nova pointed out. "He wouldn't kill him before the hit. But there has to be a connection. Have they ID'd the body?"

Keith nodded. "They have, although the police haven't made the identity public yet. We asked them to keep the case shut down until we could look into it. The vic was a Marine sergeant in the Aviation Detachment at Pax River. Worked maintenance on jet engines. His name was Jake DeRusha."

The burgundy-colored Chevy Tahoe headed out of Washington into the Maryland countryside. Bourne followed on a Kawasaki motorcycle half a mile back, his face hidden by a silver helmet.

He'd picked up Don Pine's town car outside the senator's Dupont Circle condominium, where a gaggle of national reporters was waiting. Pine emerged from the building at eleven in the morning exactly, with his chief aide, Tim Randall, half a step behind him. Bourne, dressed in the uniform of a DC messenger service, watched from across the street as Pine took questions, then announced he was heading for the Capitol.

But that wasn't where the senator went.

Five minutes later, the town car pulled into a surface parking lot on K Street, and Bourne watched as Pine and Randall discreetly exited the car's backseat and switched to a dark red SUV parked next to it. The transfer took less than thirty seconds. Then the town car returned to the street, and the Tahoe left, heading in the opposite direction, out of the city.

Now, more than an hour later, the SUV continued down a two-lane rural highway with cornfields on both sides. Bourne knew where they were going. He'd already followed Abbey the previous night to Alicia Beauvoir's country estate, in order to make sure she arrived safely. The SUV was using the identical route. It was a quiet area, mostly free of traffic, but to Bourne, the emptiness of the land made it a greater threat. The green hills provided easy vantages for snipers. The handful of roads were easy to block.

He could feel the danger in his gut. Lennon was close.

He slowed the motorcycle, watching the Tahoe approach a three-way intersection, where the highway split in two directions and a narrow gravel road led into the trees. In the distance, the horizon line marked the Potomac River and the state border between Maryland and Virginia. The Tahoe left the highway, taking the lonely side road toward the water.

Bourne waited, watching for other vehicles to close on the river road. An ambush would be easy here. The assault cars would come up from behind; by radio, they would call in support vehicles to block the road ahead of them. The Tahoe would get squeezed in the middle with nowhere to go and no escape.

But there was no assault under way. No ambush. The kill would come later.

Bourne gunned the motorcycle and took the gravel road, traveling beside a farm field bordered by a broken-down fence. He was far enough back that he couldn't see the SUV anymore, but there was no place to turn before the river. His concern now was finding the assassin's lair.

Where is Lennon?

He drove slowly, the motorcycle engine sputtering as if it wanted to go faster. Every quarter mile, he stopped to examine the green hills through his binoculars. Lennon would be camouflaged, invisible wherever he was, but Bourne knew the clues a sniper might be unable to hide. A reflection off the glass of a scope, a momentary flash on the metal of a trigger guard. He surveyed every stretch of road where the trees gave way to open ground and offered an unobstructed view from the hilltops. This was the perfect killing ground, remote, plenty of cover, nowhere for targets to hide.

But he saw nothing.

Eventually, Bourne ran out of road. The river wasn't far away. The turnoff to Alicia Beauvoir's estate was on the other side of the next hill. He took the motorcycle halfway up the slope, then silenced the engine and secured the bike in the trees. He knew the spot; he'd been here overnight. On foot, he climbed through the woods to the top of the hill, where a lingering cloud of gravel dust told him that the Tahoe had turned toward Beauvoir's house.

He saw a black sedan parked at the crossroads. Two men in orange vests stood on either side of the vehicle, both obviously armed, both private security. Bourne shook his head in dismay at the minimal protection. There should have been vehicles at both ends of the river road. Men with rifles patrolling the fields. A helicopter overhead.

Two men, one car; that was all. It wasn't nearly enough.

Bourne retreated down the hill. In the thick brush where he'd hidden the motorcycle, he located the hard plastic gun case for his Barrett M82 rifle, which he'd placed in the woods overnight. He was expecting a firefight, and he would be ready.

It would be sniper against sniper, Treadstone agent against Treadstone agent. Cain against Abel.

Just as it had been in South Ossetia years earlier.

He took the gun case and pushed through the woods. Not long after, he broke free on a ridge that led across the valley. Below him, in stretches of sunshine and shadow, green fields stretched over the land, occasionally interrupted by oak trees taking on orange-red colors. Near the river road, he saw a small lake where the seams of the hills met. Beyond the calm water, he spotted a modest farmhouse framed against sagging power lines and a dense forest grove behind it. There were no people in sight, just a white pickup truck parked on a rutted tractor road near the house.

He lifted his binoculars to examine the farmhouse more closely.

Was that motion in one of the windows? Did the curtains move?

If someone was there, they didn't show themselves again.

Bourne listened to the noises of the ridge and heard only birdsong and the whine of insects around him. It was a perfect, cloudless day. Making a full circle, he eyed the whole countryside again to watch for glimmers of light and motion. Reflections under the bright sun. Colors that didn't match the land around him. A slight disturbance in the brush. But Lennon was too smart to make that kind of mistake.

Was he looking at Bourne through crosshairs right now?

Was Lennon's finger caressing the trigger of his own long gun?

The assassin wouldn't fire. Not yet. He wouldn't risk the noise of the shot undoing his plans. But Jason could feel himself being watched. Surveyed. Studied. His instincts told him he wasn't alone. But he didn't know whether to trust his instincts, because his thoughts of Abbey kept getting in the way of his cool, objective mind.

Was that part of the plan?

Had Lennon drawn him here so that Jason could watch Abbey die? Did he know that Abbey was his weakness, his Achilles' heel?

Stop it!

He tried to anticipate Lennon's next move. He tried to put himself inside the mind of a killer. When he did, he could feel a clock ticking, counting down toward *something*. Toward death.

Jason clenched his fists and squeezed his eyes shut. Again he asked himself: *Where is Lennon?*

If it was his mission, if he was the killer, what would he do? Where would he position himself? On the near horizon, Jason spotted a slope with twin oak trees rising over the summit. His mental calculations told him that the hilltop controlled the river valley and offered a vantage on Beauvoir's estate. That was the location Bourne would have chosen for a hit, but when he examined the summit through binoculars, he saw that the green grass around the oak trees was empty. Lennon wasn't there.

Why?

What was Bourne missing?

He couldn't wait any longer. He left the valley—the lake, the old farmhouse—behind him, and he scrambled for the slope that overlooked the river. When he reached the twin trees, he slithered through the grass, staying out of view. Below him was what he expected to see—the large stone house and impeccably landscaped grounds of Alicia Beauvoir's country home. Don Pine's Chevy Tahoe was parked outside. So was Abbey's Tesla, which had been there since the overnight hours.

He set up his rifle. He wanted to get the truth about Defiance, but that was his second priority. Right now, this was about keeping Abbey alive. If Lennon appeared in his gunsight, Bourne would take the shot, even if it meant walking away without answers.

He had one mission.

Anyone who came near Abbey would die.

36

Lennon watched Cain go.

He'd felt that moment when his nemesis stared at the farmhouse from the ridge and a strange connection had passed between them. The two of them, Cain and Abel, were still like brothers. That electrical sensation across the valley was so strong that he'd jerked back, with the fringe of the white kitchen curtain falling from his hand. Lennon was sure that Cain had spotted the movement through his binoculars. He didn't miss a thing.

It was tempting to go outside and set up the final battle between them, but the confrontation would have to wait. The job came first.

In the distance, Cain disappeared over the ridge to surveil Alicia Beauvoir's estate. *You're making a mistake, my old friend,* Lennon thought, but in Cain's shoes, he would have done the same thing. That was how they'd both been trained.

If you don't know the plan, you have to play the odds.

Treadstone.

Lennon withdrew a cell phone from his pocket. Generally, he didn't like phones; he didn't like technology at all. Sooner or later, technology proved to be every agent's downfall.

They got hacked, tracked, burned, followed, and eventually captured or killed. But in this case, the phone was a necessity. He inserted a SIM card and battery and powered it on. The phone took a couple of minutes to acquire a signal, and then a chime announced that he had a new text message.

Arrival.

The source of the message was an unknown phone number, but Lennon knew it had come from Tim Randall on the other side of the valley at Alicia Beauvoir's estate. Randall had a burner phone like his own, and it would be used for only two messages.

Arrival. And in two hours, the most important message. *Departure.*

Lennon returned the phone to his pocket. He looked at the kitchen floor in the farmhouse where Mel Dawson lay on his back, a bullet hole in the middle of his throat. His wife, Catherine, lay facedown in the hallway that led to the bedrooms. She'd tried to run, and his bullet in the back of her skull had taken her down. They'd been dead since the previous day, their blood congealed.

The weapon he'd used to kill them had been taken from Walter Pepper's armory. He'd leave it behind for the police to find. He'd also taken a carton of milk from Pepper's refrigerator and brought it here, leaving it on the kitchen table. The milk would have the man's fingerprints on the carton. He'd put a half-eaten apple from Pepper's trash next to the Dawsons' trash can. Pepper's DNA would be on it.

Of course, the most important evidence would be Pepper himself.

Once the hit was done, Lennon would return to the cul-de-sac near NAS Pax River, where he and Yoko would stage Pepper's suicide. The photograph of the politician on the wall with the red *X* across the face would tell the rest of the story. The Liberty Soldiers would have claimed their first kill.

Lennon checked the window and smiled. There was no sign of Cain. His nemesis was chasing the wrong ghost.

He stepped over the bodies and headed outside. The white Dawson Farms pickup truck was parked near the garage. Better to use that, he'd decided. If someone drove by in the next two hours, the farm truck sitting near the river road would attract no suspicion. His Ford Explorer—Walter Pepper's Ford Explorer—was parked in the woods far from the kill zone.

When the deed was done, he would simply drive away.

But first he would deal with Cain.

Lennon peeled back the tarpaulin from the truck's flatbed to check the cargo. The IED was crude—a fertilizer bomb, not something he would have designed—but he wanted the components to reflect the low-tech minds of Walter Pepper and the Liberty Soldiers. It would accomplish its purpose, which was all that mattered. The only question mark was the precise timing. The electrical charge would be supplied by the phone attached to the bomb, and Lennon would activate that by making a call from the phone in his pocket. That meant he had to keep a visual watch on the site. It wasn't optimal, but it couldn't be helped. He'd receive a message when it was time to get ready.

Departure.

Lennon replaced the tarpaulin. With his gloved hands, he used Mel Dawson's car keys to fire up the engine of the pickup truck. He drove along the rutted tractor route, wincing at the bumps shuddering through his IED in the back of the truck, but his slow speed minimized the vibrations. He kept an eye on the ridge as he drove.

Cain didn't reappear.

When Lennon reached the road, he parked the truck a couple of feet onto the narrow gravel lane. The SUV would have to slow to squeeze past it. He shut off the engine, then returned to the flatbed and lifted one corner of the tarp. He leaned in just far enough to activate the cell phone inside, and it came to life with a beep.

Everything was ready. All it would take was one phone call.

Lennon walked past the lake to the farmhouse and waited.

There wasn't much of a midafternoon crowd at the tavern off Three Notch Road. Nova assessed the interior from behind her Ray-Bans. She was dressed in a black halter top that showed off her cleavage and tattoos, plus loose camouflage pants and combat boots. Her thick raven hair hung loosely at her shoulders. The handful of Navy men in the bar zeroed in on her immediately, and she could feel their eyes following her as she took a seat at one of the tables.

It didn't take long. Soon she heard the scrape of a chair pushing back, and a few seconds later, a beefy shadow fell across her table. She looked up to see a squat blond man about her age, with giant veiny biceps bulging like cacao pods. He leaned over until his forelock fell across his blue eyes.

"Hey, I'm Todd," he said. "I don't think I've seen you here before."

Behind her sunglasses, Nova rolled her eyes.

"Just passing through," she said.

"Yeah? From where?"

"I don't know. From here to there."

"Well, since you're here, how about I buy you a drink?" Todd asked.

"That depends."

"On what?"

"On whether you can help me find a friend of mine," Nova said.

"Who's your friend?"

"His name's Jake. Jake DeRusha. The word in town is that this is the off-base hangout for Pax River. I thought I might find him here."

"Sure, I know Jake," Todd replied. "Everybody does. And yeah, he's here all the time. I haven't seen him today, though."

"No?"

"No. But *I'm* here. Maybe we can get to know each other. Later you and me can go look for Jake together."

Nova didn't need to shoot him down. The bartender, a grizzled old guy who was as large as a refrigerator, showed up at the table and did that for her. "Put your eyes back in your head, Toddy. Go sit down with the boys and leave the lady alone."

Todd was twenty years younger than the bartender, but he did as he was told. He lumbered away like a puppy anticipating a kick.

"Sorry about that," the bartender told her when Todd was back with his friends. He wiped down Nova's table with a wet towel and dropped a plastic-covered menu in front of her. "I have to keep the dogs on a leash. Otherwise, they'll hump every pretty leg that comes in here."

Nova laughed. "Thanks."

"I heard you say you're looking for Jake," the bartender said. "I'm Louie, by the way."

"Nice to meet you, Louie. Yeah, I'm looking for Jake. I heard he comes in here a lot."

Louie took a long time to say anything. Then he nodded his head at the empty bar counter behind him. "How about we talk over there?"

"Sure."

Nova relocated to the bar. She slid onto one of the stools, and Louie took a shot glass and filled it with Johnnie Walker Black and pushed it toward her. Then he leaned across the bar on big elbows and spoke in a low voice.

"Let's not pretend, huh, lady? You ain't NCIS, you ain't Marines, and you don't look like a cop or a fed. Process of elimination makes me think you're a spook."

Nova downed the whiskey in a single shot. "Smart guys turn me on, Louie. And you're smart."

"Yeah, well, I figured somebody like you would show up here. I heard what happened to Jake. I got sources all over town who keep me plugged in. Nobody's saying anything to the media, but the word is, he got a bullet in his head."

"You heard right," Nova said. "Jake's dead."

"Fuck me. When did it happen?"

"Last night. Before midnight, I'm told. They found his body in a park near here."

"Jesus, he was here last night."

"Yeah? Was he alone?"

"Oh, yeah, yeah, sitting on the same stool you are right now. Why the snow job about his murder? Is there a terrorism angle? Is somebody coming after the base?"

Nova slipped off her sunglasses and fixed her dark eyes on the bartender. "That's quite a leap, Louie. Most people would figure drugs or gangs or whatever, but you went straight to terrorism. What makes you say that?"

Louie hoisted the bottle of Johnnie Walker again, but Nova waved her hand over the glass. "There was a girl in here the other night. I don't know. I had a funny feeling about her. Part of me thought she was an undercover fed, but now I'm not so sure. Either way, she was dangerous."

"Was she talking to Jake? I thought you said he was alone."

"Not last night," Louie said. "The night before. This girl came in when Jake and Walter were at the bar. She started putting the moves on Walter."

"Who's Walter?"

"Walter Pepper. Ex-Marine. Got separated a couple of years ago. Him and Jake have been thick as thieves their whole lives.

They're in here pretty much every night, complaining about the world."

"Why'd the Corps give Walter the boot?" Nova asked.

"He kept shooting his mouth off. White supremacist bullshit. The military's pretty sensitive about that stuff these days. You can think it, but don't say it, know what I mean? Jake's not much different, but he's smart enough to keep his mouth shut."

"And the girl?"

"She was all over Walter. Had her eyes on him from the get-go. Eventually, he went over to say hi, and not long after, they left together. Jake got a text from Walter, said they were hooking up. That didn't pass the smell test with me. Walter's okay, but he ain't no Romeo. A hot girl half his age doesn't meet him and five minutes later figure she's got to have some of that. Something else was going on."

"So the next night, Jake was on his own?" Nova asked. "Walter didn't show up?"

"Right. Jake was worried. He wondered if Walter was still in bed with the hottie, but you ask me, there's not enough Viagra in the world to keep Walter up that long."

Nova rubbed the empty shot glass between her fingers. "This girl.

What did she look like?"

"Black bangs, fake black, not like yours. Round face, short and skinny. Young, too. Really young, like a teenager. Like I said, not the kind of girl who would go after an old fart like Walter."

Nova's heart sped up in her chest when she heard the description. "Let me guess. Her forearm. She have a tattoo?"

"You know about that? The flag and the rifle? Yeah, Walter and Jake have the same one. Got it at some alt-right gun weekend a while back. You know who the girl is? What's her story?"

"This Walter Pepper," Nova charged ahead without answering. "Where does he live?"

"Not far. A couple of miles away." Louie rattled off an address.

Nova slid off the stool and slapped a fifty-dollar bill on the bar. She raced for the tavern door without saying another word.

Yes, she knew who the girl was.

Yoko.

37

Two hours passed. There was still no sign of Lennon.

Bourne reviewed the area again through his Leupold rifle scope. The variable magnification allowed him to zoom in on possible targets. Nothing he saw raised red flags, but the very absence of a threat was what worried him. The rolling green hills, ribboned with trails for horses and joggers, were empty under the bright afternoon sun. Beyond the hills, a dense stand of trees lined the banks of the Potomac River, but when Jason moved his sight along the bank, he saw no evidence of an ambush being readied.

He focused on the estate, but saw little activity. There was a red barn with a fenced field around it, elaborate gardens landscaped with flowers and fruit trees, a swimming pool bordered by paver stones, chaise longues, and umbrellas, and finally the house, which was three stories high, with two wings jutting off the main entrance and a large glass solarium leading to the pool and gardens. A couple of gardeners came and went on golf carts near the apple trees, but they weren't a concern. An older Filipino attendant brought champagne and appetizers on a silver tray from the house to the patio. He was harmless.

Lennon wasn't here.

Instead, Bourne saw only the same three people he'd observed for the past two hours.

Alicia Beauvoir, Senator Don Pine, and his chief of staff, Tim Randall, sat in the shade of a pergola outside the solarium. They were perfect targets, and Bourne was in the perfect spot to take them out. He could zero in on each of their faces, neatly positioned in the crosshairs of the scope. It wasn't even a challenging shot, not for a qualified sniper on a windless day. With a gentle pressure on the trigger of the Barrett, he could drill a bullet into Alicia Beauvoir's head, then disappear across the hills long before the FBI arrived.

Lennon knew that, too. The kill was waiting for him.

So where is he?

Bourne tried to read the dynamics of the meeting below him. Don Pine did most of the talking. Alicia Beauvoir listened to his pitch, her expression impassive. The senator's aide, Randall, said almost nothing, but he had an oddly jittery look about him. His eyes kept shifting away from Pine and Beauvoir, studying the grounds. A few times, his gaze landed on the hill where Bourne was watching them, and even though Jason knew he was invisible, he had the odd impression that Randall knew he was there. Randall kept a phone on the table in front of him, which he caressed occasionally with his fingers, pushing a button to light up the screen to check for notifications.

For Bourne, Randall's demeanor was the only warning sign. The man looked as if he were waiting for something to happen. An assault? A gunshot from the hills? But he was also a senior aide to a presidential candidate at a meeting that might determine the future of the campaign. Nervousness came with the territory.

Maybe it meant nothing.

More time ticked by. Two hours became three.

Finally, in the middle of the afternoon, Beauvoir said something to Pine—one sentence, just a few words—that changed the tenor of the conversation. Bourne saw broad smiles cross the faces of the two men she was with. Pine practically did a fist pump. He stood up in a rush, extending a hand to Beauvoir, who shook it while remaining in her seat. Bourne saw controlled exhilaration on the senator's face.

Randall picked up his phone and tapped out a message. Then another. And another. Jason could guess what was going on. Alicia Beauvoir had agreed to endorse Don Pine, and Randall was already spreading the news around Washington. He was leaking the news before the official press conference.

Bourne tensed. If the meeting was over, the risk was going up.

But *where* was the threat?

He watched Tim Randall excuse himself and disappear inside the house. The two politicians, Pine and Beauvoir, remained where they were. Pine looked relaxed now, refilling his flute of champagne, easing back in the chair and crossing his legs. Beauvoir, by contrast, looked stiff, her back straight, her lips squeezed into the frown of someone biting down on something sour.

The small talk continued. Pine looked in no hurry to go, whereas Beauvoir seemed impatient for the senator to leave. This was the moment, if anything was going to happen. No one was watching them. There were no witnesses other than Bourne on the hillside. If there was going to be bloodshed, an assassination and a cover-up, the time was now.

But no assault came. Eventually, Pine and Beauvoir got up and returned to the house. For another few minutes, the grounds below Jason were empty. He was alone, feeling the burn of sunshine on his neck. He checked the area one last time, but finally admitted that he'd been wrong.

Wrong!

There was no ambush planned here. No kill shot from the hill. No terrorist assault. And yet his instincts continued to scream at him that something was about to happen.

He'd misjudged the threat, but the threat was still real.

Lennon, I feel you nearby. Can you feel me?

The front door of Alicia Beauvoir's house opened. Tim Randall walked down the marble steps and stood alone in the gravel near the red Chevy Tahoe. Bourne watched him, as close to the man through the scope as if he'd been standing next to him. The aide lit a cigarette, then surveyed the grounds of the estate, his head swiveling as if to confirm no one else was nearby. His fingers twitched, the cigarette quivering. Randall checked his watch, then his phone. He wandered past the Tahoe and stood near the rear of Abbey's gold Tesla. Something about the man's attitude continued to bother Jason. He'd just closed the political deal of a lifetime. Why was he smoking like a man awaiting execution?

Randall tapped ash from his cigarette to the ground. His other hand was buried in his pants pocket. He seemed to be breathing hard, and a sheen of sweat clung to the line of his forehead.

What is he doing?

Abruptly, Randall knelt down behind Abbey's car. He was out of view only for a moment, as if he'd dropped something, and then the aide straightened up again. Randall backed away from the Tesla and flicked his cigarette on the ground. His leg shook as if he was crushing it out under his shoe. He glanced at his watch again, then extracted a cell phone from his suit and tapped out a message.

Through the scope, Bourne zoomed in on the phone in Randall's hand.

He realized Randall was using a *different* phone. For three hours, he'd watched Randall on the patio, his government-issued phone sitting on the table between Alicia Beauvoir and Don Pine. This wasn't the same phone. It was a burner.

Randall was sending a message. To whom?

And what had he done to Abbey's car?

Quickly now, the aide hurried back toward the steps that led to the house. The front door opened again, and three people emerged: Don Pine, Alicia Beauvoir, and Pine's driver. Pine and Beauvoir were engaged in casual conversation, and Randall met them at the bottom of the steps. The chauffeur unlocked the door of the Tahoe and got behind the wheel, and the back doors of the SUV both clicked open automatically.

The meeting was breaking up.

Frustration rippled through Bourne's body. He zoomed in on Randall again, and the aide's face was a stiff mask of political politeness. Bourne had seen faces like that many times. The rigid jaw. The dilated pupils. It was a mask that covered fear. Randall was scared to death.

Scared of what?

Bourne shifted his gaze to Pine, whose cheeks were flushed with victory. He seemed unaware of the odd behavior of his aide. Then Jason studied Beauvoir, and Bourne saw something in her face that he didn't understand. Her entire demeanor had become as stony as the statues in her garden. This wasn't fear, not like he saw in Tim Randall. This was something very different. What? What was it?

He didn't have any more time to think about it. The door to the estate opened again, and someone new emerged. It was a red-haired woman whose face he'd long ago memorized, whose warm, soft lips he could still taste from the previous night. The sight of her made his heart jump, and he had to wrestle down his emotion so that he could concentrate.

It was Abbey.

She was the last person he wanted to see, the last person

he wanted in the middle of this group. Because Bourne wasn't wrong. The violence was coming.

It was coming *now*.

"Ah, there you are, Abbey," Beauvoir said. "I wanted you to have a chance to see Don before he left."

Abbey held a slim laptop case in her hand, and she descended the steps of the house to join the three people gathered in the gravel parking area. Even after two years in DC, it was still disorienting for her to be among members of the powerful elite. A senior political aide who'd run in Washington circles for years, the former secretary of state and UN ambassador, and the former CIA director, current U.S. senator, and presidential front-runner. That was Washington life, but Abbey wasn't sure she would ever get used to it.

"Don, do you know Abbey Laurent?" Beauvoir went on. "She's the writer working on the book with me. Actually, the project is really all hers. I'm just providing local color."

"Don't believe her," Abbey said with a polite smile. "Alicia is a born thriller writer. She hardly needs me at all. And I'm sure you don't remember me, Senator, but we met a couple of years ago when I was writing a profile of you for the *Atlantic*."

Pine gave her the charming grin that she'd seen so often on television. It was a grin she didn't trust at all. "Yes, of course I remember you, Ms. Laurent. I definitely wouldn't forget a face like yours. Congratulations on the book project. Whatever the two of you come up with, I can't wait to read it."

"Well, that's very kind of you, Senator," Abbey replied, "but if the polls are right, I imagine you'll be too busy for much light reading next year."

"Let's hope," Pine said with another grin.

Beauvoir took out her phone and tapped a few buttons. Abbey felt the buzz of a text arriving. "Abbey, I just sent you contact information for Garrett Frith. He's a friend of mine at State. You know that scene we want to set in Hangzhou? I'm not an expert on that part of China, but Garrett lived there for almost four years. He can give us the feel of the place and answer some of our questions. But I'm afraid he's headed overseas for two months starting tonight. Would you be able to get back to DC this afternoon and talk to him? He told me he'd squeeze in an hour for you if you can be there right away."

Abbey nodded. "Of course."

"Excellent. Then come on back here, and we'll work on that chapter tonight."

"Sounds good."

Abbey excused herself from the group. She headed across the gravel driveway to the gold Tesla, but she felt a strange sensation as she did, like eyes on her back. When she turned around, she saw only the small group near the steps and no one else. But the sensation didn't go away.

Then her phone started ringing. When she checked it, she saw the name Alan Longworth, which was one of the cover identities Jason used.

Was he watching her? Was it his eyes she felt?

But she didn't have time to talk to him, not now, not here. She'd call him from the car as she drove back to DC. Abbey approached the Tesla and pulled on the door handle, which usually unlocked for her automatically. However, this time the door didn't budge under her hand. She tapped her pocket to confirm she had the Tesla key fob, but when she grabbed the handle again, the door remained locked. Fishing out the fob, she pushed the button manually to unlock the door, but again nothing happened.

Abbey frowned. She tried it several more times without any luck. Feeling the heat of embarrassment, she returned to the group near the steps. The back door of the red Tahoe was open, and Don Pine was in the process of climbing inside.

"Alicia, I'm sorry to interrupt," she said. "I'm afraid I'm having trouble with my car. It's a friend's car, actually, and the fob seems to be dead."

Beauvoir chuckled and glanced at the Tesla. "I'll have to talk to Elon about that."

"I know we're under a time crunch," Abbey added. "Do you have a car I could borrow to get into the city?"

"I'm afraid I don't," Beauvoir replied. "My husband's out with his car. Tim and I are going to stay behind to talk about the schedule for the public endorsement, but then I have a dinner to go to." She leaned toward the Tahoe. "Don, I wonder if Abbey could catch a ride with you back to DC."

The senator slid over on the seat and patted the cushion. "Of course. I'd be happy for the company, Ms. Laurent. Perhaps I can persuade you to give me some more secrets about this book you and Alicia are writing."

Abbey hesitated at the offer for only a moment.

Then she walked to the Tahoe and got inside.

38

Nova drove past the cul-de-sac where Walter pepper lived. She did that twice, not enough to look suspicious if anyone was watching the street. Then she parked two blocks away, where her car wouldn't be seen. It was a leafy suburban neighborhood, dotted with two-story houses tucked among evergreen trees. Nova found a paved sidewalk leading into a wooded park, and when she was out of sight, she headed off the trail and picked her way through the trees. Her sense of direction led her unerringly toward Walter's house.

Five minutes later, she approached the house from the back. The forest kept her in shadow. The weed-strewn yard was boxed in by a rusted chain-link fence where the mesh had come free in several places. She saw a detached garage with a long driveway leading from the street and then the house, which was in need of fresh paint. Beside her, near the fringe of the woods, was a fat oak tree with a cork shooter's target nailed to the bark. The trunk and target were pockmarked with bullet holes.

She couldn't see inside the house, but there were no signs of life, and she saw no evidence of security cameras monitoring the property. Quietly, Nova closed on the yard. She climbed the fence where one of the poles leaned toward the ground. Her Glock was in her hand. The tall grass was littered with old tools and a few empty cardboard ammunition boxes. She approached the rear wall of the house and put her ear to the wooden siding near one of the windows. No voices and no vibrations came through the wall. She pried her fingernails under the sash and discovered with a slight push that the window was open. As silently as she could, she pushed it up just high enough to provide a gap where she could squeeze her lithe body inside. Tucking the gun into her belt at the small of her back, she snaked through the window and unwound her body on the floor.

The house was cold and smelled of sweat and human waste. The only light came from the crack of the open window above her. Otherwise, the house was pitch-black. But the interior wasn't completely silent. She heard a muffled noise from one of the other rooms like the frightened squeal of a pig. Nova felt around on the floor, and her fingers closed around something heavy and glass. It had a handle—a beer stein? She took her Glock in one hand, and with her other, she hoisted the beer stein in what she thought was the direction of the noise. It landed heavily on the floor and rolled without breaking. Nothing happened. The clatter didn't bring an attack.

Nova pushed herself to her feet and took a careful step, then another, nudging her toe ahead of her to make sure nothing was blocking her way. As she got closer, the muffled noise got louder. Someone was there. A person. He was right in front of her.

Nova slipped a small flashlight from her pocket and switched it on.

In the glow, she saw a face, and the face matched the military record she'd looked up online. Walter Pepper sat with his arms and legs tied to a straight-backed metal chair. A gag in his mouth prevented him from making any sound other than that piglike grunt. The brightness of the light forced him to squeeze his eyes shut and turn away, but then he opened them again, and Nova saw that his dark eyes were filled with terror. Underneath his gag, he was trying to scream at her.

Nova understood, but she understood too late.

When she spun around, she saw Yoko behind her, frozen like a statue, waiting for her with a grin on her mouth and a Smith & Wesson M&P 22 at the end of her outstretched arms. Yoko fired, a suppressor muffling the shot to a low click, and Nova felt a strange sensation in her chest. It wasn't even pain, just heavy pressure, like a fastball thumping on her body. She stumbled backward, shook herself, and dropped the flashlight, which broke and left the room in darkness again.

Click.

More strange pressure, in her shoulder this time. Nova's brain sped up, and she finally threw herself sideways and fired her Glock. But in that fraction of a second Yoko had gone, vanishing into the blackness. Where was she? Nova fired again, completely blind, then realized she was wasting her ammunition. Her head spun, dizzy and sluggish, but her instincts made her roll away, and sure enough—

Click. Another shot.

This time Yoko missed, but Nova trained her barrel on the flash and followed the rush of air as Yoko sprinted away. She led the girl with the Glock, then fired again, and this time she got the satisfaction of hearing an expulsion of air and a stifled scream as the bullet found its mark. Yoko fell hard, but kept moving.

Nova bolted in the opposite direction, but the noise gave her away.

Click.

"Fuck!" Nova cried, unable to stop herself.

Yoko's bullet found her hip, and there was no pressure now, only agony. She stumbled hard against the slick leather of a couch, then collapsed behind it as another shot landed in the sofa and blew out a cloud of foam that landed on her face like invisible snow. Nova bit her tongue, trying to stop herself from screaming. Her hip was on fire, like an electrical charge shocking her nerve endings. Then the pain caught up to her chest and shoulder. When she inhaled, she had to clap a hand over her mouth to stop her lungs from gagging. She tasted blood in her mouth.

"You're going to die, *bitch*!" Yoko hissed from somewhere in the room. The voice came from everywhere and nowhere.

Nova's whole body stiffened, but then she spat back. "You first, little girl."

Each of them gathered their strength for the second round. Nova sat with her back against the sofa, safe for the moment. If Yoko came closer, she'd hear her. But she couldn't play the waiting game forever. Blood continued to ooze out of her, soaking her skin and clothes, and soon she'd grow lightheaded and unable to function. Yoko knew that. Wherever Nova had hit the girl, she didn't think the wound was fatal. If they sat here for much longer, Yoko was going to win.

Nova didn't know if she had the strength to fight. She'd never experienced pain like this, hot and cold, fire and ice at the same time. Her face was wet; she was crying silently from the torture. Her limbs stiffened. She was Pinocchio turning to wood.

Move! You have to move!

Her brain gave her orders, but her body lay there, lightning firing in the seared bullet holes. She took a breath, but the breath barely swelled her chest and made her want to gag. There was blood in her lungs.

"Nova."

Whose voice was that? Where was it coming from?

Then she knew—it was inside her head. She heard the voice; she saw pictures in her mind. *Oh my God,* she thought, this was her life passing in front of her. This was what you saw, felt, and heard right before the end.

"Nova."

It was Jason. He called her name as clearly as if he were right there beside her. Jason, holding her in that little bedroom near the St. Lawrence River outside Quebec City, whispering her name as he made love to her. She could feel him inside her, feel his pace quicken.

My God, she'd thought that day, *I'm in love with this man. How stupid am I to fall in love with another agent!*

The pictures in her head accelerated. Moment after moment, year after year, a bullet train sped through her memory. Her childhood. The scared girl under the bed, watching her parents die, her mother's eyes looking back at her lifelessly. Their blood soaking her clothes the way her blood was soaking hers now. Her whole life! The people she'd killed, the men she'd slept with, the drugs she'd taken, the lives she'd saved.

And Jason. It all kept coming back to Jason.

Yes, she loved him, but he didn't love her. He was in love with someone else.

Then the movie was over. She was still behind the sofa, and she was dying. Nova opened her eyes, seeing nothing. The pain turned to numbness; numbness came before death. But it was okay to die. She didn't care about that.

It wasn't okay to *lose*!

Not to this little girl.

That was the answer. That was the rule.

The most lethal enemy is the one who isn't afraid to die.

Treadstone.

Nova lurched to her feet, giving up the cover of the leather sofa. Her brain told her limbs to function, and this time, one last time, her limbs obeyed. Yoko heard her coming and started firing. *Click, click, click, click, click.* More bullets. Most went wild as Nova zigzagged drunkenly. Two struck home, one ripping off her right ear and deafening her, one shattering her left wrist. But that didn't matter. Her gun was in her right hand.

The muzzle flashes told her exactly where to aim.

And she did.

Nova fired and fired and fired until her empty magazine yielded only a hollow click. When she heard that, her fingers opened, and the Glock dropped to the floor. She spread her arms wide, expecting more gunfire, expecting the end to come. But no more bullets erupted from below her. She staggered sideways until her body crashed against a wall, then she dragged her hands along the Sheetrock, leaving a sticky trail behind her. Her fingers closed around a light switch, and Nova pushed it up. Light dazzled the room, as bright as the sun. She squinted, and then her eyes took in the scene.

Yoko was dead.

She lay on her back on the floor, eyes wide open, bone and brain sprayed on the hardwood floor behind her. Two of Nova's blind shots had drilled through her skull, leaving scorched holes like red dwarf stars. Walter Pepper was dead, too, still tied to the chair with his head slumped to his chest. A stray bullet—either from Nova's gun or Yoko's—had struck him in the heart.

Nova looked down at her own chest. There was blood everywhere, already turning dark. Her hands had begun to grow numb, and she could barely feel her legs. She didn't have much time. When she sucked in a breath, her lungs gurgled like bubbles underwater. Dizziness made her mind spin. She tried to walk, but she swayed and collapsed back against the wall. Her knees buckled, and she slid down until she was sitting on the floor.

Fuck.

But she'd always known her life would end like this. This had been her fate from the very beginning.

She stared across the room, trying to focus. Beyond the body of Walter Pepper, she noticed everything that would be found by the FBI whenever the hit was done. A huge flag of the Liberty Soldiers. don't tread on me. Handguns, cartridges, rifles, some on the floor, some on a table in the corner, like an arsenal. She had no idea how much was real and how much had been planted by Yoko and Lennon. There was also a strange sweet smell to the room that she was noticing for the first time. When she glanced at her boots, she saw orange dust.

Fertilizer.

She knew what that meant. A bomb. Crude, amateurish, and deadly.

Nova saw posters taped to the wall. Most were politicians, but there were people from the media, too. Their eyes had been scratched out. In the middle, the biggest of all, was an oversized photo taken at a campaign rally. A target had been drawn around the head, and three words had been scrawled across it, half across the poster, half across the wall.

First to die.

She struggled to find her phone. Her fingers felt thick, as if trapped inside awkward gloves. Her eyes went in and out of focus. Each breath came and went quickly, not delivering enough oxygen to her brain. She tried over and over, and when the phone finally spilled to the floor from her pocket, she pushed buttons, hoping she was doing it right. She needed Jason. She needed to hear his voice. She needed to *tell him*!

And there he was.

"Nova."

It was just like it had been when they were together. She felt the wave of memories again, the sensations washing over her body. She wasn't in a house in Maryland, surrounded by blood and death. She was in a bed with Jason.

"Nova?" he went on urgently. "Are you there? Where are you?"

"I love you."

Had she ever told him that? Had she ever admitted it to herself? And was she even saying the words out loud, or were they trapped in her head?

"*Nova!*" Jason repeated. "Are you okay? What's going on?"

"I love you," she said again, and she was sure that this time she'd said it out loud. But her voice told him everything. She couldn't hide the truth from him. She didn't sound like herself, because she sounded like what she was. A woman dying, close to crossing over. This was the end.

"Jesus, Nova, where are you? I'll send an ambulance."

"No time," she murmured. "Not a sniper. A bomb."

"What?"

"Lennon has a bomb."

"Nova, tell me where you are."

"Go. *Run.*"

She stared across the room at the bodies. The weapons. And the poster on the wall, with the target drawn in thick black marker around the head. The phone began to slip through her sticky fingers. Her eyes drifted shut.

"It's Pine," she murmured.

"What? What are you saying?"

Nova's lips curled into a dreamy smile. She felt herself sailing away, leaving one place and going somewhere new, heading for that river in her mind. Heading for Jason. She barely had enough breath to warn him.

No goodbyes, just one last mission. One last assignment, and her job was done.

"It's not Beauvoir. She's not the target. Lennon's going to kill Don Pine."

39

Bourne knew.

He clenched the phone in his hand, and he knew. He was listening to Nova die. A woman he'd loved and a woman he'd hated. A woman who'd saved his life and betrayed him. There was no mistake this time; there would be no resurrection, as there had been after the mass shooting in Las Vegas. The phone went quiet, and when he called her name over and over, he got no response.

But he had no time to grieve.

The Chevy Tahoe with Don Pine inside had disappeared down the road that led from Alicia Beauvoir's country home. And not just Pine. Abbey was with him. *Abbey* was in the SUV, too.

There were no coincidences. This was the plan. Kill them both.

Lennon has a bomb.

He took his phone again and punched in Abbey's number. He had to warn her; he had to stop that car! As it began to ring, he hissed under his breath, "Pick up, pick up, pick up! For God's sake, Abbey, answer the goddamn phone!"

But the call went to her voicemail, and he didn't bother

leaving a message. There was no time for messages. He tapped out a few words into a text—*Stop the car now!*—but the text stayed unread.

In one minute, maybe two, the SUV would be on the two-lane highway, accelerating back to the city. Bourne clutched the rifle in his fist and ran. His chest hammering, he sprinted down the slope, and wind rushed into his face. The sunshine of the perfect fall day taunted him, as if death could never come under such a blue sky.

He'd never run faster or felt so slow. He shot to the base of the hill, jumped over a wide creek flowing through the seam of the meadow, and charged up the next steep slope. Every second seemed to speed up, taking forever. When he crested the summit, he skidded to a stop, assessing the land below him. There was the farmhouse he'd seen earlier, with a small lake nearby. Beyond the fields, he glimpsed the highway emerging from a stand of trees before disappearing into the woods again half a mile later. He didn't see the Tahoe.

But he saw something else. Something that punched his gut.

A white pickup truck was parked adjacent to the highway where the green fields turned to weeds and dirt. He remembered the truck; the pickup had been near the farmhouse when he first arrived. But not now. It had been moved, relocated, placed where an SUV on the highway would have to slow down and squeeze past it. He put binoculars to his eyes and zeroed in on the truck. There was a logo painted on the door: DAWSON FARMS. Mud spattered the chassis near the wheels. The flatbed was covered with a tarpaulin, shielding whatever was below it.

It was meant to look innocent, but it wasn't. This was the trap.

But he was too far away to reach the highway in time, too far away to stop it. The Tahoe was coming. It was coming *soon.* Not even minutes—seconds! When it did, when it rolled past the farm truck, the earth would tremble, and a conflagration would consume it.

Abbey!

Bourne's gaze swept the field. The farmhouse. The lake. Lennon had to be nearby, within visual range of the truck. He wouldn't risk the delays of a remote camera feed. The bomb had to be activated manually—when the vehicle was in range, when the location was perfect for maximum destruction.

Besides, Lennon would *want* to see it happen. He'd want *Bourne* to see it. He would need to be here for the denouement.

Where was the best vantage point? Jason examined the thick trees. The long brush by the highway. The tightly rolled cylinders of hay stacked near the edge of the fields. But there was no sign of the killer. Wherever Lennon had hidden himself, his camouflage was good.

Then the taunting sunlight gave away the game. A pinpoint flash shined from the overgrown weeds at the lakeshore. A reflection—sunlight glinting on glass! He used the rifle scope for magnification and tried to hold it steady, and for only an instant, he spotted a pair of hands clutching the black metal of binoculars. Someone was stretched out in the weeds, gaze trained on the highway and the slope that led out of the trees. That was the direction the Tahoe would come as it neared the ambush. Down the hill, toward the flatland where the pickup truck was parked.

Lennon.

Jason only had time for one shot. The first bullet would warn him, and the assassin would vanish into the weeds. But he had to fire *standing up* from the breezy hilltop. He leaned backward slightly, one elbow braced against his hip as he supported the barrel. His other arm was tucked tightly against his body as his finger eased around the trigger. He sighted through the scope where he'd seen the killer's hands. They weren't there anymore, but he calculated the location where Lennon's body should be, where he had the best hope of a kill shot through the weeds.

He held his breath, then let it out slowly.

Jason held his body motionless, a block of ice. Under his finger, the trigger yielded to the pressure. The cartridge exploded with a crack, and the sound chased the bullet across the field. Through the scope, he saw a spray of red against the amber weeds. Blood. A *hit*. He'd hit him.

But how badly?

There was movement in the brush. Lennon was rolling away quickly, still alive, taking shelter behind a tree. Bourne had no shot at all there; he'd *lost*. When he shifted his attention back to the highway, he saw a new stab of sunlight, this time from the metal of an oncoming vehicle. First he saw the glinting light as the Tahoe crested the hill, and then he heard the growl of its engine.

Bourne dropped the rifle to the green grass. He grabbed his phone again and dialed the number one last time.

Abbey, for God's sake! Pick up!

The pain from his shattered ankle made him want to scream, but instead Lennon laughed. Tears of agony rolled down his face, but all he could do was laugh.

Fuck you, Cain, how did you make that shot?

He squirmed behind the oak tree where he was safe, but he had to leave the binoculars behind. There was no time to retrieve them, and he wasn't about to give Cain a second chance to land a bullet in his skull. From his new vantage, he could still see the highway. He could eyeball the best moment to set off the bomb. The phone was in his hand, finger poised to make the call. The call, the completed circuit, then the explosion. But he was guessing at the exact timing now. It would have to be enough.

His ankle howled. His foot dangled uselessly. He felt like a wolf caught in a steel trap. It occurred to him that he wasn't going to get out of this one, that he couldn't escape this time, but that didn't matter. He'd finish the assignment. He'd destroy Cain by destroying the woman he loved. His sweaty finger rubbed over the button on the phone, waiting for the right instant. His lips pursed together, and he whistled a song.

"Here Comes the Sun."

Everything was all right.

He heard the engine, then saw the Tahoe cross the summit and head down the hill toward the pickup truck. In his head, he counted down, clicking off the seconds. Five, four, three, two, *one*. Don Pine and Abbey Laurent were about to die.

There wasn't anything in the world Cain could do to stop it.

Abbey stared across the Chevy Tahoe at senator don pine, front-runner for the Democratic nomination for president of the United States. Everything Jason had said about him, all his suspicions about what Don Pine had done, ran through her head. It began with 227 people dying aboard a missing jet. Years later, people were still dying, loose ends tied up to keep a terrible secret.

This man had ordered murders all over the world. This man was behind Defiance.

A presidential campaign was a hell of a motive.

Abbey glanced out the window of the SUV. Dust from the road rose around them, kicked up by the truck's heavy tires. She couldn't see the estate; it was a mile behind them. Ahead of them was the highway and the two men from Alicia's security team, who waved them through to the main road. To the right was the Potomac; to the left was the route back to DC.

Pine was saying something, but she wasn't even paying attention. He was trying to charm her, flatter her, seduce her. For some women, power was an aphrodisiac, but not Abbey. She'd always been attracted to strength, not power. And Jason had shown her that the powerful were never to be trusted.

Before she could stop herself, she blurted it out.

"Senator, what really happened to that jet?"

Pine stopped mid-sentence. He'd been dangling promises of exclusive interviews, of a behind-the-scenes campaign novel, but the words died in his mouth. He stared at Abbey as if he couldn't believe what he'd heard.

"What did you say?"

"I said, what really happened to Flight 1342? It's just you and me here. No one's listening. Tell me the truth."

The senator blinked. "Alicia said you weren't writing about that."

"I'm not. Not yet. But my next book will be about *Defiance*, Senator."

Outside, she felt the Tahoe climbing a shallow hill. The road between the trees was barely wider than the SUV.

"I have no idea what you're talking about," Pine replied coolly, "but if you're trying to take me down, Ms. Laurent, you might as well buy a ticket and stand in line. What are you after, money? Glory? Who are you working for? Who put you up to this?"

"What happened to the jet?" Abbey demanded again, her voice louder.

"I told you, I have no idea. I've been telling people that for years, and yet the rumors keep coming my way. Directed at me, pointing the blame at *me*. I don't believe that's an accident. Someone knows, Ms. Laurent. Someone in DC most assuredly knows the truth. But you've got the wrong man."

Abbey blinked as she watched his face, the look in his eyes. Every word from Pine projected the right combination of sincerity and outrage. He was so smooth. Every politician was a smooth liar, but she found that she actually believed him. She didn't like him, she didn't trust him, but she believed him.

What did that mean?

The Tahoe crested the hill.

From the backseat, through the windshield, she looked down the slope of the highway to where the trees opened up in an expanse of green fields. Sunlight glittered on a small lake, a farmhouse in the distance. Where the pavement leveled off, a dirty white pickup truck was parked half on the shoulder, half on the road.

In her pocket, Abbey felt the buzz of a call on her phone. Again. How many times had Jason been trying to reach her? She was about to ignore it again, when her late mother's voice popped into her head.

The memory came out of nowhere. It was something she'd told Abbey when she was just a little girl.

"If it's someone you love, you always take the call. You never know when it will be the last time."

Abbey hesitated, then brought the phone to her ear. "Jason?"

His voice screamed at her like a fire alarm.

"Stop the car! Stop the car! There's a bomb in that pickup ahead of you!"

Abbey's brain processed everything at once. But she was too slow. She just didn't have time.

Jason's words rolled through her head, and she tried to catch up to what he was saying and what it meant. She saw Don Pine leaning forward to stare through the windshield. She felt the Tahoe veering to get around the pickup truck that was practically blocking the road. She was forming words through her lips; they were almost out of her mouth—*"Stop! Stop!"*—when the world exploded.

Metal tore and glass shattered. The doors flew open.

The giant heavy Chevy Tahoe blew off the ground and did a somersault in the air.

40

Jason saw it happen. He saw the blast and the smoke, saw the pickup disintegrate, saw the Tahoe flip. Even at that distance, he felt intense heat billowing across the fields. One clinical word formed in his brain.

Nonsurvivable.

Whoever had been in the SUV was dead. Abbey was dead. Miles away, so was Nova. Not just one of them. Both. He'd lost both to Lennon.

He should have been filled with rage. Or grief. Tears should have run down his face, and he should have crossed the field to where Lennon was hiding and ended him with his hands clenched around the killer's throat. But he felt nothing. He was dead, too, a shell, as empty as he'd felt when he awakened on a boat in the Mediterranean near Marseilles and realized he had no idea who he was. Right now, he would have gladly given up his memories again. He wanted to forget the past three years.

For a few brief moments, he stood stiffly in the field, unable to move. The rifle slipped from his fingers and dropped to the ground. In the distance, he already heard sirens. Someone had heard the earth tremble, seen the smoke, and called 911. He couldn't stay here, and he couldn't leave. He needed to see her, hold her, kiss her, before they came and took her away. He had to face the reality of what he'd done.

Bourne ran across the meadow toward the highway. Flames still rose from the pickup, and he had to divert around it. The forest was on fire, trees burning, the field burning. He smelled gasoline and fertilizer in the air. When he reached the road, the pavement was hot and black under his feet. The Tahoe had been blown into the trees on the opposite side of the road. It had come to rest upside down, front end pancaked, doors open, its windows broken. He stared at the ruined vehicle from twenty yards away, summoning the courage to go closer.

To see her.

He made his way to the SUV. One body, the driver, lay with his torso out the door. His head was twisted at a grotesque angle, his neck snapped by the impact. Jason fought through the smoke and had to squat to look inside the Tahoe. Senator Don Pine was there, body blocking his view. Pine was dead, too, eyes closed, no pulse, face and torso a sea of blood. Jason eased the senator's corpse through the window and stared through the smoke and shadow at the opposite side of the Tahoe.

But the backseat was empty. Abbey wasn't there. Her body had been ejected in the crash, and she lay somewhere in the dense brush. He had to find her. He had to take her in his arms one last time.

The grim search took him through the trees. His eyes swept the ground, looking for anything that would lead him to her. Clothes. A shoe. Blood. He used his hands to separate the weeds, dreading the moment when her face would be there below him. But she wasn't there. The forest was empty up to the fringe of the trees, where the green fields stretched into the hills.

Then he finally saw her. She'd been thrown at least thirty

feet as the truck flipped. Her body lay in the softness of the meadow.

His emptiness vanished, and his dead emotions came to life. His breath burst from his chest as he sprinted to her, then knelt beside her body and took her hand. Her skin was still warm. She lay on her back, angelic, no blood on her face. Her eyes were closed, her limbs motionless and peaceful. He stared at her, and his heart seized with loss and fury. Then he shoved that all aside and bent over her face and put his lips lightly against hers.

"Abbey," he murmured, his voice cracking.

There was no answer from the body below him. Finally, he said words he had never dared say, because they no longer mattered. There was no danger in saying them now. He'd already done the worst he could do to her. He'd cursed her and killed her by letting her into his life.

"I love you."

And at that moment, something impossible happened. Abbey's eyes fluttered open. It happened so suddenly he wasn't sure he was seeing what he was seeing. Her eyes blinked, moved left and right in a kind of daze, and then focused on him. Her soft lips made an effort at a smile.

She'd heard him. She was *alive*. "I love you, too."

Jason sprang to his feet. He screamed at the ambulances, police cars, and fire trucks that were wailing their arrival at the crash scene, and he called to the men who poured through the doors.

"I need help over here! Now, now, *now*!"

The ambulance took her away.

Her right shoulder and right ankle were broken where she'd landed after the impact threw her free. That was all they knew. Maybe there were other injuries; that would be for the doctors at the hospital to determine. But she was alive, which was a miracle. If she'd been trapped in the SUV, she'd be dead, like Don Pine and his driver. If she'd flown into a tree or landed on her head and neck, she'd be dead. But no. Abbey had survived.

The police refused to let him go with her. That was fine, because Jason knew there was nothing he could do for Abbey in the next several hours. However, there was something he had to do for her *and* for Nova right here and now.

In the chaos of the emergency scene, Bourne melted away. No one saw him go. He crossed the green fields toward the lake, not expecting Lennon to be there. In the lair where the assassin had been hiding, he found a large amount of fresh blood staining the weeds. The wound was serious, whatever it was. Lennon was trailing blood, leaving a path for Bourne to follow toward the farmhouse.

It was exactly as it had been years earlier, outside Tskhinvali in South Ossetia. Cain was chasing Abel. Jason's past was repeating itself.

The farmhouse door ahead of him was open. As he neared the house, following the blood, he drew his Sig and stayed low. The windows of the house were closed. He expected to draw fire, but there were no shots. He neared the door, looking for some other trap. A trip wire. Another bomb. However, he slipped inside and found the house to be utterly still. There was no movement anywhere, and the only foul element was the smell of the two bodies on the floor. An old man, an old woman, who'd been dead for a couple of days and were drawing bugs and flies as they decomposed.

Lennon was gone.

Bourne searched the house, but the killer had escaped. He'd drawn Jason inside as a misdirection to slow him down. Bourne exited the house through the back door, and outside he found the blood trail again, heading toward the woods.

Lennon's leg was dragging; he couldn't have gone far. Bourne followed quickly, pushing through the trees, his pace like a soldier's march. Adrenaline gave him ferocious energy. His eyes, his face, his heart, were all black, focused on one goal.

Kill Lennon.

End the duel once and for all, the duel that had begun in the recesses of his memory years earlier.

Pay him back for murdering Nova.

Pay him back for bringing Abbey within inches of death.

I'm coming for you, Abel.

In the thick brush, he lost the blood trail, then found it, then lost it again. But Lennon showed him the way. Through the shadows, a bullet blew past his head, and the suppressed crack of the gun rolled over him like a dull pop. Bourne took cover as more shots echoed around him. When he peered into the web of trees, he saw nothing, but then he heard awkward footsteps trampling away. A figure bobbed and weaved not even fifty yards away. Jason stopped, braced himself, and fired. The shot missed, but it slowed Lennon down, forcing the assassin to stop and hide. In the next few seconds, Bourne closed the gap between them. They weren't far apart now. Only thirty or forty feet of tree trunks and dangling vines separated them.

Two killers.

Bourne fired again. So did Lennon. The assassin's aim was good. A bullet buried itself in the flesh of Bourne's thigh, and he spun backward, sliding to the ground. The pain was immediate. He squeezed his eyes shut and pushed his lips together to fight it down. He tore off a shirt sleeve and tied the cloth around the bleeding wound. When he stood, his leg felt frozen, and it dragged woodenly as he continued the chase.

Two killers.

Two wounded men.

He heard the roar of an engine. Through the late afternoon

darkness of the woods, Bourne spotted headlights. This was Lennon's escape route. Jason didn't bother going after the car; by the time he got there, it would be gone. He changed direction, limping furiously, tree branches clutching at his skin, vines tripping him and nearly spilling him off his feet. The crunch of tires on dirt broke through the silence.

Ignoring the pain in his leg, Bourne spilled from the woods onto a narrow dirt road. He fell, landing on his back, gun in his hand. From the ground, he looked up and saw a Ford Explorer bearing down on him at high speed. The vehicle swerved, targeting him, ready to crush his body under its wheels. Jason lifted his Sig and fired five shots, aiming for the left front tire, then the right front tire, then three more into the windshield. The glass broke into popcorn. The tires shredded.

The Explorer kept coming.

Bourne tried to roll, but his leg wouldn't move. The SUV roared like a stampeding elephant, and he didn't even close his eyes for the impact. He didn't care. But the impact never came. At the last second, the Explorer lurched, wheels lifting off the ground and missing him by inches. Sharp rocks blew off the ground and cut his face. The SUV fishtailed for fifty yards before diving off the road, crashing hard against the grainy trunk of an ash tree. Its wheels kept spinning, going nowhere.

Bourne got to his feet, collapsed to one knee, then staggered after the Explorer. He kept his right arm straight and level, Sig in his hand. As Jason neared the SUV, Lennon shoved open the driver's door with his shoulder and fell out of the vehicle. The assassin rolled onto his back, lifting his head to watch Jason closing on him. He still held his Glock. Lennon raised his gun arm, but Bourne fired once, shattering the killer's wrist. The pistol fell harmlessly to the dirt. Lennon gasped with pain, then let his head fall back.

The road was deserted. The sun barely penetrated the

woods, leaving the two of them deep in shadows. The Explorer hissed steam. Jason stood over Lennon and stared down at the assassin.

"Nova's dead," he said.

Lennon breathed heavily as his blood gathered on the road. His face was cruel. "And Abbey?"

"She survived."

"A happy ending for you, Cain. How sweet."

"We don't get happy endings," Bourne said. "Not people like us. That's not how it works."

"So kill me. Go ahead, you've earned it."

Bourne knelt beside the assassin and put his Sig to the man's temple. "First tell me about Defiance."

On the ground, Lennon's mouth broke into a smile, and he laughed soundlessly. "Jesus. Why does that even matter now? Why do you care?"

"Because whoever's behind Defiance is the real assassin. The real monster. Nova died because of them. This isn't over. Not until I know the truth."

"Don't you ever learn, Cain? Nobody wants the truth to come out. Nobody will *let* it come out."

Bourne pushed the barrel harder against the killer's forehead. The heat began to burn the man's flesh like cooking meat. "Tell me about the jet. What really happened?"

Lennon stared past Jason toward the crowns of the trees. His eyes blinked open and shut with pain. His ankle was shattered. So was his wrist, his gun hand destroyed. He squirmed awkwardly as if other bones had been broken in the crash. His face was bloody where glass had cut him.

"All I know is what the scientist told me," Lennon told him with a strange sigh.

"Mallory Foster," Jason said.

"Yeah. That's her. She was called out the night 1342 went missing. She was sent to a lab to examine samples of a virus.

Something new, incredibly contagious, incredibly lethal. She said it scared her to death. If it got out? Millions would die. When the news came out about the plane the next day, she was sure that the virus had been on board. That's why the plane had to be taken down. She also knew they wouldn't let her live knowing what she did. She was right about that, too."

"Who put the virus on the plane? The Iranians?"

Lennon nodded. "There weren't many rogue nations with the scientific knowledge and the sheer barbarism to do something like this. After I killed Foster, I went to my Iranian source in New York. What she told me helped me put two and two together. It was their plan."

"*Why?* Why would they do that?"

"Vengeance for the murder of their general. Gholami."

The name exploded in Bourne's head like the launch of a rocket. Just like it had once before.

Gholami!

The Russian, Fyodor, had used that name, too, and it had set off the fireworks that came when Bourne tried to remember it. The pounding in his brain. The searing pain behind his eyes. Why did he know that name? Why was it important?

But the memory was coming back to him now.

He could see the beach in the moonlight. He could feel the warm Mediterranean breeze. Two men in black slipping toward the waterside cabana.

"A resort in Cyprus," Bourne murmured.

"That's right."

"A room on the water."

"Yes."

Then he remembered. Jesus, he *remembered*!

"*We* killed him," Bourne gasped. "It was *us*! You and me. Cain and Abel."

Lennon's eyes closed. "We were a team, Cain. We were the best. You took down Gholami. But I took out his family first."

"We weren't supposed to touch them!" Jason insisted. "We were only supposed to take out the general! I remember the mission. Holly was clear about the assignment. Only Gholami and no one else. Why did you kill them? Jesus, I heard the shots. So did Gholami. He *knew*! He saw you come in with the blood on your hands! On your face! You murdered all of them! His wife! His *kids*!"

"Your orders were different than mine," Lennon said.

"*Who* gave you the orders? Who told you to kill them?"

"It came from someone higher up. Just like Defiance. Whoever it was had the right authorizations. I don't know who it was. It was never my job to ask questions. But the order was to make sure Gholami suffered. Before he died, he needed to know his family was dead, too."

Bourne shook his head.

Fragments of memories spilled through his brain like pieces of a broken mirror. *Defiance!* Treadstone had been part of it from the beginning. It was never just about the jet. It was about the murder of children, too! Gholami's wife and children! And he'd been there when it began. It had been lost in his past.

But the past wasn't just a memory. The past was alive. Defiance had killed again. More victims. *Who* was pulling the strings?

Who'd been playing them all like marionettes for seven years?

It came from someone higher up.

Then he thought about the scene outside Alicia Beauvoir's estate as he watched through the rifle scope. He remembered Don Pine's chief of staff kneeling beside Abbey's Tesla. Disabling it.

"*Tim Randall.* He knew you were going to be targeting the car. You helped him shut down Abbey's Tesla."

Lennon blinked, long and slow. "Yes."

"What was his role? How did he find *you*?"

"An Iranian gave me the hit on Pine. One of their senior intelligence officers. Hamid Ashkani. Randall reached out to me through him. We met at the staging area. He wanted to up the timeline for the job." Lennon hesitated. "And he wanted me to add Abbey to the kill list."

"Randall is working *with* the Iranians?"

"Yes."

"To kill his *boss*?"

Lennon shrugged. "Conspiracies make for strange bedfellows, Cain. You know that. Fortunately, Ashkani never realized that you and I were behind the death of Gholami. Otherwise, we'd have been dead years ago."

Bourne's hand tightened on his Sig. He didn't know everything, but he knew enough. He knew where to go next. Lennon didn't have the rest of the answers; Jason would have to find those for himself.

There was only one thing left to do now. End the game.

This was the easy part; this was what he'd waited for. His revenge. His punishment. This was for Nova. And Abbey. And for other victims stretching back over the years. A teenager named Tatiana. A naïve cutout named Kenna Martin. People he'd tried and failed to save from this man. This *assassin*. He'd followed his trail all the way from a cottage in the snow of South Ossetia to a dirt road in the Maryland countryside.

Pull the trigger!

Kill him!

"Do it, Cain," Lennon snapped impatiently, like an echo of Bourne's thoughts. "What are you waiting for?"

Jason stared at the broken man below him. His finger was on the trigger. An ounce of pressure, and it was done. He'd come here to kill this man. He'd waited years for this moment. If the tables were turned, if Lennon were holding the gun, Bourne would die. He knew that. And still he found himself reluctant to do it. He'd killed in cold blood many times when he needed to, but what would it accomplish now? Lennon was the symptom, not the disease. The ones who needed to die were the people behind Defiance, not the soldiers they used to do their dirty work.

What would Nova say?

He heard it in her cool British voice, telling him exactly what she'd want him to do. *Murder the fucker. Hard, not soft.*

What about Abbey? If he went to her now, she'd say: *That's not who you are, Jason. You're not a killer.*

But he was. He was a killer, and he always would be.

Just not with this man, and not today.

"Do it!" Lennon insisted, his lip curling.

Instead, Jason removed the Sig and reholstered it. He eased back to sit on the dirt road. He wiped sweat from his forehead and winced as the bullet in his leg throbbed.

"Goddamn you, shoot!" Lennon repeated.

"No, I think you'll hate it more being alive, rotting in a CIA cell overseas. You know how this is going to work. They'll torture you to get everything you know, and then they'll let you waste away. They'll tell Putin you're dead, but you'll be worse than dead. Every day you spend living in the shadows and staring at the rats, you'll think of me."

The man's voice rose with fury. "Fuck you, Cain."

Bourne got to his feet, shaking his head. He wandered down the road and took out his phone. Time to call Nash. Time to bring in Treadstone.

It wasn't any kind of mercy to let Lennon live. It was cold, practical reality. The assassin didn't matter anymore. He'd never kill again; he'd never play his sadistic games. Alive or dead, he was done. And the man knew it. Lennon stared at him, his dark eyes blazing with impotent rage. He was being denied the ending he deserved. The moment of glory, the single bullet coursing through his brain.

Then something changed.

On the ground, Lennon's whole body relaxed, the taut spring of his muscles unwinding. His face softened. His angry eyes closed, a man at peace. With a huge smile, he put his lips together and whistled a fragment of a song. It took Bourne a moment to figure out that it was John Lennon's "Instant Karma."

The moment after that, he knew what was going to happen.

Jason charged back down the road toward Lennon, but the assassin moved with incredible speed, bringing the meat of his forearm to his mouth, biting like a cannibal through skin and muscle. Bourne pried the man's arm away, but Lennon had already chewed through to the capsule and sucked it down. Jason squeezed the killer's jaw, trying to force his mouth open. He punched him hard, wanting the man to vomit. But he was too late. Inside Lennon's stomach, acid dissolved the coating of the capsule and released the poison.

A long moment passed as they both waited for what came next.

Still smiling, Lennon lurched violently as tremors wracked his body. He twitched, shoulders and legs bouncing up and down off the ground. Milky foam bubbled between his lips. His eyes rolled back, leaving two white moons below his eyelids. The man's mouth fell open in a silent, twisted scream of agony.

His stomach was burning. His whole body was burning, and the fire consumed him.

Bourne swore. All he could do was watch it happen. To the man on the ground, every second must have felt like a year passing, but in a couple of minutes, it was done. The spasms vanished. The body on the dirt road went limp. No breaths came or went from his lungs. Jason reached to the man's neck and checked for a pulse to confirm what he already knew.

Lennon was dead.

41

Two hours later, Treadstone took away the body.

Jason watched the black SUV disappear down the dirt road until there was nothing left but a cloud of dust lingering in the twilight. He lay sideways in the back of a second SUV, wincing as a doctor cut into his thigh to remove the bullet. The local anesthetic wasn't enough to completely dull the pain.

That was okay. He needed to stay awake.

A mile away, the FBI had taken control of the bomb scene from the Maryland police. The investigation was theirs now. The twisted wreck of the Chevy Tahoe and the white pickup. The bodies of Don Pine and his driver, which were probably already in a government morgue. And Abbey.

"How is she?" he asked Nash. "Did they tell you anything?"

"She's okay," Nash replied. "Really, Jason. They took her to the hospital at GW. I checked in with one of my fed friends, and he says there were no serious injuries beyond a couple of broken bones. She's incredibly lucky. By all rights, she should be dead."

"I need to see her."

Nash shook his head. "Don't even try. You won't get anywhere near her. The FBI has everything locked down."

"You mean, so they can get their stories straight?" Bourne asked. "So they can convince her to stay quiet about what she knows?"

Nash shrugged and said nothing. He simply leaned on his cane and watched the doctor working on Bourne. Around them, half a dozen Treadstone cleaners scrubbed the scene. Soon there would be no blood. No DNA. No tire tracks. No Ford Explorer crashed in the trees. Nash wanted there to be nothing for the FBI to find when they expanded their search to the surrounding area.

"What about Lennon?" Jason went on, anticipating the answer.

"You know how this all works," Nash replied with a sigh. "What do you want me to say? Lennon was never here. He doesn't exist. The investigation will drag on for months—probably years. In the end, the government will send out a one-page press release that puts the blame on right-wing extremists. White supremacists. Domestic terrorists. Take your pick."

"So Lennon gets exactly what he wanted."

"Lennon's *dead*, Jason. It's over. Let it go. Pine's dead, too. He was the man behind Defiance, and he's gone now. The Iranians must have figured they couldn't let him get into the White House. From there, who knows what he might have arranged as payback for 1342? So they hired Lennon to take him out."

Bourne didn't reply.

He wasn't sure how much of Nash's speculation about the Iranians and Don Pine was true, but he knew this was *not* over. Not for him. Defiance held more secrets that he hadn't unearthed yet. He'd told Nash most of the story—but he'd left out the involvement of Tim Randall. Randall was the next piece in the puzzle, and Bourne planned to deal with him personally.

Hard, not soft.

"Have you found Nova?" he asked quietly.

Nash gestured at the wreck of the Ford Explorer, which was being mounted onto a flatbed truck. "The SUV is registered to a man named Walter Pepper. Ex–Marine sergeant, lives near Pax River. Service record shows he was forced out a few years ago over extremist ties. Sounds like the perfect fall guy for Lennon. I've got a couple of agents heading to his place now. I want to make sure we get to the scene ahead of the FBI. If Nova—well, if Nova's in there, I want her body out before the feds get there."

"No, I want to see her first," Bourne insisted.

"Jason—"

"Tell them to watch the place but not to go inside." Bourne jerked his thumb at the front of the black SUV. "I need to go. Can I take the Escalade?"

"You're in no condition to drive."

"I'm fine."

Nash glanced at the Treadstone doctor, who was finishing up work on Bourne's leg. The man rolled his eyes but didn't object. When his wound was bandaged, Jason climbed down to the road and braced himself against the SUV as he limped toward the driver's door. He shook himself and bit down on his lip to clear the fog in his head. Inside the vehicle, he started the engine and did a three-point turn. As he headed out of the woods, he saw Nash watching him, a dark expression on the Treadstone man's face.

They'd worked together for a long time. Nash knew when Bourne was hiding things from him.

A couple of miles later, Jason reached the highway that led toward DC. Darkness fell quickly as he drove, and he followed the hypnotic glow of his headlights through the empty countryside. The anesthetic in his leg wore off, and the throbbing of the bullet wound jabbed him like a hot poker.

But the pain helped him stay awake. More than an hour passed before he reached the outskirts of the city. Rather than skirt the traffic, he headed downtown along the river, passing Washington Circle. The entrance to the hospital at George Washington University was only a block away.

Abbey was a block away. Alive.

He parked near the entrance to the trauma center, but he could see that Nash was right. FBI agents blanketed the exterior, and he was sure there were more inside. A U.S. senator had been assassinated. They weren't taking chances on what might happen next. He knew Abbey was inside the hospital, and he could *feel* her close to him. He wanted to sit by her bedside and hold her hand and be there when she woke up, so the first thing she saw was his face. But based on the security outside the building, she may as well have been in a supermax prison. He couldn't get to her tonight.

So he drove away again. He made his way to Highway 5, heading south. His next journey took him two more hours. It was after midnight by the time he reached the town of Lexington Park, which was a bedroom community for the naval air station at Patuxent River. This was where Walter Pepper lived.

Walter Pepper, member of the Liberty Soldiers.

Walter Pepper, who would take the fall for the death of Senator Don Pine.

In the neighborhood near Pepper's house, Bourne found a blue Hyundai parked near a trail leading into the woods. He knew the Hyundai was stolen, because he'd helped Nova steal it outside Washington. This was the car she'd been driving.

She'd arrived here, but she'd never left.

His heart turned black, because he knew what that meant.

Jason parked behind her car and checked that it was empty. Silently, he moved through the trees. As he approached Pepper's house from the rear, he saw the first of Nash's two

Treadstone agents monitoring the exterior. The agent was a Black woman, tall and lean with brown hair streaked with purple, dressed in a dark jacket and jeans. She was smart and tough; he'd worked with her once before in Barcelona. Her code name was Vandal.

She had her gun out before he reached her. Then her face relaxed as she recognized him.

"Cain."

"Any activity?" he asked.

"No one's tried to breach the scene. An NCIS van showed up half an hour ago, but they knocked on the door, then left without entering. I assume they'll be back, probably with a warrant and the FBI in tow. If we're going in, we need to go soon."

"Give me five minutes."

Bourne began to push past her. As he did, Vandal took his arm and held him back. "Listen, Cain. Nash told us that Nova may be in there. I know about—I mean, there were rumors around the agency about you two. Anyway, I just wanted to say I'm sorry."

He nodded, his expression not changing. "Thanks."

"Remember, I can only give you five minutes," she added. "Five minutes and one second, and I'm in there, too."

"Understood."

Jason made his way to the muddy porch behind the house. There should have been a porch light over the door, but the bulb had been broken, leaving flecks of glass on the wooden beams near his feet. He found an open window and assumed this was where Nova had gone inside. He eased through the frame and pushed around the curtains. The house was dead still, but bright light streamed from the next room. His chest feeling heavy, his breath short and ragged, he headed that way with his Sig clutched tightly in his hand.

In the main room, he noted extremist paraphernalia

scattered everywhere. He wondered how much was real and how much was Lennon's invention. There were flags scrawled with white power slogans. Nazi posters. Dozens of pistols and rifles, plus boxes of ammunition. In the middle of all of it was an enlarged photograph of Senator Don Pine with a target scrawled over his face. There were also indications of a brutal fight—furniture tipped over, bullet holes in the walls.

Plus two dead bodies.

The first was an older man strapped to a chair, his head dropped forward, his shirt covered in blood. He assumed this was Walter Pepper.

The next was a woman—really still a girl—a teenager he recognized from following her in New York. She lay on her back, spreadeagle, with two shots in her forehead like an extra pair of eyes. Yoko.

But he didn't see a third body. Nova wasn't here.

A frantic stab of hope filled his mind. *Had she survived? Had she made it to a hospital?*

His gaze swept the floor, and he spotted a blood trail leading toward the side door of the house. Nova had been crawling. There were long red streaks where she'd dragged herself toward the door. He followed the trail outside across a short stretch of sidewalk that led to the detached garage. The door was ajar. Bourne slipped inside, then hunted for the interior garage light. When he switched it on, he saw a Ford Taurus plastered over with bumper stickers and American flags.

There she was.

Nova had made it to the driver's seat. The car door was open. Her body was slumped over the wheel, her lush black hair pitched forward to cover her face. Gently, he eased her back, supporting her torso. She was limp and lifeless in his arms. He checked her pulse to be sure, but he already knew the truth. He'd known from her voice on that last phone call. Her body was cold, her olive skin now deathly pale.

She was dead. He'd lost her.

Memories of their complicated relationship flooded through his mind, and he couldn't hold them back. That was the strange trade-off for losing his past. The memories he did have were vivid and clear. He thought about the missions with her. The deaths. The danger. The fights and betrayals. The sex. He could picture it all so clearly that he couldn't believe it had finally come to an end here in a suburban Maryland garage. Those years of memories stopped right now. He'd never see the fire in her eyes again, never feel her skin against his, never hear her voice.

His fingers cupped the pendant that hung around her neck. It was an old Greek coin encased in a round bezel, and he knew it had belonged to her mother. She'd never been without it. With a quick tug, Jason broke the chain and slid the pendant away from her skin. He shoved it into his pocket, then left Nova where she was.

In the trees, he returned to the agent known as Vandal.

"She's in the garage," he told her, his voice flat.

"Okay."

"You can take her now."

"Okay."

He didn't wait around to say anything more. He made his way through the nighttime woods to the black Escalade, and when he was inside, he took out his burner phone and made a call to a number he'd memorized long ago. A woman answered but didn't identify herself. He recognized the voice of Holly Schultz.

"It's me," Jason murmured.

"Cain."

"Nova's dead."

"Nash called me. I'm sorry."

A long silence stretched across the phone.

"I know about Gholami," Bourne went on. "I *remember*. I know you sent us to kill him. Me and Abel."

"The general, yes, but not his family," Holly replied. "I didn't order that."

"Who did?"

"I don't know, Cain. I'm telling you the truth. I don't know."

"Then I need your help," Bourne said. "Do you have a way to reach out to an Iranian intelligence operative named Hamid Ashkani?"

"Yes, of course." Holly's voice darkened with concern. "Why?"

Bourne checked his Sig. "Tell him I want a meeting."

42

Tim Randall glanced at his Apple watch and saw that he had fifteen minutes until the Iranian was scheduled to arrive. He wondered if Ashkani was coming to lay down new terms. To make new threats, to ramp up the blackmail. Ashkani had been as good as his word. He'd arranged the killing of Don Pine, and he'd steered the blame elsewhere. In the days since the bombing, the name Lennon hadn't been breathed once by the FBI or the CIA. Instead, the entire mainstream media was on fire about the plague of right-wing extremism and political violence. The narrative played right into their hands.

Yes, Ashkani had proved his worth, but that only meant Randall was even deeper in the man's pocket now. They both knew it.

The parking lot was empty. It would have been deserted anyway at three in the morning, but the brick warehouse on the fringe of Reagan National was permanently closed. for sale signs adorned the barbed-wire fence that surrounded the property, and sheet metal debris overflowed from two rollaway garbage bins. But the entrance gate had been open when he arrived, allowing him to drive his Cadillac inside.

Randall waited near an abandoned construction trailer.

He rolled down the driver's window, letting in damp air. The thunder of a plane taking off made the ground shake. His gaze flitted to the shadows, and he drummed his fingers nervously on the steering wheel. He told himself he had no reason to be nervous. Not now.

Defiance was done. It had been a triumph. Everything had gone according to plan.

This was his victory.

And Alicia's.

Randall flipped open the laptop he'd propped on the Cadillac's dashboard. The screen awakened, and with a tap of his finger, he replayed the YouTube video of the press conference from earlier that day. Smiling, he listened to Alicia's calm voice, the perfect political blend of reassurance and outrage.

As Americans, we're all weary of the hatred that has divided us for the past decade. Look where it's led us! The brutal murder of my good friend Don Pine. The assassination of a future president of the United States. We cannot let this stand. We cannot accept this debasement of the political process. Agree or disagree with him, Don deserved a spirited debate, a principled opposition, a free election—not the cowardice of radicals who deprived America of their ability to select the leader of their choice.

She was so good.

Seven years earlier, when Alicia was secretary of state and Tim Randall was her chief of staff, he'd thought their ambitions lay in ruins. Thanks to the Iranians, thanks to Hamid Ashkani. Thanks to 1342. But Alicia had been right about the future. She'd always been right. She'd told him her time would come again. *Their* time would come.

Now here it was.

He listened to her make the announcement they'd planned for years.

As you know, I made the decision several years ago—because of my husband's health—not to seek the presidency for myself. If this were only about me, I would stand by that decision. But the violence of Don's death has changed all of us, has demanded we alter our priorities. We cannot think of ourselves; we have to think of the well-being of the country. That is why I'm doing today what I know Don would want in the wake of his death. I'm announcing a campaign for president, and I invite Democrats and Republicans alike—all Americans—to be a part of this venture. Because together, united, we will put the era of division behind us.

The camera switched to the hordes of media covering the event. They were eating it up. Next year, Alicia Beauvoir, former UN ambassador, former secretary of state, would add the next natural notch to her résumé. Her destiny. The role she'd been planning for throughout her life and career. President of the United States.

Nothing could be allowed to stand in her way.

That was why Defiance had been necessary. To make sure all the secrets stayed buried.

And it had worked even better than he'd imagined. The polls taken after Alicia Beauvoir's announcement showed her with a fifteen-point lead over the nearest Republican challenger. *Fifteen points!*

Randall saw headlights outside the warehouse fence. A sleek black town car slid through the open gate. It approached slowly until the building wall provided cover, and then it stopped, engine still running. The high beams flashed, sending the signal. It was time. Typical Ashkani, forcing Randall to come to him. *Humiliating* him.

Someday there would be payback, he swore.

He got out of his Cadillac. Shielding his eyes against the bright headlights, he approached the town car. As he got closer, the driver's door clicked open, and one of Ashkani's bodyguards got out. The man was in shadow, his eyes covered by sunglasses, a chauffeur's hat on his forehead. The driver opened the rear door of the town car and stood beside it.

Blackmail? Demands?

How high would the price be?

Randall bent down to climb into the backseat, but then he froze in confusion. The back of the town car was empty. No one was there. He began to straighten up—*What the hell is going on?*—but in the next moment, a fierce kick propelled him across the inside of the car. His face hit hard against the opposite window, and he tasted blood in his mouth.

Someone spun him around. The back of his head slammed against the window, and a gun was shoved between his teeth. A man loomed over him, strong fingers choking off the air at his windpipe.

This wasn't one of Ashkani's guards.

The man stripped off his hat and sunglasses, and Randall recognized him. It was Cain.

"Hamid sends his regrets," Bourne told Randall. "He's a practical man. He knows when the game is over."

Randall gagged, and Bourne removed the barrel of the Sig from the man's mouth. He placed it between his eyes instead. "You came after two people I care about. You killed one. You nearly killed the other. Be glad that Abbey is alive, or believe me, this would go down even harder than it is."

The man begged through the blood trickling from his mouth. "I—I don't know what you're talking about! Please!"

Bourne had no patience for this overeducated con man. This *liar*! He'd shown Lennon mercy, but not Tim Randall. As a killer, Randall was worse than the assassin had ever been. Bourne grabbed a rag from the pocket of his coat and shoved it into the man's mouth to squash his screams. As Randall's eyes widened with the terror of what was coming next, Bourne shoved the barrel of the Sig into the man's knee and pulled the trigger. The noise was a bomb inside the limo. Muffled wailing screeched through the gag, and Jason held the man down as his whole body writhed.

He felt nothing.

He was Treadstone. He was ice.

As Randall whimpered, Bourne took a hypodermic from his other pocket. He put the needle to the man's neck and pumped the plunger just a little, delivering enough morphine to dull the agony, not enough to make him unconscious. Randall's eyes rolled. Sweat and tears poured down his face.

Jason yanked out the gag.

"Now you're going to tell me everything," Bourne said. "Start with Gholami. Treadstone sent me to kill him, but someone else reached out with orders for Lennon to kill his family, too. Who was it? Was it you?"

Randall moaned. His head swung back and forth. Bourne lifted the gun to point it at the man's other knee, and Randall made a pitiful mewling sound through his mouth.

"Fuck, no, no, no! I'll tell you, I'll tell you. Please, I'll tell you. Don't shoot. Alicia reached out to Vic Sorrento at the CIA. She had him give his man new orders."

Alicia. Bourne swore under his breath.

"Why did she want Gholami's family killed?"

"Because of Ellie."

"Ellie?" Bourne thought back to his conversations with Abbey. "You mean her daughter? The one who was killed in Israel?"

"Yes! Gholami was behind the Hizballah bombing. Gholami masterminded the whole thing! And Alicia found out—God, it was so awful—she found out that they knew."

"Knew what?"

"They *knew* Ellie was going to be in the club. They *targeted* her. Murdered her!"

"And Alicia wanted revenge," Bourne said.

"Yes! Yes! I begged her not to do it, but she was out of her mind. Don't you understand? Ellie was her whole world. She wanted them all to feel her pain. She wanted Gholami to know what she was suffering. I couldn't stop her."

Jason heard a roaring in his head. It all came back to him. Gholami, asleep in a lounge chair that faced the water. Then the man's cold, impassive eyes as he woke up and saw Cain with the gun pointed at his face. Gholami was a killer confronting a killer; he'd known this would be his end. He didn't care about his own life.

But then, from the inner rooms of the cabana, came the screams. His wife. His *children*.

They both heard the shots as Lennon executed them one by one.

That was when Gholami's face changed. Alicia Beauvoir got exactly what she wanted. Gholami knew his family was dead, and he felt the agony of their loss. A moment later, he was dead, too, as Bourne pulled the trigger.

"So 1342 was payback," Jason concluded. "Alicia got her revenge, and then Ashkani and Iran got theirs."

Randall nodded. "Except this was *personal*. This wasn't just about vengeance against the U.S. This was about Alicia. They were doing this to *her*. To destroy her."

"How?"

The man below him moaned, the morphine wearing off, the pain getting worse again.

"*How?*" Bourne repeated.

"Ashkani called Alicia for a meeting. They met in Rock Creek Park. Two limos. It was two in the morning."

A meeting in Rock Creek Park, Bourne thought.

The police officer named Billy Janssen had seen it happening.

"Ashkani told her about the jet," Randall went on. "He said—he said there was a virus on board. Their scientists had developed it. Incredibly contagious, crazy-high fatality rate. The plane was going to be landing in the U.S. in twelve hours. As soon as people got off, it would start to spread. We'd never be able to stop it, never be able to contain it. Alicia thought he was bluffing, but Ashkani gave her a sample and told her to test it. Let a scientist tell her what it was."

"Mallory Foster," Bourne said.

Spit bubbled out of Randall's mouth. "Yes! Alicia knew her through the UN. She had her check the virus, and Foster said it was legit, like a whole new plague. She said if it got out, millions would die. Don't you see? We couldn't let that plane land. We couldn't take that risk!"

"So what happened to 1342? How did you get it out of the sky?"

"The Iranians did that. They had a man on board. A martyr. The copilot, Khalaji. He brought it down. He cut off all communications, he changed directions, and then he flew it straight down into the Indian Ocean. Don't you get it? We *wanted* it to stay a mystery. We wanted it to disappear. We didn't care about rumors and conspiracies. Rumors were better than the truth."

Bourne shook his head. "And the price? What did the Iranians want?"

"Please," Randall begged. "The morphine. Please!"

"Tell me."

"I can't—Oh, fuck, it hurts so much."

"It hasn't even begun to hurt, Tim," Bourne warned him, shoving the Sig into the man's palm. He wanted to fire through nerves and bone. He wanted this man to suffer for what he'd done. To Abbey. To Nova. But he still needed information.

"They wanted to *own* Alicia," Randall went on, struggling to get out the words. "Control her. Make her their pawn."

"How?"

Randall closed his eyes. "There's a recording on my phone. Take it! Listen to it! That was the price for 1342. That was what they wanted. Ashkani met Alicia again a few hours later and made her record it. They told her what to say. Once they had that, they got word to Khalaji. The jet disappeared."

43

Bourne played the recording for Holly Schultz.

There were two voices on the tape. The first she identified as the Iranian agent Hamid Ashkani. The second voice they both recognized, as anyone in the country would. The cool, unemotional tone was unmistakable. It was Alicia Beauvoir. Her entire world was falling apart, she was staring at the murder of innocents and the threat of a global plague, and she sounded as if she were ordering Chinese food from DoorDash.

"So you have heard from your scientist now?" Ashkani asked her. *"From this woman, Mallory Foster?"*

"Yes."

"She worked alone?"

"She did, at my instructions."

"And she gave you the results?"

"Yes."

"The scientist will need to be dealt with, of course."

"Yes, of course."

Holly glanced at Bourne. That cruel, casual reply—*Yes, of course*—was the beginning of Defiance.

"So now you know we are not bluffing," Ashkani went on.

"That virus is aboard a plane headed for the United States right now. You can rest assured that every passenger is already infected. When the plane lands, the horror begins."

"If it's released, it won't stop at the water's edge," Beauvoir reminded him. *"Sooner or later the disease will come home to Iran. You're killing your own people."*

"Martyrdom has its price. We have always been willing to pay it."

"I can't believe that even you would go so far."

"You think not? Well, then you have a choice to make, Madam Secretary. You can do nothing and pray we don't mean what we say. Or you can spread the word publicly and watch people panic. Or you can end this crisis now, between us, and no one will ever know."

Alicia Beauvoir stayed silent for a long time.

"End it how?" she asked.

"We have an agent on that plane. On our command, he will sacrifice himself and bring it down."

"How many people are on board?"

"More than two hundred. Including many American teenagers."

"All because of Gholami? Is he really worth this? Don't pretend he was anything but a butcher. My daughter is dead *because of him."*

"Yes, and Gholami's wife and daughters are dead because of you, Madam Secretary. That is how the cycle of revenge goes. Now other people's daughters are about to die, too. The question is how many. A few dozen? Or millions around the world? That's your choice."

"What do you want from me?"

"It's quite simple. Read this aloud. Do that, and we end this, and no one ever knows the truth."

On the recording, they heard the rustling of paper. The only other sound was the breathing of Alicia Beauvoir, which got louder and faster. Bourne could imagine her reading the message over and over, weighing her options, trying to find a way out of the maze.

But there was no way out.

The next sound was the crumpling of paper, and then she spoke.

She'd memorized what they wanted her to say.

"My name is Alicia Beauvoir. I am the secretary of state of the United States of America. It has come to my attention that a grave threat to world health exists aboard a plane now heading across the Atlantic Ocean to the U.S. The government of Iran has offered its help in eliminating that threat by arranging for the destruction of the plane, with the accompanying loss of life. I am asking for their help in doing so, in full knowledge that Americans will perish as a result of this action. Let me be very clear: I am freely requesting that Iran perform all necessary steps to take down that jet immediately."

Holly shook her head as Bourne switched off the recording. "Jesus."

"That's why she had to make sure the secret of 1342 never got out," Bourne said. "Afterward, Beauvoir and Tim Randall launched Defiance to make sure anyone with knowledge of what happened that night—from a cop in Rock Creek Park to a beachcomber in Madagascar—never shared what they knew."

"And Treadstone was in the middle of it," Holly said. "We got played."

"That's right."

Holly stroked Sugar's head. The dog sat at perfect attention next to her, a little rumble of pleasure at her master's attention. Sunlight had begun to stream through the windows of the library as dawn broke. They were back in the McLean, Virginia, home of General Marcus Matthews, where Bourne had first confronted Holly about Defiance.

"How does Beauvoir think she can run for president with this hanging over her head?" Holly asked. "It's insane."

"I think that's why she used *Defiance* as a code name," Bourne replied. "Beauvoir wasn't going to let this incident get in the way of her life's ambition. You're talking about a woman who has wanted to be president since she was five years old. I think the murder of her daughter only made that ambition more intense."

"But she waited. She sat out the race. Why not run four years ago?"

"According to Randall, that really was about her husband. Word had gotten out about his cancer. If she ran, she'd look heartless. So she deferred her dream until now. But they still had loose ends to tie up, starting with the Treadstone agents who were involved in Defiance. And then Don Pine, too. Randall going to work for Pine gave them the perfect spy inside his campaign, but sooner or later, Pine had to go. Killing him not only cleared the field for Beauvoir, it made her look like a savior coming in to rescue the country."

"Meanwhile, Iran has her in its pocket."

Bourne nodded. "Yes. That's why Ashkani was willing to help them eliminate Pine by bringing in Lennon. I suspect Beauvoir's ego is enough to let her believe she can neutralize Iran once she's actually in office."

Holly stared into nothingness from behind her dark glasses. "What about Tim Randall?"

"He won't be seen again," Bourne told her calmly. "He'll be like 1342. A disappearance that never gets solved."

"Good."

Holly reached for a remote control with easy familiarity, and she turned on a television mounted among the bookshelves. The earlymorning news was on, and the subject was what it had been for days. The death of Don Pine and the presidential campaign of Alicia Beauvoir. She'd seamlessly taken over as the front-runner. The media had already declared her candidacy to be virtually unstoppable.

Holly clicked off the television.

"Beauvoir will win," she murmured. "First the nomination, then the election."

"I know."

"We can't allow that, Cain."

"No."

"That recording would sink her, but it can never come out. Its release would be disastrous for the country. Unimaginable. Trust in the government is already at an all-time low. The truth of 1342 would erase it for good. Not to mention the inevitable bloody war with Iran that would follow. Defiance must *not* be exposed."

Bourne nodded again and said nothing. He knew what was coming.

"I can't tell you what to do, Cain," Holly went on. "I can't give that order."

"I'm aware of that."

Holly kept stroking Sugar's head, and her voice went down to little more than a whisper. "But you know what you need to do. Don't you?"

Abbey saw the concern on Alicia Beauvoir's face. "Is something wrong?"

Beauvoir put down the phone in her hand. She took a seat at the glass table in the solarium. "I haven't been able to reach Tim Randall for a couple of days. Typically, he's never out of reach of his phone. My staff hasn't seen him at the office, and he hasn't been home. I'm worried that something has happened."

"Have you talked to the police?"

"Yes, they're looking for him, but there haven't been any reports."

Abbey sat through the silence that followed. She was in a wheelchair, her leg and right arm in casts, which left her frustratingly helpless. But the doctors had said it wouldn't be for long. She'd be free again soon.

Her laptop was on the table, but she hadn't bothered opening it because she knew why Beauvoir had called her here. Alicia Beauvoir was running for president. That meant their book project was on hold. Not that Abbey minded. Not now. She had weeks of recovery ahead of her before she could think about writing again.

She hadn't seen or talked to Jason since the bomb went off. She had a memory of him crouching above her in the field, but she didn't know if that was real or a dream. But he was still out there. A package of maple candies from Quebec had been waiting in her hospital room when she awakened. There was no note, but she knew who had sent them.

"I know the campaign changes everything," Abbey said, breaking the silence. "We can't go ahead with the book."

Beauvoir came out of her trance with a small frown. "I'm glad you understand."

"Maybe in four years," Abbey said.

"Eight," Beauvoir replied.

"Yes, of course."

"What will you do, Abbey?"

"I guess I'll write a different book. I've got plenty of ideas. Maybe this time I'll do something about the missing jet."

Something changed on Beauvoir's face. She opened her mouth, then closed it. A cloud in her eyes passed away. She smiled, but it was a politician's smile, transparent and cold. "Maybe so."

Then Beauvoir's phone rang. She checked the caller ID, and Abbey could see her relax with relief.

"Ah, that's Tim now. Finally." She went to the other side of the sunroom. Her voice was quiet as she answered the phone, but Abbey could hear what she said. "Where the fuck have you been?"

Then Beauvoir's whole body stiffened.

Abbey couldn't hear the phone call, but she watched Beauvoir become as still and hard as a statue. The woman's lips pushed together so tightly that the color seemed to vanish from them. Her eyes smoldered with emotion. Fury. Hatred. Abbey found the transformation unsettling, as if this woman she thought she knew well had become a total stranger.

Beauvoir put down the phone. Her gaze zeroed in on Abbey like a laser.

"Was it you?" she hissed.

"Excuse me?"

"It was you all along, wasn't it? A spy sent to destroy me. I should have known."

"Alicia, I don't—"

"How did you get the recording?"

"Recording? I swear, I have no idea what you're talking about."

"Do you think this will stop me?" she went on, her voice getting louder. "Do you think I'll quit? You're wrong. I haven't come this far to have you or anyone else undo my plans. I made a vow to Ellie that she would see her mother become president of the United States. I always keep my promises. People who try to stop me, people who stand in my way, get destroyed. Do you understand me?"

Abbey didn't understand any of it, but she felt a ripple of fear, hearing the icy determination in Beauvoir's face. This wasn't a mother or even a politician. This was someone who would do *anything* for power, a woman with towering ambition that erased everything else. And the threat from her felt completely real.

"I think I should go," Abbey said, but she was conscious of the fact that she couldn't walk. She couldn't run. She was helpless where she was.

"You're not going anywhere," Beauvoir snapped.

"Alicia, whatever that phone call was, I had nothing to do with it."

Beauvoir shook her head. "I really should have known. The rumors about 1342, that was all *you*. You and your boyfriend. Does he even exist, or were you behind everything from the beginning? Jesus, you asked me about Mallory Foster, too! I was foolish enough to believe your innocent girl act. I should have listened to Tim. He wanted to get rid of you right away, but all I could see when I looked at you was Ellie. Was that deliberate, too? Did you research her, act like her? You had it in for me all along, didn't you? The book was nothing but a cover to take me down. Who are you working for? Who's behind this?"

Abbey listened to Beauvoir spinning out paranoid fantasies.

"You're crazy," she murmured. "What are you saying? What's this all about?"

"It's about making *hard choices*, Abbey. That's what a president has to do. I know that better than any other politician in the country. Two hundred people versus two hundred *million* people. You weigh the options, you make your choice, you move on."

"Two hundred—" Abbey began. Then she understood. "My God, you're talking about the plane. Did you—was it *you*? What really happened? What did you do?"

"I saved this country," Beauvoir snapped. "I saved the world. That's what I did."

Abbey put a hand on the wheelchair and slowly backed toward the solarium door.

"Stop!" Beauvoir demanded.

The force of her personality, the command of her voice,

was so strong that Abbey did what she wanted. She stopped, her free hand still on the wheelchair. It felt like a kind of paralysis, as if she were a deer staring at the headlights from an oncoming car. Beauvoir advanced on Abbey across the marble floor of the solarium, her eyes filled with deranged desperation.

Abbey didn't know what she would do, but a terrible thought flashed through her mind: *She's going to kill me.*

Beauvoir passed beside the tall glass windows of the sunroom.

Outside, it was a perfect fall day, the view stretching through the green fields toward the hills. In that moment, glass shattered. There was no other sound, just the ping of broken glass. The first thing Abbey saw was a tight little starburst in one of the windows. A small hole, nothing more. Then she looked at Beauvoir and saw a trickle of blood inching down her temple, no more than a drippy streak of red paint.

Beauvoir collapsed ever so slowly. Her body caved in on itself, and she sank to the stone floor. Abbey opened her mouth to scream, but no sound came out. No breath. She rolled across the sunroom until she was beside the body of Alicia Beauvoir, and there was no question at all that she was dead. The sniper's bullet had done its work.

Awkwardly, Abbey pushed herself out of the wheelchair. She limped to the glass wall of the solarium. She had no fears for herself, because she already knew what she would see. The killer who had done this wasn't after her. She stared into the crisp distance, and on the summit of the nearest hill, between twin oak trees, she could distinguish the outline of a man with a rifle in his hands. He was staring back at her, although from where he was, she doubted he could see her through the glass. It didn't matter. He would feel her; he knew she was there.

And she knew who he was. She'd long ago memorized the shape of his body.

As she watched, Jason turned his back on the estate and walked away, disappearing on the far side of the hill.

44

Quebec city.

For Jason and Abbey, this was where they came for beginnings and endings. They'd met here three years earlier. Months later, Bourne had come back here to say goodbye to her. This time, he knew, it was the reverse. As Abbey approached along the boardwalk from the heart of the old town, he could see in her face that she was ready to end things between them.

It was December, almost Christmas. The air had a bitter chill, snow blowing in clouds from over the St. Lawrence River and making halos around the lampposts. Enough snow had fallen to leave white dust along the walkway. The Château Frontenac glowed like a castle above him in red and green holiday lights. Abbey wore a long leather coat with the collar turned up. Her tall boots left footprints in the snow, and she still favored one leg. Her hands were shoved deep into her pockets, and her chin was turned down against the wind as her red hair blew across her face. Or maybe she simply didn't want to look him in the eye.

She sat down on the bench beside him. They had the boardwalk to themselves in the late evening. They hadn't seen each other since the death of Alicia Beauvoir two months earlier. Abbey had said she needed time to think, and he'd given her the space she wanted. Since then, she'd gone home to Canada to work on another book, and he'd stayed in a safe house outside Washington, hidden away by Treadstone until they concluded he could travel again without attracting the attention of the FBI.

Alicia Beauvoir's shooting remained unsolved. No one had made the connection to Flight 1342. No one knew about Defiance.

"How are you?" Bourne asked quietly. "Are you recovered?"

Abbey still didn't look at him. "There's some lingering stiffness in my arm and leg. The doctors say it might be permanent. But it's not so bad. It's better than being dead."

He wanted to apologize for not being there for her when the bomb went off. For not protecting her the way he'd promised he would. But the words sounded hollow, so he didn't say them.

"And the new book?" he asked.

"It's going well."

"Is it about—"

She finally turned and stared at him. They were inches away from each other, close enough to touch, but they may as well have been standing on opposite sides of a wide canyon. Nothing was the same.

"Is it about a missing jet?" she said. "About a writer who's in love with a killer? No, it's not. I'm not ready to tell that story yet, Jason."

"Because you don't know how it ends?" he asked.

Her lower lip trembled. In the boardwalk lights, her eyes shined, filling with tears. "I know how our story ends. I'm sorry."

He kept his reaction off his face. He didn't say anything. But he didn't miss what she'd said.

That was the first time she'd called him a killer.

"I really thought I could handle it," Abbey went on. "I thought I could break who you are into compartments. A place for me, a place for the things you have to do. But I can't. I just can't. I'm not judging you. I'm not saying what you've done is wrong. This is me. My problem. I can't handle being part of that world."

"I never wanted you to be part of it," Jason replied.

She turned away again. Her pretty face looked stricken. She squeezed her eyes shut. "Fuck, the thing is, I still love you. That's what makes this so hard. I get the words out, and then I want to take them back."

"Don't take them back," he said.

Abbey shook her head. "What about Nova? Is Nova dead?"

"Yes."

"Jesus. So I'm leaving you with no one."

"That's not what you're doing. You're protecting yourself."

"What are you going to do next?" she asked. "Where will you go?"

"Back to Paris."

"And work for Treadstone?"

"I don't know. I never know what comes next. Usually, trouble finds me, not the other way around."

"Will you stay in touch? At least let me know how you are."

Bourne wanted to lie, but he couldn't. "No."

"It doesn't have to mean anything. Just a note sometimes."

"No," he repeated.

Abbey's eyes widened at the finality of it. She opened her mouth as if to protest, but she took a deep breath instead. "You're right. We can't keep holding on."

"No, we can't."

"But our deal still stands," Abbey said, her voice creeping lower. "If something happens to you—"

"I'll make sure you know."

She nodded. Then, with the faintest grimace, she pushed herself off the bench. Step by step, she made her way across the boardwalk to the railing above the lower town and the river. Jason followed. They stood next to each other, their shoulders brushing, flurries blowing over the cliff and dampening their faces. They turned and faced each other, but they didn't kiss. Not even to say goodbye.

"I meant what I told you three years ago," Abbey said. "What I said a minute ago, I was wrong. I was so wrong."

"What's that?"

"You're not a killer. I've seen what you have to do, but I still believe that. I'm not in love with a killer. I'm in love with *you*."

"But that doesn't change anything for us," he said. "No, it doesn't."

Abbey reached out a hand for his face, then pulled it back. She turned down her eyes. He made it easier for her by looking away toward the river. When he did, he heard the soft tap of her boots limping away in the snow. He stayed there, not moving, until the boardwalk was silent again except for the hiss of the wind. Then he finally turned around and saw that her footsteps had already been erased. There was no sign of Abbey near him anymore.

His life had come full circle, back to the way it had to be.

Bourne was alone.

About the Authors

BRIAN FREEMAN is the bestselling author of the Jonathan Stride and Frost Easton series. His novel *Spilled Blood* won the award for Best Hardcover Novel in the International Thriller Writers Awards, and his debut novel, *Immoral,* won the Macavity Award and was a finalist for the Dagger, Edgar, Anthony, and Barry awards for Best First Novel. Freeman has lived in Minnesota with his wife Marcia for over 35 years.

Follow Brian on @BFreemanbooks
www.bfreemanbooks.com

ROBERT LUDLUM was the author of twenty-seven novels, each one an international bestseller. There are more than 225 million of his books in print, and they have been translated into thirty-two languages. He is the author of *The Scarlatti Inheritance*, *The Chancellor Manuscript*, and the Jason Bourne series – *The Bourne Identity*, *The Bourne Supremacy* and *The Bourne Ultimatum* – among others. Mr Ludlum passed away in 2001.